THE DARK WIVES

BY ANN CLEEVES

THE VERA STANHOPE SERIES
The Crow Trap
Telling Tales
Hidden Depths
Silent Voices
The Glass Room
Harbour Street
The Moth Catcher
The Seagull
The Darkest Evening
The Rising Tide
The Dark Wives

THE SHETLAND SERIES
Raven Black
White Nights
Red Bones
Blue Lightning
Dead Water
Thin Air
Cold Earth
Wild Fire

THE TWO RIVERS SERIES
The Long Call
The Heron's Cry
The Raging Storm

ANN CLEEVES

The Dark Wives

MINOTAUR BOOKS
NEW YORK

This book is dedicated to teens everywhere, and especially to the Dark Wives – uppity young women with minds of their own, struggling to find a place in a difficult world.

First published in the United States by Minotaur Books, an imprint of St. Martin's Publishing Group

THE DARK WIVES. Copyright © 2024 by Ann Cleeves. All rights reserved. Printed in the United States of America. For information, address St. Martin's Publishing Group, 120 Broadway, New York, NY 10271.

www.minotaurbooks.com

Map artwork by ML Design Ltd

The Library of Congress Cataloging-in-Publication Data is available upon request.

ISBN 978-1-250-83684-7 (hardcover)
ISBN 978-1-250-83685-4 (ebook)

Our books may be purchased in bulk for promotional, educational, or business use. Please contact your local bookseller or the Macmillan Corporate and Premium Sales Department at 1-800-221-7945, extension 5442, or by email at MacmillanSpecialMarkets@macmillan.com.

Originally published in Great Britain by Macmillan, an imprint of Pan Macmillan

First U.S. Edition: 2024

10 9 8 7 6 5 4 3 2 1

Acknowledgements

A writer is only as good as the team who support her, and I'm grateful to my agents and publishers worldwide. A special shout-out to everyone at Pan Macmillan and Minotaur, and especially to Jeremy Trevathan, who has recently retired. Emma Harrow is very much a part of that team. Thanks to Jane Hartley for sharing the load and managing the Reading for Wellbeing project. If you don't know about it, check it out here: www.readingforwellbeing.org.uk. We'd love for you to join us. Isla Raynor was my advisor on everything teenager, and much of the story told from Chloe's perspective was contributed by her. Remember her name! Thanks to all the people who spread the word about books – sellers, library staff, reviewers. Most importantly thanks to the readers who pay all our wages.

Author's Note

The idea for this book was triggered by an investigative piece about private children's homes on BBC Radio 4's *File on Four*, but the novel is entirely fictitious, and none of the institutions or characters are based on reality.

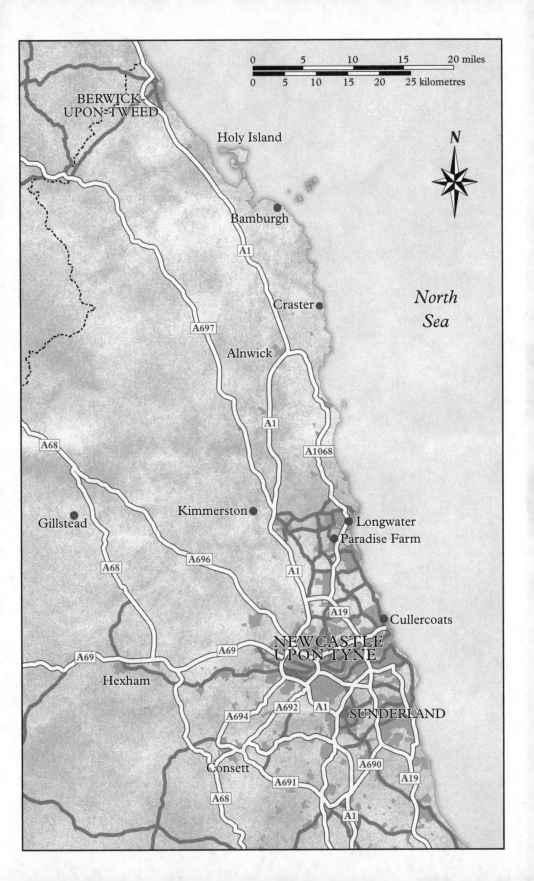

Chapter One

IT'S NOVEMBER TODAY. I HATE NOVEMBER. *Two years ago, in November, my dad ran off. A year ago, Mam stopped eating and started slipping away. She got the sack from the travel agency in town, and I caught her talking to the TV when it wasn't even switched on. She had the idea that it was talking back. There was just her and me, and I felt I was drowning. I'm only fourteen, so what could I do to help?*

I tried to tell Miss at school. I'd always thought she was okay, but in the end, she was only interested that I wasn't wearing the uniform socks and that I hadn't got my homework in on time. When I told her about Mam, she frowned and said I was making excuses. I needed to stick to the rules, whatever was happening at home. If I had real problems, I should talk to pupil welfare.

But pupil welfare is run by Mrs Saltburn, and she hates me, because she takes RE and I told her that I couldn't believe in a God that allows war and famine and anyway, what about the climate emergency?

'Salvation is an academy with a Christian ethos, Chloe. That was made clear before your parents chose it as your place of education.'

I wanted to tell her that I was getting into Wicca, which made far more sense to me, but then I'd have been in detention for the rest of the week. Also, that my parents put Salvation at the top of the list because the only other school in the catchment is Birks Comp, and a year nine kid got stabbed there, and the GCSE results are shite. But then she would have said I was being cheeky and that would have got me detention too.

Now it's November again. Mam's back in hospital, and I'm having to live here: Rosebank Home for the teenage kids nobody wants. I don't blame Mam. She's ill. And Dad's not even in the country. Apparently, he's in Dubai, making a fortune selling fancy apartments to rich people. He's not answering my calls or texts and I'm not even sure I've got the right number for him. Maybe he has a new woman in his life. A new family. Maybe he doesn't need me anymore. So I have tried talking to Miss and to Dad, and I'm not going to bother with Nana and Grandpa. They've always hated Mam and taken Dad's side and when I talk, they don't seem to hear. Nana's like Miss – only bothered about what I'm wearing and what I look like.

BUT NOBODY LISTENS.

That's not fair. Josh listens. But he's only agency staff and he's not here all the time. He listens when I tell him about the pervy guy waiting in his car outside the home – though maybe I was wrong about that – and that Brad Russell is like some sort of gangster in a crap movie, wearing that stupid parka even indoors, and dealing crack, and that I'm scared because there's no lock on my door. I'm not sure if Josh passes on the information though, or if anyone listens to him.

Josh told me to keep this diary to let out my thoughts and feelings, and we go through it when he's working and when he has time. Mostly he works in the evenings and at weekends. Today's Sunday, so he should be here, covering for Jan who's got the weekend off, but with agency staff you never know. Agency staff cost money, so sometimes Dave has to manage and it's just him and Tracey sleeping in. I don't think Dave minds when it's just the two of them.

Josh was supposed to have a shift tonight, and I thought I saw his car draw up. I was looking out of the window, watching out for him. Usually, I can see the light at the end of the quay where the coal ships used to tie up, and the big container ships heading for the docks, and the ghost ships with no crew lurking on the horizon, but it's misty, with that drizzle that feels like a heavy fog. I can't see anything. It's as if this house is on its own in the world, as if I'm on my own in the world and nobody would care if I died. Sometimes I dream about killing myself, then I think about Josh. It seems to me that he might care.

This place is worse than the bin where Mam's locked up. It's worse than prison.

Miss said I could be someone special when I started at Salvation, and my SATs were good. That was when Dad was still at home, and he came with Mam to parents' evening. She said I could be a poet or a songwriter. Then everything went wrong at home, and I couldn't concentrate, and I couldn't sleep. Miss didn't care about me anymore. Salvation only cares about the swotty kids who can make the school look good. When I got taken into care, I could tell they hoped I'd have to move to a new school, but the home's still in the catchment, and social services said I'd had enough disruption already, so they have to put up with me.

I might go down and meet Josh. We could go through the diary in the kitchen, and then he'll play cards with me if he's not too busy. The others are watching a film in the lounge. Tracey made them pizza and popcorn. But I'd rather play cards with Josh.

I think I could be in love with him.

Chapter Two

Detective Inspector Vera Stanhope looked up from the teenager's scrawl.

'It's got today's date. Chloe must have written it this evening.'

The manager of the children's home was faded, dusty. He had grey hair tied back in a ponytail. He seemed well out of his depth. Vera had seen the same ashamed look in some of her older colleagues' eyes: the people who were desperate to retire, but who couldn't quite make the jump. Because what would be the point of getting up in the morning if there were no work, nothing to get out of bed for? These were the lonely people, the bored ones, the introverts. Vera knew how they felt. She had no desire to retire, not even now when she felt like a failure. Especially now. Work was a kind of penance. They'd have to push her out.

She and David Limbrick, the manager, were standing outside in the corridor looking in at the room. The diary had been on the floor, close to the door. She'd reached in to pick it up with a blue-gloved hand, breaking every rule, but curious, because time was important now and it would take the CSIs a while to get here.

Vera was first on the scene because she'd still been in her office when the 999 call came through. Working late because she couldn't quite face driving into the hills to her empty house, so she'd sat at her desk, even though it was Sunday and the rest of the team had better things to do. Brooding about a dead young woman who'd once been a colleague, and thinking about how pointless her own life had become. Holly might have called it an existential crisis. Vera had heard the term, without understanding what it meant. Now, she had an inkling.

It was midnight and the CSIs were on their way. The pathologist would be there as soon as he could make it. He'd asked if it could wait until the morning, but she'd explained where she was, and the nature of the victim they'd found outside. And that a lass was missing. Now, it was just her and the manager. It seemed that David Limbrick slept in one of the staff rooms if he was on duty overnight, but he'd still been up when this tragedy had happened. When the body had been found, at least. Vera knew they'd be unlikely to get an accurate time of death. Paul Keating, the pathologist, made that clear every time they met. Dave told her he'd been working too. Catching up with things in the office. 'The bosses want up-to-date occupancy figures. It's all they seem to care about.' Moaning. Vera had guessed on first sight that he'd be a moaner.

Now they were both hovering outside the room, the door still open.

'I'll head outside again.' There was a uniformed officer with the body, but Vera wanted to take another look at the scene, despite the damp and the autumn chill. 'I just wanted to see Chloe's room.'

But she didn't move immediately and turned back to Limbrick.

'Anyone else here this evening?'

'Tracey,' he said. 'She was here until ten. She was in the lounge with the kids watching the movie, but she's not sleeping in tonight. It would just have been Josh and me on duty.'

'Tracey's one of the social workers?'

'Aye.'

'What time was Josh supposed to get here?'

'Eight-ish. I heard his car. He was always early.'

'But you didn't see him?'

'Nah, he was just sleeping in. Filling in for another staff member. I assumed he'd gone up to his room, and then that he was in the lounge with the others.'

'And Chloe? When did you last see her?'

He shrugged.

'You didn't notice her leave?'

'She's a wanderer that one. We never know where she is.'

The corridor ahead of them was empty, but Vera was aware of a couple of slightly open doors, young eyes peering through, muttered conversations. Muted excitement. Murder could generate excitement. She could understand that. But not here. Not this.

'Can we do anything with the other kids? Is there somewhere they can go?'

For the first time since the man had opened the main door to her, he seemed to come to life. 'No! They're only here because there's nowhere else for them. They're troubled. Disturbed.'

'I don't mean parents, families. Another home to take them in on a temporary basis. So my chaps can have a clear run.'

He looked at her as if she were mad. 'You don't understand. There is nowhere else. The whole system is falling apart.'

She thought he was being melodramatic. She'd contact social services in the morning. There must be some sort of emergency placement. She'd have to cope as best she could until then. But Limbrick was still talking. 'Most of them have been through foster care. But they're older, often aggressive. Hard to manage.'

Vera nodded down at the pages of the diary. 'Even Chloe?'

He shrugged. 'Yeah. Even her.' But he looked away and Vera could tell he didn't mean it, that he thought this hadn't been the right place for her. At least now that he'd read the girl's diary.

'You can leave me to it for now,' she said. 'Maybe you could talk to the kids. Tell them I'll be speaking to them in the morning, but that they should get some sleep.' A pause. 'Did Chloe have a special friend here?'

He shook his head. 'She was a bit of a loner.'

'Except for Josh.' Vera looked at the diary she was still holding in her hand. 'It seems that she got on with *him*.'

Limbrick didn't answer. He wandered back down the corridor. One of the kids shouted out to him through a half-open door. He gave them a few words, but told them nothing. Vera shot a quick look back into Chloe Spence's room and made her way outside.

Josh Woodburn was young. He lay on the edge of a rough path through a piece of scrub, close enough to the road for the street lamp outside Rosebank to cast a little light on his body. The PC had his back to Josh, looking out towards the sea and the lights of the town. Vera took out her torch to get a better look. Josh hardly looked old enough to be in a position of responsibility in a place like Rosebank, even if he was only on a temporary contract. He had floppy hair the colour of wheat and long, loose limbs. He was wearing jeans, a university sweatshirt and trainers. His face was turned towards Vera, but she could see the back of his head, the large round hole in the skull where he'd been hit, the blood that clotted and matted in the pale hay-coloured hair.

Oh Chloe, Vera thought. *What have you done? And where are you now? And if this wasn't you – and really there's nothing in your diary to suggest that it was – are you still alive?*

Because Chloe Spence had disappeared.

Vera stood next to the body and stared back towards Rosebank. She'd spent a bit of time volunteering in a children's home when she was a cadet. In those days, young trainee cops were sent out into the community to get to know their patch. It wouldn't hurt, Vera thought, if police training still included more good works and less sitting at a desk in the uni being talked at. The kids' home had been a big house on the corner of a leafy street. There'd been a garden with bikes and a tyre swing tied on a big tree. She'd been there in November, and they'd built a bonfire, and the house parents had let off fireworks. The children had swung sparklers around their heads, eyes wide and bright. There were potatoes baked in foil and sausages and toffee the kids had made that afternoon. It had been nothing like this place.

To be fair, the kids in that home had been nothing like the Rosebank kids. They were younger. Distressed and traumatized maybe, but easier to handle. You could cuddle a seven-year-old, couldn't you? Distract them with lights and sweets and stories. It would be hard to cuddle a fifteen-year-old lad, who'd punched his grandmother and stolen her pension to buy smack. Who'd just avoided the Young Offenders' Institution because of the tales of abuse he'd suffered. Who was handed over to social services to be cared for instead.

All the same, Vera couldn't see how being in that place was helping them. Inside, it was shabby and grey. It was as if all the light and the life had been sucked from it. Once, it had been a guest house for the workers who'd put up the new battery factory just up the coast. Before that, maybe for families who wanted a cheap holiday on the coast, though the beach here was still black with sea coal. Then it had become a bail hostel. Then a hostel for asylum seekers. And now this. A bleak house on the edge of a former pit village, with threadbare carpets and everywhere small signs of violence: a door almost pulled off its hinges, a sofa with a scorch mark, not quite hidden by a cushion. How could a child feel safe or loved here? Vera knew what it felt like to be unloved, but she'd grown up in the hills, with space and clean air, and couldn't remember ever feeling unsafe.

She said a few words to the officer, reassuring him that someone would be along to relieve him soon, and then reluctantly made her way back inside.

Chapter Three

IT WAS SEVEN IN THE MORNING and just getting light. Vera was sitting in the manager's office, waiting for more troops to arrive. Dr Keating was outside with the body, hidden from the world by a tent, surrounded by police tape. A couple of CSIs were in Chloe's room, the door now firmly shut against prying eyes.

Manager. The word stuck in her throat. The folk in charge weren't house parents now. They were managers. As if they were making widgets, not bringing up children. David Limbrick was with her; he'd been there all night too. The ponytail gave her hope. Once, perhaps, he had been an idealist. He'd become a social worker because he'd cared. The manager of a widget factory wouldn't have a ponytail.

'Tell me about the dead man,' she said, looking out of the window at the pale wash above the horizon. 'Josh Woodburn.'

'He came to us through the agency. It's hard to keep permanent staff. The company took up the references and did the police checks. That always takes for ever.' He glared at her as if the delay was all her fault. 'Josh had only been filling the gap for six weeks or so. He seemed pleasant enough.' He looked up at her. 'I didn't really get to know him. It's all firefighting here. One crisis after another. And most agency staff don't stay long.'

So it's not worth the effort getting to know them?

'And Chloe? Any history of violence?'

'Nothing physical here. Her teachers say she's aggressive at school. Challenging.'

Well, you would be, wouldn't you, Vera thought, if that was the only way to get their attention?

NOBODY LISTENS. The words on the page of the diary scorched into her memory.

'I don't understand why nobody heard anything, saw anything, last night. How did Chloe leave without you knowing?'

'This isn't a prison, Inspector.'

'But you'd want to know where they all are! And it was dark. Not late I know, but surely they're not allowed just to wander off.'

Limbrick shut his eyes. He was exhausted. She thought again that he'd been awake all night too. 'They're supposed to check in with the office, ask permission, but they're not exactly keepers of rules, these kids. This is a big house and there are ways in and out. Probably more ways than I know.'

'It sounds like chaos!'

He looked up at her with his sad grey eyes. 'Most of the time, it is chaos. We're under-staffed and under-resourced. Most of our residents have been through trauma. They need counselling and proper psychological support. But the children and adolescent mental health services are stretched too, and when the kids do get to the top of the waiting list, the process feels more like a tick-box exercise.' For the first time he seemed engaged, angry. 'In the end, most of them will come to you, Inspector. Taking up your time and an expensive prison place.'

She nodded. Now, he seemed brave to her, sticking it out, doing his best.

'What's that she says about Wicca? That's witchcraft, isn't it?'

He shrugged. 'She's got all sorts of weird ideas.' A pause. 'Never has her nose out of a book.'

'Have you any idea where Chloe might be? Friends? Extended family?'

He shook his head. 'There are grandparents, but apparently they never got on. I phoned last night, but they hadn't seen her.'

'She can't have got far, and we've got a watch out for her.' After all, Vera thought, how far could a fourteen-year-old lass get, when it was dark, and she had no transport?

A uniformed officer was standing outside, guarding the front door. Vera could hear his voice and a mutter of conversation and then the bang of a door, before a big woman pushed her way into the office. She was middle-aged, a peroxide blonde, wearing leggings and a sweatshirt with a tiger's face on it.

'What the fuck's going on outside then?' The voice deeply local and a bit amused.

'This is Tracey.' Dave gave the woman a smile. Tentative, a kind of warning. 'And this is Detective Inspector Stanhope.' A pause. 'Josh Woodburn's been murdered. A dog-walker found him on the edge of the common last night. And Chloe Spence has gone missing.'

A moment's silence. 'Dave, man, I leave you on your own for one night . . .' She looked at them both. 'Are you being serious? This is for real?'

'I'm afraid so.' Vera had taken to the woman immediately – there was something robust about her, like she'd stand up for the kids in her care – but she was also a potential witness.

'We'll need a statement. You were watching a movie with the kids yesterday evening?'

'Only with the three of them. Chloe didn't want to join in.' Tracey glanced at her watch. 'Look, can this wait until later? I want to get breakfast sorted, make sure they're out of their beds. Two of them have school to get to, and I don't like them leaving with empty stomachs.'

'Sure,' Vera said. 'No rush.' She was liking the big woman even more.

There was sunshine now, so pale you could tell that winter was on its way, and on the drive outside, two cars pulled up. Her sergeant, Joe Ashworth, climbed out of the first and a woman from the second. It took the inspector a moment to recognize her. She got to her feet and left Limbrick's office to greet the newcomers.

They stood outside the house. Vera was glad of the fresh air, the chill of the breeze from the sea. Rosebank stood on the edge of the town and she could see there were still lights on in the houses just inland. People had forgotten to turn them off when the sun came up. She nodded to Joe and turned to the other woman. Katherine Willmore, former lawyer and now Police and Crime Commissioner. A political appointment, elected by the residents of her patch. 'Ma'am.' Vera had time for the woman, but there was a question in the inflection of her voice:

What the shit are you doing here? This is operational. My business not yours.

'I was in the office early,' Willmore said. She was another woman who couldn't sleep. 'I knew this would be a sensitive case.' A pause. 'Private care homes have been in the news

13

lately. There was that TV documentary.' Another pause and then a confession. 'I'd like to bring them back into local authority control. It doesn't seem right to be making a profit from troubled children.' She looked up and gave a wan smile. 'Not that it'll happen, the way things are financially.' She looked out over the sand stained with coal dust to the grey sky. 'More likely to see a herd of pigs flying out there.'

Willmore had a daughter who was a little troubled herself. Vera nodded, but said nothing. She kept away from politics. Instead, she talked Willmore and Joe through the case as she understood it. 'A dog-walker found the body at about nine-thirty. Woodburn's car was here – the manager heard it at about eight and assumed he was inside – but nobody saw him. So we can assume time of death at between eight and nine-thirty. We won't get any closer than that, even after the post-mortem. The others were in the lounge watching a film, apparently. It's a rambling place, but they can only take four kids. They all have problems apparently. Tricky to handle.'

'And the missing girl?'

'Chloe Spence. Fourteen going on fifteen. The youngest resident of Rosebank now. Father left the family and the mam had some sort of nervous breakdown. A year on and the mother's back in the psychiatric hospital. According to the records, she'd suffered bouts of depression since she was a teenager. Chloe's an only child and there are no other relatives she's willing to stay with.'

'We think she killed Woodburn?'

'Well, she's disappeared. Hard to know if she's the killer or another victim. We need to find her.'

Joe Ashworth was lurking just outside Vera's field of view, and she could tell he was feeling restive.

'Go and see how Doc Keating is getting on.' She gestured towards the gathering around the tent. 'Then find the manager, Limbrick. He's in the office just inside the front door. He'll show you into Chloe's room.' She paused for a moment. 'We need to find the lass.'

'She's our prime suspect then,' he said. It was a statement rather than a question.

Vera didn't know what to say to that. She was remembering the diary entry. *I think I could be in love with him.* Could the lass have written that and then hit him so hard that his blood and bone spattered the thin grey grass?

'Billy Cartwright is already in there. Can you chat to Limbrick, once you've got an idea of the lie of the land? He's been up all night and I think we should let him go home as soon as we can. Get him to introduce you to the kids. Tracey, the other worker on duty, is already here getting their breakfast. She'll be on shift all day and we can get a statement from her when the kids are out of the way.'

Vera didn't want to go in yet. She needed a few more minutes to enjoy the sunshine. To give her the energy to put on a brave face.

She'd expected Willmore to follow Joe in, but the woman hovered beside her, irritating as a fly in summer.

'I hear you've made an appointment. Holly's replacement.'

That stab of guilt. *Nobody will replace Holly.*

'Yes, ma'am.'

'A local woman?'

'From Newcastle.' Brash and loud and as different from the cerebral Holly as it would be possible to be. The new DC would enjoy a night out with the lasses on the Quayside, eyeing up the footballers, getting pissed and rowdy until the make-up smudged and the shoes were discarded. 'I think she'll do very well. I've had good reports and she seems the sort to be able to look after herself.'

Willmore nodded once more. 'I'll leave you to it, then. Keep me informed.' She walked briskly towards her car. Vera took a breath and went inside.

Chapter Four

Joe Ashworth was worried. It was only weeks since Holly, their colleague, had died, and the boss was still grieving. She didn't need this. Not another high-profile murder with political rumblings. Not with Willmore sticking her neb in. He told himself that Vera should have taken some time off after the funeral. He felt sad enough about Holly, but he didn't have such a burden of guilt to carry. He'd tried his best to save her. Joe had been brought up as a Methodist and his dad was a lay preacher. He still had a sliver of faith to see him through the bad times. He thought guilt was like a weight on Vera's shoulders. Physical. It made her seem stooped and old. Never before had he thought of Vera as old.

After checking in with the pathologist in the tent, Joe made his way inside. Limbrick took him to the girl's room and then led him back downstairs into a big kitchen. Joe wondered how anyone could have thought Rosebank was a good name for the place. It conjured up country cottages, chintz and cosiness, but the house was institutional, functional. This room had a peeling laminate floor and plastic chairs around a fake wood table. The walls were pale purple and clashed with the colour of the furniture. It looked as if someone had found a pot of leftover paint to cover stains which weren't quite hidden. A woman was standing by the stove frying sausages, and the smell made Ashworth realize that he'd not had breakfast. There was the background sound of a washing machine. Kids were helping themselves to cereal from catering-size boxes. There was lurid orange juice in a plastic jug. The plates were plastic, though these were teenagers not toddlers.

There were two lads and one girl. She wore leggings and a shapeless black school jersey, black gym shoes. There was something frail and haunted about her. When she reached for the jug of juice, her sleeve fell back, and Joe saw cut marks on her wrist. He wasn't one for flights of fancy, but he thought she'd been born scared. One of the lads, thin and weedy, looking younger than the others, was in a traditional uniform, with a tie and blazer. It was Monday, and in Joe's house the beginning of the week meant clean uniforms, everything newly ironed, smelling fresh. The kids might not stay tidy for long, but they started out looking good. Here, the uniforms were faded as if everything had been stuck in the wash together. Joe could have wept.

The last kid didn't wear uniform at all. He was in a rip-off Newcastle shirt over trackie bottoms. He was the leader. He had fierce, angry eyes, but there was something appealing about him too. An energy. He was good-looking in a romantic rebel kind of way. James Dean for a fresh generation. The sort lasses might love, but parents would hate. He nodded to the adults as they came in, and flashed a quick smile at Joe.

'What's going on then, Dave?' He couldn't quite keep still and was bouncing on the balls of his feet, like a boxer before a bout. 'I need to be in town.'

Joe wondered if he was high, or rattling, desperate for a fix, or maybe he was just the sort of lad who needed more space than this. Joe had been to school with boys like that, boys who couldn't be contained. They'd become runners, athletes, soldiers.

'Josh is dead,' Limbrick said. 'I explained last night. This is DS Ashworth. He wants to talk to you all.'

'Just a few words,' Joe said, 'before you get off. We'll send someone in to school this morning to take proper statements.'

Vera had wanted the kids out of the way as soon as possible.

'I'm not at school.' That quick smile again. 'No one will have me. And I'm nearly sixteen anyway. I'll be leaving soon.'

'Then I can talk to you in a bit, can't I?' Joe fixed him with a stare. 'We're looking for Chloe. She might be in trouble. Does anyone know where she could be?'

There was a silence. The woman lifted sausages out of the pan and stuck them into sliced bread, put the sandwiches onto a plate and set it in the middle of the table.

The boys took one each. Still, nobody answered. The girl in the over-sized jumper made no move. Joe took a seat next to her. 'Were you and Chloe friendly?'

'Not really.'

'What's your name?'

'Mel. Melanie Hunter.' Her voice was scarcely more than a whisper.

'Only two lasses in the place, you'd surely have stuck together.'

'Not really,' she said again.

Joe waited for some explanation, but none came.

'Were you at school with her?'

Melanie shook her head. 'I'm at Birks. She goes to Salvation Academy.'

Joe had heard of Salvation. It had the best exam results in the region. Not selective. Not allowed to be. But choosy. You needed an interview to get in.

'Any idea where she might be?'

Melanie shrugged and picked at her nails. Joe was a father. His Jess was almost a teenager, and she could be pretty inscrutable. But he had no idea how to get through to this girl, with her blank eyes and flat voice.

He gave up with the lads in the end too. Nobody had heard or seen anything unusual. They were in the common room all evening watching a film. Josh was okay, they said. They didn't expect him to stay long. Agency workers came and went.

Each bit of information was squeezed from them in grunts between mouthfuls of sausage and oozings of tomato ketchup. Joe couldn't be sure they hadn't fixed their story before he arrived.

In the end, he said they could go, and Mel and the weedy lad went out to get the bus to school. The woman followed them. Joe was left with Dave Limbrick and super-cool Brad.

'Just answer the sergeant's questions.' Limbrick sounded exhausted now. 'Then we'll leave you alone.'

'I've got to go into town. Now. Appointment with my social worker.' This time the smile was challenging. He knew he wouldn't be believed.

'Answer the questions first.'

Brad shrugged. 'Sure. What do you want to know?'

'Tell me about Chloe.'

'She thinks she's better than the rest of us.' A pause. 'She has something about her. Posho voice, big fancy words and that. Always dressing weird. Who's even a goth nowadays?'

'Chloe's a goth?'

'Kinda. Black hair and black stuff on her eyes. Looks like a witch. Not when she went to that fancy school like, but the rest of the time.'

'So you didn't mix much?'

'A bit.' Joe thought he could sense a tinge of regret. Had Brad tried it on? Been rejected? 'I thought we might get on when she first came. She had more about her than some of them. But mostly she hid away in her room. Reading books.' As if that was totally weird.

'Anyone here she was friendly with?'

'Only Woodburn. You could tell she was into him. Big style.' This time there was definitely an edge to his voice. 'I couldn't get it. He was just a tosser. Wet, you know.'

'What time's your appointment?' Limbrick's words were sharp.

'Uh?'

'With the social worker?'

'Oh, now. I'd best get off.'

'I could come in to the session with you,' Limbrick said. 'Check progress.'

'Nah, you're all right.' He gave another, complicit grin, before slinking out of the room.

'What's going on with him?' Joe made no effort to keep the antipathy from his voice.

'Brad's been exploited all his life. First by his father, then a foster carer and now by some thugs with pretensions to set up a county lines gang. He's a petty dealer and a user. Not very bright and completely screwed up. His mother died when he was a kid. He stayed with his grandparents until he stole from them. He's been chucked out of every institution he's been put in.'

'But you've hung on to him?'

'Yeah. You might not believe it, but he's improved since he came here. He can be quite likeable. Funny. He winds the other kids up at times, but he's started to rub along with them.' Limbrick shrugged. 'It's a kind of success.'

Joe thought that didn't sound like any sort of success to him. 'In her diary, Chloe talks about him peddling drugs in the place. Also, about someone pervy hanging around in a car outside the home. Do you know who that might be?'

Limbrick shook his head. 'It could just have been someone waiting to pick up a staff member after their shift.'

'Did Chloe mention it to you?'

There was a pause. At the other end of the room, Tracey was loading the dishwasher. She'd put the radio on low. Radio Two. Some love song.

'When Chloe first came here,' Limbrick said, 'she was demanding, lippy. Her background was different from most of the kids. Perhaps because her mother and the school found her behaviour challenging, she was used to attention. She'd come into the office with stories. Some had a bit of basis in truth, but others were so wild they were unbelievable. Strange conspiracy theories picked up from social media. Fantasies just created in her own head. Maybe she believed the lies she told, but in the end, I couldn't take her seriously.' He looked up at Joe. 'She was lonely. She struggled to make friends here. She was cleverer than most of the kids we get and made fun of them, or got in their faces. She probably lied to them too. After a few weeks, she spent most of her time in her room.'

'You didn't believe there was a guy hanging around in a car outside?' Joe was imagining grooming or the kind of county lines that Brad had been sucked into. The lass had been missing

all night, so perhaps someone had picked her up, offered her shelter, an escape from the police.

'I'm not saying that, but I didn't see anyone.'

'She seemed close to Josh Woodburn.'

'Josh hadn't worked here long. He hadn't had a chance to get cynical.'

'Why don't you get off home?' Joe said. The man's gloom had started to affect him. He felt it settle like dust on his skin and his clothes. 'Get some kip and a shower. Come back later.'

Limbrick nodded and walked away. Tracey, the other social worker, came back into the kitchen and started clearing plates.

'You were in the lounge with the three kids all evening?'

'Yeah. Sunday's film night. A kind of ritual. They've never had any sort of routine, so we try to create one.'

'They were all with you all night?'

'Well, they wandered in and out during the evening, pretending they needed the toilet or to fetch something. I'm sure Brad would have gone out for a sneaky drag of weed. Mel vapes, and she knows I can't stand the smell. None of them are used to sitting still for long. Except George. The youngest lad. He hardly moves at all. I went into the kitchen to make a brew and to bring in cans of pop for the kids. But I can't see that anyone was away long enough to kill Josh. And why would they? It was a chilled evening.' She paused. 'I was pleased Chloe decided to miss it. She's angry most of the time. Confrontational. Likes to provoke a scene.'

'You think she was angry enough to kill Josh?'

Tracey gave a little laugh. 'Nah! She worshipped him.'

* * *

As Joe was looking for Vera, he bumped into Brad Russell who was on his way out. Swaggering. No coat despite the cold. Playing the hard man.

They stood, looking at each other for a moment. A kind of stand-off.

'Have a good day,' Joe said. 'See you later.'

Brad said nothing and walked outside.

Vera was in the office. Joe leaned against the desk beside her.

'I've just sent the manager home.'

She looked up from a sheaf of files. 'Yeah, he called in on his way through.'

'Cheery soul.'

'Would you be? Working here.' She closed one of the files. 'I've got an address for Woodburn's next of kin at last. Limbrick didn't have it on the files – admin doesn't seem his strongest point – and I had to go through the agency. It's the same as his home address apparently. We couldn't track it down until someone showed up at the agency's office this morning. You okay to notify the death?'

'Okay.' It was a role Joe hated, but at least it would get him away from this place.

'The new woman's on her way here. You could take her with you. See how she gets on.'

She'd just finished speaking when they saw a car pull up outside. It didn't quite screech to a halt, but it was going faster than it should have been in the narrow drive and there was a scattering of gravel when it braked. It was red. Long black boots appeared from the driver's door, then very tight jeans.

'Is that her?'

'Yeah,' Vera's voice was flat. 'That's Rosie Bell. You'd best go out and welcome her to the team.'

Chapter Five

NINE O'CLOCK IN THE MORNING AND there was still no news of Chloe. They'd been texting and calling all night, leaving messages for her, but the phone must be switched off, because they hadn't been able to track her movements through it.

Vera had walked round the building the night before, looking for possible exits out of the reach of the limited CCTV. The kitchen door was locked on the inside, and she suspected that would be the route the kids would use if they didn't want to be seen from the office.

It occurred to Vera that the girl might just turn up at school as if nothing had happened. With some story about where she'd been. Everyone said she was good at stories. Her uniform might be wrapped up in a bag. There might be some school friend she'd stayed with after legging it from the home. Vera hoped she had a friend. She'd been about to phone the school, when Joe Ashworth had appeared after chatting to the kids, and then Rosie Bell turned up in her flash red car. Vera waited for them both to drive off before grabbing her coat and leaving the building herself. She was interested to meet the 'Miss' who'd been more concerned about the state of Chloe's uniform than the fact that she was at home alone with a woman going through a serious psychotic episode.

She felt a moment of relief, almost of joy, driving away from Rosebank. The cloud had cleared overnight and the sunlight was reflected in the puddles in the narrow road. She was thinking how good it was to be out of the building, before the guilt kicked in.

We shut these kids away so we can't see them and don't have to deal with them.

She was briefly cheered by the thought of what Joe's wife, Sal, would make of their new DC. Holly had been no threat, but Rosie was a very different sort of woman, quite gorgeous if you liked fake tan and stick-on eyelashes. And she had the kick-ass attitude to go with the looks. Joe wouldn't know what had hit him.

But the guilt and the sadness that had haunted her since Holly's death soon returned. Holly had died working on a case, and Vera knew she was responsible.

The school was on the other side of Longwater, the town where the children's home stood. It had been built twenty years ago on a brownfield site which had once held a steel plant and employed hundreds of people, one of the first round of academies when they were sponsored by companies and individuals. It still looked good though. Freshly painted and well maintained. Inside, it was like walking into a fancy office building, all shiny plants and a reception desk with a shiny woman behind a glass screen. The photograph of the person who'd first sponsored the academy smiled down on her. Vera paused to look at it. Then she was reminded of tinpot countries, where the photos of leaders were prominent in every public building. The pupils were dressed in bottle-green blazers with badges and black trousers and skirts. Black-and-green striped ties. The plants had been chosen to match the exact same shade of green as the uniforms. As the last arrivals walked down the corridor, all in the one direction, they seemed unnaturally quiet.

Vera introduced herself and asked to speak to the head.

'I'm afraid all our teachers are busy this morning. We have a very special assembly. Our sponsor comes once a term to talk to the school and give out awards to the students who have made most progress. The trustees are here too.'

'Will it take long?' Now she was here, Vera didn't want just to piss off back to the police station.

'Only half an hour,' the woman said. 'We don't want to interrupt our students' education.'

'I'll wait then.'

She wandered up the corridor. The door to the hall had been left open and she could see what was taking place inside. The stage was ahead of her. On it, a row of chairs on which sat about a dozen people. All smart. These must be the trustees, and perhaps some of the senior staff. In the centre the sponsor, whose photo had been displayed in reception. She was in her forties, power-dressed in a skirt and jacket. She'd have looked more at home in a boardroom than a school.

A different woman got to her feet and stood at the lectern. She introduced herself as Susanna Hepple, chair of trustees. She was slim, well dressed and neatly groomed, but her attire wasn't as formal as the other trustees. She was in her thirties and seemed to Vera to be very young to hold such a position.

'I'm going to ask Helen Miles, our sponsor and founder, to give prizes to the students who have made most progress over the term so far. As most of you will know, Miss Miles was born and grew up in Longwater. She struggled to make her way in the world, and founded the school to give children in the area the start that she never had. Helen, we're all very grateful for your generosity.'

There was an orchestrated round of applause. Helen Miles got to her feet and beamed out at them, so she looked just like her photograph.

Her voice was local. Success hadn't changed that. 'I'm delighted to be here. As you know, I spend a lot of time in the school and the ethos we've created – hard work backed by Christian values – is absolutely mine. I'm grateful to the wonderful staff who, every day, turn my vision into reality. I hope you understand how lucky you are to attend this magnificent academy. Congratulations to all the award winners.'

The rest of the ceremony passed very quickly. Certificates were handed over and blushing children returned to their seats. Vera was willing to bet that Chloe Spence had never been invited to the stage. She wandered back to the lobby.

Ten minutes later, the receptionist called over to her. 'I've just spoken to the head teacher's secretary and I'm afraid that, immediately after assembly, he'll be in a meeting for the rest of the morning. But Miss Miles would be happy to speak to you.' The last statement was spoken with a mix of astonishment and awe.

Immediately, Vera heard the clack of heels on polished floor and Miles appeared. She was even more impressive close to: no inch of spare flesh, and cheekbones you could cut a cake with. If ever a mouthful of cake crossed her lips, which seemed unlikely. She led Vera into a small and wonderfully tidy office. It had a view of playing fields, with the grey sea in the distance.

'The head's said we can use his room. He'll be interviewing all morning.' That voice placing her roots in the former coalfield of south-east Northumberland.

'I'm here about Chloe Spence.'

'Ah yes, Chloe.' As if she could have guessed that Vera was interested in that particular child.

'You've heard of her? I thought your role was . . .' Vera struggled to find the word, '. . . honorary.'

'All the teaching is entirely independent, obviously. I make no attempt to interfere. But this is my project. I want to be involved. I understand that Chloe has had problems here.'

'Is she in school today?'

Miles tapped on the computer on her desk and frowned. 'No. She's been marked down as absent.'

'I'd like to talk to one of her teachers. A form teacher, perhaps. The person who knew her best.'

The woman who said she could be a songwriter or poet.

'That would be her tutor.' Miles looked up from the screen. 'We work a tutorial system here to provide some continuity throughout our students' journey.'

Vera wondered what that must be like if you disliked each other: to be stuck with someone you couldn't stand for all those years. She restrained from smiling. It would be just like her team and her. You'd have to learn to rub along as her colleagues had to.

'Could I speak to the tutor then?'

'Let me just check Miss Wiseman's timetable.' Miles looked up briefly again. 'The tutor's Rachel Wiseman. You're in luck. She's free this period. I assume she'll be working in the staffroom.' She got to her feet and asked, pretending not to be too interested: 'What's Chloe been up to?'

'We don't know that she's been up to anything. But she's missing and she's a vulnerable child.'

'Of course.' The perfect face expressed manufactured concern followed by the same thin, tight smile.

Rachel Wiseman was on her own in the staffroom, sitting at a table, marking a pile of exercise books. She was young, plump, smooth-faced, more like a student herself, Vera thought, than a teacher. She stood up when Helen Miles walked in. As if the sponsor was royalty. Miles introduced Vera, then seemed inclined to stay and sit in on the interview.

'We won't keep you.' Vera saw that there was a filter machine with a jug full of coffee next to the sink. Besides, she could tell that Rachel Wiseman would be terrified – this was the founder of the school – and certainly she'd talk more easily without the woman earwigging. 'I'm sure you're busy.'

Miles flickered another smile. 'If you're sure . . . Let me know if I can help when you're finished.'

She's a control freak. Then: *It takes one to know one.*

When Miles had left the room, Vera poured coffee for her and for Rachel without waiting to be asked. 'I don't suppose there are any biscuits knocking around? I'm bloody starving.'

The young teacher smiled. 'In the blue tin in the cupboard. My own secret stash.'

'I wouldn't want to deprive you . . .' But Vera already had the cupboard open. 'I'm here about Chloe Spence. You're her tutor, so you probably know her better than anyone else. She's gone missing in difficult circumstances and we're desperate to trace her.'

'Poor Chloe. She and I started at Salvation at the same

time. I was a newly qualified teacher and she was a bright eleven-year-old.'

'Tell me about her.'

'At first, she was much like all the other kids in the class. Eager, enthusiastic. I taught her English as well as being her tutor. She had a real way with words. She read more than any other kid in the school. Sometimes she got a bit lost in the stories. I think she spent a lot of time on social media, reading other students' stuff. Fan fiction, you know, and weird conspiracy theories, almost believing that stuff was real. Maybe wanting to believe it, to belong to the group.'

'She said she was into Wicca. That's some kind of witchcraft?'

The teacher laughed. 'She never mentioned that! I guess she needed to escape to another world. You can understand why, with everything that was going on in her life. But I thought she'd do well here.' Then she paused. 'She'd come to us with very high SAT results from primary school though.'

'Isn't that a good thing?'

'Well, of course. But the thing about Salvation is that they're recognized for their value added.'

They not we. Vera thought Rachel Wiseman was already looking for another job.

'I don't understand.'

'Well, if the children come with high SATs and they don't improve, it doesn't reflect well on the school. It looks as if the trust isn't fulfilling its role to build standards from a lower base.'

'It's hard for your work to improve if your father's left home and your mother's going through a psychotic episode.'

'I know.' Rachel Wiseman shifted awkwardly in her chair. 'I tried to explain to management that Chloe was going through a hard time, but they insisted that the rules should still be applied.'

'Uniform socks.'

'It sounds ridiculous, but the theory is that if we get the small things right – like uniform – then good behaviour and a strong work ethic will follow.' She was blushing now. 'I did try to intervene on Chloe's behalf, but I was told that I was getting too emotionally involved. The head always says: "We're educators not social workers. The best thing we can do for these kids is give them a good education." It kind of made sense, and there are so many kids here with difficult families and mental health issues that we all feel a bit swamped. I was told that if I was worried about a safeguarding issue I should pass the information on to the teacher in charge of welfare.'

'Miss Saltburn. The teacher of RE, who'd already had a run-in with Chloe.'

'You know about that? She told you?'

'Not directly.' Vera paused. She'd done a bit of googling in the early hours of the morning. 'I thought that academies had to admit children of all faiths and none.'

'Miss Miles has a strong evangelical faith. We admit children to reflect the entire local region, but parents understand that Salvation has a strong Christian ethos.'

Vera didn't reply directly to that.

'The school must have been told that Chloe had been moved into a care home. They'd have been invited to the child protection meetings.'

'Yes . . .' Rachel hesitated.

'But that would have been Miss Saltburn too.' Vera finished the sentence for her. Rachel nodded.

'And she wouldn't have been very sympathetic.'

'Chloe wasn't the easiest after her father moved out. It was as if she set out to be confrontational. She picked fights with the other kids she claimed were laughing at her. Real fights, hitting and scratching.'

'She was physically violent?'

Violent and strong enough to kill a grown man with loose limbs and wheat-coloured hair?

'She had a short fuse. And when she lost her temper, she really lost it.'

'Of course, that provided ammunition for Miss Saltburn.'

'Yeah,' Rachel said, 'along with Chloe's apparent belief in her own fantasies and the whole conspiracy thing. Sometimes, they came across as excuses for poor behaviour, lies. The management team would have liked to exclude her permanently, but the social worker persuaded Salvation to give her one last chance.'

'Were the kids laughing at her?'

'Oh yes!' Rachel looked directly at Vera. Her words were bitter. 'Conformity is prized at Salvation. Chloe isn't interested in conforming, and the children pick that up.'

'Did Chloe have anyone on her side?' More than anything now, Vera wanted there to be someone who cared for Chloe, and not just because that might make it easier to find her.

'When she first started here, she was great friends with Esther Sullivan. They'd been at primary school together. But as Chloe's behaviour deteriorated, Esther started to distance herself. Partly, I suspect, because of pressure from her parents and other teachers, partly because she was, by nature, a rather shy girl. A keeper of rules. Chloe's notoriety would have scared her.'

Vera made a note of the name. It was possible that, at a time of danger, Chloe would have turned to her oldest friend. Her only friend.

An electronic bell rang. There was the sound of doors opening and shutting, murmured conversations as pupils made their way to different classes.

'I'm sorry,' Rachel said. 'I'm teaching next period. I have to go.'

They stood for a moment.

'Will you stay here?' Vera asked. 'Try to make a difference?'

Rachel shook her head. 'Nah, I'm too much of a coward. Or too much of a realist. I start at Birks after Christmas. I know it's rough and it won't be easy, but at least there, the teachers seem to like kids.'

Helen Miles was waiting for Vera in the lobby, lean and predatory like a hawk.

'Is there anything else I can help you with, Inspector?'

'Not at the moment, thank you.'

Miles looked at her watch. 'I'll head off then.' She added: 'I'm on a flight to London this afternoon.' Just to show how important she was.

Vera waited until she'd left the building before turning to the receptionist. 'I'd like Esther Sullivan's home address.'

'I'm not sure . . .'

'This is a police inquiry.' Vera smiled. 'And a child is missing. We all want Chloe back safe and well, don't we?'

'Of course.' The woman knew when she was beaten. 'Of course.'

Chapter Six

THE SOCIAL WORK AGENCY HAD GIVEN Josh Woodburn's home address as Cullercoats, a village on the coast, part of the sprawl between Tynemouth and Whitley Bay. A sheltered bay held between two piers, once it had been a fishing village. The American artist Winslow Homer had painted the boats and the fisherwomen and the storms coming in from the sea. Now only one row of picturesque fishermen's cottages remained, the rest knocked down and replaced in the seventies by a small estate of flats and terraced houses. These days, Cullercoats was famous for wild swimming, kayaking and paddle-boarding, and property prices put it well outside Joe's reach, even if he'd wanted to live there. Older locals still took out small boats for lobster and crab.

Rosie had talked at him most of the way there. Holly had been a private woman, taciturn. Throughout their time of working together, he'd found out little about her personal life. Over the years, she'd become even more reserved, more silent. Often Joe had wanted to yell at her to talk to him, to get through her shell to the woman inside. Today he'd wanted to yell at Rosie to shut up.

There was a story about a hen night in Edinburgh. *We were mortal by the time the train left Alnmouth. Jenny had brought everything for making cocktails in one of those hampers you get in Fenwick's for Christmas. Shakers, glasses and more varieties of booze than I've seen in my life before. I dunno what happened after that, but I do remember dancing down Prince's Street at four in the morning.*

Then there'd been the questions about Vera. *She's a bit of a legend, isn't she, your boss? Is it right she's never had a bloke? Gay, is she?*

'No!' Joe had answered that immediately. That was the way rumours started and there were enough of those surrounding Vera anyway. 'She just likes her own company. And she's wedded to the job.'

'Oh.' Rosie had seemed dumbfounded.

'What about you? You in a relationship?' Because it was better to have the endless anecdotes about Rosie Bell than endless questions about Vera Stanhope.

'I was. Not anymore.' And then she'd fallen uncharacteristically silent. For which Joe was profoundly grateful.

In Cullercoats, they stood for a moment outside the house. Since the clocks had moved back, it was lighter in the mornings and the sun surprised him with its strength. Looking out at the sea, he had to squint.

'They must be minted.' Rosie was eyeing up the house, not the view.

Joe agreed. It was a large Victorian end of terrace on the corner of the seafront and the street leading inland to the village. He could see there was a long garden at the back, with mature trees, taller than the wall that surrounded it. Some of the houses in the street had been converted into flats, but this was still intact: three storeys, long windows looking out at the bay. The rooms at the front would be full of light at this time of the day. Joe could see inside to a front room: solid furniture, paintings, a log-burner and on each side of the chimney breast shelves full of books. This wasn't a place that an agency carer would afford.

'I think it belongs to his parents.' He thought it unlikely that anyone would be in. Josh was young; his parents would still be working. He rang the bell and heard the sound echo inside. There were footsteps and a man in his fifties opened the door.

'Yes?' He was wearing jeans and a hand-knitted jersey, specs. His voice was impatient, but he wasn't thrown by two strangers appearing on the doorstep. He had, Joe thought, no suspicion that his life was about to change.

'Mr Woodburn?'

'Yes.' He was curious now. His head was tilted to one side. Joe introduced himself. 'We're here about Josh.'

At last, it seemed, the man realized that this was serious, but still not the possibility of tragedy. 'What's happened? Where is he?'

'Could we come in?' Rosie's voice was more gentle than Joe would have thought possible. 'We'll explain.'

And it was Rosie who took over the interview at first. She found out immediately, as they stood in the hall with its original patterned floor tiles, that Anna, the man's wife, was at work in Gateshead. She was a GP and Chris was an accountant for an investment company. He worked from home, he said, and led them not into the living room Joe had seen from the pavement, but into his office on the first floor. As if they were clients, rather than police officers. The room was at the back. There was a long window, with a wrought-iron balcony looking out over the garden. He took his seat at the desk behind his computer, a barrier between them. They sat on leather chairs.

'I'm so sorry,' Rosie said, 'but Josh is dead. His body was found last night in Rosebank, the children's home where he was working.' No kind or misleading words. Joe approved of that. He'd learned from Vera that the best way to break bad news was to be straight.

'There's a mistake.' Chris Woodburn sat very still for a moment. Frozen, Joe thought, by shock. Then he gave a tight little laugh. 'Josh doesn't work. He's a student. There must be somebody else with the same name.'

'His employer gave us this address,' Rosie said. 'Was he home last night?'

'No, he doesn't live at home. Not at the moment. This is his permanent address, but in term time he stays in the city. He's got a flat there with three friends. He wanted to stay local to study, but he still wanted the student experience. We could understand that. And he still comes home of course. Most Sundays for his mother's roast dinner. When he needs his washing done.' Anxiety seemed to be making him voluble.

There was a photo propped on the bookshelf behind Woodburn. A middle-aged couple looked out at the lens and between stood them a young man. With long, loose limbs and wheat-coloured hair.

Rosie nodded towards the picture. 'Is that Josh, Mr Woodburn?'

'Yes, it was taken on the beach here. Anna and I love it.'

'That looks very like the young man who was found dead last night in a children's home up the coast in Northumberland. He'd been working there for six weeks. Mostly night shifts. Could he have been supplementing his income? Doing something useful at the same time?'

'No! He would have told us.' Then, turning to Rosie and

almost begging for confirmation: 'We were close. Every month he and I went walking in the hills together. He's our only child. You can see that he would have told us?'

'Perhaps it was something to do with his course,' she said. 'What was he studying? Psychology? Sociology?'

'No! He was doing art history. And he was an artist himself. He made film. That was his thing.' A pause. 'I need to see him. I can't believe it until then. None of this makes sense.'

'Of course,' Rosie said. 'We'll need a formal identification as well.'

'I have to tell Anna. She'll want to be there too.'

'Would you like me to make the phone call?'

Joe couldn't believe that this tactful woman was the individual who'd shared stories about throwing up outside bars in Edinburgh, whose skin was orange with fake tan.

The man thought about that for a while. 'No,' he said at last. 'But I'll do it in the living room. I can't have an audience.'

She nodded. 'If Anna can get here, we can take you both up to the hospital in Kimmerston where Josh's body is held. You do understand that there'll have to be a post-mortem?'

Woodburn nodded, but Joe thought he hadn't really heard the words. He was planning how to tell his wife that their son could be dead.

'We can provide a lift here for Anna if she doesn't feel up to driving from Gateshead herself.'

This time, Woodburn did seem to take in the words. 'I think she'll want to drive herself. That's how she is. Independent.'

He took his phone from his pocket and retreated from the room. They heard his footsteps on the stairs.

When he returned to the room, they could see that he'd been crying. He took off his glasses and dried his eyes with a handkerchief. 'Anna will be here in half an hour.' He stuffed the handkerchief back into his jeans pocket. 'She wanted to know how Josh died. If that young man is *our* Josh. I was in so much shock that I didn't ask you, but she's a doctor, you see, and he's always been so fit. She needed to know.'

'We don't think that your son died of natural causes.' Rosie paused, reached out and put her hand on his arm. 'We think that he was murdered.'

Anna Woodburn must have broken the speed limit on her way down the coast road, because she was there long before Joe was really expecting her. He'd asked if he might take a look in Josh's room and was pointed in the direction of the third floor. It was flooded with sunshine from the skylights, full of colour. The student's own paintings hung on the walls, with photos and clipped-out pieces from magazines. No space between them. There was room for a double bed and then a sofa against one wall covered by an Indian cotton throw. A recycled wardrobe, stripped and painted eggshell blue. An ensuite bathroom. Not tidy, but clean. No festering pizza boxes or empty beer cans.

It occurred to Joe then that the Woodburns would certainly employ a cleaner. And someone to look after the garden. Joe was still looking, not touching, because the search team would come in, but getting a feel for the place and the young man – he'd learned that from Vera too – when he heard the front door bang and a woman's voice. Hoarse with pain, demanding answers, hardly human. He waited for a moment – let Rosie deal with this too – and then he went downstairs.

In the hall, he found a thin woman with short curly grey hair in Rosie's arms. The woman was crying.

★ ★ ★

The Woodburns sat in the back of the car. Joe had phoned Vera, and confirmed that Josh's body had been taken to the mortuary in Kimmerston. The couple gripped each other's hands as they got into the car. All the way north, they were silent, apart from a couple of muffled sobs from Anna. Joe was driving and didn't look behind him. He thought they deserved at least that much privacy. Rosie too said nothing. When they got to the hospital, she stayed in the car with the Woodburns, while Joe went inside to check that the mortuary team were ready for them.

The body had been laid out so the wound at the back of the head was invisible, but Josh was obviously dead, not sleeping. Joe's dormant faith returned once more and he thought the soul of the man was no longer there. Anna howled as soon as she saw her son, then stuffed her fist into her mouth to stop the noise coming out. Chris was so pale that Joe thought the man might faint.

'Would you like some time on your own with him?' Rosie's voice was hardly more than a whisper.

'Yes! Yes, please.' Anna was howling again, but this time with words.

Rosie and Joe sat outside the room on a hard bench. Rosie took out a make-up bag and redid her lipstick with a little brush. It was very red, and he thought it clashed a bit with the almost orange skin.

'You're good at all that,' Joe nodded towards the door. 'Tactful, better than I'll ever be.'

She rubbed her lips together and gave a final look in the mirror. 'Plenty of practice,' she said. 'If you're the woman in the team, you get the job, don't you? Anything the lads don't want to do they pass on to the girls with the excuse that we'll be more sympathetic.' She turned to Joe and fixed him with a stare. 'Just don't get any ideas.'

He was about to say that he'd never be as good as Rosie, however much practice he had, when the Woodburns came out. He thought he'd have to tell the boss, then said he'd arrange a lift home for them.

'We'll give you a family liaison officer,' he said. 'Someone who'll keep you informed about the investigation, keep the press off your backs.'

Anna turned to Rosie. 'Will that be you?'

Rosie shook her head. 'It's a specialist role.'

'We don't need anyone else then,' Anna said. 'We need to be on our own for a while.' She reached out and took Rosie's hand between two of hers. 'I trust you to tell us if there's any news.'

Chapter Seven

By LUNCHTIME VERA WAS BACK IN the police station. She didn't need to be in Rosebank. Mel and George were in school and the CSIs were still working the scene. Keating had already agreed for Woodburn's body to be removed to the hospital, so they could get a positive ID from the parents. She'd sent Charlie, another DC attached to the team and one of her favourites, to Birks Comp to get statements from the two Rosebank kids:

'Get that done today before they have any longer to put together even more of a story.'

She'd spoken to the duty manager at social services on the phone, begging for different accommodation for the care home children. 'There must be somewhere they could go.'

'Not within the North-East, and really you can't want me to disperse them all over the country while you're working.' The woman, Kathleen Oliver, was refusing to relent. 'It would be a terrible disruption for them and anyway I don't have the budget. Do you know how much these places charge? Rosebank is bad enough but it's at the cheaper end of the scale.'

'I need to speak to Chloe's social worker.'

'She's off sick. Just signed off for another ten days. Stress.'

'Her manager then.'

The woman sighed. 'That'd be me.'

'Can I come in? It'd be easier than over the phone and there might be paper records.'

'I suppose so. Four-ish? I'll see what's left on the system. Don't hold your breath though. She was cracking up big style, before I persuaded her to take some sick leave. Stress gets to us all in the end.'

But Kathleen Oliver sounded strong and competent. Vera thought *she* at least would survive the pressure.

Chloe's school friend, Esther Sullivan, lived on a small executive estate not far from the Salvation Academy, built on the same brownfield site. It was windswept and exposed, and something about the cracked streets and the brown, salt-laden gardens made it seem unfinished, or finished and then deserted. Perhaps, Vera thought, everywhere looked like that in November. There *was* colour in the Sullivans' garden: a red maple still with a few leaves, a couple of crab apple trees and a bush with orange berries. A bright plastic slide, which Esther must have grown out of years before. Of course, there could be younger siblings, and that meant that somebody might be at home.

She could hear them before she saw them: loud children's voices. Vera rang the bell and a woman shouted: 'Sorry, I won't be long.' Then the door opened. The woman inside was still talking before she looked up. She had a toddler on her hip. 'You're a bit early today! But James is nearly ready. Let me just find his jacket.'

Then she saw Vera. 'Are you his grandma? I can't just give him to you, you know. Not without confirmation from Gavin or Sue.' Her voice was just a decibel louder than it needed to be. She had dyed red hair and there was something theatrical about her.

'I'm not anybody's grandma, pet. I'm a police officer.'

'Oh!' There was surprise on her face. This was a person whose emotions were expressed clearly and without embarrassment. Everything about her was a little larger than life. She reminded Vera of some of the actors she'd seen in amateur theatre. 'You'd better come in then. I need to shut the door before any of the small people escape.'

It seemed that Gaby Sullivan was a childminder. She looked after three kids in her home, two toddlers and a three-year-old. Now she put them in a row on the sofa in the living room full of toys, and switched on the television. 'CBeebies. A ritual at this time of day. Half an hour in the afternoon. A brief moment of peace.'

She and Vera sat at the dining-room table. Double doors were open to the children's space, so Gaby could keep an eye, but they seemed either exhausted or transfixed. One little boy put his thumb in his mouth and fell asleep.

'His mother asks me to keep him awake so he'll sleep early in the evening. But honestly, she hasn't seen him all day – he's here by seven-thirty every morning – and he's knackered. You'd think she'd want some awake time with him when she gets him home. I let him have a little nap and I only tell her if she asks.' She seemed nervous. 'Why are you here? Is there a problem with one of the kids? I haven't noticed anything. No sign of abuse. Nothing like that. And I'm all legal. Properly registered. I trained as a nurse and turned to this when my own kids were young.' A pause for breath. 'There hasn't been a complaint?'

Vera shook her head. 'I'm investigating a murder. One of the workers at Rosebank, the care home for teenagers, was killed yesterday evening.' She paused, looking for a reaction, some sign of recognition, but there was none. 'One of the residents, Chloe Spence, has gone missing. We know she used to be friendly with your Esther. I wondered if you'd heard anything from her.'

'You think she's killed someone?' She sounded shocked, but there was something else. A kind of relief?

'We don't know what's happened at this point. She could have run away, scared by the assault. She could have been abducted. But yes, it's possible that she could be a suspect.'

More than possible, but I've come to like Chloe. I hope that's not what happened.

'I'm sure Esther hasn't heard anything from her,' Gaby said. 'They've not been close for more than a year. I didn't know Chloe had gone into care. Esthie was a very loyal friend. There were three of them, all living in this part of town, all at the same primary. Chloe, Esther and Alice. Alice's parents moved away inland to the Tyne Valley. They work at the uni and were always a bit posh for us . . .' She looked up at Vera. 'Sorry, I'm rambling. I talk too much. We were so pleased Chloe and Esther got into Salvation. Birks doesn't have the best of reputations and Paul and I don't believe in private education, so we wouldn't have chosen that route, even if we could afford it.'

'What went wrong?'

'Chloe's family life fell apart. Her mother was ill and her father lives abroad. We did what we could. She came for sleepovers most weekends, but then she started getting into bother at school.' Gaby looked up at Vera. 'She's braver than Esther and wouldn't put up with all the crazy rules. Part of me was cheering her on: *Go, girl,* I'd think when she challenged the teachers. But then the head asked us to go in. He said they were worried about Esther's progress and that she was being led astray by Chloe. Esther's brother had started there by then, and he was flying! So we pulled away a bit. The school suits Esther. She's a conformer, eager to please and their exam results are truly spectacular. They get kids into Oxbridge every year and that's unheard of in the other local schools. We didn't want to put our daughter's whole future in danger, and we asked her to widen her friendship group. But I felt bad about it. Guilty, I suppose, that we were deserting Chloe when she most needed help and support.'

Vera thought that explained the relief she'd heard in Gaby's voice when she'd mentioned the murder. How much easier it would feel to have prevented the friendship between the girls if Chloe was a killer. Then Gaby could consider herself a sensible mother, perceptive and protective, rather than someone who'd let down a child in need.

'Can you ask Esther if she's heard from Chloe? The lass's phone seems to be switched off, but she might have found a way to communicate with Esther. We don't think she had any other friends.'

'Sure. Of course. Poor girl.' Gaby was almost in tears.

'Here's my card. Please give me a ring if you hear anything. Even if it's only a rumour.'

Vera let herself out. Looking back through the window, she saw that Gaby had joined the kids on the sofa. She had her arm around one of them and bent down and kissed the top of her head. A gesture of grief, almost of apology.

Oh, pet, Vera thought. *It's a bit late to be sorry now.*

✶   ✶   ✶

She got to the social services office exactly at four o'clock. She didn't want Oliver to have any excuse not to see her. It was in a children's centre in the middle of Longwater, not far from the docks. Once it had been part of a smart new Sure Start project; now it was looking a bit worse for wear, with peeling paint and stained concrete. Parents were picking their children up from the nursery, chatting to the workers, laughing at a joke one of them had made. It felt reassuring. Normal.

The social worker was reassuring too.

'Call me Kath. Everyone does.'

She was plump, about Vera's age, so not that far from retirement. She wore sensible shoes, and seemed solid, grounded. The only flash of vanity came in the form of long enamel earrings and a clunky bead necklace.

'I've dug around in her files a bit. I'm not sure that there's anything helpful. Nothing recent, at least. Have you been in touch with the father? It seems he works abroad.'

'I left a message with his employer. Apparently he's away on holiday.'

'Back in the UK?'

That hadn't occurred to Vera and it stopped her in her tracks for a moment. 'I'm not sure. Of course, we're checking.'

Or we will *be checking.*

They were sitting in a meeting room on comfortable chairs. There was a box of tissues on the coffee table. This was where parents were comforted and confronted. The low afternoon sun was hidden by the buildings on the other side of the road. Vera felt very tired and briefly thought she was too old to be awake all night and still working. Her brain wasn't as sharp as she needed it to be.

'Tell me about Chloe's mam,' she said. 'What's going on there?'

The woman had been on her mind since they'd realized the girl had disappeared, since she'd read the diary.

'Her name's Rebecca. Becky. She's always had moods swings and bouts of depression, controlled pretty well with medication and some talking therapy according to the GP. But when Chloe's dad left, she became really ill. There were delusions, and she was hearing voices. Eventually suicidal thoughts. She was referred to a psychiatrist and the community mental health team took over. But you know how stretched they are. Chloe became a carer more than a child. Then six weeks ago there was another crisis, a suicide attempt, and Rebecca was admitted to hospital, sectioned.'

'That's when Chloe moved into Rosebank?' *At about the same time as Josh joined the staff.*

'Yes. It's very much a temporary move. We hope Becky will be home soon, and then Chloe can move back.'

To be a carer again . . .

'There was no other family willing to take the lass in?'

Kath nodded. 'There are paternal grandparents, Gordon and Pam, but there was a breakdown in relations after Becky and John divorced. Everyone taking sides. Pam finds Chloe tricky, and Chloe refused to go there, so she ended up in Rosebank. I hoped they might find some sort of reconciliation, once the original drama was over, but Chloe's a stubborn young woman.'

'She's kept in touch with her mother though?'

'Of course,' Kath said. 'We've set up regular visits. They're very close.'

'Does the mam know that Chloe's missing?'

'Yeah, I went in this morning to tell her.' Kath paused for a moment. 'I said that there'd been a death at the home, and we thought Chloe had been upset and taken herself off. Becky seemed quite calm about it. She's still heavily medicated though. I don't think Chloe has been in touch. She certainly hasn't been to the hospital since the last official visit.'

'Has Chloe gone AWOL before?' Vera thought if it was a routine occurrence, Becky might not be too panicky. 'I can't find any details of a missing person report.'

'She went walkabout a few times when she first arrived at Rosebank. But she was never out overnight. Always back by midnight, looking a bit wild and dishevelled but calm enough. Claiming she'd just needed to be on her own for a while.'

'The home never contacted us?'

Kath shrugged. 'It's not unusual for kids to be back later than they're supposed to be, and Chloe's independent, used to looking after herself. The staff would have been on the phone to the police every night . . . You'd have loved that.'

'Any idea where she went?'

'Chloe told the staff she was just out walking. I'm not sure. Maybe she wanted to get away from the other kids. It's happened less recently.'

You wouldn't know though, would you, even if it had been happening? The home only puts in a report if they're away overnight. But perhaps you're right, and the lass was sticking around because she had Josh to talk to. And if she cared that much about him, surely she wouldn't have hit him on the head hard enough to kill him.

'Tell me about the home,' Vera said. 'Rosebank. Who actually runs it?' She couldn't see Dave Limbrick in charge of the place, even if there were only four kids staying there.

'It's owned by a company called Seaview. Based in Barrow, and they have places in Blackpool and Whitehaven too. They buy up places in run-down seaside towns and set up kids' homes.' Kath looked up at Vera. Her eyes were feverish with anger. Vera recognized the mood, the fizzing fury. She could get like that herself. 'They put people like Dave Limbrick in charge. He'll be compliant and do his best for the kids, but not make any fuss. He'd struggle to survive working for us in the field with a full caseload, and he's too young to retire.'

'So it's all about making profit?'

'Private care homes have taken two hundred and fifty million pounds out of local authority children's services,' Kath said. 'So yeah, it's mostly about profit, no matter what the glossy brochures say.'

'I'll need to talk to the manager, wherever they're based.'

'Well, good luck with that,' Kath said. 'I want to talk to them too. But they're slippery.' A pause. 'We had a bairn in their Barrow home. There was no space in Rosebank, and it was the closest place we could find. They knew she was a suicide risk, but somehow she managed to get hold of a kitchen knife and slit her wrists. They found her in time, but it should never have happened. Apparently, the important information wasn't passed on to the staff on the ground. Who weren't qualified anyway to deal with young people with severe psychiatric problems. I'm still waiting to get a satisfactory answer.'

Vera tried to think of something to say but knew that whatever words she came up with wouldn't help. Instead, she changed the subject.

'I went to Chloe's school today. Salvation Academy.'

'What did you make of it?'

'If I'd been there, I'd have run away.'

Kath gave a laugh. 'So would I.'

'Not very Christian, is it? Caring more about the uniform than a kid in pain.'

'They claim that they're raising expectations and breaking a cycle of poverty. I'm sure some of their students do brilliantly under the regime. They head off to university and change their lives for the better. But they pile a load of stress on their pupils and not all of them are strong enough to cope. There's no allowance made for stuff that might be going on at home. There's an epidemic of teenage anxiety and depression all over our region. The North-East has a horrific record of suicide. Salvation says it's not their role to tackle poor mental health, but sometimes all the kids need is to be listened to.' She looked up, her face bleak. 'We don't have the resources to deal with it. Have you seen the waiting list just to get a CAMHS appointment? And often that counselling session is worse than useless, inexperienced counsellors going through the motions.' She paused and looked out of the window at the approaching dusk. 'Sometimes I'm tempted to take early retirement, but if I go, there'll be one fewer person fighting for the families. The new recruits to social work just look like kids themselves to me. Bright and sparky, but with no lived experience.'

'I know the feeling.'

'Sorry to rant.'

'Rant away, pet, if it helps. Sometimes there's nothing else we can do.'

'So we just battle on,' Kath Oliver said.

'Yeah, we just battle on.' They looked at each other with a complicit smile. Vera left the building thinking she had an ally. When this was over maybe she'd invite Kath up to the cottage she'd inherited from Hector, her father, when the drink had finally killed him. She'd take one of her neighbour's game pies out of the freezer and they'd eat it with a bottle of good red wine.

Chapter Eight

ROSIE BELL HAD WANTED TO WORK on Vera Stanhope's team since she'd started as a detective. She was a city girl, always had been, growing up in Fenham and now living in Heaton, loving the buzzy vibe, even though it had been taken over by students and arty young professionals these days. But Vera's rural base seemed romantic to her. She'd come across a book in the school library when she'd been in primary school, old and tatty and pushed to the back of the shelves. It had been about the Romans on Hadrian's Wall, and a local British lass who'd become friendly with a daughter of one of the soldiers based there. It had made rural Northumberland seem wild, a place of adventure. Somehow the vision had stuck. And then, as she'd told Joe Ashworth, Vera was a legend. Someone she could learn from. Rosie Bell had ambition.

That didn't mean she planned to change. Her mam was on the checkout in Asda and her dad was a postie, working in the sorting office these days. Rosie wasn't going to start wearing waxed jackets and wellies or spending her free time tramping over heather moors. She wasn't about to become middle-aged and boring before her time. Her best friends were still the lasses she'd gone to school with – she loved the weekend nights out, the gossip and the fun. Through work, she'd met Holly, strait-laced and sober, dressed like a business executive, and heavily into healthy living. Rosie wasn't going to become Holly mark two, running five miles before work every day and living off lettuce and fresh air. Vera's team would have to accept her just as she was, and she would have to prove to them that she was a better bloody detective than Holly would ever have become. Of course, it was dreadful that a fellow officer had died, but her death had given Rosie this brilliant chance.

She'd been expecting a full briefing at the close of the day, but in the end it was short, matter-of-fact. The CSIs were still working at the locus and in Rosebank. Billy Cartwright, the crime scene manager, was in the ops room with them, feeding in what information they had – which at this point was fuck all as far as Rosie could tell. There was no evidence that a stranger had been in Chloe's room, but no evidence either at this point that an individual from outside hadn't made their way into the home. They'd found the hammer that had killed Woodburn close to the body, thrown to one side, but it was clean of fingerprints, and they were checking for DNA, in case a drop of sweat or saliva had fallen onto the handle.

'But don't hold your breath for the results.' Cartwright had looked out at them with a grin of resignation.

You know how slow the system is.

'One strange thing,' Cartwright went on. 'We haven't found Woodburn's phone. A lad that age, you'd think he'd be tied to it. They use it for everything, don't they? To take notes, pay for stuff. But my chaps have searched everywhere – pulled

the
their
until
nger

been through the common room and the

in the student flat where he lives.'

ood to find it.'

had a reputation too, as a wizard when it

eived
chool
eling.
ssion
they
need
, her
e has
resort
m and
ing to
ebank.
hope

crime, but also as a bit of a lech. Word on
ad to clean up his act since Willmore had
Her mission to root out misogyny and
famous. She couldn't afford an old-school
his banter and his over-familiarity with
get in the way. Not now. Not after the
oly Island murder, and Holly's death.
neeting, Rosie could see that there *was*
about Cartwright. He didn't have the
it he had charisma and wit. She could
n might fall for it. Not for a long-term
a bit of fun.

ther regular member of Vera's team. He'd

talk
e

osebank kids in their school. Rosie thought
imal, a shrew or a mouse. He had a pointed
e eyes. You'd never pick him out of a crowd
sit next to him in the bus for half an hour
able to describe him afterwards. You'd just
nary'.

l he'd been good at talking to the kids though.
talking to anyone. You could imagine a stranger
versation with him in an old-fashioned pub or
n. He'd seem interested.

ned in his chair so he was facing the room, not
not making a big fuss about his feedback, but
the information clearly and briefly.

'The two kids I spoke to both go to Birks. I chatted t
SEN teacher there too and she was able to fill me in on
backgrounds. Mel is Melanie Hunter. She's fifteen, and
recently she was living at home with her parents and you
brothers. She's been diagnosed with ASD.'

'What's that when it's at home?' Vera asked.

'Autistic Spectrum Disorder. She's only recently rec
the diagnosis, but she's been struggling at home and at s
for a while. She can come across as rude, disengaged, unfe
In fact, her teacher thinks she's been living with depr
for a while. Her brothers are three-year-old twins, and
have much more severe autism. They're non-verbal and
constant supervision. Because Mel's less demanding
parents hadn't understood the extent of her problems. S
a history of self-harm and was taken into care as a last
for her own safety. She's seen the psychiatric crisis tea
they were worried she might be a suicide risk. Accord
school, she seems a bit more settled since she came to Ros
She has regular weekend leave with her parents in the
that she can get back there full-time.'

'Poor lass.'

There was a moment of silence before Charlie started
again. 'The other lad, George, is the same age as Chlo
fourteen, but much less mature, physically and emot
According to the teachers, he's still just a kid. He seem
doing okay at Birks. Not a high-flyer educationally, bu
and well behaved.'

'So how did he end up at Rosebank?' This time, Ro
the nerve to stick up her hand and ask the question.

'His parents died in an RTI on the A1. A Scottish lorr
on his phone swerved into their lane on the stretch

Morpeth and Ellingham where there's no dual carriageway. George was taken into foster care. The foster parents had their own younger kids and found him a bit much to handle. He had meltdowns apparently whenever he left the house. Nightmares that kept the whole family awake all night. He's been seeing a psychologist and it seems he's doing better. There, he has a room next to one of the staff, and if he wakes in the night, they'll hear him and can calm him. He finds it easier to be in an institution like school or Rosebank than with a family.' Charlie looked out at them. His voice didn't change. 'He was in the car when his parents and his baby sister were killed.'

'That's great background, Charlie, but did any of them have anything useful to say about the night Woodburn died?'

'They say not, and really, ma'am, you can see why. All except Chloe, they'd just settled down in the common room to watch a film and stuff themselves with popcorn and pizza. Mel says she saw Josh's car arrive – she'd gone to the downstairs bog and saw it through the window in the hall – but they didn't see the man himself.'

'Nobody thought to ask where Josh was?'

'He was there on sleepover duty. They thought he'd just gone to his room.'

'So the kids can alibi each other?'

'Looks like it. I'm guessing one or other of them went to the bathroom, or out for an illicit smoke, but it seems that nobody came back covered in blood.' A pause. 'Doc Keating says there *would* have been blood.'

'I've spoken to Chloe's social worker,' Vera said. 'Rosebank is managed by a private company, Seaview. They're based in Barrow and own a few homes in Cumbria and the North-East. It might not be relevant, but I want to know all about them.

Specifically, the contact details of the owner. Charlie, are you okay to have a dig?'

Charlie nodded. Rosie was relieved that task hadn't been assigned to her.

Joe stuck up his hand then. 'Chloe must be our prime suspect, mustn't she? It's too much of a coincidence that she disappeared at the same time as Josh died.'

Vera frowned. Rosie thought she wasn't used to being challenged. 'We just need to talk to the lass,' Vera said. 'We can't assume anything until we've found her.'

The briefing was over by six-thirty. Rosie approved of the way Vera had rattled through it. There was a bottle of Sauvignon in the fridge waiting for her – she'd got it specially to celebrate the first day of her new job – and she was looking forward to climbing into her PJs and watching *Love Island* on catch-up.

Vera, it seemed, had other ideas.

'I'm starving. I'll not make it home without falling asleep if I don't have something to eat. You going to join me?' The invitation was thrown to Joe and Rosie. Charlie had already slid away. He was, Rosie thought, the invisible man. And this was less of an invitation than an order. Vera was marching ahead of them out of the building, assuming that they would follow. Joe was muttering something about his wife expecting him home for dinner, but Vera pretended not to hear. She turned briefly and gave Rosie a wink.

They ended up in a little pub, down an alley from the cop shop. It was quiet. No music and no screens. The sort of place Rosie's nana and grandad might go.

'The pies are good,' Vera said. She looked over the table at Rosie. 'You're not a veggie, are you?'

'No way.'

'Not that I've got anything against veggies, but it's not easy to be picky if you're out and about.'

'I'll eat anything, me.'

'Pies then. And chips. You going to the bar, Joe?'

'My shout.' Rosie got to her feet. 'New girl and all that. What do you want to drink?'

Vera went for a half and Joe a Coke because they were driving.

'Cheap round,' Rosie said, only half joking. At the bar, she ordered the food. She was tempted to ask for a G&T for herself. She was finding her first day in the new team harder than she'd expected, and she thought a drink might relax her. Since she'd parted from Daniel, she hadn't been so easy in company. But she didn't want to cock this up before she'd really started, so she went for a soda and lime.

The room was almost empty now. The post-work drinkers had wandered off for their tea. The meal turned into an extension of the briefing, informal but demanding.

'So what are your thoughts?' Vera was poised, a piece of stewing steak on her fork, looking across at them.

'Have we chatted to the guy who found Woodburn's body? Did he see anyone else about?'

'Charlie did the interview this afternoon,' Vera said. 'Nah, the man didn't see a soul. He told Charlie the weather was so foul that he wouldn't have left home if he hadn't had to empty the dog.'

'Limbrick could have slipped out of the office without anyone noticing.' Rosie pictured the layout of the home. 'The office is right by the front door and the body was only a couple of minutes away.'

'Maybe.' Vera drained her glass and looked wistfully at the bar. 'I don't see him having the nerve though. And besides, why would he?'

'I still think the lass is the most likely,' Joe said. 'Maybe Woodburn tried it on with her. Or she was hoping he would, and was disappointed . . .'

'And she just happened to have a hammer in her hand?'

'She's the only person to have done a runner!' Joe shot back.

'We don't know that Chloe ran, do we?' Rosie said. 'She could have gone down to meet Josh and seen the attack. It's possible that she was abducted to stop her raising the alarm.'

Vera nodded. Her mouth was full of pie now so it was hard to make out what she was saying. 'Yeah, that's possible. Whatever happened, we need to find her.'

'If Josh was the target, and it wasn't some random piece of violence, a former client with a grudge against the care system maybe, could it be someone from his other life, the student life, who's the killer?' Rosie wondered if she was talking too much for a new girl. Perhaps she should just be listening to her superiors.

But Vera nodded, approving. 'So that's two lines of inquiry for tomorrow. Joe, you talk to Limbrick. Is there a former resident who hated the place so much that he was prepared to have a go at one of the staff?' Vera pushed away her glass before speaking again. 'And let's see if John Spence is back in the UK. We know he's on holiday and Emirates flies direct into Newcastle. I'm not saying he's the killer, but Chloe could be with him. She might have fallen out with her nana and grandpa, but we know from her diary that she'd been trying to get hold of her dad. Rosie, you check out Josh's place in

Jesmond, chat to his flatmates.' A pause. 'And I'll see if we can find the poor lass. Whether she's alive or dead.'

Vera got to her feet. Rosie wondered if she was heading for the bar to get a round in, but she was making for the door.

Chapter Nine

VERA WATCHED ROSIE WALK AWAY TO fetch her flash car. The woman had a bit of style to her. She wanted to be noticed. Joe was about to follow, but Vera called him back. The temperature had dropped and she was keen to get home, to light a fire and pour herself a nightcap. She needed to sleep, but she was curious about the new member of the team. And determined to give her the support that she'd failed to give Holly.

'How did she get on today?' Vera nodded towards the disappearing back but Joe would have known already who she was talking about.

'She did really well.' He pulled his coat round him. For a lad born and brought up in Northumberland, Joe *did* seem to feel the cold. Vera thought central heating would do that to you: make you mardy. His smart new house was always roasting. No thought for the planet.

'She was great dealing with Josh's parents. They loved her.'

'That's good then.' Vera thought she'd keep an eye out for the lass all the same.

* * *

She drove home in a blur, exhaustion starting to bite now and strange thoughts rolling around in her head. Because she'd read Chloe's diary, she imagined that she could hear her voice, and because she'd seen photos, she could picture her: short for her age and round, hair cut in a long smooth bob, a pale face and heavily made-up eyes. Black skirt with net over the top, scuffed Doc Marten boots that she'd probably found in a chazza shop and a black lacy corset affair pushing up her breasts. All making her seem older than fourteen. Though the look on her face, cheeky and shy at the same time, had made Vera realize she was still a child. According to Joe, Brad Russell had called her a witch. If that was the case, she was very much a witch in training.

Vera arrived at the cottage in the hills, without being aware of the drive at all. On autopilot. Out of the car she stopped for a moment. It was dark and silent. No moon. Air you could get drunk on. Flecks of starlight in the sky and from the farm-houses in the valley below. A single light in her neighbours' house. Jack and Joanna, the best friends a woman could have. Her only friends outside the job. She thought briefly of Kath Oliver the senior social worker. Perhaps she would be another. Someone she could have a laugh with, someone to share right-eous indignation about the world's injustices.

Inside, she switched on the light. It felt colder in here than it did outside at the front of the house. That was the damp. She was tempted to pour herself a whisky and go straight to bed, but it wasn't eight-thirty yet and if she went now, she'd wake up at crazy o'clock in the morning. She put kindling and logs in the grate, crumbled in a firelighter, then tossed in a match. For a while the fire didn't throw out much heat, but it was cheery to look at. She got herself a drink and sat in her coat until the room warmed through, told herself that she was as bad as Joe, wondered once again about getting central heating installed. Then knew, as she always did, that she'd hate the mess and the intrusion.

Eventually, it was late enough to go to bed. Her last thought, before falling asleep, was of Chloe Spence.

I hope you've found somewhere warm, pet. I hope you're not cold.

Vera was up and out early, calling in to the station on the hands-free phone as she drove to work to check if there'd been news of Chloe. Nothing. Not on the town's CCTV or even any reported sightings.

'Eh, man, it's as if she's disappeared into thin air.' Then, a spur-of-the-moment decision: 'I'm going straight to see her mother in St Margaret's. Give me a shout if you hear anything.'

All the leaves had changed colour now and were dropping. They blew in dry waves across the narrow roads when she passed through woodland. St Margaret's was an old hospital, on a side road just out of Longwater. It had been taken over by the psychiatrists when general medicine moved somewhere new and more convenient. It was tall and forbidding and had the air of a workhouse. A group of individuals stood outside, smoking as if their lives depended on it. It was impossible to tell if they were patients or staff.

Vera had phoned ahead, and the hospital was expecting her. Becky Spence was sitting at a table by the window of the day room. She must just have washed her hair because it was still wet. She hadn't dyed it for a while and there were long grey-ing roots.

'Have you found Chloe? Is she okay?' She seemed sharper

than Vera had expected from Kath Oliver's description. Perhaps they were weaning her off the medication a little before letting her home.

'Not yet. But the whole service is aware she's missing. Everyone's looking out for her.' Vera sat opposite. There was a jigsaw on the table, the edges complete. 'I was hoping you might have some idea where she might be.'

'You've looked in our house?'

'The first place we tried when we realized she'd gone. Your neighbour let one of my colleagues in.' A pause. 'She said that she'd give us a call if she saw the lass. We'll go back though and check for ourselves.'

Because if you were scared, you'd go somewhere you felt safe, wouldn't you? Somewhere familiar.

They sat in silence for a moment. Somewhere in the distance a young man was singing. It could be a radio, but there was no accompaniment. Just the voice. A beautiful voice.

'I don't know where else she might be. Not anymore.' Becky looked up. She had watery blue eyes, skin so pale and translucent you'd imagine you could see the bone. 'I've been such a terrible mother.'

'You've been ill and that's something altogether different.' Vera thought she knew about terrible parents. But her mother had died. Vera could hardly blame her for that, and perhaps Hector, her father, had been ill too, right from the start, even before the drink had taken hold of him. Perhaps she should have been more tolerant. 'When did you last see Chloe?'

'At the weekend. We'd planned to go out for a walk, but it was raining, so we just sat in here. She helped me with the puzzle.'

'How did she seem?'

Becky shrugged. 'I don't know. I wasn't so well when she was here that afternoon. It was a bad day. I was too wrapped up in myself to take any notice of her.' Guilt seemed to tense her body like a stab of pain. Vera knew about guilt too.

'Was there anywhere special that the two of you liked to visit? Where she'd been happy. Somewhere she might go back to?'

There was a long pause while the woman seemed to be thinking. Vera thought there'd be no answer, but at last Rebecca spoke. 'She loved it up at Gillstead.'

Vera knew Gillstead. It was a hamlet on the other side of the valley from Vera's house. Nothing there but a few farms and one street of cottages, which had once belonged to the big house. On the fell, three standing stones – the Three Dark Wives – that pulled in the occasional history buff. She'd always loved the legend of the Dark Wives. The story was that three crones had been turned to stone by a giant who'd thought they talked too much. There were times when Vera thought of herself as a crone, and she hoped something horrible had happened to the giant. At least the crones were remembered, and he'd disappeared from the story. An ancient pub stood in the middle of the street. It held a couple of large scrubbed pine tables, so the drinkers had to be sociable. And there was the big house itself, changed now into a fancy hotel with a swimming pool and spa. Famous for hosting weddings. Vera had never been, but she'd seen the adverts.

'John's parents have got a place there. His dad was a farmer – the family had been on the land for generations. Pam wasn't really a country woman, and in the end, she persuaded him to sell up. They kept a place there though. A second home. Nothing fancy, like. More of a bothy, somewhere to camp out.

We didn't go much. John liked his creature comforts. When I worked at the travel agency, we got discounted holidays abroad and he preferred a hotel in the sun.'

'But Chloe liked it?'

'When she was younger, yeah. It had a big open fire, and we'd toast marshmallows.' Her voice was dreamy and Vera thought that in her head, Becky was there, sitting on the hearth with a toasting fork in her hand, remembering the good times. 'Only one bedroom but a kind of loft over the living room where Chloe used to sleep. A tin bath for washing. There were deer on the hill and bats in the roof.'

'Where is this place exactly?'

'Oh, I'm not sure. It's years since we went. John's parents might have got rid of it by now or the place might have fallen down.'

'I could take you to Gillstead. We could drive round and find it.' Vera was excited now. She could imagine the girl, resourceful, scavenging the place for firewood, baking stolen potatoes in the embers. A character in a children's adventure story.

'She won't be there.' The woman's voice was tender. It was as if Vera was the woman with the lost child, and who needed to be comforted. 'She wouldn't be able to find it any more than I would, and how would she get all the way up into the hills by herself?'

Vera knew that Becky was right. There would be no bus to the hamlet, except to bring the bairns in from the school in Hexham. Even if the girl could find it by herself after all these years, there would be no way of getting there. Still, she couldn't quite let the image go. 'Has Chloe kept in touch with John's parents?'

'Not really. I tried to maintain contact with Gordon and Pam when John first left us – my parents are dead and it seemed important that she knew one lot of grandparents – but in the end, they made things difficult. They were critical of Chloe, the way she dressed and behaved. Picked away at her. Chloe was angry when John went so suddenly and perhaps she took it out on them. She's not easy. In the end she refused to go.'

All the same, Vera took down the contact details. If the girl were desperate, she might have turned up on their doorstep, especially if her father had arrived in the UK and was staying with her grandparents. She would want to see him, wouldn't she, no matter how angry she was?

'Have you heard from John recently?'

The woman shook her head. 'I've heard nothing since he left.' Her eyes filled with tears. It seemed to Vera that she was more distressed by her husband's absence than by the disappearance of her daughter, and that caused a moment of doubt, of suspicion.

'You're sure you've not heard from Chloe?'

Becky shook her head again, but she didn't speak.

In the Land Rover, Vera looked at her phone. There was a missed call from Joe and she rang him back.

'You were right.'

'I usually am, pet, but what am I right about now?'

'John Spence is back in the UK. He flew in on the Emirates flight from Dubai a week ago.' A pause. 'Business class so he's not short of a bob or two.'

'Do we know where he went when he arrived?'

'We do! Emirates organize a driver service for their fancy-pants customers. They had the address on record.'

'Come on, Joe, lad. Don't keep me in suspense. We want to find Chloe, don't we, and I haven't got all day.'

Joe rattled off an address in Whitley Bay. Vera checked her notes. 'That's where the grandparents live. I'll head off there now.'

Chapter Ten

ROSIE WOKE WITH A BIT OF a thick head. She'd opened the wine when she got in. The first day in her new role deserved some kind of celebration, after all – a new start after the debacle with Daniel – and it had been there, waiting for her. She hadn't finished it. Not quite. But had drunk enough to make her fall straight to sleep and then to wake in the early hours, before dozing again. She'd have to watch herself. She needed to stay sharp for the new team. If Vera Stanhope put in a good word, it shouldn't be long before she got promoted to sergeant.

It seemed that Josh Woodburn's student flatmates had been drinking the night before too, because they were still there when she rang the bell, both looking worse for wear. The door was opened by a willowy young woman in pyjamas and a fleecy top. Mascara stains on her face and a mass of tangled hair.

'Who are you?' A Southern voice. Rude. Newcastle Uni had its share of entitled rich kids these days. A lot of them lived in Jesmond, with its Victorian terraces and fancy bars.

Rosie explained who she was. Bluntly. She didn't have to put up with any shit from some student.

'Oh, you'll be here about Josh.' The girl stepped aside to let Rosie into a living room, scattered with the detritus of a night of partying: empty bottles, candles half burned, stray items of clothing. There was a grate where a fire had been lit, and ashes remained. 'Sorry about the mess. We had a few friends round for drinks to, you know, celebrate his life. His parents told us that he was dead. Poor Anna and Chris.'

'You know them?'

'Yeah, they're really cool. Josh was the only one of us who's local and they'd have us round sometimes for Sunday lunches. They were *so* generous. We'd walk on the beach, go swimming in the summer. Have a barbecue in their garden after. They've got a *fab* house. Josh is an only child and I think his parents liked to have the house full.'

She looked wistful. Perhaps she was thinking there would be no more free lunches, no more summer barbies.

'You are?'

'Lizzie. Elizabeth Stirling.'

'You were his girlfriend?'

'No! God, no! I'm with Pete, but he's a language student and he's doing his year in France, lucky sod.'

'Did Josh have a girlfriend?

'Not really, not since I've known him. There were mates of course, but I don't think there was anyone special. Not now. He fell in love with someone when he was still at school, and I think they were still seeing each other when he started here. She broke his heart apparently. Stella. He still talked about her when he'd been drinking.' Elizabeth didn't quite roll her eyes.

'Who else lives here?'

'Just Miggy while Pete's away. Miguel. His parents are Spanish. He's doing English like me.'

71

'What was Josh doing?'

'Art history.'

'Could you dig Miguel out of his pit and perhaps make us all some coffee?'

Despite his name, Miguel spoke perfect, unaccented English. He was slight and dark with the grace of a dancer. Lizzie disappeared into the kitchen, leaving the door open so they could continue the conversation, and sorted the coffee. Real coffee made with a fancy machine.

'Josh's parents were upgrading so they gave this to us.' Lizzie must have seen Rosie looking at it.

Of course! Rosie thought this was a different fucking world.

'So,' she said. 'Tell me about Josh.'

And they did. Lizzie did most of the talking. She'd met Josh when they were in their first year. They were in halls together. He could have lived at home, but he'd wanted the real student experience and his parents could afford to cough up. He didn't need to work to pay his way through uni, because they were minted, but he'd got a job in a bar for a bit, just to fit in. She thought he'd found other work recently, but he hadn't told them what he was doing. That was just like Josh. He was always a bit secretive.

'Why did he choose Newcastle, if he wanted the real student experience? Why stay so close to home?'

'I dunno.' Lizzie shrugged. 'Northerners are like that, aren't they? Passionate about home.' She sounded a little supercilious. Rosie bit her tongue.

'So you didn't know he was working in the care home?'

'Not really.'

'What does that mean?' Rosie decided Lizzie was really getting on her tits now.

'I knew he'd got a job, but I thought it was something to do with his art. He had all sorts of projects going on. That was his real love. Making art. Mostly film. Activist film. Ken Loach was his hero.' Lizzie looked up. 'And that's a bit weird if you've had a comfortable life.' A pause. 'I suppose that's a Northern thing too, isn't it? Believing that you're part of the downtrodden masses when you've been brought up in a very nice house close to the sea, with wealthy parents who love you to bits.'

'So Josh hadn't told you exactly where he was working?'

'No, he said it was shift work. I thought maybe he was working in a theatre or indie cinema, something like that.' Lizzie leaned back in the battered armchair, shut her eyes, and drank her coffee. 'We were mates, you know, but we had our own lives.'

'Had he fallen out with anyone? Any problems?'

'No! That wasn't Josh. He was a gentle soul. Not very good at standing up for himself. Not the most resilient. He got on with the whole world.' She made an expansive gesture with her arms.

'So nothing out of the ordinary happened in the past few weeks?'

'There was that weird guy who turned up at the door for him.' Miggy uncoiled himself from his chair, stood up and stretched, reached out for the mug he'd put on the windowsill.

'What weird guy?'

'Kind of ageing hippy. Long hair and scruffy clothes. Jeans and a jumper and a long coat that looked as if it had come out of a charity shop.' He spoke with the voice of someone who'd never had to use a charity shop.

'Name?'

73

Lizzie shrugged. 'Josh didn't say. It was all a bit mysterious.' She turned towards Miggy. 'Josh seemed shocked to see him, wouldn't you say? He wasn't expecting a visitor.'

'But they knew each other?'

'Yes, I think so.'

'Did they have a conversation?'

Did you eavesdrop?

Josh didn't invite him in. Miggy and I just saw him through the window and it was already getting dark. They chatted for a bit and then they went off together. Josh came back about an hour later. When we asked him about the guy, he said it was something to do with work. Like I said, it was all very mysterious.'

Rosie thought the description might match Dave Limbrick. Or the man might have been from the care agency. The latter seemed unlikely, unless the employer needed to check an address. Wouldn't any interview take place in the office? Rosie thought it would be easy enough to find out. She wondered why Josh had kept the visit secret from his flatmates if it was work-related. If you had any sort of social conscience, and it seemed that Josh did, wouldn't you be proud of working with a bunch of screwed-up adolescents?

She sipped the coffee and thought maybe she should get one of those machines. 'Have you seen Josh's phone? It wasn't with him, and we wondered if he'd left it here.'

The question was directed to them both, and they both shook their heads. 'That wasn't like him,' Miggy said. 'He was super organized.'

'Is it okay if I have a look at his room?'

'Sure, go ahead.' Lizzie stood up. 'I'll show you. I need to move my arse anyway, have a shower and dress. Get my head together. I've got a seminar at twelve. *Othello*. It's time to channel my inner feelings of jealousy and revenge.' She smiled. Rosie thought that despite the drinking of the night before, Josh's death had hardly touched her.

His room was a small double and looked out over the street. It showed none of the personality of his room in Cullercoats. It had the air of a temporary residence, a place in an Airbnb and Rosie wondered why he'd felt the need to move out. She couldn't imagine Chris and Anna Woodburn cramping his style and there was a regular and efficient metro service into town. On the desk under the window, she found a laptop which she bagged to take away.

The only other furniture was a pine wardrobe with a few clothes, and a shelf of textbooks. These were large, with photos of paintings, or they were biographies of twentieth-century artists, of whom she'd never heard. Next to the bed a pile of books which seemed to be his reading of choice. Again, mostly non-fiction: memoirs by actors and film-makers. Josh seemed to have been a serious young man, conscientious. She couldn't imagine how he could have provoked anyone to violence. She made a thorough search of the room but there was no sign of the phone.

By the time she went back out, Lizzie was dressed and about to leave. She was wearing leggings and a big sweatshirt, chunky boots, a bag slung over one shoulder. Her face made up. Rosie could understand that. No matter how informally she was dressed *she'd* never leave the house without make-up. It would feel like going into the world stark naked.

Miggy was still in the living room, curled in the same armchair. He was eating a slice of toast.

'One last thing,' Rosie said. 'The older guy who came to talk to Josh. Did you see what he was driving? Or was he walking?'

'I think he got out of a bus,' Lizzie said. 'At least, he was walking from the bus stop at the end of the street. I was just coming home from uni. I didn't realize he was coming here at that point, but I noticed him because he looked a bit out of place. Too old to be a student but too untidy to be a Jesmond resident.'

'Do you know what number bus he was on?'

'God, no! He was just walking in that direction.'

'Thanks.'

Out on the street, Rosie wandered to the corner to check out the bus stop. It was the number twenty-two, which ran from the coast into the city centre. She thought that this probably had no significance at all, but she'd done her research into Vera Stanhope and had learned that there was nothing she liked more than detail.

Chapter Eleven

CHLOE'S PATERNAL GRANDPARENTS LIVED ON A pleasant leafy street in Whitley Bay, just inland from Park View, the main shopping street. The houses were spacious, Edwardian. The atmosphere of the place, Vera thought, wasn't very different from the community in Cullercoats where Josh Woodburn's parents lived. The houses were only a couple of miles apart, a gentle stroll along the coast. She wondered if the families might know each other, if that might provide a link between Josh and Chloe.

This couple, it turned out, was quite different from Rosie's description of the accountant and the medic. From different worlds. There was no university education here. Gordon, Chloe's grandfather, owned an abattoir further north, not far inland from Longwater. His son, John, had managed it before he'd run away to the sun. Pam, the grandmother, ran a women's clothes shop in Whitley Bay, and she was at work.

Gordon was in his sixties, taciturn, monosyllabic. Vera thought that might be anxiety. Chloe was his only grand-child. He must be beside himself. John, Chloe's father, was prematurely silver-haired, handsome, and he showed little sign of anxiety or stress. Only a nervous tic, a twitch of one eye, gave away the tension.

'We're very concerned about Chloe's safety.' Vera had been shown into the living room. Everything there was big and soft and comfortable. Giant sofas and a giant television set. Not a book in sight. 'She's been missing for two nights. And the care worker was beaten to death.' She wanted to provoke a reaction.

'You think she's been taken? Kidnapped?' Gordon was still standing in front of the marble fireplace.

'It's a possibility that we have to consider.'

'She couldn't just have run away?' For the first time John seemed uneasy, defensive. 'She did that a couple of times when she was at home. Becky couldn't control her.'

'As I understand it,' Vera said, her voice softly menacing, 'Becky was ill and in no state to control anything.'

'We offered to have her.' Gordon, the grandfather, was ill at ease and defensive too. 'We told the social worker that she could come here when Becky was ill. We've got the space. She'd have had everything she needed.'

'But Chloe didn't want to come here.' Vera genuinely couldn't understand the girl's refusal to move in with her grandparents. Wouldn't this house with its comfort have been so much more pleasant than Rosebank? 'Why was that?'

Gordon answered first. 'She and my Pam never really hit it off once she became a teenager. Different generations. She was such a bonny thing and Pam thought she should make more of herself.'

There was an awkward silence before John spoke. 'There was more to it than that, Dad. You know there was. Chloe blames me for Becky's illness. I'm the monster in the room.

My parents took the flak too. Adolescents see everything in black and white, don't they? There's no shade of grey.' He was silent for a moment. 'But it wasn't fair. Becky had bouts of depression even before I left. I tried to hold things together, but in the end, it was too much. I didn't even *like* her anymore, not as a wife, a partner. It's a hard thing to admit, but she'd just become a burden, someone I had to care for.'

'So you just ran away.' Even as she spoke the words, Vera wondered if she was being too harsh. She'd been tempted many times to run away from Hector's increasing demands. She just hadn't had the guts to do it. But deep down she knew that, even if she *had* made the break, guilt would have dragged her back.

'Yes!' John was defiant now. 'I just ran away. And Chloe blamed me and she blamed my parents. She wanted to hurt us.'

'She'd tried to get in touch with you though. I've seen her diary. She'd tried to text you and call you, but you didn't answer.'

There was another silence. 'It's hard to explain. I know it looks bad. But she wasn't part of my life anymore. When I thought back to my time in the UK, it was like some kind of dream. Or nightmare. My life was in Dubai – I've met someone there. It was sunshine, making a life for myself. And it was work. Hard work. The company I'm with is global, and the targets are high. Great rewards, mind, but it takes all my energy.'

He paused, expecting some sort of response from Vera. When none came, he continued, more quietly: 'I suppose I didn't want to be reminded of what I'd left behind. I was afraid I'd be pulled back by some idea of guilt or duty. So I deleted the texts without looking at them, and I never took the calls. Anyway, I thought social services would be taking care of it all.' He looked at his father. 'I'm sorry.' The brash defiance had gone. 'She will be all right though, won't she? She's strong, our Chloe. Always has been since she was a baby. She's a survivor.'

'What brought you back to the UK for this visit, Mr Spence?' *If you were trying so hard to forget it.*

He shrugged. 'I suppose I was just a bit homesick for the place.'

'Were you planning to tell Chloe that you were here?'

He flushed red. The shame was sudden, and shocking. 'No,' he said. 'I was going to, but I want to leave the past behind. I'm paying the maintenance every month – more than I need to – and I thought that's enough. I don't want to get tangled up with all their problems again.' He looked once more at his father: 'I'm sorry.' Then to Vera: 'Please find her. I want to put everything right.'

Vera wasn't sure what else John Spence wanted from her. Some form of absolution? 'If you hear from her, of course, you'll be in touch.'

'Of course!'

She was on her feet, making for the door, when she turned back to them.

'Becky said there was a place Chloe liked to go, up at Gillstead. A cottage or a bothy. Do you still own it?'

Gordon smiled. 'Aye, we do, though it's never used much these days. We held on to it when we sold the farmhouse and the land. It was no use to the new owner, and it was senti-mental, I suppose, like I was holding on to a bit of the heritage. My grandparents had farmed there, and my parents, and so did I for a while, until the butchery side of the business took up most of my time. It was a wrench to leave, though Pam never really settled in Gillstead. She grew up on the coast and this is home for her.' He stopped talking for a moment, surprised perhaps that he'd said so much.

'And the bothy?'

'It's ancient. It was probably there before the farmhouse, built into the hill. I let the family camp out there when Chloe was a bairn, but you were never keen, were you, John?'

John shook his head, gave a wan little smile. 'I never saw the point of roughing it.'

'It was bonny though,' Gordon said. 'A grand view over the moor. I could see why the bairn was so fond.'

'Would you take me up there?' The question was directed to the grandfather. Vera didn't think she'd keep her temper during a car ride with the man's son. 'It's a long shot. But just in case.'

'Aye.' His face brightened. Perhaps Gordon himself had had enough of John. 'We'll go now, shall we? Like you say, just in case.'

Vera was tempted, but this was such a long shot and she still had more important immediate things to do. Besides, she didn't want to send one of the team and miss out herself. It would be her form of escape.

'Tomorrow,' she said. 'I'll pick you up early. We'll go then.'

Gordon seemed about to say something else, as if a thought had just occurred to him, but in the end he stayed silent, and she left.

On the way back to Kimmerston, Vera stopped at the house in Longwater where Chloe and her mother had lived, trying to hold things together after John Spence had left them. It was in a little estate of substantial 1930s homes, an established community. Vera thought it had been built with the professionals attached to local industries in mind – the deputies at the pit, the draughtsmen in the shipyards. Someone had mown the front lawn, so from the road at least, it looked as tidy as the rest. The street keen to keep up appearances. The neighbour holding the key was elderly, lonely and eager to chat.

'I've been looking out for the lass, but there's been no sign of her.' A pause. 'She's a lovely girl, you knaa, despite all the make-up and the strange clothes. Kind. I've known her since she was a baby.'

Vera nodded and took the key.

Inside, there was a dusty, unloved feel to the place, and Vera sensed immediately that it was empty. The officer who'd first gone in to look for Chloe had picked up the mail from the doormat and put it in a heap on a small table in the hall. Vera thought that letters had gone unread long before Rebecca had ended up in hospital. Most were junk mail, flyers. Or bills. There was one with a Salvation crest on the envelope. Vera opened it. The tone was brusque. It demanded to know why Rebecca had missed an appointment to discuss Chloe's behaviour and her future in the school.

In the living room and dining room, the furniture was solid and tasteful. It had probably been bought while both parents were still working. The conservatory looked out on a jungle of a garden. The kitchen was small but filled with gadgets that felt like boys' toys. Vera suspected that this had been John's territory. There were no mucky plates, no stinking bins. Vera wondered if that was Chloe's doing, that she'd been told of the move to Rosebank and had cleared up before she left. It said something about the girl.

Upstairs there were three bedrooms and a bathroom. Rebecca still slept in the bed she'd shared with John. It had the fusty smell of unwashed sheets. Chloe's room was at the back with a view of the garden. The walls had been painted black, but there were fairy lights hanging from the ceiling and the bedspread and curtains were brightly coloured. This wasn't a child wallowing in despair. The smell here was of joss-sticks, and faintly of weed.

Vera wondered if the girl had been using in Rosebank, if her relationship with Brad Russell had been more complex than either had let on. Though, Vera knew, the stuff was ubiquitous, and Chloe had probably been able to get hold of it through someone at school. Or even one of the parents, who smoked themselves and saw no harm. Better weed, some of them would say, than alcohol.

She let herself out of the house, and stood for a moment, enjoying the fresh air. She was tempted to stick the key through the elderly neighbour's letterbox and drive quickly away, but compassion, or guilt, made her ring the bell. She might be the only person the woman spoke to all day.

They stood for a moment chatting on the doorstep – Vera knew better than to allow herself to be lured inside.

'Was it one of your people who came to the house yesterday?' the woman said, just as Vera was making her excuses to go.

'The uniformed officer who came to you for the key?'

The woman shook her head. 'Nah, no uniform. Driving a black car. I thought it might be the press. You wouldn't want one of them sniffing through your life.'

'Quite right,' Vera said. 'I don't suppose you noticed the registration number of the car?'

'Nah. *Pointless* was about to start on the telly. I do love *Pointless*. When it had finished the car had gone.'

Vera handed over a card. 'If it comes back give me a shout. You've been very useful.'

The woman beamed and waved as Vera walked down the path.

Chapter Twelve

BACK IN HER OFFICE, VERA FOUND a message from Katherine Willmore, the Police and Crime Commissioner. Would the inspector be free to meet her? Informally over a cup of tea? She named a place in Longwater. The marine centre. One of the few attempts to level up the town, it was an exhibition space with a café attached. She named the time and Vera thought it wasn't really an invitation. She'd be expected to go.

She set out early, thinking she'd like to get an idea of the place, a sense of the geography. It was mid-afternoon, but the November sun was already low. Some of the naturalists Hector had hung out with talked about ground-truthing – understanding the relationship between theory and reality, checking the landscape for what was really there. That was what she was doing here, walking in the Rosebank kids' footsteps, seeing the town through their eyes.

The town was built on one bank of the estuary, a long, narrow inlet where the water was deep enough to have let the coal boats in. Vera parked in one of the residential streets on the edge of the town. The houses were solid, built of grey stone, with windswept gardens and views of the water. She walked along the edge of a council estate, and on to the main drag, with its charity shops and betting shops and the shuttered windows of premises that had been closed for years. A homeless young woman in a sleeping bag was sitting in the doorway of one of the empty shops. Her eyes were empty too. Vera hardened her heart and walked on past; she was probably a druggie, wasn't she? Or an alcoholic? The charities said not to give money directly to individuals.

But further down the street, there was a greasy spoon and Vera went in for two takeaway coffees and a bacon sandwich. She told herself that this wasn't charity. It was work. It hit her that the woman had probably been in care herself, and that some of the recent Rosebank residents might end up here, on the street. She squatted by the woman and handed over one of the coffees, and took a sip of her own.

'What's your name, pet? I'm Vera.'

The woman was eating the sandwich daintily, holding back her greed, making it last. She looked up, suspicious.

'What do you want, like?'

'A lass has gone missing from the care home up the road. Only fourteen. I wondered if you'd seen anyone new on the streets.'

There was a moment of silence while the woman's attention was focused on the sandwich. Then she shook her head.

'Any idea where a homeless lass might end up?'

'Nah. Not that age. If she turned up at a hostel, they'd just call social services.'

Vera got to her feet. Her knees creaked. 'Thanks anyway.'

She'd moved several yards down the road when the woman called after her: 'And thanks for the scran. I hope you find her.'

Vera gave her a little wave and walked on.

At the end of the street, she turned into a cobbled alley and emerged on a promenade where the river was at its widest. The town was more optimistic here. People were walking their dogs, chatting when they met. A young mother pushed a pram, while a child was on a scooter beside her. There was a veggie café, brightly painted, with a few customers inside, and a gift shop selling local crafts.

Rosebank was in the distance, solitary, on a headland at the point where the river joined the sea. Once, Vera thought, it must have been rather grand.

The marine centre was on the same level as the promenade. It was glass and concrete with a design of flying gulls painted on the wall near the entrance and on the noticeboard outside. Vera stared at the logo for a few minutes, trying to work out what species had been portrayed, then gave up. This was like no gull known to man. But perhaps it didn't matter.

She was on time, but Willmore was already inside, in the café. Vera had to walk through the exhibition space to get there. The displays were about the women who played their part in the miners' strike. The images brought back memories for Vera. She'd been a newly qualified officer at the time of the strike, she'd dealt with some of the women, and still had mixed feelings about that time. She saw Willmore as soon as she walked into the café, but the woman waved and called her over. There was an elderly couple at a table at the far end of the room, but otherwise it was empty. The place would be reaching the end of its working day.

'Thanks for coming,' Willmore said. 'I know you're busy with the Woodburn case. I thought this would be convenient.'

Vera didn't say she'd had to drive out of her way. There was a moment of awkward silence.

'How's it going?' Willmore seemed anxious, edgy.

Vera shrugged. 'We've still not found the lass. I've been talking to her family. The father's back in the country, but claims not to have been in touch. The mother's still in hospital. The school's not sympathetic, but the social worker's good.' Willmore didn't reply immediately, and Vera went on:

'How's it going with you and Eliza? I heard you've both moved back to Kimmerston?' Eliza was the PCC's daughter. She'd been at the heart of an investigation earlier in the year.

'Yes! She's decided to do an MA in Newcastle and I still had my house in Kimmerston. So we're back living together. A bit like old times.' She looked across the table at Vera. 'I almost resigned. I'm still not sure it was the right thing to stay.'

'I'm glad that you did.'

'Really?' Willmore brightened. 'That means a lot. I'll leave it to the electorate to make the decision when the time comes.' She paused. 'But you can understand why this case is so important to me. Another sensitive investigation and the press already breathing down my neck. We can't let this drag on, Vera. Really. We need a result or I'll be forced out of post, and you'll be landed with someone who gives you a much harder ride than I do.'

Vera felt a stab of resentment. Why had the woman dragged her here, just to pile on the pressure? All that could have been said on the phone. It occurred to her then that Willmore was lonely. After the Holy Island case, she'd be considered toxic, and her allies would have drifted away.

Vera didn't answer. She felt some sympathy for the woman, but she wanted Chloe found because there was a child in danger. Not to save the PCC's political neck.

Chapter Thirteen

JOE WAS BACK IN ROSEBANK, FOLLOWING Vera's instructions. He'd found Limbrick in his office again, frowning, hunched over a computer keyboard. There was no sign of the kids, not even Brad Russell. Joe imagined the teenager lurking on the streets of Longwater, picking out victims, the addicted and the sad who needed something to see them through the day. It occurred to him that he should point the local cops in Russell's direction; the lad would surely have enough on him for them to make an arrest. But what good would that do? A night in the cells and an appearance in the magistrates' court might result eventually in a custodial sentence. But only a short one. And then Russell would be back, harder, with more knowledge of the system, and a list of contacts to move him up the pecking order of offenders.

Limbrick looked up when Joe knocked at the open door.

'Sorry to disturb you.'

'That's okay. I'm glad of the interruption. These days, my job seems to be all about targets and budgets. Not really what I signed up for.'

'A bit like policing then.'

They walked through to the kitchen. There was no sign of Tracey or any other staff. Limbrick made instant coffee and reached into a high cupboard for a tin of biscuits.

They sat at one of the tables. 'We were wondering if there was a former resident with a grudge against the place,' Joe said. 'Someone unstable enough to take out their anger on Josh Woodburn.'

Limbrick gave a small, sad smile. They'd checked out the manager of the home of course. No criminal convictions. Divorced. No children. He lived in a former council house in Longwater. Not one of the rough estates. Pleasant enough on the edge of the town. No debt that they could see, and surely money couldn't be the motive here. Who would benefit financially from Woodburn's death? Joe had put the word out among his local colleagues, asked about rumours, their impressions of Rosebank and the manager. They would have had contact with the man over the years, picking up missing kids or using the home for an emergency placement if there just happened to be space. They hadn't had any strong views either way, but there was nothing bad. No hints of skeletons in the cupboard, improprieties which Woodburn might have discovered and threatened to expose.

'We've had a lot of angry young people in our care, Sergeant, but not anyone who knew Josh. He'd been here for such a short time. Only two residents have left since he started. They were with us as short-term placements, and I can't see either of them being angry enough to lash out with a hammer. They were eleven-year-old twin girls. A foster placement was found for them after three days.'

'The hammer that killed him,' Joe said. 'You told the CSIs

that you had no idea where it could have come from. Have you had any other thoughts about that?'

Limbrick shook his head. 'All our maintenance is done by contractors, and that's organized from head office, so we have no need to keep tools on site. I can't say for certain that it wasn't here somewhere, in the shed in the garden maybe, but I hadn't noticed it.'

'Can we have a look at the shed?'

'Your forensic people have been in there and checked it out.'

'All the same.' It occurred to Joe that Chloe Spence might have sneaked back on to the premises after a couple of nights in the cold. A shed might not be cosy, but it'd be better than the open air. The kitchen door might be locked from the inside at night, but there could be other ways in, known only to the kids. Joe pictured Chloe hoping to sneak in when everyone was asleep, to raid the pantry. Besides, he wanted to be out of the house, which smelled of fried food, disinfectant, and all the institutions he'd ever been in.

'A quick question.' Rosie had been on the phone about a visitor to Josh's student flat in Jesmond: *The description might fit Limbrick. Untidy. A bit of an ageing hippy.* 'Did you ever visit Josh at home in Newcastle?'

The man shook his head. He seemed astonished by the idea. 'Of course not. Why would I?'

'We're just following leads.' He got to his feet.

Limbrick led him out through the kitchen door. There was an area of scuffed and scruffy grass, surrounded by a brick wall. A line of trees against the far boundary had almost shed all its leaves and they were gathered in heaps. A football net had blown over.

'Do the kids use the space much?'

Limbrick shrugged. 'Nah, not this bunch. They'd rather be inside on their screens. In the summer, the lasses come out occasionally to sunbathe and chat. Josh made an effort to persuade them into the open air.'

The shed was in one corner, substantial, built with wooden slats, a glazed window on one side. The door was bolted but not padlocked shut. Joe reached out to open it. Inside, there were a couple of rusting bikes and a go-cart. A barbecue, which hadn't been cleaned since it was last used, still with pieces of burned charcoal, the grille covered in grease. But no sign of a fourteen-year-old girl. No clothes or sleeping bag. No tool box where a hammer might have been kept. There was still fingerprint dust on the door and on some of the surfaces. The CSIs would have found any trace of an intruder waiting here before heading to the common to wreak violence or vengeance. Joe made a mental note to speak to Billy Cartwright at the briefing that evening.

'Anything else I can do for you?' Limbrick looked at his watch, a hint that he had better things to do than stand here in the cold.

'Yeah, I'd like to see the files of any residents who left in the past six months. This might not have been an attack specifically targeted at Josh. More a general rage, someone wanting to lash out at the home in general.'

Though, Joe thought, if one of the former residents was going through some sort of psychotic episode and felt the need for revenge, wouldn't they come inside and go for the common room where the three kids and one of the care staff were sitting, watching a film, filling their bellies with popcorn? If someone had had bad experiences here, that would wind them up, wouldn't it? An assault in the common room would provide an immediate target and a big hit. An audience. Like the school shootings in the US. A day of fame. Would the intruder really hang around outside looking for a stray care worker and a girl?

'Sure.' Limbrick didn't sound very interested. 'It'll take ten minutes or so to track them down. Do you want to wait in the warm while I'm looking?'

'Nah, you're all right. I'd like to get a sense of the place. I've never seen it properly in full daylight.' Joe knew this to be an excuse. He didn't want to be back inside. Limbrick's depression and sense of hopelessness were contagious. 'I'll call back in when I've had a look around the neighbourhood.'

'There's not much to see. But suit yourself.' The man ambled back towards the house.

There was a side gate leading from the garden to the drive, and a gravel patch where Joe had parked his car. In full sunlight Rosebank looked even shabbier, more in need of repair. In a gale, the wind would carry salt spray up over the low cliff, and Joe imagined it eating away at the fabric of the place. The whitewashed render was stained and peeling away from the brick. Through the office window, Joe saw Limbrick standing next to a filing cabinet. He thought that if this building was the man's castle, it was crumbling around him.

The front of the house was unfenced. The children's home was at the end of the road. Joe looked back down the potholed street towards the town and the water. There was a pier where even in *his* lifetime boats had waited to be loaded with coal to power the nation. Beyond Rosebank, the road petered out leading to a track into a patch of scrubby land, uneven, covered with bramble, the blackberries shrivelled and rotting now in late autumn, small, fragile trees, and wild roses which might have prompted the name of the home, but now had nothing left but the hips. This was where Josh Woodburn's body had been found and though it had been taken to the mortuary, a strip of police tape remained, marking the spot, along with a few bunches of dying flowers.

Once, Joe thought, there'd been a pit here, and this scrubland was the spoil heap, rewilded. But not through planning or to save the planet. It had just been left, neglected when the colliery had closed, and had been reclaimed by nature. There were traces of wire-mesh fencing, but that had been pulled down long ago and now there were winding paths through the undergrowth and signs that local children had built dens and set fires.

Joe knew that a search team had been through the area the day before, and had found no sign of Chloe. They'd come across debris of course – the skeletons of several prams, tyres, discarded children's shoes and clothes, the remnants of fires – but nothing that had seemed relevant to Chloe's disappearance. All the same, Joe found a pair of wellies in the boot of his car and went for a wander himself.

In a clearing, he found a pair of lads aged about ten. They were hacking branches off some of the bigger surrounding trees using a blunt kitchen knife. They stopped when they saw him and stared. Not scared and not in the slightest bit intimidated.

'You a birdwatcher?'

'No. Why aren't you at school?'

The first lad, dark-haired, with shrewd, watchful eyes, chose not to answer the question, but continued with his own train of thought.

'We get birders in here sometimes. Spring and autumn.'

'Shouldn't you be in school?' Joe repeated.

'Teacher training day.' It came out automatically, a standard excuse.

'What's your name?'

'Alfie.' The speaker nodded towards his mate. 'He's Noah, but he doesn't talk much.'

'What are you doing?'

'Nearly Bonfire Night, isn't it?' He narrowed his eyes. 'What are you doing here if you're not a birdwatcher?' A pause. 'You a pervert?'

'I'm a cop.'

There was a silence, but still no sign of fear. This was *their* territory. He was the intruder. 'What you doing here, like?'

'There was a murder here. You'll have heard?'

'Saw the cars. All the pigs walking through the common.'

'That's what this is called? The common?'

The boy nodded. 'It's what *we* call it.' A pause. 'They didn't see us though. Not in our den. We heard them coming, with their big boots, all talking and shouting. If they were looking properly, they should be quiet, shouldn't they?'

'You two would be good cops. I bet you notice things that other people don't.'

For a moment the boys didn't respond. They knew he was softening them up, but all the same they were enjoying the flattery.

Joe persisted. 'You come here a lot?'

'Yeah.' Then quickly: 'After school. Weekends. Teacher training days . . .'

'Even when it gets dark? Aren't your parents worried?'

'Nah, we're always back on time.'

'I'm looking for a lass,' Joe said. 'Fourteen. Dresses like a goth. She's gone missing from Rosebank. We need to find her.'

'Chloe Spence?'

'You know her?'

'She comes here sometimes. Sits in our den and reads. Says she likes the peace.' He looked up at Joe. 'We don't mind. She's sound.'

'Have you seen her in the past couple of days?'

'Nah.'

'Can I look at your den?'

They shared a look. 'You won't tell anyone where it is?'

Joe shook his head. 'Not unless it helps find Chloe.'

That seemed good enough. 'It's canny well hidden. Not even the cops found it when they were doing their search.'

They set off so quickly that Joe found it hard to catch up. They knew this place intimately, every twist in the path which Joe would never have guessed even was a path, every twisted root protruding above ground to trip up the unwary. They were sure-footed as goats. Soon, Joe had lost his bearings. He couldn't see beyond the scrub and the tangled bushes to the world outside.

They stopped suddenly on the edge of a huge thicket of bramble, higher in the middle, caused, Joe decided, by a mound in the uneven ground.

'Well?' Alfie was triumphant. 'Can you see?'

'Not a thing.' It was what they wanted to hear, but it was also true.

They circled the thicket and stopped once more. Still, Joe couldn't make out what they were looking for. He could see that there was more dead wood here, dying leaves. The boys reached in and pulled aside a big dead branch, thick with twigs.

'It came down near the road in the big storm a couple of years back. Arwen it was called. We pulled it all the way here. We knew it would hide the entrance.'

Now, he could see there was a narrow path through the bushes, and again the boys ran ahead. In places Joe had to stoop so low that it would have been easier to crawl. They came at last to a wooden door. It looked magical, a door into the hill – a hobbit house – and he could see why it had excited them. He'd loved building dens when he was a kid. Like these boys, he'd been allowed out to play, no questions asked. He and Sal liked to know where their children were, preferred organized events, sleepovers with families they knew. It occurred to him briefly that perhaps *his* kids were more deprived than these boys, with their dirty faces and tatty clothes. Deprived of their freedom and the possibilities of adventure.

The mound that he'd seen when they'd come across the thicket was this – a tiny building no bigger than the shed in the Rosebank garden. The undergrowth had grown over it, hiding it completely.

'Wow,' he said, his admiration genuine.

The talkative boy opened the door with a flourish. 'This is the den.'

Inside it was dark; there had been windows, but they'd been grown over and only a shadowy green light came in, with a smear of sunshine through the door. Alfie reached in and found a torch on a shelf and switched it on, shone it round the space so Joe could see the wonder that they'd created.

'How did you know it was here?'

'The council were doing some filming on Longwater and they were using a drone. It went down in there. They paid us to go in and look for it. And we found the den. It took us a canny while to get the path cut properly.'

There was a piece of faded carpet on the floor. 'Someone just chucked it on the edge of the common,' Alfie said. 'They're always hoying out their rubbish.'

Brightly coloured cushions had been piled in one corner to form the only seats. 'Were they thrown out too?'

Alfie tried to look shamefaced. 'Nah, I nicked them from my gran's. Her house is full of crap. My mam says she's a hoarder. She didn't miss them.'

'Can I borrow the torch and look inside?'

Alfie pretended at reluctance. 'Okay.'

Inside there was barely enough height for Joe to stand. This must have been a storeroom of some sort. It hadn't been built as a place for people to work. At first there was no sign that Chloe had been here. Nothing that might have belonged to her.

Then, carefully folded and left on the shelf that ran around the room, he saw a piece of paper, torn from a notebook. Joe held it with gloves and shone his torch so he could see it properly. He recognized the writing immediately. There were the same swirls and circular dots on the 'i's as in Chloe's diary.

He went back through the door and stood with the boys. He held out the bag with the paper inside.

'How long's this been here? Do you know?' Trying to make it sound as if it wasn't important at all.

'Nah, haven't seen it before.' Alfie was getting bored now. Joe thought they wanted to go back to slicing down branches for their illicit bonfire.

'If you see Chloe, can you let me know? We're worried about her.'

'How do we get hold of you?'

'You got a phone?'

'Course.'

'Give me the number and I'll ring you. Then you can save mine.'

Alfie pulled a phone out of his jeans pocket and shouted out the list of numbers. The ringtone sounded odd, out of place in this small piece of wilderness. Joe realized that, in his head, he was still in his own childhood and he wouldn't have had a phone when *he* was out playing.

Alfie saved Joe's number with surprising speed and efficiency. Then the boys led the way out of the bramble thicket and pulled the dead branch back over the entrance so it was, once again, completely hidden.

They stood just outside the secret entrance. 'We'll be sending in some CSIs,' Joe said, 'to test for fingerprints.'

'CSI? Like my gran watches on the telly?' Alfie tried not to sound too excited.

'Something like that. We might have to take your prints too, but I've got your number now. Can you stay out of the den for a bit, until the forensics team have been in?'

'Okay.'

'And if you see Chloe, or anyone else nosing about, you must be certain to let me know.'

'Sure,' Alfie said. 'Cool.'

Joe walked back to Rosebank and Dave Limbrick, feeling somehow less depressed and more optimistic, even when the man handed him a pile of dusty files.

Chapter Fourteen

VERA CALLED JOE AND ROSIE INTO her office before the evening's briefing. The inspector knew that she'd made mistakes in her handling of Holly. She'd kept the DC in the dark, without quite meaning to. Holly had resented being left out of important decisions, when Joe had been included in the discussions. Vera could see how that would have seemed unkind. It *had* been unkind. Now, she remembered clever quips and unthinking words of criticism, which rolled into her head like an incoming tide, washing with it the inevitable guilt.

Vera and Joe had always been close. Holly must have felt she had something to prove, that she had to be brave to be noticed. Vera didn't want that on her conscience again, so she'd promised herself that with Rosie she'd try to be more open, to communicate more. If she managed it, at least she'd be able to claim it as an improvement in management technique when it came to this year's appraisal. There was no harm in keeping Watkins, the superintendent and her boss, happy. Playing the game.

She perched on her desk, letting Joe and Rosie have the

two chairs. The office was tiny, the one radiator either freezing or scalding hot, but Vera held on to the room with grim determination. It was her space. No open-plan working or hot-desking for her.

'So what have we got to report? Rosie, you went to Josh Woodburn's place in Jesmond and spoke to his flatmates?'

'Yeah. Miggy, real name Miguel. Spanish parents, but he's a Brit. And Elizabeth. Josh wasn't in a relationship with either of them, or with anyone else as far as they knew. Elizabeth has a boyfriend who stays there sometimes, but he's studying in France at the moment. They'd had friends around last night to get pissed and remember Josh, but really, I didn't have the impression that they were best mates. It seemed more like an excuse for a party.'

'You don't hit someone on the head with a claw hammer, just because they're not your soulmate.' Vera was talking to herself but then realized that might sound critical. 'Useful to know though, to understand something of the background.'

'Josh didn't come across as the sort to make enemies,' Rosie went on. 'He was quiet, self-contained. The students seemed very happy to take advantage of his parents' hospitality – the Sunday lunches and barbecues – but I don't think they were particularly close to him.'

'You're saying that they were using him?'

'Maybe. Something like that. Or that they were a bit dismissive of him. Like, they were sophisticated Southerners and although his parents were professionals, minted, he couldn't quite match up.'

'You haven't got a bit of a Geordie chip on your shoulder, pet?' Vera thought that some things needed saying, even if she was trying to be kind.

'No!' Then Rosie seemed to reconsider. 'Well, only a small one.'

'As long as it doesn't cloud your judgement.' A pause. 'So, no enemies. Did you get anything else out of them?'

'Only that he had a visitor last week. A middle-aged man. Too old for a student and too untidy for a Jesmond resident, according to Elizabeth. He came to the flat and asked for Josh. Josh went out with him for about an hour. No communication with the other two about who the guy was and what he wanted. They assumed it was something to do with Josh's new job.'

'It couldn't have been Limbrick? A kind of informal appraisal or catch-up?'

'That's what I thought.' She leaned back in her chair.

Joe jumped in then. 'Rosie phoned me before I got to Rosebank and explained about the guy. I asked Limbrick, but he says he'd never been there.'

'Did the students notice a vehicle?'

'Nah,' Rosie said. 'Elizabeth thought he'd got there on the bus.'

Vera didn't think that sounded much like Limbrick. He could have walked to work from where he lived, but his clapped-out red Corsa was always parked outside the home. It'd be an effort getting to Jesmond from Longwater by public transport.

Rosie was still talking. 'I picked up Josh's laptop from his room, and I've dropped it off at digital services. There's a hell of a backlog though. They said not to expect anything until next week.'

'I'll give them a ring.' Vera had been in the service so long that she had favours to call in. 'See if they can shove it up the ladder a rung or two.'

'Thanks, boss.' Rosie sounded impressed. Vera liked that. It had been hard to impress Holly.

'Joe? You went to talk to Limbrick. What did you come away with?'

'Well, he couldn't hand me a likely psycho who'd attack Josh for the hell of it. Or the glory. Or as some form of revenge against the whole childcare system. But Limbrick *has* given me a heap of files of residents who've been in Rosebank and have left in the past six months. I haven't read them all yet, but I'll do that after the briefing.' A dramatic pause. 'I did find this though.'

Joe set a scrap of paper in its clear evidence bag on the desk in front of Vera. She had a sudden image of a cat, bringing in a mouse as a gift for its owner. But there was a moment of pride when she recognized the writing. Her boy had done it again.

'Where did you find this?'

Joe described his encounter with the lads on the common.

'And the search team missed the building altogether?' Her voice sharp now. She'd have a word with the team leader.

'Honestly, you can't blame them. There's no way I'd have seen it if the lads hadn't pointed me in the right direction.'

'We don't know when it was left in the boys' den?'

'No, they couldn't help with that. The paper's relatively dry though and the place is damp. It hasn't been lurking there for months.'

'You think she was hiding out there?' Vera thought that was a bit speculative. 'The night after Josh Woodburn died?'

'Nah, I'm not saying that. Worth checking it out though, in case there's any other DNA. The lads and Chloe are the only people who've used it, so anything else would be of interest.

And we might find Josh Woodburn's blood. If Chloe did kill him, she could have gone there to change out of stained clothes.'

'Aye.' Vera didn't want Chloe Spence to be the killer and had to force herself to keep an open mind.

'I've got one of the lads' mobile number,' Joe said. 'We'll need them to get access to the building. I don't think I'd find it again on my own.'

'You weren't in the Scouts then, Joe?' An attempt to lighten the mood. She still felt weighed down by the possibility that Chloe was a killer.

He shook his head. 'No. Boys' Brigade.'

She looked at him quizzically.

He grinned. 'Run by the Methodists. Scouts with a moral conscience.'

Ah, she thought. *That's still you then, bonny lad.*

The mood in the briefing room was gloomy. This was the third day and still they had nothing. No witness to a stranger approaching or leaving Rosebank on the night of Woodburn's murder. No possible motive. No sign of the girl. And a growing sense among the team that when they *did* find her, it would be as a body and not a live child.

Vera passed on the new information she'd gained during the day. 'John Spence is back in the country from the Middle East. He claims not to have seen Chloe, but let's check out his phone calls and see if she's been in touch with him, using a mate's mobile or a public landline.'

'You think he might be hiding her somewhere?' Rosie threw in the question.

Vera thought the new lass wasn't turning out to be a shrinking violet. Which was a good thing, wasn't it?

'It's a possibility, I suppose, but I didn't get that feeling.' A pause. 'I met the grandfather too. They live in a nice house in Whitley. Very upwardly mobile is Whitley Bay these days, and his wife owns a fancy clothes shop in Park View. He still runs an abattoir not far from Longwater, but it seems that the couple is upwardly mobile too and moved out to the coast five years ago. The grandparents offered Chloe a home when Becky, her mam, went into hospital, but she refused to go. She blames her dad and by extension her grandparents for her mam's illness. And Pam, the grandmother, disapproves of the way she looks and dresses.'

Vera looked out at the room. Rosie was taking notes.

'Becky told me that Chloe's favourite place was a bothy in Gillstead, which used to be on the family land, and which they still own. It doesn't seem too much of a stretch to imagine that the den on the common where she'd go to escape Rosebank reminded her of the place where she was so happy. It's an outside chance, but I'm taking Gordon, the grandfather, up to Gillstead tomorrow. Just to have a look round. While you lot carry on with the real policing.'

Someone in the room gave a little chuckle. Vera liked that. 'It'd be good to track down the middle-aged man who visited Josh at his house in Jesmond. The description doesn't sound like a family friend. Then why haven't we found the details of the car parked outside Rosebank and described by Chloe in her diary?' She looked out at them, challenging. 'A similar car was parked outside the lass's family home in Longwater. A neighbour thought it was the press, but maybe it's too much of a coincidence?' A pause. 'Can we check CCTV in the neighbourhood and see what we come up with?'

Again, Vera looked out at the room. It was time to bring a

bit more energy to the group. She raised her voice. 'Now I'm going to hand over to Joe Ashworth here, who'll tell you all about that den, and I'd like to know how our *specialist* search team missed it, when my detective sergeant came across it within minutes of having a wander around the place.' She paused and waited for their response. There was a smattering of ironic clapping directed at Joe, and more subdued laughter. 'And now he'll show you the one piece of useful evidence we have to date, and he'll read you a message from Chloe Spence.'

The big, overheated room fell silent.

Chapter Fifteen

IT'S ODD BEING HERE IN THE dark. I've only been here in daylight before. The watery light coming through the window. The leaves outside like seaweed. I imagine myself submerged under waves. Lost. Tonight, it's pitch dark outside. There's no moon and no stars, and I wouldn't see them in here even if they were shining.

I'm waiting to be found.

While I'm waiting, I'm trying to make sense of the confusion. The guilt. Wondering what I've done. I shouted but again nobody was listening. I sometimes have nightmares when I'm screaming and no sound comes out. It was like that. So close to a houseful of people, you would think that someone would hear you. But perhaps it was like the dream and I hadn't actually made any sound at all.

I don't know what the time is. I don't own a watch and my phone's run out of charge. I'm cold now. I brought my coat. The good one Mam bought for me in Marksies in town before she got ill again, but still I'm freezing. I'm not sure how long I can stay here, waiting to be rescued. Perhaps I should have a plan in case nobody comes.

You'd expect this place to be quiet. Silent. But there are sounds here, scuffling noises, animals in the undergrowth. Not cute animals. Alfie says there are rats here, as big as small dogs. And I heard a tawny owl in the distance.

Then it must have rained in the night, and the elder trees are still dripping. My great-gran used to pick elderberries and make them into syrup for the kids and wine for the grown-ups. The sound of dripping rain made me want to pee and I went outside and walked along the path a little way.

I had a torch to see my way and that's how I saw it. A body, covered in blood. At least that's what I thought. A kid's body. Small. The blood dark as night. But when I got closer, I think it was just a pile of clothes. I was too freaked out to look too closely. But the blood was real. I'm sure of that. Is it a sign? Is someone trying to scare me? Well, they've done a good job because I'm properly terrified now. And I still need a piss but I'm not going out again until it gets light.

There's one good thing: I won't have to go to fucking school tomorrow.

Chapter Sixteen

ROSIE LISTENED TO JOE READING OUT the lass's writing, and could imagine Chloe outside in the dark, hiding in her den in the middle of a huge patch of brambles, scratched and cold and scared. Vera broke into her thoughts.

'What did you make of the pile of bloodstained clothes?' The inspector looked at Joe. 'Did you see anything like that, Joe?'

He shook his head. 'And I would have done if they were close to the path. The boys would have mentioned it too.'

'Maybe her imagination was running away with her,' Rosie said. She thought *her* imagination would be running wild, on her own in a place like that.

'Maybe,' the inspector said. 'It's *all* a bit poetic, don't you think? A bit contrived. If you were that scared, would you get out a pen and paper and write about it? If she'd just seen Josh Woodburn's skull bashed in by a hammer, wouldn't she just head back into the building sharpish and let Limbrick know? She wouldn't sit there in the middle of a bush, waiting to be rescued.'

'What if she was the one to hit Limbrick over the head?' Joe asked. 'You seem to have dismissed the lass as a suspect.'

Vera shot him a hacky look. 'I've dismissed nothing, Sergeant.' Her voice icy. 'But these don't sound like the words of a young killer.'

'You told us her English teacher said she could be a poet or a songwriter,' Joe said. 'Perhaps she's just telling stories. Putting us off the scent. She knows we'd find her hideout sometime.' A pause, because of course Joe Ashworth was soft as clarts, and he couldn't really see a young lass as a killer. 'Or it could be her way of processing trauma.'

Rosie thought that was bollocks but knew better than to say so. The boss made a kind of snorting sound. She obviously thought it was bollocks too.

The words had been blown up and projected on to a screen, so they were all able to see what Chloe had written.

'It might have been a piece of imaginative writing,' Rosie said. 'She thinks of herself as a goth, doesn't she, and this is pretty gothic. She could have written it anytime. It could be part of an essay for an English class.' She paused. 'If it wasn't for that last sentence about bunking off school.'

Vera looked across at Rosie and beamed her approval. 'I thought that too. That was real, wasn't it? We know that she hates school, but she hasn't missed any lessons since she started living at Rosebank. I checked when I talked to the teacher. No absences at all until the day after the murder.' She looked out at the group. 'Which means?'

Rosie knew the answer of course but let Joe reply. It wouldn't do to look cocky. Not straight off. And he jumped in straight away.

'That she was there, in the lads' den, the night that Josh Woodburn was killed.'

There was a long silence, and now Rosie did think she could

raise her hand and ask a question without pissing off a more established member of the team. 'So who was she waiting for? Who did she think would come to rescue her?'

Vera narrowed her eyes. 'Well, that's the question, isn't it? And more importantly, where is she now? With her mysterious rescuer? Or out there somewhere on her own?' The boss looked out at the room, and the next sentence emerged as a shout: 'This is a fourteen-year-old girl. With important information and in danger. I want her found.'

There was a silence before Vera switched her attention to Charlie.

'Have you got a name for the person in charge of Seaview Care?'

'It's hard to track down ownership. Some private equity firm based in the Middle East seems to be getting involved. But the general manager of all the kids' homes is a chap called Charles Stamoran. He says he'd be happy to have a Zoom call with you if that would help.'

'Would he now?'

'He's sent over some times when he'd be available.'

'Good of him.' The boss was clearly being sarcastic. 'Let's see if I can fit him into my equally busy schedule.'

After the briefing, Rosie hovered at the door of the operations room. She wasn't sure if there'd be another invitation to the pub for a meal, if that was a regular fixture during a murder inquiry. But Vera just gathered up all her bits of paper and stuck them in a Morrisons carrier bag. 'I'm off then. See you bright-eyed and bushy-tailed in the morning.' Joe had already disappeared – wary, it seemed, of being trapped again, of facing the wrath of his wife by being late home.

Rosie ran after Vera and caught up with her in the car park.

'I wondered if it would be okay to call in on the Woodburns. It's almost on my way home.'

'Not quite, is it, pet?' The smile was friendly enough but Vera's eyes were sharp.

'They turned down the offer of family liaison, and I got on well with them, that first day when we told them Josh had died. We know a bit more now. About his friends in Jesmond and the older guy who called on him. They might be able to throw some light.'

'So they might!' Vera said. There was a moment of almost awkward silence. 'Go ahead then. Call in to offer our support and ask a few questions.' She paused again. Rosie was about to go on to her car. 'But you've nothing to prove to me, you know. You're doing okay.'

And then Vera was off, marching across the car park towards her filthy Land Rover.

Rosie arrived at the Woodburns' home at the worst possible time, just as they were about to sit down to dinner, but Chris, who opened the door, still seemed glad to see her. Perhaps he was hoping for information, or at least that she would distract them both from their grief.

'Come in!' Then: 'You will join us? I've made loads and neither of us has much of an appetite at the moment.'

So she found herself sitting at the breakfast bar in their smart kitchen, eating pasta with courgette and parmesan. She wasn't sure if there was any rule about accepting a meal from potential witnesses, but Rosie thought that Vera wouldn't be one for rules. But she did turn down the offer of a glass of wine, though she would have been glad of one to help her through the awkwardness of the situation.

Anna looked thinner, even more tense than when she'd dashed across from her Gateshead surgery to learn of her son's death. She leaned across the bar towards Rosie. Her eyes were slightly unfocused. Rosie thought she'd been self-medicating with booze, but that it wasn't helping.

'Is there news? Do you know who murdered him?'

'I'm afraid not. We're trying to find one of the Rosebank residents though. She disappeared the night Josh was killed.'

'You think she might be the killer?' Anna's voice was too loud, almost hysterical. She was even more drunk than Rosie had first thought.

Rosie didn't give an answer. 'She could be a witness. She's a fourteen-year-old girl called Chloe Spence. Do you recognize that name?'

Chris answered. He was holding things together better than his wife, but he was almost rigid with the effort of keeping calm. 'We didn't even know he was working in that place. He certainly didn't talk about any of the individuals living there.'

'I've been to chat to his flatmates in Jesmond. They didn't know anything about his job as a carer either. Have you got any idea why he might have wanted to keep that secret?'

The parents looked at each other, and Anna answered.

'None at all. We'd have been proud of him, taking on such an important task. I'm a doctor, for fuck's sake. I work with troubled people every day. But he was never a child who confided much in us. In me, at least. He was always closer to Chris. They went walking and cycling together, and when he was little, I always seemed to be at work.' She looked across at the fridge, where there were photos stuck on with magnets. Rosie saw images of a small boy with a bike, of a teenager on the top of a mountain, of an almost-adult with his father, a backdrop of three monumental stones, grinning into the camera as a selfie.

Anna was still talking. 'Otherwise, he was a bit of a loner, a dreamer. Lost, somehow, in a world of his own. And he never had particularly close friends. He wasn't bullied, nothing like that. But he was self-contained. He drew when he was a child, endlessly, from life and odd cartoon characters. Then as he got older it was all about film. Watching it. Making it. We always joked that he'd turn out to be a famous director, that we'd go with him to Hollywood to see him picking up his Oscar.' She screwed up a paper napkin and scrubbed at her eyes.

Chris Woodburn's mobile rang. He looked at the number. 'Sorry, work. I'll have to take this.' He didn't seem sad to have an excuse to leave the room. He pulled the door to behind him, but it was still slightly open, and Rosie heard him talking to someone on the end of the line, his voice suddenly a little more assertive. 'That wasn't what we planned. Really, we need to reassess the situation. I'm sure you understand that I can't talk now. It's a dreadful time for us. I'll call back in the morning.'

If wine was Anna's means of escape, Rosie thought, it seemed work was her husband's.

He returned to the kitchen and his meal, apologetic. 'I'm sorry. Even now, some clients are incredibly demanding.'

'Just turn off your phone.' Anna was snappy. 'Let someone else deal with any crisis. Nothing is that important. Not now.'

Rosie could tell that Chris would continue working though. It seemed like a thread to sanity, to a world before his son had died.

'Josh had a visitor to the Jesmond flat,' she said, 'the week before he was killed. An older man, rather scruffy. We think he'd come into town on a bus from the coast. They went out together for about an hour and Josh didn't tell Miggy and Elizabeth who the man was. I wondered if you'd know.'

Anna sat with her elbows on the table, her head in her hands. Her eyes closed for a moment and Rosie wondered if she was falling asleep. 'Could it have been one of his lecturers?' Anna turned to her husband, awake after all, but dreamy. 'Wasn't there someone who looked like that at the exhibition we went to?'

'What was his name?'

They looked at each other. 'Honestly,' Anna said, 'I can't remember, but surely the university would know.'

'Of course.' Rosie made a mental note to check it out.

'There is one other possibility.' Chris looked at his wife. 'It sounds a little like Stella's father.'

'Stella?' The name rang a bell for Rosie, but she couldn't quite remember where she'd heard it.

'When Josh was at school, she was his girlfriend. His first real relationship. She's a couple of years younger than him, and I suspect that was why he chose a university close to home. It meant that he'd be able to keep in touch with her. We were the ones to suggest that he live out, so he could have a real student experience. Left to himself, he'd have stayed here, meeting up most nights with Stella, not making any real friends of his own.'

'And that would have been a bad thing?'

'No! Not at all!' Something in Anna's voice, though, made Rosie think that Stella wasn't an ideal potential daughter-in-law. 'We just thought that Josh was too young to be so serious about someone. So intense.' There was a pause. 'And poor Stella hadn't had a conventional childhood. She was brought up by her father in a kind of hostel. When Stella was eleven, her parents separated, and he started this project here in the North.' A pause. 'One could hardly blame the woman. He can't have been the easiest man to live with.'

'The mother left Stella with her father?'

'According to Josh, Stella chose to move north with her father. I believe it was a kind of misplaced loyalty. The mother still lives in London, I think.'

'And you think that the stranger who turned up on Josh's doorstep was Stella's father?'

'It could have been, couldn't it?' Chris's question was directed to his wife.

Anna shrugged. 'It could have been anyone! As we said, someone from the university.'

'But he came here once, looking for Josh,' Chris said. 'He claimed that Josh was pestering his daughter, sending unwanted texts and emails. He asked us to make him stop. Quite ridiculous, of course. Josh had been the one to end the relationship when he started at the university.'

'Are you sure?' Rosie remembered then where she'd heard the girl's name, during the conversation with Lizzie in the student flat.

Josh would talk about her when he'd been drinking.

And perhaps his work in Rosebank had been a way of proving to Stella that he was worthy of her love.

It took the couple a moment to answer. Rosie sensed the hostility bouncing between them. This had been a subject of discussion and anxiety long before Josh's death. 'Could Josh have been sending unwanted messages to the lass?'

Chris set down his wine glass and put his hand over his wife's. It was a tentative gesture, as if he thought she might push him away, but she allowed it to rest there, and even shot him a grateful little smile.

'I don't understand –' Anna's voice was angry now, barely controlled, and she seemed to be speaking for them both – 'how this could possibly be relevant to Josh's murder. You can't start blackening his name now he's dead.'

'We have to follow every possible contact.' Rosie suspected that the couple's fury was more about the loss of their son than about the direction that the investigation was taking. 'Can you give me the contact details for Stella and her father?'

'You think one of them might have killed our son?' Anna's voice was so quiet that it was almost a whisper.

'Not at all. It's just a procedure to follow. We'll need to talk to them, since we're talking to most of the people who knew him.'

Chris tore a sheet of paper from a notebook on the bench and scribbled on it, before almost throwing it at Rosie. 'Perhaps you'd have the courtesy to leave us now to remember our son as we knew him.'

Rosie got to her feet. 'Of course. But one last thing. If you remember anything that might help us to find Chloe Spence, the missing girl, you will get in touch?'

Both parents nodded their heads, but Rosie thought they'd hardly heard her. They were too wrapped up in their own grief to care about another lost child.

She stood up to go then, saying she'd see herself out. She left them, sitting among the remains of the barely eaten meal, hand in hand.

Outside, it was strange for a moment to find the world un-altered. Cars still drove down the road along the coast, their headlights shining on people walking along the pavement to the cafés and bars. Far out in the bay, ships were waiting for the tide before docking in the container port, south of the Tyne, their lights steady, unmoving. Rosie tried to process the emotions she'd experienced in the gleaming kitchen with its gadgets and appliances. In the end, she thought, perhaps guilt was at the bottom of it. The Woodburns had thought that they'd rescued Josh from a relationship that had been damaging to him. But it seemed that he'd died lonely and sad, desperate to have her back.

Perhaps his relationship with Stella had no relevance at all to his murder. It could, though, explain the student's decision to find work in the care system. It would be interesting to see the place where Stella had grown up. Perhaps Josh too had felt guilt, a sort of survivor's guilt because his childhood had been very different from hers. He'd been comfortable, loved. Rosie wondered if she should put any of these thoughts into her report about the visit to the Woodburns. In her old team, she might have been mocked for that kind of speculation:

You're not a psychologist, Rosie Bell. Stick to the facts.

Vera was different though. Rosie thought that Vera might understand.

Chapter Seventeen

JOE WAS IN THE STATION EARLY. He knew it was ridiculous but he felt that he had to prove to Vera that he was still her right-hand officer. The boss had never really taken to Holly. She'd admired the woman, but they'd been so very different in every way – Holly wasn't local, she'd been a fitness freak, had been cerebral and logical, and a little scared of Vera's impulsiveness – and there'd been no closeness or friendship. Rosie was brash, a looker, and he'd thought she'd annoy the boss. Instead, it seemed they'd already developed a mutual respect, even affection. Of course, Joe knew he should be pleased. They'd be a stronger team if they all got on. All the same, he felt a competitive streak and a tinge of jealousy. He was determined to up his game.

His first call was to the digital team. He went down in person; he knew that Alison who ran the section was a lark. A nerdy lark. She was always in early.

'Josh Woodburn's computer. Have you been able to get into it?'

'Sure. Didn't your colleague tell you?'

'What colleague?' Knowing it was ludicrous, but feeling his hackles already rising.

'The new Holly. Rosie, is she called? There was a message on my voicemail when I got in.' Alison was still staring at a screen, unaware of the effect her response was having.

'I haven't seen her yet.'

'No, you wouldn't have done. She was on her way in when I called her back. We chatted on her hands-free.'

'What were you able to tell her?'

Now she seemed to sense the impatience in his voice, and she looked up. 'Shouldn't you ask her that?'

'Alison! We're working on the same investigation. This isn't some sort of competition!'

Alison gave a little nod of agreement, but Joe wasn't entirely sure she believed him. 'Rosie was asking me if there was any evidence on the laptop to suggest that Josh Woodburn was hassling a former girlfriend.'

'And was he?' He was too poor an actor to keep the surprise from his voice. Besides, it seemed out of character for Josh Woodburn.

'You didn't know? Apparently Rosie visited his parents last night and they told her the lass's father had tried to warn him off.'

'What did you find on the laptop?'

'There were lots of emails to her. She's called Stella, Stella Marsh. Nothing obscene or abusive, but he's certainly been persistent.'

'Does she answer?'

'Yes, but not frequently and the tone is regretful rather than angry. Unless he's been stalking her in other ways, I can't see that any crime would have been committed here.

There's been nothing threatening in the student's contact with the lass.' Alison paused and looked up at him. 'The last email from her is very interesting. It was sent a couple of days before Josh Woodburn died. It refers to a phone conversation that they'd had. It suggests that they should meet.' There was another pause. 'Rosie has all the details. You need to talk to her.'

And with that, Joe had to be satisfied.

In the open-plan office, he found Rosie already at her desk. Vera, who was standing behind her looking down at the screen, looked up and called him over.

'Look at this! It seems our Josh is still smitten with his childhood sweetheart.' A pause. 'And it seems he's been making a nuisance of himself. According to the young woman's father, at least. Rosie got that gem of info out of the parents yesterday. The man turned up on the Woodburns' doorstep asking him to control their son.'

'I know.' Joe knew he sounded churlish. Childish. 'I've just been to chat to Alison.'

'Rosie, can you follow it up? Go and talk to Stella and her dad. Let's see what was going on there.'

'Sure.' Rosie was on her feet, but still talking. Still, Joe thought, showing off. 'I've checked out the father. William Marsh. No previous convictions, not even a ticket for speeding. The daughter's known to us though. A caution for breach of the peace after some eco demo.'

She reached out for her coat, but Vera held up her hand to stop her leaving the room. 'Take Joe with you. I'd like this to be a two-hander. It could be the most important lead we've had so far. Then you can both go and chat to Josh's tutor at the university. He might not be the chap who visited the lad in Jesmond, but he might know what took him to work in Rosebank.'

The address for the Marshes was on the border of Northumberland and North Tyneside, on the flat coastal plain, too close to the former industrial heartland of the region – and just too far from the sea – to be pretty or appealing. A few miles inland from Longwater. All the same, it wasn't what Joe had been expecting. Rosie had talked of a sort of hostel, and he'd pictured a terraced house in one of the towns: bedsits, homeless people with no job and no ambition. A Rosebank for adults.

There was nothing smart about this place, but it wasn't like that. It was rural, up a pockmarked track, with a windblown hedge on each side. The track led to a gate with a hand-painted sign: *Welcome to Paradise Farm*. White lettering on a green background. Quite classy. More classy than the surroundings. Rosie was driving, so Joe got out to open the gate. Inside there was a cracked concrete yard, with free-ranging hens that gathered around his ankles in the hope of food. There was a barn, open on one side to the weather, containing an old, small tractor and a quad bike, and another barn, sturdier. After closing the gate, Joe looked through the window. Inside, half a dozen bunks, a couple containing sleeping bags and pillows, but otherwise unoccupied. On each barn roof solar panels, and beyond the main farmhouse a small wind turbine. Another small outhouse that might once have been a pigsty.

The house itself seemed well cared for. It was built of grey stone with a grey slate roof. Symmetrical with a porch at the front. Small in comparison with the barns but solid. A young woman in jeans and a sweater appeared from behind it.

'Can I help you?'

'Are you Stella Marsh?'

She shook her head. 'Stella will be in school. I'm one of the volunteers.'

'Her dad around?'

'You'll probably find Will in the house.' She walked away, the hens following her.

The door to the porch was open. They stood inside and knocked. The man who answered met the description they'd been given of Josh Woodburn's mysterious visitor. William Marsh was middle-aged, lanky. He wore faded jeans and a large hand-knitted sweater, frayed at the hem.

When he spoke, the voice was unexpected: deep, melodic, educated. 'How can I help you?'

Joe explained.

'Of course, we heard about poor Josh. Do come in. Let's sit in the kitchen. It's the only warm room in the house.'

They sat at a scrubbed pine table where it seemed he'd been working. There was a laptop and a pile of papers.

Joe decided to take the lead on this one. 'Josh was a friend of your daughter's.'

'Yes, they were very close at one time. They were in school together in Whitley Bay High. He was older, of course, taking A levels when she was in her GCSE year.'

'But the relationship ended?'

There was a pause. It had seemed to Joe to be a very simple question, but Marsh was considering.

'They maintained contact, but Stella's an independent young woman, very intense, passionate about the values we follow here on Paradise Farm. An eco-activist, I suppose you'd call her. If you check your records, you'll see that she's been cautioned by the police for disrupting a meeting of the local council, when fracking was under consideration. I don't think she found the same commitment in Josh.' He paused and smiled. 'Though she'd probably say I lack commitment too. I'm prepared to make compromises, work with big business if they can help us. Take their sponsorship. She talks about greenwash. She's very young, very idealistic. Perhaps she'll mellow with age.'

'Josh couldn't accept that the relationship with Stella was over?'

'He adored her,' Marsh said simply.

'What is this place?' Rosie's question wasn't rude. Not quite.

Marsh seemed unoffended. 'It might be helpful if I give you a bit of background. I started off in IT and ran my own business very successfully for many years. I'm a local lad, but went to London to make my fortune, as lots of us do. Got married. We had Stella. I was living, I thought, my dream life, until my wife found a new partner and took my daughter with her. Suddenly, I was alone, very depressed, losing myself in alcohol and prescription drugs.' He looked up at them and smiled. 'Just very, very sorry for myself. Then my father died, and I came home for the funeral. This place was for sale. I bought it on a whim, and I never went back to the city.'

Joe thought this was a speech the man had given many times before.

Marsh continued:

'When I took it on, most of the land was brownfield, a former open-cast mine, worked out several years ago. The house and the barns were left over from its former agricultural existence. We've brought it back to life. We have a smallholding, a little herd of sheep, a polytunnel where we grow our own fruit and veg, with enough left over to provide fresh stuff for the local food bank. And patches we're rewilding. The soggy meadow has become a flood plain, where waders come to breed.'

'We?'

'I've had help, of course. More recently we turned a barn into a bunk house where volunteers can stay, learn new skills, escape their problems and have a taste of country life, even though we're so close to the coastal towns and former pit villages.'

'Stella lives with you now?'

'Yes. At first, she came for holidays for several weeks at a time. We lived too far apart for conventional access. Her mother and I have a civilized relationship these days. When Stella was fourteen, she decided she wanted this to be her permanent home. She loved being a part of the project. She was never really happy being a city girl, though of course she goes back to stay in London and to visit her mother whenever she feels like it.'

'Why did you go to see Josh Woodburn's parents to warn him off seeing Stella?'

'Is that what they told you?' Marsh seemed a little amused. 'I went to the house in Cullercoats to see him, not them. I hadn't realized that he'd moved out to Newcastle, until they told me. It was interesting to meet the parents. All very suburban perfection. It explained a lot.'

Joe would have liked to ask what that meant, but before he could frame the question, Rosie was asking one of her own:

'I still don't understand why you felt the need to see Josh. Didn't your daughter think you were meddling in her private business?'

'I'm sure she would have, if she'd known what I was doing. But I liked the lad! He was in danger of losing Stella as a friend as well as a girlfriend. She's stubborn. She needed time to make up her mind about him. By contacting her so often, he was simply irritating her. I said he needed to find a project of his own, something he was passionate about, so he wouldn't come across as quite so needy.'

'He found a job as a childcare officer in a kids' home.' Joe wanted to stand up for the young man who'd listened to Chloe Spence and given her hope for the future. 'He was making a difference there. He was killed just outside it.'

Marsh stared across the table at them, horrified. 'So in one sense I contributed to his murder.' His voice was very low. 'I thought that Josh would throw himself into his art. That was his passion, and Stella understood how much it meant to him. I didn't think he'd follow such a different, such a dramatic path.'

'We'll have to speak to Stella of course. When would be a good time to see her?'

'She'll be home from school at four-thirty. She rarely strays far from the Paradise when she's back, so any time after that.'

Chapter Eighteen

VERA HAD TO DELAY HER TRIP to Gillstead with Gordon Spence to fit in the Zoom call with Stamoran, boss of the company that owned Rosebank. She phoned Chloe's grandfather to explain and could tell he was disappointed.

'Give me half an hour,' she said, 'and I'll be there. This is important.'

She hated Zoom and fretted while she waited for the connection. Stamoran let her into the call at precisely the time they'd arranged. He was sitting in an office with a bookshelf behind him. Nothing personal. Nothing to indicate exactly where he was. He was in his early forties, slick black hair and an unseasonable tan, wearing a suit jacket and shirt, but no tie, managing to give the impression of a man who was professional but relaxed and confident.

He spoke first. 'This is dreadful business. Many of our residents can be challenging, but we've never had this kind of aggression directed at our workers. They've been trained to manage violent behaviour and are usually capable of diffusing difficult situations.'

'I hope you're not implying that Josh Woodburn was somehow responsible for his own death.'

'Of course not!' His voice was confident too, and equally hard to place, but Vera thought she detected a trace of Geordie. 'I just wanted to assure you that we take employee safety very seriously.'

'What sort of training do you provide?'

There was a moment's hesitation. 'Of course most of our staff have recognized social work qualifications. For temporary workers like Josh, there's an online session explaining our aims and responsibilities. He completed that course with flying colours.' A pause and a smile showing a row of impossibly white teeth. 'We are regularly examined. Most of our homes have been rated as good or above.'

Vera thought she could follow that up with Kath Oliver. 'Why have you assumed that Josh was killed by one of your residents?'

'I understood that one of the teenagers had run away. It seemed a logical assumption to make.'

'The teenager's name is Chloe Spence and we're looking for her. She's a witness and potential victim. She's not a suspect at present.'

This time the silence lasted longer. 'I'm sorry. I didn't realize. I only had the information passed on to me by the manager of the home. Of course we'll help your inquiry in any way we can.'

'When was the last time you visited Rosebank?'

'One of our team was there three months ago. Most of our staff supervision sessions are online but we meet in person every quarter.'

'You didn't go yourself?'

He gave an awkward little laugh. 'I'm very much a back-room boy.'

'So you weren't in the North-East earlier this week?' Vera put the question because she knew it would annoy him.

'Certainly not, Inspector. My wife and I have only just come back from a cruise in the Caribbean, soaking up a little sunshine before the worst of the winter. We arrived back in Cumbria yesterday.'

'Business must be going well.'

'We need to make a profit, Inspector, to invest in our facilities.'

Homes! She wanted to scream at him. *They're supposed to be homes!*

Instead, she thanked him for his time, and ended the call. Kath had been right. He was a slippery bastard. But he couldn't have anything to do with Josh's death. It seemed he didn't care at all about the kids in his care or the staff who looked after them. Why would he go to the effort of killing one?

When Vera parked in the leafy street in Whitley Bay, Gordon Spence, Chloe's grandfather, was waiting for her, coat and boots on, eager to go. There was no sign of Chloe's father, but Pam, the grandmother, was there, in full warpaint: thick mascara and lipstick the colour of holly berries. She was dressed in a floaty black number, topped off with a number of equally floaty scarves. On her feet, little high-heeled boots. Vera, who had never worn heels in her life – had never seen the point of them – supposed that this was uniform of a kind. If you ran a clothes shop, you'd feel obliged to display its wares.

'I'm just off to work, or I'd come up to Gillstead with you.' Pam hesitated at the door, and Vera wondered if she'd change her mind, even now, and ask to come with them to the country.

Something about the woman reminded Vera of Chloe, of the photos she'd seen of the girl at least. It was the round face and the small frame, the slightly reluctant smile.

Gordon gave his wife a peck on the cheek. 'I'll let you know if we find anything.'

'We should have brought her to stay here, whatever she said. She was only fourteen. What fourteen-year-old knows her own mind?' Pam's voice almost broke. 'And I should have let her wear what she wanted whenever she came here for her tea. I was only teasing.'

'Eh, pet, we did what we thought was best. We didn't know the sort of place they'd send her. When we find her, we'll bring her home.'

Then, when they were all in the front garden, the woman turned away from them, fidgeting in her black-and-gold handbag for her keys. Vera could still see the tears though, trickling through the powder on her cheeks.

On the way inland, Gordon gave Vera a full family history. It was a kind of nervousness. On first meeting she'd thought him taciturn, but here in the Land Rover, he spoke easily enough. Perhaps he'd become used to her and no longer saw her as someone in judgement. Vera was happy enough to listen. She said that an investigation was all about background and context.

'I grew up on the farm at Gillstead. My father had been brought up there and knew nothing else. It wasn't easy, mind, right at the edge of the village. It's not far away from the city, but we still weren't linked to the electricity grid even when I was a bairn. Power came from a generator that Dad kept going on a wing and a prayer, and even then it would break down. In the winter, often I'd come in from school and stick on a head torch to do my homework. Water from a bore hole that tasted of peat. As I was growing up, I was more business-minded and set up the abattoir. We slaughtered beasts from all over the north of the county, supplied the butchers and some of the supermarkets. We survived foot-and-mouth, and recently, folk like to know exactly where their meat comes from, so business has been good. You can charge a premium.' He paused for breath. 'I still lived on the farm though, until I met Pamela, and even for a while after we were married.' He gave a little chuckle. 'But it wasn't for her. She comes from Blyth, and she likes her creature comforts.'

'When did you move to Whitley?'

'Oh, only five years ago, once I decided to take a back seat with the business. Before that we were in Amble, not too far from the premises. I've got a great manager now. I trained him up myself. I don't need to be there every day. Soon after we moved to Whitley, Pam bought into the dress shop. At first it was a kind of hobby, but she loves it. She's found her passion late in life, but she was lucky to get there in the end.'

'And your passion was always meat?'

He looked at her, wondering if she was mocking, but saw that she was serious.

'Aye. Raising the animals with care, killing them not too far from home.'

'It's important,' Vera said, 'these days of climate change.'

He gave a little laugh. 'Seems the world has finally caught up with me.'

'So your John mostly grew up in Amble?'

'Nah, we were still in the hills even when he left home. I hoped he might take over the business, but he never showed any real interest. He was always good at selling – he worked for an estate agency in Newcastle and finally set up on his own, ended up with a small chain along the coast.'

'And now he's selling property in Dubai.'

Gordon nodded. His disapproval of the new role was clear from the tone of his voice. 'He's not his own boss anymore. He's working for some anonymous company with fingers in too many pies. Not just property. Global finance, whatever that is. It wouldn't suit me.'

'Have you got any other children? Someone who might take over from you?'

'Nah. Just the one son. I'll pass the business on to my manager when the time's right. Give him a good deal. He's earned it.'

They drove in silence for a little while and Vera thought that it was a disappointment to Gordon not to keep the abattoir in the family, though he wasn't a man to brood.

When they got to Gillstead, the village was looking its best in the low autumn sun. Vera had remembered it as a grey, lonely place in the shadow of the hills and a towering, rocky outcrop. Now, briefly, it was flooded with light, and the dying leaves glowed with colour. There was an old church with a left-behind poster advertising the harvest festival flapping outside. A row of grey cottages along the main street, with a pub in the middle. Vera had been there a few times. It was the nearest pub to her cottage, and she'd been called by the landlady to collect Hector who'd drunk himself into an aggressive stupor, before he'd been banned alto-gether. The school had been closed for years and had been turned into the village hall. A pair of older women carrying yoga mats were walking in that direction, but otherwise the village was empty. Someone looking like Chloe would surely be noticed here.

There were posters in some of the cottage windows in the main street. The image of an eye, stylized, black on white. Wide open. Staring.

Gordon chuckled when he saw the posters. 'It's that time of year again. Witch Hunt. Eh, I loved it when I was a bairn. Though most years I scared myself shitless.'

Vera knew all about the Witch Hunt, a kind of glorified game of hide-and-seek. It was one of those village traditions that start off just for the locals and turn into an attraction for visitors throughout the county. And a business proposition for hospitality venues, like Gillstead Hall.

Gillstead Hall had once been the big house, owned by a friend of Hector's parents, but much of the estate had been sold off and now it was a hotel with a famous chef and a spa. Visitors came from all over the country to stay, but they seldom wandered beyond the grounds. Besides, Vera thought, none of them would look like a fourteen-year-old lass, who dressed like a witch herself, and who'd spent the night camping out in the middle of a bush. She'd stick out like a sore thumb anywhere in Gillstead.

Gordon directed her down a narrow road to the farm where he'd lived until he married Pam. There was grass growing in the middle of the track, a cattle grid, and a gate he jumped out of the car to open. The house must have been very different when it had belonged to him. Now, everything looked repaired and refurbished. There were new ridge tiles on the roof, fresh paint on the woodwork, and to one side of the house, a hot tub. In the porch a pile of logs. But it looked empty, dead.

'The guy who bought the farm from me kept the land and

sold off the house. It's owned by a couple from Newcastle now. A second home. They rent it out to holidaymakers in the summer.' Gordon's voice was flat, but Vera thought it would be hard for him, knowing the house was empty for much of the time.

'So there'd be nobody there this time of year?'

Nobody to see Chloe walking down the lane, looking for her place of safety. Her own den.

'Nah!'

Vera parked in front of the house. Sunlight reflected from the windows, but she was curious and peered inside, shielding her eyes with her hand to cut out the glare. Everything was very tasteful. The original doors and floors stripped and waxed, coloured rugs, art on the walls. She turned back to Gordon.

'Eh, I bet you see a difference.'

'It was a different time,' he said. 'A different place.'

'Let's see this bothy of yours.'

The place was tiny but more substantial than Vera had been expecting. It might have been built as a home for a farmworker and his family, centuries before, in the days when everyone lived in the same room, with the second saved for the animals brought in during bad weather. She imagined a shepherd living here, close to the hill where the sheep would graze. There was a steep path to reach it and it was built into the slope of the fell. It was made of rough stone with a stone-flagged roof, a squat chimney still grimy with soot. A quad bike might reach the place, but she thought even her Land Rover would struggle. They were both out of breath when they got there.

The view made up for the effort and they stood for a moment, leaning against the wall, looking down into the valley, at the river twisting through the village and the road that followed it. On the other side of the valley, she could see the standing stones, an ancient monument, Northumberland's answer to Stonehenge. They were known as the Three Dark Wives, and they'd triggered legends and stories and songs. About three uppity women, turned into stone by a giant to stop them nagging their husbands. Hector had passed on the tale as a kind of warning, because she'd always been uppity, even as a kid. In the background there was the sound of sheep and a curlew in the distance. A buzzard calling overhead.

'You'd see anyone coming for miles,' Vera said. She thought this building might even have been here since the days of the reivers, when the border with Scotland was debatable and shifting, and raiding clans fought for land and livestock. It could have been some sort of lookout post when it was first put up.

She pushed herself upright and looked for a way in. Gordon stood quietly, letting her explore the place for herself. She thought he was remembering happier days, when Chloe had been young and had loved being here.

The door was made of solid wood. No lock or bolt. It was well made and fitted snugly enough. Vera had to pull hard to get it open. There were no windows, and the only light came through the door.

'Chloe!' She couldn't see at first and it took her eyes a moment to get used to the gloom. 'Are you here, pet?'

Then it became clear that *somebody* had been here recently. The ashes in the grate could have been there for years. They were cold, but that meant nothing either way. The fire could have been lit the night before, but it was chill here and once it had gone out the embers would quickly cool. But on the makeshift table there was half a loaf on a wooden board. If it had been here for more than a week it would be mouldy or nibbled by rodents. Vera knew better than to touch it, but she stepped further into the room, and it looked fresh to her.

On the table too she saw a jar of instant coffee. By the side of the fire, a blackened kettle stood on a flat stone. This could be a visiting homeless person though. In the countryside poverty might be hidden behind picturesque cottage doors but it was still present. Vera stood where she was, and using the torch on her phone she shone a light into the corners. She saw nothing to suggest that Chloe had stayed here. No diary or novel. Nothing that looked like the clothes belonging to a teenage girl.

An open door led to a tiny second room, which was entirely empty apart from a few sacks of animal feed.

Vera knew she shouldn't jump to conclusions, but it was surely too much of a coincidence that a stranger had wandered into the space which the girl had loved so much.

Still Gordon stood outside. She was aware of him waiting, holding his breath now. Perhaps praying that she would find his granddaughter.

A rough wooden ladder was propped against the opening to the loft, where Chloe had slept as a child. Vera checked that it was firm and then climbed a few steps.

'Chloe! Chloe, love.'

Because there was a mattress up here and a sleeping bag, or blankets. It was hard to tell. Vera was holding on to the ladder with both hands and couldn't shine the torch at the same time.

'Is she there?' Gordon shouted into the bothy. His voice was painful with hope.

'Could you just move away from the door for a moment, hinnie? You're blocking the light.'

Vera climbed into the loft. The roof was so low here that she had to crouch, even at the apex of the eaves. She switched the torch back on. The mattress was a double and took up most of the floor space. On top of it a sleeping bag, with someone or something inside. If it were a person, the bag had been pulled right over the face. To keep out the cold?

'Chloe.' Vera's voice was gentle, hardly more than a whisper. She didn't want Gordon coming in, blocking the light again, causing a fuss.

No response. Vera touched the sleeping bag and felt something hard. Bone. Muscle. She pulled back the bag, so she could see what was inside, and was already thinking of the words she could use to break the news to Gordon. But it wasn't the soft round face of a nearly adult girl looking out at her. It was that of a young man. Dark-haired, with a smudge of moustache. Good-looking in a brooding kind of way. Even in death he looked at once very young and dangerous. Vera stared down at the face of Brad Russell.

Chapter Nineteen

AFTER THE VISIT TO PARADISE FARM, Joe dropped Rosie at the station in Kimmerston.

'Check out Stella Marsh and see if she's been involved in more of the environmental protests than her father's admitting to. I want to go back to Longwater and get a full statement from the lads who play on the common. The ones who knew Chloe Spence.'

'Won't they be at school?'

Joe wasn't sure about that. He thought the boys were completely feral. They'd only be in school if they felt like it.

'I've got a number for one of them, Alfie Armstrong. I've arranged for him to be home at lunchtime and for an adult to sit in.' A pause. 'You know the boss won't be in the station. She's taking Chloe's grandfather up to Gillstead, to see if the lass made it to the bothy where they used to camp out. When they were still playing happy families, before her dad ran away and her mam fell sick.'

Rosie had the car door open and was climbing out. Joe shouted after her. 'It's probably a complete waste of time, but our Vera's always up for a jolly to the hills.'

★   ★   ★

It turned out that Alfie and his mate Noah lived on the same estate as Dave Limbrick, below the common, close to the coast, a short walk from the town centre. A post-war council house, which must have seemed palatial when it was built and still felt more solid than many of the newer private developments. Joe arrived at midday.

'I don't *have* to go into school today,' the boy had said when Joe had phoned to make the arrangement. 'It's important to help the police, isn't it? They'll understand.'

'School's important too. Can you get out at lunchtime?'

'Sure.'

'Will your mam be in?'

'Nah, she works as a cook in the old folks' home. But Dad'll be there. He does shifts at the bakery.' A pause. Joe had heard the shouts and jeers of other kids in the playground, waiting to go into school. 'He doesn't know it was a teacher training day yesterday.'

'I understand.'

'So no need, like, to say we were on the common yesterday.'

'I get it.' Joe hadn't been able to restrain a smile.

The house was neat, spotless. A coal fire in the grate. The estate had been built to house the miners at a time when nobody was worried about a climate emergency. It looked out on an area of grassland, with a couple of wild-looking horses tethered in the middle, despite a notice informing the public that this was prohibited. A small flock of gulls padded their feet on the grass. Vera, who was an expert in these things, had once told Joe that the dance was an attempt to bring worms to the surface.

Alfie's father was large, tattooed, gentle. His name was Kevin. Kev. He looked knackered.

'What's he been up to this time?' His voice resigned.

'Nothing. He's been very helpful. But we need a statement from him. A lass from Rosebank has gone missing, and he might have some information to help us find her.' Joe turned to the boy. 'We think she stayed in your den the night she ran away. So just tell me again about the last time you saw her. And it would be useful to know about any other regulars on the common. Dog-walkers, joggers. Perhaps you could help with that too, Kev.'

The man didn't answer directly. 'I told you to keep away from those Rosebank kids, son. They'll get you into bother.'

Joe thought that Alfie could get into bother without any help from the Rosebank residents. The boy repeated the story he'd already told on their first meeting. Joe believed him. He had no reason to lie. Then he turned his attention to the father.

'Can you think of anyone who used the common? Someone who might have seen Chloe? She's only fourteen and we're anxious about her.'

'There's Jimmy the birdwatcher. He's there early mornings, putting up nets to catch the migrants.' Kev paused. 'Sometimes he'll catch something rare and a whole gang of his mates turn up. It's wild then. Cars parked all the way down the street.'

'Has he been there recently?' Joe directed the question at Alfie.

Alfie shrugged. 'He's there early and at weekends. I don't always see him. You just see the grass flattened where he's been checking his nets.'

'Where can I find him?'

This time Kev answered. 'In the health centre in the village. He's a doctor. Canny enough. Jimmy Hepple. He lives up the coast, somewhere a bit fancy. I was at school with him. He was always a bright lad.' He nodded towards Alfie. 'This one reminds me of him. He runs rings round us all.'

Hepple, the GP, was based in a flat-roofed concrete building on the same estate, and found time to see Joe between patients. He had a restless energy that made him speak very quickly, his childhood accent intact. He never seemed still, even sitting in his chair in his room in the surgery.

'Birding saved me,' he said. 'Kept me out of trouble. I bumped into one of the old guys in the Northumberland ringing group when I was about Alfie's age, and he showed me a willow warbler in the hand. Completely magical. I was hooked and I still feel the same if I catch something I've never seen before.'

'You must have gone away to study. What made you come back?' Joe didn't think anyone would choose Longwater if they had an alternative.

'I love it. Not just for the birding, but the community.' He gave a wry grin. 'I know Longwater has a bit of a rep for being rough, but there's a kindness. I'd live here if I had my way, but my wife's from the South – I met her at uni – and she wanted somewhere a bit classier. More academic schools for the bairns and bougie coffee shops for herself. Though with the work and the birding I spend more time here than I do at home. She understands, I think. That was part of the deal. She says that you don't marry someone if you want to change them.'

'Did you ever meet Chloe Spence out on the common? She was one of the Rosebank lasses.'

'Small? Trying to be a goth but ending up a bit chavvy? Always has a book with her.'

'Aye.'

'She was with Alfie and his silent mate a couple of times, but I didn't really get to know her.' He smiled. 'She's more interested in reading and writing than natural history. I always hope I can catch some of the local kids with the magic of nature, but it hasn't worked so far.'

'I don't suppose you saw her on the common two days ago? Early in the morning. She went missing the night that the worker at Rosebank was killed. We think she spent the night in Alfie's den, but she's disappeared again, and we're concerned for her safety.'

Joe was aware of thoughts rattling through the doctor's brain, speedy flashes of memory. 'I was there that morning. There'd been a day of easterlies and then rain. It's a bit late in the autumn, but I thought something interesting might have come in. In the end, there was a fall of thrushes and a few woodcock, but nothing particularly rare.'

'You didn't see a pile of bloodstained clothes anywhere?'

Hepple looked shocked but shook his head. 'But it's a big area. It doesn't mean there was nothing there.'

'And you didn't come across the girl?'

There was a moment of intense concentration. 'No, but I had the sense that someone was around when I set up the nets. A sound. Sounds. Footsteps perhaps, though it was damp underfoot so I don't think it could have been that. A jacket brushing against the undergrowth maybe.' He was determined to be accurate and looked up at Joe. 'But I could have imagined it. I was expecting someone to be out on the common because of the car.'

'What car?'

'I always park on that piece of wasteland at the end of the

track just past Rosebank. Later in the day the runners and dog-walkers use it too, but there's usually nobody there when I arrive, just before dawn. That morning, the one you're asking about, somebody else had parked there. It was empty. Nobody inside. But it was unusual. Rosebank staff always park on the care home drive.'

Joe remembered Chloe's diary, the piece about the pervy guy in the car hanging about outside the home. 'Have you seen it there before?'

There was another silence. Another attempt to be completely accurate. 'I don't think so. If it had been there later in the day along with a bunch of other vehicles I probably wouldn't have noticed.'

'Can you describe the car?'

Hepple closed his eyes briefly. 'It was big and black. A Volvo. Local registration, so starting with ND. Sorry. I can't remember anything else.'

'That's pretty impressive!'

'Detail matters, professionally and in birding. Besides, I'm nebby. Always have been. And I had my torch ready to walk to the ride where I wanted to set up the net, so I could see the number plate.' Now he was fidgeting again, on his feet. 'Look, I'm sorry, there's a waiting room of patients and if I don't crack on, I'll be behind all day.'

'Of course. If anything else occurs to you, could you give me a ring?'

'Sure.' But Hepple was already back in GP mode. He followed Joe into the waiting room, and told an elderly woman using a walking frame that he was ready to see her now, and that he was sorry about the delay.

Chapter Twenty

VERA KNEW IMMEDIATELY THAT THIS WOULD be a logistic night-mare. A body in a building with no power or water and so far from the road. They'd need to trace the owner of the farmhouse to let them use his land for parking and as a base for their team. They'd probably have to bring in a generator, because it'd be getting dark by the time the whole circus arrived and they'd want lights. She could see no immediate cause of death, but the lad certainly *was* dead, even if she couldn't be the person to call it officially. At least there was a little mobile signal, and she phoned Joe and told him briefly what she'd found.

'Get yourself up here. Doc Keating too. And Billy Cartwright's team.'

The implications of the discovery – that the lad had died in a place that was miles from anywhere, known to Chloe, but not, as far as Vera knew, to anyone else connected with Rosebank – was so mind-blowing that she couldn't even think about it yet. What she *could* think about, was the certainty that Chloe Spence couldn't be the killer, despite Russell's body

144

having been found on her home territory. How could she have
lured him there? And this was a sophisticated murder. Planned
to confuse. Chloe might be a storyteller, a liar even, but she
wouldn't have engineered this scenario.

'Shall I bring Rosie?' Joe broke into her thoughts. 'She's
back in Kimmerston. I can pick her up on the way.'

'No, tell her what's happened, but leave her there to lead
on the detail. I need an accurate timeline for Brad Russell.'
Vera wanted the old team with her for this, not the new officer
she had to be careful with. 'She'll have to put off her research
into the Marsh family until we've got things sorted here. It's
hard to see how they could be involved now. This takes us
straight back to Rosebank.' She paused, her thoughts racing.
'Bring Charlie with you. He'll be useful, a place like this. He
can start to canvass the village.'

But first she had to sort out Gordon Spence. He was still
doing as he'd been told, standing a little way from the house,
waiting for information. She climbed down the ladder, her legs
a little unsteady, and went outside.

'Well?'

'I'm sorry, pet. Chloe's not there.'

'Oh.' He seemed to shrink a little. 'I thought I heard you
talking. And you were gone for so long that I thought you'd
found something.'

'I did find something. A lad.' She hurried on in case he
started asking questions she wasn't ready to answer. 'He's dead.
Name of Brad Russell. He lived in the same care home as
your Chloe.' A pause. 'Does the name mean anything?'

He shook his head. 'What was he doing all the way out here?'

'Well, I'd really like to know that too. It's not somewhere
you'd stumble into.'

And Brad Russell wasn't the sort of person Chloe might chat to about the happier times of her childhood. Was he? I can't imagine the pair having a heart-to-heart over a late-night cocoa. And he didn't strike me as a country boy. But there was something about him. A kind of charm that might have pulled her in if she was vulnerable, and susceptible to flattery. Her diary didn't suggest that, but how could I know what was going on in a young girl's mind?

'It'll be a bit of a hoopla now,' Vera said. 'We need to find out how he died, and all the experts will pile in. Let's wander back to the lane, shall we, and see about getting you a lift home.'

Walking back down the hill, she kept her eyes peeled for vehicle tracks on the sheep-cropped grass. There was no way the young man had walked all the way here from Longwater. In life, Brad had the manic sort of energy that had set him twitching, bouncing on his toes, but Vera knew he'd not have the stamina for a thirty-mile walk. Someone had driven him to Gillstead and left him with supplies. No tracks that she could see as they'd walked from the farm. Although she hadn't looked closely, Vera knew for certain that Russell's death wasn't accidental. While she'd seen no obvious cause of his demise, she was sure that somehow, Brad's dying was linked to Josh Woodburn's murder. Anything else would be a ridiculous coincidence. The only connection between Woodburn and Gillstead was Chloe Spence, and Vera had already decided that this put the lass in the clear.

She chatted to Gordon as they walked, moving things on, while she had him with her.

'What's the name of the guy that owns the farmhouse now?'

'I don't know. I don't think I ever heard.'

'But you know the chap that bought it off you and kept the land.'

'Yeah, that's Matty Raynor, but like I said, he sold the house on.'

'We'll need his number, if you've got it.'

'Sure.' They stood for a while for him to check in his phone and for Vera to make a note in hers.

Vera looked down into the valley to the village, at the warmth of the colours and the smoke rising straight from cottage chimneys, and thought there couldn't be a greater clash of worlds than between this place and Brad Russell. She couldn't imagine how he'd turned up here.

When they reached the farmhouse, she sat Gordon in the Land Rover and stood outside making more calls. One was to Willmore, who was already going through a tough time, and needed the heads-up. The commissioner was businesslike, efficient, but Vera could detect a note of despair in her voice.

'Someone else connected with one of our care homes killed?'

As soon as Vera ended the call, Joe phoned to say that they were on their way and would be there in thirty minutes. Vera got back into the Land Rover and drove towards the village. Parking at the end of the lane, she saw that the pub, the Stanhope Arms, was just about to open. Hector had loved the name, and had reminded the landlady, when he was banned, that he had a stake in the place.

The landlady had been unmoved.

'I'll be waiting for you in the Land Rover at the turn-off to the farmhouse,' Vera said to Joe. 'You won't miss it. There's only one street. Gordon Spence will be in the pub. We'll need a car to take him home. And I need to track down the owner of a holiday rental property. Cragside Farm. The previous owner, Matty Raynor, might be the quickest route to him.' She passed on the number. 'Get Rosie on to it.'

It was the same landlady holding court in the pub. She was older, of course, but with the fighting spirit that Vera remembered. Small and wiry and tough as old boots. Marie Fenwick. Known to her customers as Ma, though it was hard to imagine anyone less maternal.

She peered across the bar. 'Vera Stanhope as I live and breathe. What are you doing here in the middle of the day? Don't you have to work like the rest of us?'

'I'm here to claim my inheritance, Ma.' A standing joke.

'Bugger that. What'll you have?'

'Whatever this gentleman would like and a coffee for me. White. Two sugars.'

'We don't have any of those fancy machines. It'll be instant. Out of a jar.' Which reminded Vera of the bothy. Surely there'd be fingerprints on the coffee jar. You wouldn't hold that with gloves.

'Instant's how I like it,' she said. 'Can I get it to take away?'

'This is a pub, not bloody Starbucks.'

'I'll bring the mug back when I'm done. And settle the bill then. Just look after this gent until the cavalry arrives.'

'What's going on, like?' Ma was serious now, leaning forward to Vera over the bar.

'Ah, pet, you'll know soon enough. Just make sure you've got staff on for the next couple of days, and someone to cook. You're going to be busy.'

'I'll be busy enough anyway come the weekend. It's the Witch Hunt.'

Vera swore under her breath. She'd briefly forgotten about the Witch Hunt. Hundreds of incomers drawn to the village.

It was the last thing she needed. She stamped over to the table where Gordon was sitting. 'I'll have to get back and make sure nobody wanders up the hill to trample on my scene. Ma here will look after you.'

The man nodded, a little dazed.

'Don't worry,' Ma said. 'Gordon and I are old friends.'

In the road, Vera leaned against the Land Rover, squinting at the sun, looking up at the hill. The same sheep wandered past the bothy. There was no sign of a human. She was still standing there when Joe arrived, Charlie beside him. Charlie, the most reliable member of the team now, though he'd gone through a bad patch when his wife had left him years earlier. Loneliness could do strange things to you, Vera thought, if you were the sort who was used to company. She started talking to them before they got out of the car, handing out her orders:

'Charlie, you start in the village. This is the nearest vehicle access to the farm. Anyone noticed a strange car drive down here in the past couple of days? Or they could have parked outside the pub. It'd be less conspicuous there.'

Charlie slid away towards the Stanhope Arms, which was, she thought, the best place to start. He'd just crossed the road when Keating and Cartwright arrived. They drove in convoy up to the farmhouse. She closed the gate behind them, though it wouldn't be much of a barrier against a hoard of curious reporters.

Walking up the hill again in their scene suits, she decided that to the villagers they must look like alien invaders. News would get out, making Willmore's life even more difficult. They were hardly inconspicuous. The press would arrive, filling

Marie Fenwick's bar. She and Joe stood just outside the bothy door, while the pathologist and crime scene manager climbed into the loft.

'Rosie's on the case, tracking down the owner of the farm,' Joe said. 'And I've asked her to talk to Limbrick. We need to know when Russell went missing from Rosebank. She'll contact us as soon as she's got an answer.'

Vera thought about that. 'You'd think that the man would have the brains to let us know if the kid went AWOL in the middle of a murder investigation.'

Joe shrugged. 'We don't even know if Limbrick was on duty last night. He must be entitled to the occasional evening off. And I bet Russell disappeared quite regularly, so the staff probably wouldn't think much of it.'

'Aye, maybe.' Vera still thought it was odd. 'There's something a bit strange about Limbrick though. I can't quite get a handle on him. What's such a loner doing in a job that's all about interacting with other people?'

Joe looked at her and chuckled. 'Well . . .'

'I know! Folk could say exactly the same about me. All the same, get Rosie to have a little dig. The care staff provided the alibi for all the kids on the night Woodburn died, and we've mostly only seen Rosebank through Limbrick's eyes. Tracey, the other social worker, seemed a bit more clued up. I know someone will have taken a statement, but I bet she'd talk more informally to our Rosie.'

Joe raised an eyebrow. She could tell that the *our* had thrown him. Well, Vera thought, he'd just have to suck it up.

She looked down into the valley and saw that more cars were arriving. Uniformed officers stood in a gaggle close to her Land Rover, apparently unsure what to do.

'Go down and sort them out, Joe. We'll need one of them to give Chloe's grandpa a lift back to Whitley. Billy and the doc won't be done today, so we'll need a rota to cover the locus overnight. Keep the ghouls and the press out of the way. Someone on the gate of course. The troops won't be happy, but I'll get Ma at the pub to sort them out with food and hot drinks.' A pause. 'In fact, you're in charge here. Ma has a couple of rooms, so book yourself in. I know Sal won't be pleased that you're having a night away but tell her you're SIO at the scene and she'll think you've been promoted.'

'What are you doing?'

'I'll get first impressions from the experts in the loft, then have a little sniff round the village. After that, I'll head back to Longwater.'

Because Longwater was Russell's natural habitat. Vera wanted to understand him. After all, he hadn't been born a petty drug dealer. He had a history in the same way that Josh Woodburn in his fancy house in Cullercoats had. It occurred to Vera again that Josh and Brad were only a few years apart in age and with a different upbringing, the student could have been lost and damaged just like Brad. And then she thought that Josh might actually have been lost and damaged too, but in a very different way.

She watched Joe Ashworth stride down the hill towards the gathered officers, and was grateful that there was nothing damaged or lost about him.

She waited until he'd reached the road, then she pulled her mask over her face and stuck her head inside the bothy.

'Well?' The mask muffled her words, but she knew they could hear her. She had a voice like the Tynemouth foghorn when required. 'First impressions?'

Keating climbed down the ladder to join her by the door. Shouting was beneath his dignity.

'No immediate sign of violence. Very different from the young man in the care home. I take it you are linking the two?'

'It would be a bit of a coincidence otherwise. I'm only here because the lass who went missing from Rosebank knew this place and we thought she could have been hiding out here.'

'Mr Russell isn't a healthy individual. Regular drug user?'

Vera nodded. 'And small-time pusher.'

'My best guess at this point would be an overdose.'

'You're saying it was accidental?'

'Not necessarily. It's hard to tell, isn't it? A kid like that. His head already mixed up. Willing to try anything to numb the reality of his life. I suspect he'd take whatever was offered.'

That made sense to Vera. 'Poor lad,' she said. She could tell that he'd been an irritating sod, frustrating to the workers who'd tried to care for him. But he didn't deserve this.

'I'm heading back in a bit,' she said. 'I'm assuming you'll need him here overnight for Billy and his team to do their best for him.'

'I think so,' Keating said. 'There's no rush on the post-mortem and it'd be impossible to get him down from here without contaminating the scene or the body. Best do what we can in situ.'

'Joe's in charge until tomorrow. I need to see if he had any relatives who should be informed of his death.'

I do hope that there's someone who'll grieve for him. If not, I'll shed a few tears for you, bonny lad, for a wasted life and a sudden death.

* * *

Vera was halfway down the hill when her phone rang. She thought this must be one of the few parts of the county with reliable phone signal. One blessing at least. It was Rosie.

'Sorry to interrupt, boss, just to let you know what we've got so far. Not much, I'm afraid, though I've got the name of the new owner of Cragside Farm.'

'Can you let Joe know? I'm leaving him in charge here.' Vera stumbled on a bit of uneven ground and swore under her breath.

'Boss?'

'How are you doing tracking down a next of kin for Brad Russell? I presume Limbrick can help?'

'I can't get a response from him. The staff say he's got a couple of days' leave.'

Vera thought about that. It was interesting that Limbrick's days off coincided with Russell's death, but perhaps she shouldn't make too much of it. Even she took a day off every now and again.

'Talk to Kath Oliver, the senior social worker in the safeguarding team. She should be able to help. And let me know if you get a result. I'm heading back to the coast now.'

In the end though, Vera didn't head east immediately. She drove the Land Rover back through the village and past the long stone wall that marked the grounds of the Gillstead Hall hotel. She was still thinking about the mysterious black car that had been seen close to Rosebank and perhaps again outside the Spence house. That would surely belong to someone with a bit of cash, and Chloe had mentioned it in her diary at the same time as she'd talked about Russell's dealing. If he was Russell's killer, perhaps he'd have stayed locally. He wouldn't have taken Russell up the hill to the bothy in daylight. Everyone in the village would have seen.

Gillstead Hall would be an anonymous place to spend a night. A place for smart businessmen looking for something a bit special to stick on their expense accounts, even if it meant a drive away from the A1. For somewhere to take a secret lover, or for couples escaping the kids for a while. And Russell's killer might well have had an accomplice. Russell had been a petty drug dealer, but the person at the top of the heap would be wealthy. A stay at the Gillstead Hall hotel wouldn't come cheap, but they'd be able to afford it. Perhaps that was what this was all about. Perhaps Josh had become aware of Russell's activities and threatened to go to the police. Vera felt as if she was groping towards a motive at last.

Outside the hotel, she parked next to a car with a personalized number plate, and spent a moment looking at the vehicles. No big black Volvo. It was only the beginning of November, but inside, there were already posters advertising their Christmas menu. *Book early to avoid disappointment.* It was very hot, and Vera felt sweaty after her walk up and down the hill. Her boots were muddy. The receptionist was beautifully made up with sleek hair and a patronizing air. Vera showed her warrant card and asked for a list of the customers who'd checked in over the previous two nights.

'If you'd just print it out for me. With the contact details.'

The young woman slid into the office behind her, leaving Vera to wait. There was a café bar to one side of the lobby and the smell of coffee almost tempted her in. This wouldn't be instant, and she saw pastries crisp and dusted with sugar. Then she thought of Brad Russell, still and quiet at last, and she took the list from the young woman and headed for the Land Rover. As she drove away from the village, the single eyes on the Witch Hunt posters seemed to be watching her progress.

Chapter Twenty-One

APART FROM THAT FIRST FLEETING VISIT on the morning after Josh Woodburn's death, Rosie hadn't spent any time in Rosebank. Now she was back here, following the boss's instructions and chatting to the second in command, a woman called Tracey who'd lived in Longwater all her life.

'No need to tell her that Brad Russell's dead. Not yet.' Vera had shouted orders down the hands-free phone as she was driving. 'I want to be there when she finds out what's happened. Get some background. But find out when Brad was last seen.'

They were in the kitchen. Tracey was stuffing a pile of sheets into the washing machine.

'They're supposed to do their own laundry. But in the end, it's easier to do it myself than to nag.' Tracey looked up. 'Besides, kids that age in their own homes, I bet the parents would be doing it for them.'

The house was quiet.

'Where are they all?' Rosie asked.

'Mel and George are at school. Who knows where Brad is?

He went out yesterday afternoon and he's still not back.' She scooped powder into the machine and started it off.

'Shouldn't someone be looking for him?'

'I phoned the police just now, but they know what he's like. He'll be leaving care soon and we won't be able to chase after him then.'

'What sort of lad is he?'

'You asking if he could have killed Josh Woodburn?'

'Yeah,' Rosie said. 'I suppose I am.'

Tracey didn't answer immediately. She turned away and switched on the kettle. 'Fancy a brew?'

Rosie waited.

'He's the only kid I've ever been really scared of,' Tracey said at last. 'He's got that lovely smile, and it pulls you in, but there's nothing behind it. No warmth. And he's unpredictable.' She turned away to pour water onto the teabags in a pot. 'Like a dangerous dog. You never know when it's going to bite.'

Rosie was shocked. It seemed a horrible thing to say about a kid in her care. But Tracey was still talking.

'Not his fault. His mam's an addict, and she was still using when she was pregnant. He's been moved around since he was a baby. No stability. No real support.' She poured the tea. 'But we've had other bairns with troubled backgrounds and eventually we can get through to them. Brad says all the right words, but in the end, he'll do anything to get what he wants.'

For a moment, they drank their tea in silence before Rosie asked:

'How did you get into this business?'

She let Tracey chat. She was genuinely interested, and besides, it was easier than talking about the damaged boy.

'I didn't get on at school. Too much of a rebel and couldn't see the point of learning stuff I would never use again. I left at sixteen and went into a textile factory in Blyth. It was okay. The machinists were all friends, and we had a laugh. I met my bloke, and we had a couple of bairns.' She looked up. 'But when they started school, I wanted more out of life. Mike's a lorry driver and he's away a lot. I was bored.' She stretched. '*So* bored. I decided I might be able to learn if it was stuff that mattered, so I started evening classes. Psychology. Sociology. Then it was off to college to train. I've always been a nebby cow and social work makes it all right to nose into other folks' business. And I ended up here.'

'When was that?'

'Five years ago, when the home opened. I live just down the road. This place had been empty for a while, then we heard it had been sold, but we didn't know who'd bought it. Turned out it was going to be a children's home, and I'd just qualified. It seemed meant to be.' She looked across at Rosie. 'It sounds daft, but I love it. It's tough, and frustrating, because we don't have the resources to do the job properly. The owners are all about profit, not about doing a good job for the kids. But some days I think I've made a difference, and I never had that in the factory.' A pause. 'I suppose your job is the same.'

'Occasionally!'

Tracey laughed. 'Sometimes I think I'll be found out – what do they call it? Impostor syndrome? – and they'll send me back to the machines. Though those jobs are all being done by robots now.'

'You're not planning to move? Go for promotion?'

Tracey shook her head. 'There's just me and Dave left from the beginning. The other workers come and go, so there's no continuity, but we're still here.'

'You get on well with Dave?'

'Oh aye. Though he's worn down with the pressure of it. The kids kicking off on one side and the management on his back at the other. It's all about budgets these days, isn't it, wherever you're working? Sometimes I bring treats in myself if we can't make the cash stretch. A bit of baking I've done at home. A cake if there's a birthday. A present. Some of the little buggers who end up here, we're the only family they've got.'

'Tell me about the evening that Josh Woodburn was killed.'

'I've already told that other guy. Ashworth.'

'I know, but I'm interested in hearing it from you.'

'We have a film night every Sunday. A bit of a treat. Even Brad usually comes along to that. And Dave, though that evening he didn't because he was stuck in the office. Management demanding numbers that he had to work on. I always do pizza. We can't run to takeaway, but I get nice ones from Morrisons. I just stick them in the oven, and we eat in front of the telly. Jan was due to sleep over, but she'd called in sick. Josh was on the rota and had agreed to come in, so I knew I wouldn't have to stay. I left before they found the body.'

'Chloe wasn't watching the film either?'

Tracey shook her head. 'She knew Josh was coming. She had a crush on him, and she'd rather spend time with him, talking about books or art or film.'

'Was it wise of Josh to encourage her?'

Tracey didn't answer straight away. 'He was naive, idealistic. He thought he was helping.'

'Did you hear Chloe go out?'

Again, Tracey shook her head.

'The other three kids were with you all evening?'

'Well, they were in and out, you know. Brad and Mel aren't very restful. We paused the film a couple of times for vape and fag breaks. They have to go outside for that. But neither of them came back covered in blood.'

'And Dave?'

'He was in the office all evening.'

'But you wouldn't see him, would you, from the lounge? He could have gone anywhere.'

The question hung between them, but Tracey didn't answer.

'What did you make of Chloe Spence?'

There was a pause for a moment. 'I couldn't see what she's doing here. She's intelligent. Sparky. A bit lippy, but then I'd be lippy. A place like this, you need to stand up for yourself to survive. She told me her mam was in hospital, but Dave said she had grandparents. You'd have thought there'd be someone to care for her.' Another pause. 'She was a brilliant mimic. She could take them all off.'

'Any idea where she might have gone? Friends she mentioned?'

'Nah. She wasn't chatty. Not about anything personal.'

It was then that the door opened, and another voice boomed through. 'I hope there's more tea left in that pot, because I'm gagging.' And Vera Stanhope strode in, still in her coat and hat. They both stared at her. 'Don't worry, pet. I took off my boots at the door. They were covered in sheep shit, and I see you've got a nice clean floor.'

Tracey reached behind her and pulled down another mug. 'I'll stick the kettle on again. This'll be stewed.'

'Champion.' Vera stretched out her legs and Rosie saw that there was a hole in one of her socks and that a large toe was poking through. The nail needed cutting. 'I've got some bad news for you, Tracey. It's about Brad Russell.'

Rosie ended up making the tea, while the social worker sat at the table and stared into space.

Vera got little more information from Tracey than Rosie had, and she batted away all the social worker's questions about Brad's death.

'We need to talk to your boss,' Vera demanded in the end. 'Any idea where he might be?'

'He's on leave. Do you know how much stress he's been under? Leave him in peace.' Tracey was fierce. Protective. 'He'll be back on shift tomorrow evening.'

Later, the detectives sat in Vera's Land Rover to talk. Vera asked the questions and Rosie answered as best she could.

'Have we got an address for Brad's next of kin?'

'Yeah, his mam. Well, a sort of address. She's in a hostel for homeless women on the Southgate estate in Shields. I spoke to Kath Oliver, who gave me a bit of family background. The mother, Sharon, is an alcoholic. Brad was first taken into care when he was five. Since then, Sharon has had two more kids, both taken away from her at birth by the safeguarding team because of the danger of neglect and abuse.'

Rosie paused and wondered what that must be like. The emptiness. Your body would think you were a mother, wouldn't it? Making milk. Racing hormones. Wouldn't you want to fill that gap by getting pregnant again? Her sister was a new mother. She'd found the early weeks exhausting, but if anyone had tried to take the baby, Faye would have fought like a lion. Then Rosie thought about the kids she'd heard about, seen photos of, so skinny their ribs poked through the skin, beaten, bruises and broken bones. Of course the social workers had to act. She'd seen them crucified in the press for doing too little.

'What about grandparents?' Vera broke into her thoughts.

'Brad stayed with them for a bit when he was younger. But they had health issues and couldn't really cope. They're older. They washed their hands of him completely when he started stealing from them.'

'Is the father still around?'

Rosie shook her head. 'He left before Brad was born. Soon after, Sharon started living with another man, who according to Kath was edgy and controlling. He was abusive towards her and the lad, but Sharon was always too scared to press charges. He was the father of the next two kids, who were taken into care and adopted as babies. Sharon finally walked out on him six weeks ago and since then she's been living in the hostel.'

'Has she had any contact with Brad while she's been there?'

'Kath didn't know.'

'We'd better go and see her then, let her know that her lad's dead.' Vera started the engine and Rosie found herself being carried away towards North Shields, her car left stranded outside Rosebank.

The refuge was anonymous. Two semi-detached houses had been knocked together to form a bigger establishment, but from the outside it looked like any other building on the run-down sixties estate. The door was opened by a young woman in jeans and a long sweater, hair pulled back, specs. She could have been an earnest student. And that, it seemed, was what she was.

'There's a paid warden, who lives in, but the rest of us are volunteers.' She opened the door wide to let them in. Perhaps it wasn't unusual to have police officers turning up on the doorstep.

'It's good of you to give up your time, pet.'

Vera walked inside; Rosie followed in her wake. Through an open door they saw a living room, furnished with comfortable sofas. Three women and a couple of toddlers. A plastic laundry basket full of brightly coloured toys. The television on, some kids' programme, but ignored by everyone in the room. The student walked on and let them into a large kitchen, where two women sat at the table, talking. One was older, in her mid-sixties, round-faced and short. The other, in early middle age, was painfully thin, and Rosie thought she could see the shadow of Brad Russell in her dark eyes and brown hair.

'These detectives want to talk to Sharon.' The student slipped tactfully away.

The younger woman looked up at them. Her hands were trembling. 'I've already told you. I don't want to press charges. He'd slaughter me.'

'This isn't about your bloke, pet.' Vera took a seat at the table. Rosie stood in a corner and tried to be unobtrusive. 'It's about your son.'

'Brad?' Sharon looked defeated, and her voice was panicky. 'He's too much for me. I can't look after him. I told the social worker.'

The older woman, the woman in charge of the refuge, looked up. 'Honestly, Sharon's got too much going on now to be responsible for her son.'

'I know. This is information you need to hear though.' Vera looked across at the older woman. 'I wouldn't be here if it wasn't important.' She leaned across the table and took Sharon's hand. Rosie thought the bones were thin as twigs and looked as if they might snap under the pressure. 'Brad's dead. We found his body this morning.'

The room was silent. Next door a child started crying, and they heard a mother comforting him.

'What happened?' The older woman was speaking. Sharon still stared at Vera, her face blank, stony.

'We're not sure yet,' Vera said. 'It looks like an overdose.'

Two round tears ran down Sharon's face. 'It's my fault.' The words muttered under her breath. 'I was using when I was pregnant. He was always going to turn out to be an addict, wasn't he? And then I should have left Ryan years ago. I was never there for my boy.'

Rosie thought Sharon was right. It *was* her fault and it was a bit late to start feeling guilty now. But of course she said nothing.

'Have you heard from Brad recently?' Vera asked. 'We're trying to find out exactly what might have happened.'

'I told him I'd left Ryan and that I was living here. I sent him a text.' She looked up at Vera. 'Saying that I'd done the right thing at last.'

'Did you hear back from him?'

'He texted back. Just a thumbs-up. But that was enough to know he was proud.' A pause. 'In the past, he only got in touch to ask for cash, so I thought it was a sign. That things might be getting better for him too.'

'We found him out in the country,' Vera said. 'A village called Gillstead. Does that mean anything to you? I wondered if you might have family living that way?'

Now Sharon just looked confused. 'No! We've always lived on the coast.'

'Might Brad have been in touch with his father? Could he have been back in the boy's life?'

'No way! He pissed off as soon as he realized that I was pregnant, and I haven't heard from him since.'

'We'll find out exactly what happened to Brad. I'll come and tell you when I know.' Vera took away her hand and leaned on the table to push herself to her feet.

'Can I see him?' Sharon was suddenly more animated. 'I'd like, you know, to say goodbye.'

'Of course. But not yet. When we've got him back to the hospital. We'll let you know, and Rosie here will take you.'

Terrific, Rosie thought. *I get all the best jobs.*

But she smiled. 'Of course,' she said. 'Of course.'

Chapter Twenty-Two

ROSIE RESENTED BEING LEFT BEHIND, STRANDED on the coast while the others were in the hills, investigating another murder. She felt like a child stuck at home while the older siblings were taken out for a treat. Vera had disappeared after the meeting with Brad's mother – though she had dropped Rosie back in Longwater first – and Rosie suspected that she'd headed back to Gillstead too.

It seemed that the lead *she'd* discovered – Josh Woodburn's relationship with Stella Marsh – was no longer considered important. But Rosie thought it was worth following up and besides, she'd told Will that she'd be back to speak to the girl. The light was fading when she made her way to Paradise Farm, and the place was quiet, a strange oasis of peace between a main road and a new housing estate.

When she knocked at the door it was the girl, Stella, who answered. She'd changed out of her school uniform and was wearing big cargo trousers and a sloppy khaki jersey. Her frizzy hair was tied back in a loose ponytail. She looked white and drawn. Rosie thought she was grieving for the lad who'd been her boyfriend. Who might have been her boyfriend again if he'd lived.

'Dad said you'd be coming.'

They went into a different room, small, cosy, with a fireplace, an old sofa and a couple of armchairs. A dog sat on one of the chairs. Stella squeezed in beside it.

'I'm sorry,' Rosie said. 'I know you two were friends.'

'More than friends for a while.' Stella looked up. 'I had a massive crush on him when I first started at the high school. He was two years older. Quiet. Shy. We were both into art and the teacher let us use the art room at lunchtime and after lessons. We talked, you know. I dreamed about him. He asked me out on my fifteenth birthday. We went for a pizza in Whitley, and then to the Jam Jar cinema. Held hands. He drove me home. He'd just passed his test and his parents had bought him this car. Dad and I don't have a car. Don't believe in them. So I wasn't sure what to say when Josh offered and I got him to drop me at the end of the track, so Dad wouldn't see.'

'Was that why you broke up?' Rosie asked. 'The clash in principles?'

'Something like that. Or maybe I just felt I was too young to settle with one bloke, that there was more to life than what he was offering. I didn't want to end up like his parents: complacent breadheads with nothing more on their minds than the colour of their walls and the next foreign holiday. Josh already seemed to be thinking marriage and kids, and that freaked me out.'

Rosie chuckled. 'His mam's a GP. I don't think she's dreaming of interior design all day!'

Stella smiled back. 'Maybe I could be a bit arrogant. Full of myself.'

Rosie could see why Josh had fallen for her.

The girl was still talking. 'I was exploring options for uni. My chosen subject was ecology, and I wanted to look at the best places, not the ones closest to home. I had dreams of travelling, to see a bit of the world. I couldn't see how Josh might fit into all that.'

'So you dumped him?'

'Well, it wasn't that brutal. I still wanted him as a friend. He gave me confidence, helped me believe in myself.'

'You wanted to have your cake and eat it? The admiration and support without the commitment?'

There was that disarming grin again. 'Yeah, I suppose.'

'How did he respond?'

'He was kind of sad. He kept sending me messages. I mean, nothing weird. He wasn't *stalking* me or anything. Any excuse to keep in touch. Sometimes I answered and sometimes I didn't.'

'Your dad went to see him, to tell him to cool it.'

'Yep, though I didn't know he was planning to see Josh until after he'd been.' A pause. 'I don't think he was warning Josh off. Nothing like that. Just to give him a bit of advice, to tell him to leave me alone for a while. Give me a bit of space.'

'Did he?'

Stella nodded. 'Then about a month ago he got in touch again. He said he'd got a project of his own. Something he could be proud of. He was very mysterious and said he'd let me in on it when he was more sorted. Then there was nothing. Of course, I was curious. I thought it would be something to do with his art, but there might be a green agenda some-where in there. He'd realize that would appeal to me, and we'd discussed stuff like that when we were both still in school.'

'So you suggested that you meet up so he could tell you all about it.'

Stella looked up at the detective. 'I was missing him. I wanted to see him.' She paused. 'Honestly? Finding out about the project was just an excuse.'

'Did you meet up?' Rosie held her breath. It had been impossible to tell from the email trail if the meeting had taken place.

'No. He was going to pick me up from school earlier this week. He didn't show. I was angry, then anxious when he didn't reply to my texts. It wasn't like him. I only learned later that evening from a friend that he was dead.'

'He'd got a job in a children's home,' Rosie said. 'Supporting mixed-up teenagers. It seems that he was very good at it. I guess he thought that was something that would make you proud of him. Not art, but real life. As real as the things that you and your father do here.' She looked across at Stella, who was burying her face in the dog's fur to hide her tears.

The girl looked up to speak. 'I would have been *so* proud. So very proud.'

'We're looking for a lass called Chloe Spence. Did he mention her at all? Maybe when you were chatting on the phone?'

There was a moment's hesitation and then Stella shook her head. 'We didn't talk for long. I could tell he wanted to save all his news until we were together.'

'Brad Russell?'

Again, she shook her head.

'If you can think of anything that might help, give me a ring.' Rosie held out her card.

They stood up and Stella wiped her eyes on her sleeves.

'Or if you just want to talk.' Rosie knew she was being soft, but she couldn't help herself. 'I'll let you know when there's any news.'

At the door, Stella reached out, put her arms around Rosie, and gave her a hug.

Chapter Twenty-Three

WHEN IT GOT DARK, JOE AND Charlie had an informal briefing in the Stanhope Arms in Gillstead. There'd been a magnificent sunset over the moors to the west, setting the bracken on fire and filling the village with a strange red glow. They'd had an early dinner in the bar, but they hadn't discussed the investigation there; it had been packed with locals and the press, all earwigging, and desperate for news on the murder.

Now they sat in Joe's room, the curtains open to let in the last of the light. There was a view up the hill of the bright white rays of spotlights powered by the generator that Billy Cartwright had arranged to be delivered by tractor and trailer. It was so quiet outside that Joe thought he could hear the hum of the engine. He sat on the bed, while Charlie was on the only chair.

'The boss will want an update before she finishes for the night,' Joe said. 'Have we got anything for her?' He'd been organizing the team, sorting out the logistics. Rosie had tracked down the owner of the farmhouse who'd given them permission to use it as a base. For a fee. It seemed that Ma had a key.

'We use the same cleaner,' the owner had said. 'Marie is keeping an eye on the place for me.' His voice was rich, and he'd seemed to consider the whole episode something of a joke. An entertainment at least. 'I'd come myself but I have to be in London for business.'

'When were you last here?'

'A couple of weeks ago, to shut the place down at the end of the season. We'll open for business again over Christmas, but this is a good time to do any basic maintenance and spruce the place up.'

'Have you had anyone working there in the past week?'

'No. It's bloody impossible at the moment to get any of the local trades to commit to anything. The whole world seems to want an extension or a new roof. So much for a cost-of-living crisis! I might have to ship in some workers from the city.'

The man had never heard of Brad Russell or Chloe Spence, though her family name had triggered a memory. 'Didn't they own the land at one time? I remember seeing it on the deeds.' He'd had nothing more to contribute.

Joe hoped that Charlie's afternoon had been more productive. What Charlie did best was let people speak for themselves. He understood the reality of their everyday lives.

'What have you got for us, Charlie? Any of the locals seen anything?'

There was a moment of silence. Charlie couldn't be hurried. 'It might be worth speaking to Mary Lister. She's a widow, lives on her own two cottages down from here. Insomniac since her husband passed away. Spends a lot of the night sitting up in bed knitting and listening to the radio. Doesn't draw the curtains because she's nebby too. Likes to see who's leaving the pub together and what they're getting up to. It makes her feel she's still part of the community. She's sharp as a tack and said there was a car in the village that she couldn't recognize. I said you'd probably be in tomorrow to chat to her.' He paused. 'Her tea's like gnat's piss, mind. Best avoided.'

'I'll remember that.'

'There wasn't much else though. Nobody'd heard of Brad Russell, and you'd hardly miss him, would you? A place like this, full of folk who can work from home and staying in the fancy holiday rentals.' Another pause. 'The hotel has pulled the active elderly into the village too. They come for a spa weekend and fall for the place, then choose Gillstead as a perfect retirement destination. I met a few of those. They're running the village now – members of the parochial church council and community hall committee. The farmers and their families don't have the time on their hands.' Another pause. 'I suppose it keeps the place alive.' Though he didn't seem too sure that was a positive thing.

Joe thought this was slim pickings: one elderly woman staring out of her window.

Charlie looked up at him, with a question of his own. 'Anything from the CSIs?'

'Not so far.'

A silence. Joe was pondering small communities with long memories. 'Did anyone remember Chloe Spence? She'd come here as a young kid, and they'd know her grandfather.'

'Yeah, the real locals all know of Gordon. He was well liked and they were sorry when he sold up. The farmers still keep in touch with him through the abattoir. They weren't so fond of John, the son.'

'Of course. He'd have grown up here too.' Joe waited for Charlie to continue. He knew there'd be more information.

'He was an only child. Spoiled rotten according to the folk here. Arrogant. Thought himself better than the other kids. Someone who was at school with him described him as sly. He often stirred up trouble, but somehow it was other people who got the blame.'

'Doesn't mean he turned into a killer though. Did they know his first wife? Becky. Chloe's mam.'

'Aye, she was well liked. They thought she was a sensitive soul. Bonny, they said. Too good for him.'

'And now he's living the life of Riley in Dubai and she's in St Margaret's psychiatric hospital.'

There was silence. Joe felt awkward for a moment, because Charlie had needed psychiatric help himself in the past. He'd been swamped by a wave of depression when his wife had left him, and none of the team had realized how close he was to drowning. Outside, the sky was completely black, except for a three-quarters moon and a sky full of stars.

'But nobody's seen Chloe in the past few days?' Joe wished they could find the girl. It would freeze tonight and she could be outside with nobody to care for her. If she was still alive.

Charlie shook his head and looked more morose than usual. He had a daughter too. 'I showed people a photo of her. Nobody recognized her as the lass they'd known. They change so fast, don't they, at that age? Suddenly they're grown up. But there have been no unexpected teenagers wandering around the place. If she was here, she's kept herself well hidden.'

'They'll all know the Spence family though? They'll have been here for generations.'

'Yeah, everyone liked Gordon and Pam. They reckon that Gordon was making a go of the farm and the butchery. Pam was more of a town lass. She stuck it out here for a bit, and was friendly enough, but she could never settle to the country life, so Gordon sold up. Putting the family's wishes first, the locals I spoke to said. He still comes back and stays at the Stanhope for special nights out with his friends apparently. It sounds as if he misses the place.'

'Has he been back recently?'

'A retirement do here in the pub three weeks ago. Another farmer giving up the ghost and selling up. Gordon stayed over.' Charlie looked at his watch. 'I'm heading home now. Get a few hours' kip before I have to be back. You'll let the boss know?'

'Aye, not that there's much to tell.'

That was Vera's reaction too, when Joe phoned her.

'That's all you've got for me?'

'We've sorted out the farmhouse as a base and Charlie's been out in the village for most of the day. He's just gone home now. If there'd been anything to find, he'd be the person to dig it out.'

'Talk to Ma,' Vera said. 'Wait until she's got shot of all the punters and then go down and buy her a drink or two. She listens to the customers' gossip, and if she likes you, she'll fill you in.' A pause. 'Interesting that Gordon was there only three weeks ago. He didn't mention that.'

Joe had been hoping for an early night, but he'd learned long ago that there was no point arguing with Vera. Not in the middle of a murder investigation. Not ever. He made coffee in the hope of staying awake and listened out for the drinkers leaving. His room was over the door, and he thought he'd have been woken by the shouts of farewell, even if he'd managed to sleep. At last it was quiet and he made his way downstairs to the bar.

Marie was wiping tables. She must have sent all her staff home. She looked up as he came in. 'I thought you might come down. Any friend of Vera Stanhope would be fond of a drink.'

'She's my boss,' Joe said. 'Hardly a friend.'

She seemed not to have heard him. 'Large whisky, is it?'

He didn't usually drink spirits, but she'd poured it before he could answer. 'You'll have one yourself? Add it to the bill.'

This, he thought, could go onto expenses. Vera had better sign it off.

'Why not? It's been quite a day.' She shot him a quick grin. 'Not bad for business though a shame about that poor lad who died.'

They sat on tall stools at the bar.

'You'll have heard that we're looking for Chloe Spence. Her father grew up here.'

'I've asked around,' she said. 'Nobody's seen her, or anyone matching her description.'

'Gordon was here three weeks ago.'

'Aye. Three weeks to the day.' She paused. 'He got bladdered with his farming pals.'

'Got a drink problem, has he?'

'No more than most of us.'

Which didn't, Joe thought, help very much.

Ma had finished her drink and poured herself another. He added water to his from a jug on the bar.

'There are a group of them who get together every now and again,' Ma went on. 'Mourning the loss of their land and the way farming has gone. Blaming everyone from the EU to rich incomers.' She looked up at him. 'I don't have much sympathy. It's tough for everyone and it's the young I feel sorry for.'

'Did Gordon mention Chloe while he was here?'

'Towards the end of the evening. He said he should have held on to the land. His son would never be a farmer, but his granddaughter might have taken to the life.' Absent-mindedly Ma stuck her glass under the optic and added in a double. 'Gordon said he'd sprung her from her care home once and brought her up to remind her of the place where her father had lived as a bairn. The place that could have been her inheritance. It seemed a daft thing to do. What was the point when he'd already let it go?'

Joe thought that was interesting. Both Vera and the lass's mam had thought Chloe wouldn't be able to make her own way here. But if she'd been here recently with her grandfather, she might have done it. Taken the bus to the nearest village and walked it from there. He'd check the nearest bus stop and see if there was signal for satnav. Another line of inquiry that might just keep Vera off his back for a while.

'What's he like, the guy that bought the farmhouse?'

She shrugged. 'Bit of a tosser. Pots of money. Arrogant with it.'

'He said you share a cleaner.'

'Yeah. Josie. But she'll be no good to you. She's got seven grandbairns and an elderly mother with Alzheimer's. She's got no time for gossip.' She downed the whisky. 'I'm heading to my bed now and I need to lock up.'

He took the hint and left her to it.

Chapter Twenty-Four

THE NEXT MORNING, VERA WAS UP early, out of her house and driving down the track towards civilization before it got light. If you could call Longwater civilization. The night before, Limbrick still hadn't been answering his phone, and the uniforms who'd visited his house hadn't got a response either. Vera thought the care home manager was playing silly buggers. Did he want them to consider him a suspect? Then she'd start treating him like one. Russell's death and Chloe's disappearance had caused a simmering anger within her that was ready to explode.

When she arrived on the estate where he lived, there was a pale dawn. There'd been frost in the hills, but here, close to the coast, it was milder. Even here in the town, she could smell damp earth and sodden leaves. A light shone upstairs in Limbrick's house. She could see it round the edges of the curtains. She banged on the door with her fist. The curtain moved. She couldn't see his face, but he'd be looking down at her.

There was the sound of the key in the lock and the door opened. Limbrick was wearing grey tracksuit bottoms and a black vest. His face was grey too, the hair lank around it. He looked different without the ponytail. Wilder. Less controlled.

'Where the fuck have you been?' Vera pushed past him and into the house. 'We've been trying to get hold of you since yesterday lunchtime.'

'It was my day off. I don't switch on my phone. There'd be no peace. I need a proper break. For my mental health. That was what my doctor told me.'

'Your doctor's Jimmy Hepple?'

Joe had told her about the interview with the Longwater GP, and the name had rung a bell in her head: Hector coming back from a trip ringing birds one autumn, talking about a sparky young lad who'd found a dusky thrush. It had been the first of its kind her dad had seen in the UK and he'd been buzzing, words tripping over themselves as they left his mouth.

He had the worst binoculars you've ever seen in your life. Must have been used by the army in World War Two and picked up in a junk shop. I don't know how he saw anything through them. But the best young birder I've ever met.

Hector's admiration for the boy had been clear. Vera had been jealous. She'd always known that Hector would have loved her better if she'd been like Jimmy Hepple. A boy and a birder. Her father had gone back to the same spot the next morning with an old pair of his own binoculars.

They're not brilliant, but they'll be better than the things he's using at the moment. Who knows what he might find now?

Limbrick was staring at her. 'Yeah, Dr Hepple. I've got high blood pressure. He says it's stress. Why?'

She just shook her head. She needed to focus. She couldn't let the ghosts of the past come in to haunt her.

'When did you last see Brad Russell?'

'Why?' Limbrick seemed wary, a little sharper now, but not much. Vera thought he'd been drinking the night before. She could smell the alcohol oozing through his pores, along with the stink of cheap Chinese takeaway. She couldn't blame him for needing to escape. He'd had quite a rough few days.

She didn't answer immediately. 'Stick the kettle on, pet. You need some coffee.'

He did as he was told.

'On the piss last night, were you?' She looked at him, brown conker eyes, bright and sharp. 'And the evening before? On your own or with anyone?'

He handed her a mug. 'What's this about?'

'Best tell me if you had a friend to play. Is she still here?' Because Vera had seen the smudge of lipstick on Limbrick's mug. He might have rinsed hers under the tap, but he'd not bothered to wash his own properly.

He blushed, suddenly and dramatically, like a teenager.

'Fetch her down, pet. She could be useful to you.' Since arriving, Vera had sensed someone else in the house. It was Limbrick's jumpiness, a slight creak on an upstairs floorboard, that could have been nothing, or might have been someone creeping to the landing to earwig. Also, a woman's coat draped over the banister at the bottom of the stairs was a bit of a giveaway. Fake fur. Large.

She must have been listening in, because she appeared before Limbrick could call for her.

She'd been drinking the night before too and seemed to be suffering. Mascara was smeared across her eyelids. She was wearing a man's dressing gown – Vera presumed it was Limbrick's – and little else. It was Tracey, the Rosebank social worker.

'You look as if you could do with a coffee too, love. A bit of a night, was it, once the other carer came in to do the overnighter?' She looked out at them both, her gaze jumping from the woman to the man. 'It doesn't seem as if you've been grieving. You didn't tell Dave here that Brad Russell was dead? I can't believe you didn't pass on that little bit of information. You've got a spare place in the home now. Or were you holding your own personal wake for the lad?'

'We've done nothing wrong.' Tracey had more fight to her than her boss. 'We both needed the comfort. Consenting adults and colleagues.'

'True,' Vera conceded. 'But I seem to remember you're married. Husband the open-minded sort, is he?'

'He's a lorry driver, and he does lots of trips to Europe for work.'

'And what the eye can't see, the heart doesn't grieve over?'

Tracey laughed despite herself. 'Aye,' she said. 'Something like that.' She settled at the table.

'How long have you been here?'

'Two nights, when I wasn't at work. Dave was in a dreadful state after poor Josh Woodburn's murder. I thought he needed cheering up, and my Mike isn't back for another night.'

'When was the last time either of you saw Brad?'

'I saw him the day before yesterday,' Tracey said. 'I told the lass who was talking to me when you came in.'

'Did you notice anything unusual about him?'

'I've been thinking about it since you told me he was dead. He was on his own in Rosebank before Mel and George came back from school. We had a sandwich together because he said he was in a rush and wouldn't be in for his tea. There was something he had to do. Making a big deal of it, saying he had an important meeting, making out he was a big-shot businessman.'

'Did he say where he was going or who he was meeting?'

Tracey shook her head. 'Nah, he turned it into some grand mystery. I think he wanted me to ask, but that day I'd had enough of his games and his showing off. I was still thinking about Chloe and I didn't have the patience.' She paused. 'I wish I'd listened more carefully. Of course I do. He was angry and mixed up, but he didn't deserve to die.'

'Did you see him leave?'

'No. Like I said, he was in a hurry. I thought he'd be up to no good. Meeting a dealer. And I thought if I did ask what he was up to, I'd only get more lies.'

'Did you notice any car outside?'

Tracey shook her head. 'I heard the door bang, but I was still in the kitchen.'

'What happened?' Limbrick asked. 'How did he die?'

'It looks like an overdose.'

Limbrick nodded as if he'd thought as much, as if the lad's death had almost been inevitable.

'It's more complicated than it seems though,' Vera said. 'For one thing we found him out in the wilds. A village called Gillstead. So who took him there? And why?' She looked at Limbrick. 'Any idea? Did he ever mention the place?'

Limbrick shook his head, then considered again. 'Chloe did though. She went there with her grandad not long after she moved in with us. He took her for a day trip. She said he used to own the land.'

'Was Russell there when she was talking about it?'

'Yeah, they were talking over supper when she got back.' A pause. 'Brad was being a pain as usual, mocking her, but kind of flirty at the same time, saying it was just another of her stories. And it did seem like one of her tales. She was telling them all about the Gillstead Witch Hunt. It didn't happen at Hallowe'en. Later into November, she said. The first Saturday past Bonfire Night. One of the adults dressed up as a witch and hid on the fell close to those standing stones. The kids had to find her. Sounds like a health and safety nightmare, all the grown-ups in the pub and the bairns wandering around on the hill in the dark. I can't imagine it was really like that.'

But Vera thought Chloe had pretty well got it right. She'd taken part in the Gillstead Witch Hunt once, when Hector had needed an excuse for a drink in the Stanhope Arms. Marie Fenwick had been a youngster then, probably too young to be a real barmaid, but collecting glasses. Working for her aunty. Vera could remember the adventure. Stumbling around on the hill with the village children close to the Dark Wives standing stones. And suddenly this woman in a witch's costume, jumping out from behind a crag with a horrible howl, and terrifying them all.

'An old tradition. It goes back centuries apparently.' Vera finished her coffee and pulled her attention back to the present. 'I need you two to get dressed, and come to Rosebank with me, whether it's your day off or not. I want to look inside Brad's room. One of my chaps should have sealed it and I want a neb. Let's see if we can find anything that took him out of his comfort zone and into the wilds.'

Brad Russell's room in Rosebank gave nothing away. It stank of teenage boy and weed. He'd hung a dartboard on the wardrobe door with a bent nail but had missed the board more often than he'd hit the target, and the plywood was covered in holes. Inside, a few clothes lay on the cupboard floor. He hadn't bothered to hang them up. The room was at the front and looked out towards the common. He might have seen the encounter between the victim and his killer. But when Josh Woodburn had died, Russell had been with the others, the closest he'd ever had to a family, watching a film and eating popcorn and pizza. Though, Vera thought, there'd been gaps in the evening. More than she'd first realized. Tracey had admitted that.

Standing in the miserable room, it struck Vera that the lad's death seemed completely pointless. A bit like his short, cruel life. That last thought seemed overwhelmingly painful, and she tried to banish it from her mind.

Chapter Twenty-Five

JOE WAS UP EARLY, BUT THE Stanhope's landlady was in the pub before him. The bar was clean, smelling of cheap disinfectant, and the tables were laid for breakfast.

'You've got other people staying?'

'A couple of reporters. One lass, all the way from London.' Ma gave a quick wink. 'Murder's good for business. Apparently there are more of them staying at the hall. I couldn't put them all up here.'

Joe had learned from Vera that Gillstead Hall was the fancy hotel on the edge of the village. Maybe the Southern reporters had bigger expense accounts.

Remembering the dreadful coffee of the day before, he ordered a pot of tea, and after a moment's hesitation, the full English. Sal had been on a healthy eating kick for months, and he relished every mouthful of the food put in front of him. He was leaving the bar to go back to his room when the other guests started trickling down.

He waited until nine before going to see Mary Lister. If she suffered from insomnia, she might sleep in. He was just about to leave the pub when Vera phoned:

'It seems Limbrick and Tracey were having a bit of a fling. When her husband's away for work, she stays at his place. To cheer him up, she says. To keep him company. More likely what you young things call a recreational shag.'

'You think that could be a motive for murder? If Josh and Brad found out what was going on? You can imagine Brad Russell trying his hand at blackmail, threatening to tell the husband.'

'You can, but it doesn't seem Josh Woodburn's style. Besides, I imagine the relationship is an open secret. Tracey has grown-up kids living at home. They must know that she disappears to her boss's house every time her bloke's driving his truck across Europe. I wouldn't be surprised if the husband didn't have a similar arrangement.'

Despite himself, Joe was shocked, not just by Tracey's easy infidelity, but by Vera's amused tone. His marriage and his kids meant everything to him. His colleagues might think him stuffy and old-fashioned, but he'd made vows that he wasn't prepared to break. 'Limbrick's bosses might not like him having a relationship with a colleague. Brad could have threatened to tell them. So could Josh, even if he didn't have blackmail in mind.'

This time, Vera laughed out loud.

'Kids go missing overnight, a lad's dealing drugs in the place, and they just let our Dave get on with it, as long as social services are footing the bill and the place is making a profit. I hardly think they're going to care if he's screwing a colleague. In his own time and off the premises.' She paused to catch her breath. 'What are your plans for today?'

'Charlie found an insomniac old lady who might have seen something. I'm just on my way out to chat to her.'

'Brad was still in Rosebank the day before we found his body, so it'd be good to know if she saw anything that night.' There was a moment's pause. Joe waited for more instructions. 'Head back to Kimmerston after that. Let's get the team together and share what we know. There are so many lines of inquiry that I'm in a proper muddle, and I need to talk everything through. Clear my mind.'

Mary Lister was bent with arthritis and walked with a stick. She was very small, very prim. She'd spent her working life doing the books for farmers and landowners.

'I'm not an accountant, you understand, Sergeant, but I prepared the accounts and saved the farmers a bit of time. And rather a lot on their accountants' bills.' She'd been married but her husband had died ten years before. There'd been no children. This information she passed on without a trace of self-pity. 'Though I say it myself, I always found mathematics easy.' Now her voice *did* become wistful. 'I would have liked to read it at university, but it wasn't possible. Not then. Not for the daughter of a tenant farmer. I was needed to help at home. And it did become very useful, my ease with figures. I rather think that it saved my family's business.' She paused. 'But that was only arithmetic of course. I would have loved to study the mystery of numbers, the magic of pure mathematics.'

Joe, who had scraped through maths GCSE and heaved a sigh of relief to give it up altogether, regarded Mary with something like wonder. She led him into a living room with a view of the street. Her chair was obviously the one by the window. Next to it was a small table with a pile of sheets torn from the classier papers. 'To keep my brain active,' she said with a smile. 'Number puzzles and crosswords. I struggle sometimes with the crosswords, but the numbers are still there, making sense, forming patterns. And I continue to earn a little pin money bookkeeping for a couple of local businesses.' She nodded for him to take the other easy chair in the room. 'But you're here about the murder up at the Cragside bothy.'

'My colleague thought you might be able to help.'

'Because I'm a nosy old biddy?' She gave a little smile. 'Though I call it interested not nosy.'

'We're interested too. Especially in the night before last. That was when the lad went missing.'

'I don't sleep well,' she said. 'The arthritis. The doctors give me painkillers, but they don't altogether help, and I prefer to keep a clear head. I read at night and listen to the World Service on the radio.' There was a pause. 'But my bed is by the window in the room just above this one and I keep the curtains open a little. Just to watch the world go by. To feel that I'm still a part of it. Do you understand?'

'Of course.' Though Joe couldn't imagine what it must be like to be alone in the house. No Sal and no kids. In pain and awake. Watching the world at sleep.

'There was a car,' she said. 'Not very late, before midnight, but after the pub had closed. Some of my friends complain about noisy customers leaving the bar, but I rather like it. It marks the passage of the evening, and they seem so jolly, so full of life.'

'You never consider going into the pub to join them?' Joe knew he should ask about the car, not about this lonely woman's life, but he couldn't help himself.

'Oh no, Sergeant! When my husband was alive, I'd go with him, but not now. What would I do? Sit in a corner away from the fire and watch everyone else have fun?'

'But you'd know most of them!'

'Some of them,' she admitted. 'And I expect they'd be kind and try to include me, but it wouldn't be easy. It would feel like charity.'

'So you watch them from your window.'

'I do, and some of them I recognize. Some of them I went to school with, and some were friends of my husband. But the village was quiet by the time I saw the car.'

'Can you pinpoint that time precisely?'

'Not absolutely,' she said. 'But I'd say between eleven-forty and eleven-fifty.'

'Can you describe the car?'

'Black,' she said. 'A saloon. Smart and clean. Not one of the farm vehicles.' She looked straight at him. 'I couldn't see the registration number. Not all of it. But it started with ND. So local, I thought. Before that, I'd decided it could be an incomer, heading perhaps for Gillstead Hall. I'm afraid I make up these stories in my head. All speculation.'

'Very useful speculation,' Joe said.

'Of course, Newcastle people stay at the hotel too, but they usually arrive earlier, for dinner, or to treat themselves to the spa. So then I had the fancy that it might be a businessman arriving the night before a conference. The Hall hosts a lot of conferences.'

'Where did the car go?'

'In that direction. Towards the hotel.'

'Not towards Cragside Farm?'

'Well, it's the same direction. It did cross my mind that it could be full of visitors staying at the farm. It's become a holiday let now, but I'd heard that it had closed down for the season, so I dismissed that idea.'

'Could you see how many people were in the car?'

She screwed up her eyes, an attempt to visualize her view of the vehicle.

'There were two men in the front. I couldn't see in the back.'

'Definitely men?'

'Oh! Perhaps that was an assumption. I'm not sure.'

'We haven't found the car in the village at all. Did you see it return?'

Mary shook her head. 'But that doesn't mean it didn't come back. I do doze a little. I'm not wide awake all night.'

'Of course.'

There was a moment of silence. An older couple walked past the window on the pavement outside.

'The dead lad was in care,' Joe said, 'and a young woman is missing from the same home. Her name is Chloe Spence. Perhaps you recognize the name? Her family once owned Cragside.'

'Of course, Gordon and Pamela. I worked for them for a while. They ran a very successful business.'

'Chloe is their granddaughter. They're very anxious about her.'

'They will be, but I can't help you, Sergeant. I haven't seen her since she was a very young girl. That would be years ago.'

'Apparently Gordon brought her to the village last month. You didn't see them?'

She shook her head. 'But I might not notice. I'm up and about during the day. I don't spend all my time staring out of the window.'

'Of course,' Joe said again. He stood up. He had a little information for Vera, but not as much as he might have hoped. 'You've been very helpful.'

'The Spence lassie?' Mary pulled herself to her feet. The movement twisted her face with pain. 'You say she's gone missing. Is the assumption that she's dead too?'

Joe paused before answering. 'We don't know. But either way, we need to find her.'

They met in Vera's office, crowded in. Charlie was there, but they were just her core team. The main briefing with the other agencies would come later in the day. This was one of the tiny office's ice-box days, and Joe kept his coat on. Vera seemed not to notice the cold. She sat behind her desk, the others perched around her.

'What have we got? Concrete stuff, that I can understand. No stories. Not yet.'

'There's still no sign of Chloe,' Charlie said. 'Her face has been on the telly, and all over the local press. Nothing. It's as if she's disappeared into thin air.'

'So she's either bloody good at playing hide-and-seek, or we're looking for a body now.' Vera snapped her mouth shut and sat, stony, staring out at them. 'Or somebody's helping her.'

'Nobody's seen her in Gillstead, though we know her grandfather sprang her from the home to bring her to the village for a day trip,' Joe said.

'And he didn't mention it to me, even though we spent a couple of hours together yesterday.' Vera was angry now. 'I'll be speaking to him as soon as we've finished here.'

'The black Volvo,' Joe said. 'The one Jimmy Hepple saw at the common where Chloe spent her first night, and probably the one that Chloe mentioned in her diary as hanging around outside the home. I think the same car was seen in Gillstead the night before you found Brad Russell's body.'

'How do we know it was the same vehicle?' Vera sounded sceptical. 'Plenty of big black cars around.'

'Not in Gillstead at eleven-thirty at night. Not with a local registration plate.'

'True, and something similar was seen outside Chloe's mam's house too.'

'You got that info from Mary Lister?' Charlie had the knack of seeming to speak without opening his mouth.

Joe thought he'd make a cracking ventriloquist. 'Aye. She thought there were two people in the front of the vehicle. Men, she said at first, but when I questioned her, she wasn't so sure.'

'I'm surprised she was sure about anything,' Vera said. 'Pitch black and hurtling through the village.'

'There are street lights right outside her house.' Joe knew better than to allow Vera to wind him up. 'And it wouldn't have been hurtling. There's no off-street parking in the village and you'd have to slow right down to get past all the parked cars. Not unless you wanted to lose a wing mirror.'

Vera nodded to accept the argument. 'So we need to find that car. Let's check out the vehicles owned by everyone involved in the case. See if anyone owned a black Volvo with an ND plate. If Brad was there, we should be able to find a trace of him.'

'That lets Stella Marsh and her father out then,' said Rosie. 'Neither of them owns a car. A matter of principle.'

'Let's check if they have a driving licence. No reason why they wouldn't hire one.'

'A bit unlikely surely,' Rosie said. 'You wouldn't hire a car and let it sit outside Rosebank night after night. And Joe said Dr Hepple was a model witness. I think he'd have noticed a rental sticker.'

'Maybe.' Vera paused. 'Brad Russell left Rosebank in the afternoon the day that he disappeared. If you're right, Joe, and the car your witness saw had Russell in the front seat as a passenger, where did they spend the remainder of that evening?' They looked at her blankly. She raised her voice and spoke slowly, a primary school teacher spelling out the obvious. 'Let's check CCTV and vehicle recognition. If Joe's right and the car is crucial, let's see if we can find it! I want to know if it stopped anywhere between Longwater and Gillstead too. There was half a loaf of bread and some instant coffee in the bothy, but nothing else. That could have been meant for breakfast. Can we check pubs and restaurants en route? They might have stopped to eat. Brad was very much a city rat. He'd have stuck out like a sore thumb in any of the country pubs. It's possible too that they met up with other people.'

'You think more than one person is involved in these killings?' Joe said.

Vera shrugged. 'I don't know anything about these killings, so I have to keep an open mind.' A pause. 'Rosie, can you take on the search for the car?'

'Sure, boss.' But Joe thought the new girl was disappointed. She wouldn't enjoy being stuck in front of a computer screen all afternoon.

'Before then, Rosie, tell us about the Marshes. Father and daughter. We know that he was the person to visit Josh Woodburn in the student flat in Jesmond, and that she was Josh's girlfriend. The love of his life. We need to keep an open mind. Brad's death might have shifted the centre of the investigation geographically, but Rosebank is still at its heart.'

'They're both eco-warriors, living in a kind of green commune just off the spine road. They have the farmhouse but there's a barn full of bunks for the volunteers. Stella dumped Josh because, I suspect, he was too clingy and because she saw him as too much a part of the establishment – wealthy parents, comfortable existence. He might have felt the need to prove himself, and that might explain his decision to start working in the kids' home.'

'We're in story territory here,' Vera warned. 'Speculation.'

'Perhaps, but it agrees with what Stella told me. She'd decided to meet up with Josh, so he could tell her about his exciting new project. He'd told her she'd be proud of him.'

'When were they going to meet?'

'The day after he died.'

'Have either father or daughter got a motive, do we think?'

Now it was Rosie's turn to shrug. 'Not that I can see. All the evidence from their digital contact is that Josh was a bit pathetic, but not abusive. I can't think that a sparky young woman like Stella would have felt in any way intimidated by him, and the father genuinely seemed to like him.'

'Any chance that either of them could have known Brad Russell? He couldn't have been placed in the hostel they run on the farm?'

'I wouldn't have thought so! I can check with social services, but the bunk house is for volunteers who want to work on the smallholding. It would hardly be Russell's sort of thing.'

'Unless he had a social worker who thought it might be good for him.' Vera was almost talking to herself.

'I can't think why either Marsh would want to kill him though.'

The answer came unbidden into Joe's head. *Because he was an irritating little shit.* But he said nothing and turned to Vera instead.

'What do you want me to do this afternoon?'

'Get in touch with Brad's social worker and find out all you can about the lad. Legally he was still a child and in the care of the local authority.' Vera gave him a phone number. 'This is the direct line for Kath Oliver, the senior safeguarding person. If anyone can fill you in, it'll be her.' She paused and seemed deep in thought. 'I'll go and talk to that doctor of yours, Jimmy Hepple. He seems to know the community well. Russell might even have been a patient if he was a long-term resident at Rosebank.'

Joe was surprised by the offer. 'You don't want one of us to do it, boss?'

'Nah,' she said. 'You're all right.' It was as if she had reasons of her own for wanting to meet the man. 'You say he lives further north up the coast? I can call in on my way home this evening.'

They sat for a moment. Water gurgled in the radiator that still gave off no heat.

'Let's find the lass,' Vera said at last. 'I can't bear not knowing where she is. Even if she's dead I want to find her.'

It was a kind of dismissal and they all stood up. Rosie turned back to the boss, just as they were about to file out of the room.

'Is it okay if I tell the Woodburns that Russell's dead? It's already all over the news, so they must know, but they'll connect it with their son's death, and I think they have a right to hear some of the details from us. Chris will be at home, even if his wife has gone back to work, though she'll surely be on compassionate leave. She was a real mess last time I saw them.' A pause. 'I'll still have time to focus on the car later.'

Vera took a while to answer. Joe thought – hoped – she might refuse. But in the end, she just nodded.

'Don't let it take up too much of your time though.'

Chapter Twenty-Six

VERA LEFT FOR WHITLEY BAY AS soon as the others had gone. She felt betrayed. She'd liked Gordon Spence and she'd thought she understood him. Like her, he'd grown up in the hills, surrounded by space, long horizons and big skies. She hadn't expected lies and secrets.

He opened the door as if he'd been expecting her. This morning he was wearing old man's clothes, suburban clothes, slacks and a cardigan and tartan slippers.

'Pamela's at work.'

'No matter.' Vera had already marched across the doorstep. 'It's you I want to talk to.'

She carried on, without being invited, into the sitting room, and landed on one of the huge sofas like a ship at dock. Then rather spoiled the effect by having to stand to take off her coat. The room was far too hot for her. Gordon followed her in and hovered.

'Would you like some tea?'

'I don't have time for tea! I've got a double murder to solve and more importantly, I need to find that lass of yours.' She glared at him. 'Why didn't you tell me you'd taken Chloe up to Gillstead?'

He looked like a child hauled up in front of the head teacher.

'Well?' She shouted the word, and finding that she was almost enjoying the drama of the moment, felt a stab of guilt.

'It was a kind of secret,' he said at last.

'So you'd not told Pamela that you'd taken Chloe up there for a jaunt?'

'I couldn't tell her. She'd not have approved. She always took John's part in the divorce. Her only son could do no wrong. You know what mams are like with their boys.'

No, not really, pet. I never had one of those.

'Pamela always spoiled him rotten.' He paused. 'I wanted to give the lass a day out. I knew she'd always loved it up at Cragside.'

'And you'd not have minded a day in the hills too?'

He gave a sheepish grin. 'I miss the place. Don't get me wrong. There's nothing wrong with Whitley, but I'm a country boy at heart. I'm not used to all these folk.'

'So tell me what happened?'

'I did it right. All above board. I phoned the office in advance and spoke to one of the staff.'

She jumped in quickly. 'Which member of staff? Dave the manager?'

'I don't know. Some young lad. Well-spoken, you knaa.'

'Josh?'

'Aye. Josh. That's it. And he said he'd put it in the diary so if he wasn't on duty, they'd know what was happening. But when I got there, that Saturday we did our trip, he *was* on duty, so he just waved us off, all cheery like.'

'Josh Woodburn was the first murder victim. You didn't recognize the name from the news?'

'Nah.' Gordon seemed genuinely shocked. 'I don't bother much with the news. It's all politics, isn't it. Depressing. I used to get the local paper for the mart prices, but I don't even bother with that anymore.'

'Tell me everything you did on your day out. And sit down, man – you're making me uncomfortable. This is going to take a while.'

He sat, obedient as a dog, on a large armchair and twisted it so it was facing Vera and not the television.

'There's nothing much to tell. It was just a day out. Pamela was working in the shop all day and then going out in the evening with her staff, because one of them had a birthday. I picked Chloe up at about ten-thirty and we headed off. I'd made a picnic for our lunch. It was a bright day, clear and cold. One of those days when you know winter's not far away.'

'Which way did you drive?'

'We went on the back roads. We were in no rush, and I wanted the views. The empty spaces I'd been missing. I thought Chloe might like them too, after being cooped up in that home with all the other kids.'

'Can you show me on a map?' Vera wondered if people still did maps. The younger members on her team would have got themselves lost every day without their smartphones.

'Sure.' Gordon was desperate to help now. He pulled a battered road atlas from a shelf to show her the route they'd taken.

'You won't have bumped into much traffic along those roads.'

'Nah, we got stuck behind a tractor every now and again, but that didn't bother us. Like I said, we weren't in a rush. There weren't many other cars about. There never are up there.'

'You couldn't have been followed?' *By a black Volvo?*

Gordon shook his head. 'Nah, I'd have noticed.' A pause. 'Why would anyone want to follow us?'

Well, pet, that's the question, isn't it?

'What did you chat about on the road?'

'Not much to start with.' He paused again. 'Chloe was prickly, resentful, and trying to make out that she didn't really want to be there. "I'm only here because Josh said I should come." That was what she said. She always blamed us for taking John's side against her mam. I could understand that. But after a while, she opened up. She talked about the home and what a shambles it was. And school, and how much she hated it. I let her talk. She deserved a good whinge, all she'd been through. It seemed to me that nobody had listened to her in a long time.'

Except Josh, and now he's dead.

'What did you do when you got to the village?'

'It was nearly midday. Quiet on the street. We parked close to the farm – the house looked empty – and walked up to the bothy. She sprinted ahead of me.' He smiled. 'She reminded me of cattle let out after a winter indoors. All frisky and kicking, you knaa. The fresh air making them young again. By the time I got there, she'd made herself at home, up in the loft where she used to sleep.'

'Any sign that anyone had been there recently?'

He shook his head. 'It was tidier than I'd expected. The grate clean and a pile of kindling and logs in a basket.'

'Did you light a fire?'

'Nah, it wouldn't have been fair, would it, if someone had trekked up the hill carrying all that wood. I might still own it, but I don't mind walkers and climbers using it.'

'So what *did* you do?'

'We had our lunch outside in the sunshine. It was sheltered there, and warm enough. I'd brought pop for her, and a beer for me.' He looked sharply at Vera. 'Just one mind, because I knew I was driving.'

'What happened then? Nobody saw you in the pub. You didn't want to catch up with all your old mates there?'

Gordon shook his head. 'It was our Chloe's day. I wanted to give her a treat. There's a lass who was with her in primary school in Longwater, before the family moved to Gillstead. A year older than our Chloe but the two of them were always pals. So we met up with her and I took them both to the Hall, the hotel, and bought them a treatment. Some facial thing they fancied.' He looked up at Vera and smiled. 'Pamela always asks for a spa day for her birthday, and I thought Chloe would enjoy it.'

'Did she?' Vera could think of nothing worse. She tried to imagine what it would be like, some stranger rubbing stuff into your face. Having to lie still while they were doing it.

'Aye, they both did! Said it was dead relaxing.' He smiled again. 'I'm not sure what they made of Chloe though in her ripped baggy jeans and panda eyes. Their customers are mostly smart older women.'

'Did you bump into anyone you knew there?' Vera was still trying to work out how Brad Russell had ended up in Cragside bothy. That coincidence was eating away at her.

'It's not really the sort of place where my farming friends would go.' He added, a kind of admission: 'I had a nap while I was waiting for them. It was hot in the hotel conservatory where I was sitting, and there was nothing else to do. I only woke up when they came out of the treatment room.' He paused then. 'I was tempted to take them into the Stanhope then. I thought some of my old friends would be there for a pint straight after work. But I wasn't in the mood. It's hard, you knaa, to realize what you've lost.'

'You must love your Pamela very much to have given all that up.'

There was a moment's silence.

'Aye,' he said simply. 'I do.'

'What time did you get Chloe back to Rosebank?'

'It would have been about seven-thirty. We stopped for our tea in a place in Kimmerston on the way home. Fish and chips.'

'Was Josh still on duty?' Vera wasn't sure how important all these details were, but she waited anxiously for the response. Somehow, she thought, the away day in the hills was significant.

'He might have been, but I didn't see him. There was an older guy in the office. Dave. He said he was the manager. He was pleasant enough and asked if we'd had a good day out. We had a bit of a chat about Chloe and how she was getting on there.'

'Did you tell him you'd been to Gillstead?'

Gordon had to think about that. 'Honestly? I'm not sure.'

Vera hoisted herself to her feet. 'Is there anything else you've not been telling us? Anything else that might help us find Chloe? Your last chance before I head out.'

'No! Really!' He'd become the schoolboy again, swearing his innocence.

'Where's that lad of yours?' She had a sudden panic. 'He's not gone back to Dubai?'

Gordon shook his head. 'He's got another week.' He looked at Vera sadly, a confession. 'Pamela will miss him, but I'll not be sorry to see him go.'

Gordon saw her to the front door. Now he seemed reluctant to let her leave, to be alone again in this house, which still didn't feel quite like home to him. 'You will get in touch, as soon as there's any news?'

'Of course, pet. And you give me a shout if you hear from Chloe, or you get any idea where she might be.'

'I will! Of course I will.'

Chapter Twenty-Seven

CHRIS AND ANNA WOODBURN WERE OUT when Rosie arrived, and she kicked herself for not phoning first. They could be anywhere. She crossed the road and looked down at Cullercoats Bay, trying to decide what to do next. She supposed she should return to the station and do as she was told. Check out that black Volvo that the boss was so obsessed with. But she couldn't quite bring herself to get in the car and drive straight back. Instead, she wandered out to one of the little cafés on the street where the Woodburns lived, bought a takeaway coffee and a sandwich and sat on a bench looking down at the beach. It was cold and there were a few dog-walkers, a kayaker paddling between the two piers.

A group of older women emerged from the sea after a swim, and they ran over the sand to the bottom of the lifeboat station where they'd left their clothes. The cold water had turned their bodies pink. They were big and their skin was wrinkled with cellulite, but they seemed not to care. Rosie didn't want *ever* to look like that, but she envied them their freedom, the laughter as they wrapped themselves in big towels and brightly coloured Dryrobes and drank coffee from a flask.

She threw her cup and wrappers into the nearest bin and walked back towards the car. She'd give the Woodburns one last go, before heading off to Kimmerston and the tedium of a screen in the big open-plan office. As she turned the corner into their street, she almost bumped into the couple on the pavement. They were approaching the door of their house, keys in hand. They were wearing waterproof jackets and their boots were sandy.

'Were you looking for us?' Chris seemed almost embarrassed that they'd been caught outside, enjoying a walk on the beach. 'We both felt that we couldn't stay cooped up in the house, that we needed some fresh air.'

'There have been some developments,' Rosie said. 'I thought I should bring you up to date.'

'Another boy dead!' Anna stood in the entrance hall, balanced, apparently with ease, on one leg while she pulled off a boot. Her socks were patterned, a fancy Nordic design. 'We saw. So dreadful!' The other boot came off. 'Come on through.'

They took Rosie to the upstairs room where she'd first sat with Joe, after passing on the news of Josh's murder. The shock and disbelief experienced then by Chris Woodburn seemed to linger in the place, like a ghostly haunting. The photograph of the family was still in pride of place on the shelf over the fire.

It appeared that Chris felt uncomfortable here too. 'I'll make some coffee, shall I?'

'Not for me,' Rosie said. 'I'm sorry but I can't stay long. I just wanted to let you know what's been happening. Besides, there's a chance perhaps that you can help.'

'Sure.'

Today, Anna looked as if she was holding it together better than her husband. Perhaps because she hadn't yet started drinking, and the sea air had brought some colour to her cheeks.

'Of course, we'll help if we can.'

'The boy who died was called Brad Russell,' Rosie said. 'He was one of Josh's clients at Rosebank. He was troubled, known to the police since he was a young child. We think he'd been groomed by a drug dealer and was a user himself.'

'Oh.' Anna was in one of the armchairs, her legs tucked underneath her. 'How very sad! Such a terrible waste.'

'I assume that the name means nothing to you?' Because, after all, they hadn't even known that Josh was working at Rosebank. Again, Rosie thought how odd that was. Surely helping troubled youngsters was something to be proud of? Why the secrecy?

The couple shook their heads.

'His body was found in a bothy in rural Northumberland, near the village of Gillstead.'

Again, she was expecting blank faces or bemused expressions, but now there was a flash of recognition.

'Josh would have known it,' Anna said. 'Wouldn't he, Chris? Even I've been there once or twice when Josh was younger, and we'd go walking as a family. More recently Chris and Josh would mostly go off hiking on their own together. It had all become a bit strenuous for me, and I quite liked my restful days home alone.'

Chris nodded. 'We've always been keen walkers. Not members of a group, but we loved to take ourselves out into the hills. When Josh moved out to uni, it was a way for me to keep in touch with him, to stay close.' He looked up at Rosie. 'The village is just inside the Northumberland National Park, and we've followed several of the suggested trails.' He gave a little smile. 'I'm a bit old for camping out in bothies though.'

'Did you stay in the Gillstead Hall hotel?'

Chris shook his head. 'Nothing that flash. In the Stanhope Arms. It's a real village pub, full of characters, and they don't mind a bit of mud on our boots.' A pause. 'Josh loved it there. He said it would make a great subject for a short film about the reality of country life.'

Rosie was distracted for a moment by the notion that Vera might have a pub named after her. Then she remembered that Gordon Spence had been a regular in the place and still had friends there. She wondered if that was another coincidence or had any significance to the investigation. The boss would be pleased with the information anyway.

'I stayed there once,' Anna turned to her husband, suddenly animated. 'Do you remember? It was his eighteenth birthday, and we offered to take him away for the weekend. Anywhere he wanted in the world. I was thinking Paris, Berlin, Barcelona, but he chose a walk in the hills and Gillstead.' She smiled.

'He brought Stella Marsh with him that day,' Chris said.

'So he did.' A pause. 'It was his special birthday treat. We could hardly refuse. He couldn't keep his eyes off her.'

Another coincidence?

'I'm sure Stella would have loved the weekend in the country,' Rosie said. 'I met her at Paradise Farm and it's her passion, isn't it, the whole green thing.'

'It didn't exactly make for the fun weekend we were expecting,' Anna grumbled. 'She turned it into a walking lecture and guilt trip, banging on about over-grazing and bird of prey poisoning, as if we were somehow responsible. We just wanted the exercise and fresh air. A few beers at the end of the day. We work hard and we were there to relax and to give Josh a great time.'

There was a silence before Chris spoke. 'He did have a great time. He said it was the best birthday ever.'

There was another silence before Rosie changed the direction of the conversation:

'I went to see Stella and her father. I don't think they were accusing Josh of stalking her or pestering her. Will seemed to like him.'

'That wasn't the impression he gave when he came here,' Chris said. 'He was rather rude actually, demanding to see our son. We had guests in for drinks, colleagues of mine, and he caused a scene.'

'He didn't give me the impression of being the sort of man to cause a scene.'

'Perhaps that's not quite the right description,' Anna said. 'It was embarrassing. I suppose that appearances shouldn't matter, but he looked like a tramp! He'd cycled apparently, and it had rained, so he stood there in the hall in a strange yellow cape, water dripping on the floor, that lank hair plastered to his face. We didn't know who he was at first. Chris didn't want to let him in, but when we realized, what could we do? Chris spoke to him there in the hall, but the door to the living room was open and everyone could see.'

And you didn't want your smart mates thinking he was a friend of yours, that his daughter was going out with your son.

It occurred to Rosie that Will and Stella had been judged, just as Chloe had been judged by her grandparents. Both the Spences and the Woodburns were concerned about what neighbours and friends would make of these people. They would want the pictures on social media to be of beautiful young women becoming part of their family – not Chloe with her ripped fishnet tights and goth make-up or Stella with her baggy combat pants and boots. Rosie couldn't blame them. She was jealous of the images posted by her friends. The pictures weren't of kids, not yet. But of fit boyfriends, fabulous holidays, weddings. All there just to make people like her envious.

'When was the last time you were at Gillstead?' Rosie directed the question to Chris.

The couple looked at each other. Rosie couldn't tell if they were really trying to work out an accurate timeline, or if they wanted to be sure their stories would be the same.

'About a month ago?' Chris answered. The question was for Anna. 'I was on my own. It was just a day trip. I parked on the edge of the village and walked the footpath along the river, and then into the hills. It had been a stressful week at work, and it was just what I needed. I didn't stay over.'

'I remember. You'd asked Josh if he wanted to come but he said he was busy. I suppose he was working in the care home.' Anna paused. 'Why didn't he tell us about his new job?' The question came out as a cry. 'Surely he knew we'd be proud of him.'

Rosie thought that it was Stella their son had been eager to impress, not his parents, but she said nothing. She got to her feet and waited for Chris to show her to the door.

Back at the station, Rosie found Vera still in her office.

'You back then? How are the grieving relatives?'

Rosie thought of the immaculate home, haunted by memories of family gatherings and laughter. 'Still grieving.'

'Not your role to fix that though.' Vera's voice was firm but not unkind. 'Time to get on to that car that seems to have been lurking on the edge of the inquiry from the beginning. It's starting to bug me, and surely it can't be too hard to track it down if it belongs to any of our people of interest.'

'Some coincidences did come out of the conversation with the Woodburns.'

'Oh?' For the first time, Vera moved her attention away from the screen. She was intrigued, as Rosie had hoped she would be.

'The Woodburns are walkers. They know Gillstead. They enjoy doing the Northumberland Park trails.'

'Well,' Vera only sounded mildly interested. 'Lots of folk enjoy a hike in the hills.'

'They've stayed in the Stanhope Arms.' Rosie paused for dramatic effect. 'Anna stopped going with them a while ago, but it seems to have been a regular overnight stop for Josh and his dad.'

'Was it now?' Vera leaned back in her chair. 'So that gives us another link between the scuzzy kids' home on the coast and a village full of local farmers and the retired wealthy in the hills. Just a coincidence, do we think?'

Rosie didn't answer the question. She was waiting to pass on the most vital information and didn't speak again until Vera was upright. 'On one occasion, they took Stella Marsh with them. Josh's eighteenth birthday treat.'

'Did they? You're right. That is very interesting.' A long silence. Rosie could sense the thoughts churning in Vera's mind, but it seemed she'd come to no conclusion and when she did speak, her tone was dismissive. 'Now get back to your desk and find that car.'

Rosie turned, disappointed. She'd expected a better reaction. She was almost out of the room when Vera shouted after her: 'Good work, pet! I think you'll be an asset to the team.'

Chapter Twenty-Eight

Joe Ashworth had never much liked social workers. He'd not met many in his time – though one had been a victim in an early case he'd investigated with Vera – but he'd always seen them as ineffective, supporting the sinners rather than the sinned against. He viewed the boss's instructions to talk to Brad Russell's key worker as a waste of time. In his experience, social workers' main function was to hold meetings. There was a lot of talk and little action.

When he discovered that Chloe and Brad shared a social worker and that she was on sick leave through stress, he began to have a little sympathy. Surely one of those troubled adolescents would be a full-time job on their own. When he was told that there was a caseload of a couple of dozen other children and young people, who now had to be shared out between already overloaded staff, his perception shifted again. Even a complex murder investigation sounded simpler than dealing with a bunch of arsey teenagers with a history of trauma and neglect.

The team leader, Kath Oliver, squeezed him in between meetings. They met in the community café on the ground floor of the building. She was drinking tea from a large mug and eating a piece of carrot cake. Joe thought she was a social services version of Vera, though definitely better dressed. She offered to buy him a tea, but he could tell that her time was already tight, so he refused.

'Brad Russell,' he said. 'You'll have heard that we found his body up in the wilds of Gillstead.'

'Yes.' She looked at him over her mug, her voice serious. 'Brad was an enormous drain on our time and resources, but he was a young lad who'd been through a dreadful time, and he'd never had the care that he really needed. If I thought too much about it, I'd weep.'

Joe didn't know how to react to that, so he went on. 'The pathologist says that an overdose killed him, but it seems a coincidence after Josh Woodburn's murder and Chloe's disappearance.'

'So you think someone doctored the drug he was taking?'

Joe nodded. 'The boss asked me for a bit of background.'

'Of course. As I explained, it makes rather a depressing story. His mother is an addict, and his father was never part of the picture. Midwives and health visitors expressed concern about the care the baby was getting soon after birth and we were involved within the first month. We were granted a care order, and Brad was placed in foster care. And when that broke down, with his maternal grandparents. He's been under the supervision of social services throughout his life. His grandparents tried their best, but they weren't good at providing boundaries, especially as he got older. He learned how to charm them, and always managed to get his own way. The grandmother had health issues, which meant she had limited mobility.' She looked up at Joe. 'They had no life of their own at all. They wanted to do their best for the boy, though in the end it was unsustainable.'

'Was he seeing his mother during this time?'

Kath shrugged. 'Contact was sporadic and unreliable. It depended on the whim of the boyfriend she was living with at the time. She has a knack of choosing controlling and violent bullies.'

'But she's in a refuge now?'

'She is and seems to be doing well. That was positive. In time, she and the lad might have got together.'

Joe remembered Brad with his hyperactivity and strange, insinuating smile and couldn't see it. 'You never thought adoption might be an option?'

'Brad had been in a number of foster homes, but none of the placements worked long term. It always started well enough, but then there were outbreaks of anger and violence. We didn't think adoption would be suitable. I know it's hard to believe, but he was doing better at Rosebank than in any other placement. He was more settled over the past months than at any time in his life. Something made him want to stay there.'

'You say he had outbreaks of violence and anger. Would he have been capable of attacking the care worker in the children's home?'

Kath took her time in answering. 'I hate to say it, but I think that he would. He had very little impulse control, especially if he'd been using. Could he lash out suddenly if someone had annoyed him? I think that he could.' She looked up at Joe. 'But if you're saying he was murdered rather than that he took an accidental overdose, surely the same person killed him and Josh? I find it hard to believe in two murderers with a connection to Rosebank.'

Joe nodded to accept the point. 'We wondered about black-mail.'

'You think he saw Josh being killed and tried to extort money?'

'Yeah, would he be bright enough to do that?'

'Oh yes.'

They sat in silence for a moment.

'As I said, his body was found in Gillstead, up in the hills. Did he have any connection with the place? Family from there?'

Kath shook her head. 'He might have been taken on a trip from the school referral unit, when he was still attending. They try to get the kids out for a bit of fresh air and exercise, but there's nothing in the records to suggest a family history away from Longwater and the surroundings.'

'How about Paradise Farm? That eco place off the spine road. Could he have had any contact with the Marshes?'

She raised her eyebrows but didn't demand a reason for the question. 'Not as far as I know. They take some of our older kids as volunteers occasionally, but we'd never recommend someone like Brad. It wouldn't be fair to them or to us. They'd never consider one of our kids again.'

'What about Chloe?'

She took a moment to think about that. 'Well, not once she moved to Rosebank. That's all about crisis management. They don't have the time or resources to do much extracurricular stuff. But when she was living at home, she was a member of our young carers' group. There are more kids than you'd think who look after a parent with a physical or psychological illness. The group tries to widen their horizons, let them be kids for a bit, and mix with people their own age. I know Chloe went there when Paradise Farm hosted days out for them.'

Joe tried to imagine his kids having to take responsibility for a disabled adult. They struggled to look after themselves.

'What do you make of the set-up there?'

'I think it's great. Everyone who works at the Paradise has all the usual background checks. It's close to towns and villages where most of our young people are based but it gives them a real sense of the outdoors. It teaches them a bit of responsibility. And where their food comes from.'

'So you're a fan?'

'I am. I've even volunteered myself once or twice. Not to sleep in the bunk house – those days are long gone – but on their open days.' Now she did ask: 'How are Will and Stella involved in your investigation?'

'Stella was Josh Woodburn's girlfriend until quite recently. They were going to meet up the day after he died.' No need for her to know that William Marsh had been looking for Josh in Cullercoats, or that he'd called on the lad at his Jesmond home, advising him to back off his daughter for a while.

'Oh!' Kath was more shocked than Joe had expected. It seemed she was closer to the Marshes than she'd let on. In her role she'd be used to sad news, and this seemed personal. 'Poor Stella.'

'Did you ever meet Josh?' He was curious now. 'At the farm or at Rosebank?'

'Certainly not at Rosebank. My role is supervisory now, or chairing child protection core group meetings. I seldom get out into the field. I might have come across him at Paradise Farm, but I don't think we were ever introduced. I know Will better than Stella.'

Joe was even more curious now. Could there be a romantic attachment between the green activist and the senior social worker? The idea amused him, but he supposed that was probably no business of his. He'd got what he'd come for. There'd been no connection between Brad and the father and daughter at Paradise Farm.

He was about to end the conversation when Kath spoke: 'Would you like to talk to Brad's grandparents? Even when he was at Rosebank, he did keep in touch with them. Not very often and usually when he wanted something from them, but they were closer to him than anyone else.'

Joe thanked her and made a note of the address. 'You can just call in,' Kath said. 'They're always at home. I think they'd be pleased that you'd bothered to visit. They got very little thanks for all the work they put in over the years.'

He went straight to Brad's grandparents. They lived in a miners' welfare bungalow in a village not far from Longwater. Once, the only point of the village had been the pit. Now, it seemed to have no point at all. In the single street, there was one corner shop that served too as a post office and a working men's club that had seen better days. Behind the main street stood three terraces of houses and the bungalows, with their grab rails and ramps. Many of the retired miners who'd once lived there had died, but other elderly people had taken them over.

Joe knocked at the door and waited. Kath was right and the couple were there. He could hear a television inside. It was loud enough for him to tell it was a programme about a dream life in the sun. It just took Brad's grandfather a while to get to the door.

He was thin and bony, with a hard, sharp face. Not very old. Seventy perhaps, but he'd had a tough life, and his face was grey and lined.

'Who are you?'

'I'm police. Here about Brad.'

The man nodded as if he'd thought as much and stepped aside to let Joe in.

A woman sat in a large armchair in the corner of a small, cluttered room. She was fleshy and soft, with long grey hair and the most swollen legs Joe had ever seen. A walking frame stood next to her. There was a box of tissues and an ashtray on a coffee table within easy reach. It took Joe a moment to recognize the smell in the room – cigarettes. Nobody he knew smoked now. Certainly not indoors.

They were Hilda and Jack.

'I'm sorry,' Joe said, 'about your grandson.'

At first, Jack did most of the talking. 'There've been times,' he said, 'when I've wished him dead, but now I just remember him as a small bairn, and the pain hits us. While he was living there was always a chance that he'd turn his life around.'

Hilda pulled a tissue from the box and wiped her eyes. They were red-rimmed and sore.

'We blame ourselves,' Jack went on. 'Maybe we shouldn't have turned him out. But you can see how it is here. Hilda needs more care than she gets from the council, and I'm not fit myself. I'd wake up worrying about what he was up to and go to bed with the same anxious thoughts. He stole from us over and over again, but always denied it. Gave us that lovely smile and said he would never do such a thing. That saps your strength, makes you think you're going mad. We had no life. So we told the social worker that he'd have to go. Most of the time we didn't know where he was anyway.'

'When was the last time you saw him?'

'A couple of weeks ago. It was Hilda's birthday. Brad turned up with a card and a box of chocolates.' A sad smile. 'He ate most of them himself, but never mind. He'd remembered.'

'How did he seem?'

At last Hilda spoke: 'Excited. He told us he'd been offered a job.'

'What kind of job?'

'He didn't tell us,' Jack said. 'I thought it'd be something to do with those dealers he'd been conned by since he was a kid. But he said no. Nothing like that. Something respectable.' He looked up at Joe. 'But I didn't believe him. He was always full of shit. You could believe nothing he said.'

'They said he died from an overdose.' Hilda pulled herself up in her chair and winced at the pain. 'He's been addicted to that muck since he was a small lad. It's the dealers who killed him, but they'll never be charged. It was a kind of murder.'

'There's some question over his death.' Joe chose his words carefully. 'The overdose killed him, but we think the drugs had been given to him. Because of the context. What led up to it and where he was found.'

'What are you saying, lad?' Jack's voice was sharp. 'That it really *was* murder?'

'A care worker was killed at Rosebank, the children's home where Brad was staying,' Joe said. 'You must have seen it on the television.'

Jack shook his head and looked blank. Someone else who didn't bother with the news. 'One of Hilda's carers was rabbiting on about a lad being murdered in Longwater, but it didn't sink in that it was where our Brad was living.'

'It seems a coincidence that your grandson should die too.' Joe paused. 'And then, there was the place where he was found.'

'Where was that?'

It seemed that the information which had been given to the couple had been minimal. Another drug user had taken an overdose. Another wasted life. That would have been the story given to the local uniforms, and they wouldn't have bothered to find out any more of the details.

'His body was found in a bothy in a village called Gillstead. Out in the wilds. Halfway up a hill. Does that sound like a place Brad would visit alone?'

Hilda started laughing. It turned into a racking cough, and it took her a while to catch her breath. 'No way! He acted as if he was big, but a bus trip into Newcastle was an adventure to our Brad. We took him to Tynemouth once when he was small, and you'd have thought it was the moon. His eyes as big as saucers looking at the fancy shops and the priory.'

'He never went to Gillstead? On a school trip, anything like that? You've no relatives living out that way?'

The shook their heads in tandem. 'We're like Brad,' Jack said. 'None of us have moved far from home.'

'What about a place called Paradise Farm? It's just off the spine road not far from here. Does that mean anything to you?'

'What's that then? Sounds like the sort of place where they grow all that cannabis?'

It was Joe's turn to smile. 'Nothing like that. It's a small-holding. They teach local kids about sustainable living and have volunteers in to work on the land. It's run by a father and daughter called Marsh. Some looked-after kids help out there. I wondered if Brad had mentioned it?'

'That wouldn't have been for him,' Jack said. 'He couldn't see beyond what *he* wanted at the time. I think he was born that way, and we can't blame him. Or maybe we didn't do the right things when he was small. The social worker was always talking about setting boundaries, but he'd kick off, and sometimes we just wanted an easy life. She didn't have to live with him and put up with his temper.' He looked straight at Joe with his narrow slatey eyes. 'Sometimes, I thought he might kill someone. I never thought that *he'd* end up a victim of murder.'

Chapter Twenty-Nine

VERA WAS SITTING AT HER DESK in her tiny office. She was leaning back in the chair and her eyes were shut. Anyone looking in from the open-plan office outside would suspect she was asleep. But she was thinking. The information that Rosie had passed on about the Woodburns' passion for traipsing the hills close to Gillstead could be important or completely random. But the fact that Josh had known the place and that Stella had been there too, was at least interesting.

If Vera hadn't wanted to check out Jimmy Hepple, she'd be tempted to head straight to Gillstead. Chloe had spent time there recently, had met a friend and had been spoiled by her grandfather in the hotel. The friend was interesting. Hadn't Esther's mam mentioned an Alice, said that the three of them had been close when they were young? They'd need to track *her* down. Chloe had proved herself to be resourceful. It was still possible that she was hiding out there. She was a storyteller. She could have told a story to persuade someone sympathetic to help her.

Vera pushed herself upright, opened her eyes and made a note that one of the team should check out any teenagers still living in the village. But that wasn't a job for *her*. She was too old and too abrasive. She'd send Rosie. Surely the youngsters would relate to the younger detective, and it'd be good for the woman to get a feel for the whole patch where she'd be working, not just the coastal plain.

Then there was that eco place. Paradise Farm. That must surely fit into the picture somewhere. Vera couldn't work out what the Marshes were doing there, playing at saving the planet. How could they earn a living from a small patch of land with a handful of sheep and some farmyard hens, when *real* farmers in the hills were struggling? Did they get funding from some charity or other? Could Josh have discovered they were fiddling the books once he started at Rosebank? Vera thought it'd be interesting to find out how they survived financially. It might even be possible to get a forensic accountant to look at their books. If they had nothing to hide, then surely they wouldn't object.

Again, Vera was tempted to rush out and visit the place. She'd never met the young woman who'd turned Josh's head, who had, it seemed, persuaded him to take up good works and apply for a post in the children's home. But a senior officer turning up out of the blue might put Marsh on his guard. Best to wait. Best have a discreet dig into the financial background of the outfit.

That decision left Vera restless. There were plenty of things that she should be doing, though she preferred to be out, walking the land, listening to conversations. She sighed and switched on her computer screen. If she got the admin backlog cleared now, she could head out on the following day. A treat or reward to keep her going. And she still had the birdwatching doctor to meet. He was on the very fringe of the inquiry, but he might have memories of Hector. Positive memories to share.

Her phone rang. A woman's voice that she thought she'd heard before but couldn't immediately recognize. A voice that was slightly louder than necessary, a little theatrical.

'Is that Inspector Stanhope?'

'Yes.' Vera was slightly suspicious. She wished she could place the voice.

'This is Gaby Sullivan. My daughter, Esther, was Chloe's friend.'

Of course, the childminder who was used to catching and holding the attention of toddlers. Whose interaction with her charges was a constant performance.

'I wonder if we could meet.' Then, when Vera didn't respond immediately: 'This isn't something I can discuss on the phone. I'll be interrupted by the children. And I don't want you coming to the house again – my neighbours are intensely nosy and will be asking about you. There's something I want to show you.'

'When were you thinking?' Vera remembered the madhouse of the woman's home. The toddlers only briefly quietened by their half-hour of television. Gaby was right; it wasn't the place for a serious interview.

'I have an early finish today. A couple of my parents work from home at the end of the week and the other is part-time. And Esther isn't home from school until four. There's a café on the estate. In that row of shops by the supermarket. I could meet you there just after three.'

So Vera was released from her desk and her screen after half an hour. She left for the estate where the Sullivans lived, not expecting much more than an escape from the station and a fancy coffee.

She arrived there before the childminder. The shops must have been built when the first houses went up, because they seemed more established than the part of the estate where the Sullivans lived. There was a little boutique, selling the sort of clothes that Vera would never dream of wearing, a post office and a chemist, a small supermarket and the café. There was one elderly woman at the table nearest the counter, chatting to the owner. Vera supposed that this was school pick-up time, so the yummy mummies were otherwise engaged. She ordered a cappuccino and a cheese scone and felt righteous because she'd resisted the temptation of tray bakes covered in butter cream.

Gaby arrived just as the coffee was being delivered to Vera's table by the window. She seemed flustered, but somehow excited as she called across to the owner.

'The same for me too please, Lily.'

So she was a regular.

Vera waited until they were settled and the conversation by the counter had continued.

'Why did you want to see me?' Vera wasn't expecting much. This was a woman with a melodramatic bent, thrilled by the prospect of contributing to a police inquiry.

'It seems that I was wrong, and that Esther had maintained her friendship with Chloe, even after we asked her to keep her distance.'

Good for Esther!

'Does she know where Chloe is?'

Gaby shook her head. 'She claims not.'

'You don't believe her?'

'I don't know what to believe. I can get inside the head of a three-year-old, but teenagers become a mystery, don't they? Hormones kick in and they think they're invincible. That they know everything.'

Vera said nothing. What did she know of the teenage mind? Except that she'd been one herself, and had been at once timid and rebellious, and only determined that Hector would no longer rule her life.

'Perhaps you could tell me exactly what happened.'

'I went into Esther's school bag last night. Not prying. But looking for stray games kit to put into the wash. And I found the letter.'

'A letter from Chloe?' Now Vera was tense, alert. A foxhound with the sense of the hunt in her nostrils.

Gaby nodded.

Vera kept her voice even. Best to play this down and to limit her own expectations. 'A recent letter? Written since Chloe went missing?'

'It's not dated, but certainly that's what it reads like.'

'Of course, you've got it with you?'

'I have.' Gaby reached into a large bag. Vera saw disposable nappies, a couple of soft toys. And a large plastic freezer bag, with a couple of rather crumpled A4 sheets of paper, covered in what was recognizably Chloe's writing. 'I wasn't sure about fingerprints. I only touched the corner once I realized what it was.'

Vera took it and put it into her bag. She'd read it in private, not here with Gaby looking on, wanting a reaction.

'Did you talk to Esther about it?'

'Of course! I couldn't believe that she'd misled us. We were never a family with secrets.'

Oh, bonny lass, if there's one thing I've learned in my life, it's that all families have secrets.

'And what did Esther say?'

'That Chloe had been her best friend since primary school,

225

and she wasn't going to betray her now because Salvation Academy was being unreasonable. It seems that they'd got together secretly. When I thought Esther was at an after-school club or doing her homework in the library because it was quieter than at home, they were hanging out together there, or in the park or in a greasy spoon in Longwater.'

'This was after Chloe had moved to Rosebank?'

Gaby nodded. 'In one way, I'm proud of Esther. She knew Chloe was going through a tough time and stuck by her. I just wish she'd told us what was happening.'

'What would you have done?' Vera wiped scone crumbs from her mouth. 'Would you have told her that she was doing the right thing? Or flown off the handle and demanded that the meetings stop?'

Gaby looked up and smiled. 'Probably that. I'd have been scared of upsetting the school. We've become paranoid about Ofsted ratings and exam results. I care deeply about the happiness of the tinies that I work with, but we just pile on the pressure when they get older.'

'Has Esther seen Chloe since she ran away from Rosebank?'

'She says not, and really I believe her. Now it's come out that they've been meeting outside school, what reason would she have to lie?'

Because sometimes made-up stories are better.

'But they have been communicating since Chloe went on the run?'

'Yes, not by mobile phone though. Esther said Chloe insisted on that. She said if she used her phone she could be traced.'

Vera wondered if Chloe had picked up that gem from the scallies at Rosebank or from television drama. 'So what did she do then? There aren't many phone boxes working anymore.'

'They wrote to each other.'

'If Esther had got a letter through the post, surely you'd have noticed?'

And the mail doesn't deliver that quickly!

'Of course. It's only circulars and bills in the mail these days. I'd have seen a handwritten letter.' Gaby paused. 'No, it seems that they'd devised a system for passing on notes, even before Chloe ran away. They left them in a book in Longwater library. Esther was telling the truth when she said she did go there to do her homework. She just hadn't mentioned that Chloe was there too. They'd chosen an obscure title that they thought nobody would ever borrow.' She looked up at Vera. 'It was quite clever actually. Like something in a spy novel.'

More like something out of the Famous Five *and Enid Blyton.*

Though, Vera thought now, hadn't Enid Blyton first given her the idea that she might become a cop? It was the possibility of sorting out muddles and bringing some clarity and certainty to her world.

It seemed to Vera too, that the library might be a good place for Chloe to hang out during the day now she was on the run. A warm space where nobody would bother her. It would, at least, be worth a look.

'When did Esther last see Chloe?'

'She claims not to have met up with her since Josh Woodburn's murder.' Gaby slowly spooned cappuccino froth from the bottom of the mug.

'You don't believe her?'

'I want to believe her, but really? I just don't know. She seems to have become very good at lying. She's not my well-behaved little girl any longer.'

'Someone else has died,' Vera said. 'A lad who lived at Rosebank with Chloe. His body was found out in the wilds, so there's no connection with the Woodburn killing been made by the press yet, but there must be a link. I don't want to go to your Esther, all heavy-handed and scary, saying she'll be putting Chloe's life in danger if she doesn't tell us everything she knows. I think you'll get more out of her than I will. But if she has any idea where Chloe is she *has* to tell us.'

Gaby was pale and close to tears. 'She'll be home from school soon. I'll talk to her as soon as she gets in.'

'Let me know what she says.' Vera looked up at the woman. 'This is important now. Not a game any longer. If you think she's not telling you everything, we'll have to bring her into the station and talk to her there.'

'I'll make her understand.' The woman's voice was quiet now, hardly more than a whisper. The childminder, used to jollying her charges with her large personality, had disappeared.

'You told me there was another lass, someone they were both friends with. Alice who moved to the Tyne Valley. Do you know exactly where she lives now?'

'Yeah, a village called Gillstead.'

'One more thing, pet. What was the name of the book they used to hide their notes?'

'It was called *Pitmatic: A Study of Regional Coalfield Accents*. By someone called Geoff Milburn.'

'Not exactly a raging bestseller then.'

'No.' Gaby gave a little smile. 'Not quite that.'

The library in Longwater was modern, part of a community hub with a café and a leisure centre. Vera felt an ache of nostalgia for the quiet Victorian building where she'd gone as a child to borrow books. It had been her escape then, and later when she'd joined the police as a cadet. Before doing anything else she found a quiet corner in the reference section and read Chloe's letter through the clear plastic of the bag. It was interesting – and Chloe's voice was so strong that she could almost hear the lass speaking – but it gave no real clue about her present whereabouts. She'd share it with the team at this evening's briefing.

The place was buzzing. At one table a group of women were making proggy mats, and at another some teenagers were sitting around the computers, earnestly doing homework. Chloe wouldn't have been noticed here – even, Vera thought, during school hours. There were discreet corners behind shelves, and besides, it was a place where everyone seemed welcome, and nobody was challenged. A man who was clearly homeless was sitting drowsing over a newspaper.

She flashed her warrant card at the young man behind the desk. 'Have you got a few minutes?'

'Sure.'

'We're looking for this lass.' She got Chloe's photo up on her phone. 'Has she been in recently?'

'Yeah, she's a regular. She's here most nights straight after school, staying sometimes until closing. Sometimes with a friend, but *she* doesn't stay for so long. They're not in today.'

So the library had been Chloe's escape too. From home when her mam was poorly and from the chaos of the children's home. Esther's day was more regulated though. She wouldn't get away with staying out until it closed.

'Was Chloe ever in here when she should have been at school?'

He shrugged. 'I don't remember noticing her here then. Sometimes in the holidays though.'

'When did you last see her?'

He thought for a moment. 'About ten days ago. But I've only just come back from leave.'

'Is there anyone else on duty who would have been here when you were on holiday?'

'Sure, I'll find somebody for you.'

He returned with a middle-aged, motherly woman. The library manager. The badge on her lanyard said she was Laura, and she was there to help. 'You're asking about Chloe?'

'We're concerned about her. She's gone missing.' Vera looked across at her. 'You haven't seen our appeals for information?'

The woman shook her head. Vera thought that she'd over-estimated the efficiency of the police's publicity department. But then headlines changed, and the world moved on to the next drama or catastrophe.

'She was in two days ago,' Laura said. 'She spent most of the day here.' The woman had a Scottish accent, and a brisk, no-nonsense manner.

'Even though it was a school day?'

'Better here than wandering the streets! Some Salvation Academy kids get suspended for the day for relatively minor offences. I'm not going to embarrass them by asking.'

'Did you notice anything unusual the last day she was here?'

'She spent most of the day in her regular haunt in the local history section. It's quiet there, and there's a corner where she can work in private. She came out to get lunch in the café.'

'She had money for lunch?' Vera thought that was positive. She'd imagined Chloe cold and exhausted after her night in the den on the common, perhaps begging like the homeless woman she'd met in Longwater.

'She wouldn't need much to get a decent meal,' Laura said. 'It's run on a not-for-profit basis by volunteers.'

Vera had asked Dave Limbrick if Chloe had money with her when she went on the run, but he'd just shrugged. It was possible, perhaps, that Esther had given her a little cash.

The library manager was still talking. 'This is a safe space. If our readers come in just to use the bathrooms to freshen up, that's their business. We make no judgement here.'

'Is that what Chloe was doing on her last visit?'

Laura gave a little smile. 'I saw her go to the loo. She was a bit tidier when she came out than when she went in. But that wasn't the object of her visit. She spent most of the time she was with us reading. And writing.' There was a pause. 'Because she'd seemed a bit dishevelled when she got here, I meant to go and chat to her and check that she was okay, but it was really busy, we were short-staffed and I was on the counter all morning, so I never quite got round to it. I feel dreadful about that now.'

'Did she meet anyone?' Vera asked. 'Another lass?'

'Not this time. Sometimes she was here just after school with a friend. A quiet slip of a thing. But not that day.' Laura paused and frowned. 'She left before I was expecting her to. It was surprisingly busy in the library. There were several people I didn't recognize. Something seemed to spook her, and she disappeared through the back door into the car park.'

'You think she recognized somebody, and ran away?'

Laura shrugged. 'I could be blowing the whole encounter out of all proportion. I read a lot of crime fiction. I make up exciting stories in my head.'

'Could you describe any of the individuals?'

She shook her head. 'There were a couple of guys and a

woman, but I can't say any more than that. I don't think they came in as a group though.'

'You must have CCTV. Could we take a look?'

'Sorry, it hasn't worked for months and our budget's so tight that we haven't been able to get it fixed.' Laura looked up. 'Perhaps you shouldn't take what I've said too seriously.'

'Well,' Vera said, 'you've been very helpful. You won't mind if I have a browse myself?'

'Of course not! And if you're not a library member, we'll be very happy to join you up.' Laura looked at her watch and disappeared.

Vera wandered across to the local history section. That would surely be where she'd find a book about local dialect. On the way, her attention was caught by other titles, and she stopped occasionally to read the blurb on the back. She didn't want any of the staff to notice exactly what she was looking for.

As Laura had said, this corner was quiet. There were a couple of desks with chairs, where readers could do their own research. And there it was: *Pitmatic: A Study of Regional Coalfield Accents*. A surprisingly large book for such a niche topic. Nothing about it would attract the attention of the general reader.

Vera held it by the covers and shook it gently. A sheet of paper floated to the floor.

The note was short. Nothing like the long letter that Gaby had found in Esther's school bag. It looked as if it had been written hurriedly.

Sorry. Can't meet after all. I think I'm being followed. It's all too weird. Will get in touch as soon as I can but need to disappear for a bit. Then a big curly C and a row of kisses.

Chapter Thirty

SOMETHING HORRIBLE HAPPENED LAST NIGHT. *I can't believe it and I don't know what to do. This is grown-up stuff and I know that it's too much for me to cope with alone, but I don't trust any of the grown-ups around here. It's like there's NOBODY I can trust. Even the people you think would never do you any harm. Like they've all turned into monsters, or vampires or zombies, and they're just pretending to be human. Like they're empty inside with no feelings and no conscience. I can't stay in Rosebank. That's where all the shit things started. I'm hiding out. I won't tell you where in case someone finds this letter. I've come to the library today just to let you know that I'm okay.*

Josh is dead. I was waiting for him, and he didn't come and then I heard from some kids that the police had been in Rosebank all night and searching the common. I told you about Josh and how amazing he was. He was kind and funny and I think he liked me but not in a creepy way. Just like I was a sister or something. He was interested in me, and in the other kids at Rosebank and what was going on there, and now he's gone. I am so well out of that place now. But I'm scared. What if they come after me? I think they're already looking for me.

I can't stay where I am. I don't want to stay with Nana and Grandpa. She hates me and anyway my father is there. I have to hide. I know too much.

Shall we meet in the library? I need to see someone friendly. I feel so lonely. I'll go there during the day. Come straight after school.

Thanks for being such an amazing mate. I don't know what I'd do without you.

Love you loads

Chloe xxxx

Again, the words had been projected onto a screen so the whole team could see them, but Vera read them out anyway. She turned into the room.

'It's not dated, and I guess she's losing track of time now. I certainly am. When do we think this was written?'

Rosie stuck up her hand. Vera was pleased to see that. The lass was becoming more confident within the group.

'I think it's the day after she spent the night in the den on the common. Later she went to the library and left this for Esther.'

Vera nodded. 'You're probably right. The girls probably met up the following day, but the next afternoon Chloe didn't wait for Esther to arrive. Why? Because she was spooked by someone she recognized? So she ran off but left that hurried note for Esther to find. We don't know where she'd spent the night before. She was probably roughing it somewhere, because she went into the toilets to tidy herself up.'

Vera wondered how it had been possible for the lass to avoid the CCTV in the town. She wouldn't have been like the dealers and thieves who'd know where they were all positioned. Perhaps she'd made herself anonymous. Wrapped in a big coat with the hood up, without the distinctive make-up, she'd have been just another kid.

'Now for the big question. Where is she now?'

Again, it was Rosie who answered. 'Could Esther be sheltering her somewhere? A garden shed, a garage?'

'Not at home,' Joe said. 'They wouldn't need the palaver with the notes in the book if Chloe was just on the doorstep.'

'That letter was written a couple of days ago. She could have moved on from there now.'

'If she's staying anywhere close to the Sullivan house, Gaby will find her,' Vera said. 'She's shocked that her lass has been keeping secrets from her. They'll be having a heart-to-heart this evening, and I've asked her to check any places local to her.'

'What about Paradise Farm?' Joe threw out the suggestion. 'There are plenty of outbuildings there and if Chloe still had a bit of money left, there's a bus that goes right past the entrance.'

'How would she know about that place?' Vera was dubious.

'I spoke to Kath, your mate the social worker, earlier today. Before Becky, her mam, went into hospital, Chloe was part of a young carers' group. You know, for kids that take on extra responsibility within the home because of a parent's illness or disability. The group were taken for trips out, and Chloe definitely spent time at the farm.'

Vera tried to process that. It seemed to her that three places were deeply involved in this investigation – Rosebank, Gillstead and Paradise Farm – though the connections between them still seemed tenuous. She'd still not been to the Paradise and the place intrigued her.

'I wonder if Josh talked about Stella to Chloe,' she said. 'In one of those heart-to-hearts they had. He was still in love with her, and he seemed the sort of lad who could get a bit soppy. Chloe might have seen the place as a sort of haven.' She looked first at Rosie and then at Joe. 'You've both talked to Stella. Would she have told you if Chloe was hiding out there?'

His response was immediate. 'Absolutely not!'

'Why?'

'It would be a matter of principle to her. She's one of those eco-warriors who ties themselves to motorway gantries. We're members of the establishment and not to be trusted in any way.'

'I didn't find her quite that dogmatic.' Rosie sounded tentative, unsure. 'Not unreasonable at least. But Joe's right. I think her first impulse would be to protect a friend, especially someone connected to Josh, rather than to persuade her to go to the police.'

Vera stared out at them all, aware that the silence was dragging on, making some people in the room uncomfortable. But she was thinking about the best approach here. Joe was right and Paradise Farm was a potential hiding place for Chloe. Should they go in with a search team and dogs to sniff out the girl as if she was a criminal? A girl who was already vulnerable and scared.

'It sounds as if you got on okay with Stella, Rosie. Why don't you and Joe pay a little visit when we've finished here? They won't be expecting anyone to turn up this time in the evening. If they're sheltering the lassie, surely they'll take her indoors for something to eat, and a bed for a night, even if she's hiding in one of the farm buildings during the day.'

'Sure!' Rosie was all set to leave immediately.

'No rush,' Vera said. 'Let's see what progress we've made during the day. Billy, I think you have some news for us.'

The crime scene manager nodded. 'We found Josh Woodburn's phone with Brad Russell's body. It was in an inside pocket of his jacket. Confirmation, if we needed it, that the cases are linked.'

'Does that make Brad Josh's killer?' Rosie threw out the question.

'The lad could have nicked the phone earlier in the day, but that seems unlikely.'

Vera still couldn't get her head round that one and moved on:

'Any news on the Volvo Dr Hepple noticed on the common?'

Rosie answered. 'Nothing that links to anyone involved in the investigation.'

'Let's keep digging, shall we? See if a similar car has been linked to any criminal activity.'

'You're thinking drugs?'

'The big-boy dealers do love their macho toys.' Vera looked at Joe. 'How did you get on?'

'I spoke to Brad Russell's grandparents.'

'And?'

'It was just really sad. They'd tried to do their best for the boy when he was growing up, but he ran rings round them. They saw him quite recently. He turned up for the grandmother's birthday with a card and chocolates. They said he seemed positive. He claimed to have been offered a job.'

'What sort of a job?'

Joe shook his head. 'They couldn't be specific. They didn't believe it could be anything real. Anything worthwhile.'

'I want you back up at Gillstead tomorrow,' Vera said.

'You *and* Rosie if we don't find Chloe at the Paradise this evening. We know she had some money at least. Probably enough for a bus fare to somewhere within hitching distance.' She looked out at them and had a sudden thought. 'Do people hitch anymore?' It had been how she'd got about when she was a kid and Hector had refused her a lift.

Both Rosie and Joe looked at her with pity – apparently *nobody* hitched these days – so she continued. 'And she'd been to the village recently. I can't think why Brad Russell would have been there if there were no connection with the girl.'

'What do you want us to do when we're there?' Joe asked.

'According to her grandfather, she met a friend at the hotel spa.' Since talking to Gaby, Vera had realized just how important that information might be. 'I think it was a lass called Alice, who'd grown up in Longwater. It's Friday tomorrow. Just make sure you're in the village when the school bus gets in and catch the youngsters on their way home. Track down Alice.' A pause. 'I'd tell your folks it'll be an overnighter and book a couple of rooms at the Stannie Arms. The journos will have moved on to another story, so I'm sure there'll be space. If you can't get a handle on the kids tomorrow evening, you might catch them on Saturday during the day.'

Vera wondered what country kids did these days. Were they still into ponies? The young farmers' club? Drinking illicit cans of strong cider and lager in one of the parents' barns? Or were they like their town counterparts and holed up in their bedrooms shooting people remotely on screen?

She could tell that neither Joe nor Rosie was delighted at the prospect of a night away in the wilds of Northumberland, and that gave her a little moment of spiteful joy. It would do Rosie good to get a glimpse of the outer reaches of their patch.

Now though, it was time for them to head out for the strangely named Paradise Farm, in case Chloe Spence had been close to home all the time. And for her to visit Dr Hepple in his home on the coast. On the way, she called Gordon Spence, but there was no reply.

Chapter Thirty-One

VERA HAD PHONED THE SURGERY EARLIER in the day.

'I need to speak to Dr Hepple.' Introducing herself and making it clear this was urgent.

'He's with a patient at the moment. I'll ask him to call you back.'

Yeah, right. She'd had skirmishes with doctors' receptionists before.

But five minutes later the call had come through. It had been a local voice, friendly but professional. She'd wondered if he might recognize her name, but the conversation was brief, and she could sense that he was busy. Perhaps it hadn't registered, or perhaps he no longer remembered the birdwatcher who'd gifted him a pair of binoculars. After all, he'd moved on a long way since then. He'd agreed that Vera should call at his home that evening.

'You'll have to take us as you find us, mind. It's a bit of a madhouse.'

The Hepple family lived in Warkworth. A bonny village with a castle at one end and the river running through it. A stately main street, a mix of beautiful homes, B&Bs, cafés and small shops. A couple of hotels. A tourist village, as different from Longwater as it was possible to imagine. The doctor's family lived in a modern house just out of the village, on a wooded hill with a view of the sea. It was dark when Vera arrived, but she could see the light buoys in the water. When she got out of the Land Rover, there was the autumn smell of damp leaves and salt.

A woman opened the door to her. She was familiar, but it took Vera a moment to place her. She'd been on the stage at Salvation Academy as chair of the school's trustees, and she'd introduced Helen Miles, the founder, at the prize-giving. Close up, she gave the same impression of professional competence as she had then. She seemed younger than her husband, but Vera thought she was the sort to age well. She had dark hair pulled back into a loose ponytail, jeans and a navy knitted sweater. Nothing showy, but everything well made, classic. The look that Vera would never have been able to achieve, even if she tried.

'You must be Inspector Stanhope! Come in. I've just made a pot of coffee and the kids have retreated to their rooms.' She was friendly too, though not local. Unless her family had been too grand for her to have acquired an accent. 'Jimmy's in the living room. Just through that door. I'll bring the coffee in.'

Despite the age of the house, the room had an air of solidity and grace. There was a fire burning in the grate and it was lined with shelves made, it seemed, of reclaimed wood. On the shelves, books she recognized – field guides not just to birds but to butterflies, moths and plants, monographs about single species, travel guides. Hector's library hadn't been so extensive, but the two men had clearly shared a passion. There were blinds at the windows, but they hadn't been lowered. Jimmy sat at an old oval table reading a magazine. He was wearing specs, which he pushed onto the top of his head when she came in. He jumped to his feet, held out a hand.

'Inspector, take a seat. I'll just shift this stuff out of the way.' He moved a pile of files and notebooks from a chair close to the fire.

'Isn't everything online these days?' She took off her coat, folded it onto the arm of the chair and took the seat.

'Oh, for work, though you'd be surprised how much is still waiting to be digitalized. But this is my private passion. I'm writing a book on the natural history of the Longwater Valley, and I'm looking at the old records. Some of this is personal from local birders, the rest is made up from newsletters and natural history society reports.' He grinned. 'Sometimes I think I must have been mad to take it on but then I've got this far so it would be madness to give up.'

Vera thought he wasn't the sort of man to give up easily.

The woman came in with a tray.

'You've met my wife, Susie. She tolerates my madness.'

Susie rolled her eyes at Vera.

'I've seen you before,' Vera said, 'at the Salvation Academy in Longwater. That's where our missing lass goes to school.' A pause. 'Helen Miles didn't tell you?'

'No.' The woman frowned. She clearly thought she should have been informed but felt the need to be diplomatic. 'I'm not really hands-on. My role is more supervisory.'

'How did you get involved with the place?'

'Through Helen, the founder. The academy was her idea, her baby. I'm an employment lawyer and our company has worked with her over the years. She's a very impressive woman.

She grew up in Longwater, left school with no qualifications, and even had brushes with the law when she was young. She started off building up her own scrap metal business – very much a male preserve even now – but her real talent is in finding the right companies to back. She turned her life around and wanted to give something back, to give local kids the opportunities that she never had.' Susie looked up at Vera. 'We don't only work together, we also worship at the same church. Her faith is what drives her.'

Vera was tempted to ask if pupils wearing the right colour socks was a tenet of faith but managed to resist. There was a moment of silence before Susie smiled and spoke again.

'I'll leave you to it and check the kids are actually doing homework and not killing each other on their screens. Don't let him lecture you about the importance of the Longwater Valley to migrating wading birds, Inspector. He's ruined many a good dinner party. My colleagues are very wary of coming anywhere near.'

She left the room. Jimmy Hepple watched her go affectionately. 'She doesn't mention that I find *her* colleagues equally tedious. I'm not entirely sure how we get on so well. We have nothing at all in common. She teaches in Sunday school, and I'm a committed atheist. Luckily, she gave up trying to convert me years ago. And I've stopped dragging her out on my birding trips.'

He poured coffee and took one of the other comfortable chairs. 'You might be interested in my magnum opus though. Some of your father's records are in here.'

Vera looked up at him, not knowing how to react.

'You are Hector Stanhope's daughter? There can't be that many Vera Stanhopes in Northumberland.'

'He mentioned me?'

The doctor nodded. 'I was very young of course, but Hector was kind to me. He made a difference. And perhaps because I was just a child, he talked to me, about the fact that you wanted to join the police.' He looked up. 'Another reason why I knew you must be his daughter.'

'He gave you a pair of binoculars.'

'He did! And the world suddenly became clear. I always had good eyesight, but I started picking up details that I'd missed before.' There was a pause. 'I lost touch with him as I got older. I focused more on my academic work. Besides . . .'

'. . . he had a reputation as an egg thief and a trader in raptors stolen from the wild. You wouldn't want to be known as his friend.'

'I wasn't just worried about what the others would think. I disapproved of what he was doing. Violently. And it was such a waste! He was a brilliant naturalist. But his records were accurate, and they'll go into the book. That'll be some sort of legacy, of rehabilitation.'

'Let me know when it's published. I'd like a copy.'

'Of course. But I'm sure you're not here to talk about Hector or me. How can I help you?'

'Someone else attached to Rosebank has died. Brad Russell. He was registered with your surgery.'

'I heard about it,' Hepple said. 'News spreads on the estate. He was still on the books of his family doctor close to his grand-parents' home, but I saw him a few times, talked about his health, tried to give him advice about drugs.' A pause. 'He tried to con a script for methadone from me, but he must have realized he didn't have a chance. I told him to discuss it with his own GP. That was the impression I had of him – he was a chancer.'

'We found his body in Gillstead.' Vera paused for a moment. The coffee was too good to be hurried. 'A car similar to the one you saw close to the common was seen in the village. Of course, it could be a coincidence, but we'd like to follow up the possibility that it was the same vehicle. Have you been back birding since my sergeant spoke to you?'

'Yes, this time of year, I'm there most mornings before I start work. Especially if there's an easterly wind and a bit of drizzle to bring in the migrants. As Hector's daughter, you'll understand the excitement.'

Vera had never shared Hector's passion, and she shook her head slightly. 'Have you seen the car again?'

'No.' Hepple was quite clear. 'There was nothing else parked close to the common on either of the mornings I was there. I went after work on Tuesday too. There was a car then, but it was a regular, belonging to a dog-walker I see all the time.'

'What time were you there on Tuesday evening?'

'Earlier than usual. Five-ish. I was gone by six. It's starting to get dark early now, and I had a meeting in the evening.'

So even if the Volvo had been there to pick up Brad, Hepple might have missed it by a few minutes. Vera got to her feet. She wanted to be home and there might soon be some news from Joe and Rosie's visit to Paradise Farm.

Jimmy and Susie came to the door to wave her off. She thought she'd probably gained nothing relevant to the investigation, but still, it hadn't quite been a waste of time. There'd be a book. Something to remember Hector by. And she'd met a man with at least some fond memories of her father.

Chapter Thirty-Two

THEY DROVE TO PARADISE FARM IN Joe's car. Rosie thought at least they weren't in Vera's battered Land Rover, which she was sure broke all sorts of rules. If cops were using their own cars, they were supposed to be roadworthy and relatively new. The boss's vehicle must have something wrong with the suspension – it bounced and rattled – and the heating didn't seem to work. Certainly, every time Rosie had been inside, it had been bloody cold. It had become a bit of an obsession, wondering how Vera got away with it. She was tempted to ask Joe, but she'd already realized that he would never speak ill of the boss.

The gate to the farm track was closed and Rosie had to get out and open it and then stand in the cold while Joe drove through. He'd brought a thick jacket and a scarf, but *she* wasn't dressed for a late-night adventure. She never felt chilly in the city, even when there was a frost and they were out in the early morning after a night clubbing. Geordies were famous for it. This was different though and she wished she'd brought a coat.

Although it was dark, there was a glow on the horizon to the south and the west. They were so close to the conurbations that the sky was polluted by their street lights. All the same, there were stars above her that were never visible from her flat in Heaton, dizzying.

Vera had given them detailed instructions, which of course Joe followed to the letter.

Don't park too close to the house. It doesn't matter if you block the way. There'll be no tractors coming through at this time of night, and you don't want to warn them that you're there. Not until you've had a good look round any of the outhouses.

He pulled into the side of the track a hundred yards from the gate. They walked in silence towards the house, but Joe stopped at the edge of the yard. 'Let's have a quick look in some of the outbuildings, shall we?' He was whispering, but Rosie could tell he was uncomfortable. Obedience to Vera was challenging his natural reluctance to break any rules. 'See if there's any sign that the girl has been here.'

The big barn was open-sided, and they could see that nobody was hiding there. Joe moved on to the smaller outbuildings. These were bolted shut from the outside, but not locked.

The bunk room seemed empty, and the concrete floor had been swept clean. Rosie stood inside and pointed her torch into every corner. Joe was outside. She could tell he was shitting himself in case anyone should come out of the house. For a brief, heart-stopping moment Rosie imagined a girl's body on one of the bunks, but she could tell a moment later that it was a pile of blankets.

The former pigsty or stable was unlocked and unbolted. Half of it contained logs, neatly stacked, ready for use in the fire in the house. In the other half there was hay, loose not baled.

Rosie was poking it with her foot, looking for anything that might be hidden underneath. Joe followed after her to see what she was doing, forgetting for a moment his caution and anxiety. There was sudden white light and a yell.

'Hey! What the fuck do you think you're doing?' It was a young voice. A girl. For a moment Rosie thought it might be Chloe, because surely she'd be the sweary kind. But when she turned, she realized it was Stella. She was carrying a wicker basket and must be here to collect logs. She'd switched on the light near the door.

Beside her Joe seemed frozen. Rosie found that she was trembling with shock, but she channelled her inner Vera. 'We're looking for a missing child.'

'You could have come and asked permission first!'

'We could have done.' At last Joe seemed to have found his voice. 'We just thought we'd have a little look before we disturbed you. I take it that it's all right if we come into the house for a chat.'

'I don't know! Have you got a warrant?' Stella stared at Rosie. 'I should have known better than to trust you. You're just like the others.' Spitting out the words.

'Don't blame her.' Joe seemed to have discovered his inner Vera too. 'I'm the senior officer here. This was my decision and my responsibility.'

'You don't need a warrant, officers.' The voice came from just outside the shed. Will Marsh was standing there. 'It wasn't very courteous to start searching without our permission, but we won't make an issue of it. Will we, Stella?' The last question held a note of warning. 'Why don't you come into the warm and you can explain how we can help you?'

★　★　★

They sat in the little living room where Rosie had talked to Stella on her last visit. No offer of tea or coffee this time. Both Marshes made it clear that they weren't welcome guests. Will remained standing, with his back to the fire, until Joe spoke:

'I'm sorry. Of course it was rude not to come and ask you first.'

Marsh nodded an acceptance of the apology and took the remaining seat. 'Could you tell us what you were doing, searching our property?'

'We're looking for the young girl, Chloe Spence. She's only fourteen but she's been missing since Josh was killed.'

'Why would you think she'd be here?'

'Apparently she came here as a volunteer. She was part of the young carers' group before her mother went into hospital and social services took over.' Joe paused. 'We thought she might see it as a safe place, and there are plenty of places to hide out.' He looked across at the man. 'You haven't taken pity on her? Taken her in?'

Marsh didn't reply directly. 'Why would she have run away?'

'Josh's dead body was found on the common near Rosebank. It's possible that she saw the killer, or at least suspects their identity. We believe that she's scared for her own safety.'

'Why wouldn't she just go to the police?' Stella asked.

Rosie jumped in now. 'Would *you* go to the police if you were in trouble? You don't have much faith in us, do you? And poor Chloe's been let down all her life by people in authority. According to her teachers, she's given to weird conspiracy theories. Maybe she's decided she's better on her own.'

'You mentioned Chloe,' Stella said, 'when you came to talk to me about Josh.'

'I did. Josh was kind to her. He made a difference to her. I think she had a bit of a crush on him.'

'He was kind to everyone.'

'Do you remember her?' Joe said. 'Apparently she came a few times with the young carers' group. She might well have stood out. A bit gothic in dress, make-up and temperament.'

Stella shrugged. 'They're all a bit that way inclined.' As if, Rosie thought, she was an old woman commenting on the youth of today, not a teenager herself.

'Kath Oliver the safeguarding team leader brought her along. It seems she's a big fan of your project.'

'Ah,' Will said. 'We're a great fan of hers. She comes to volunteer even if she's not bringing a group.'

'So neither of you remember Chloe and you've not seen anyone like her hanging around the farm?' Joe was persisting with the question, which still hadn't been properly answered.

'We haven't,' Will said. Rosie noticed that Stella made no comment. 'Of course, if we see her, we'll get in touch with you. Won't we, love?' That question was directed to his daughter.

'Yeah,' Stella said. 'Of course.'

'If that's all,' Will said, 'we'll see you out. We have to be up early in the morning to care for the animals.'

Rosie got to her feet – she'd be glad to get home – but Joe didn't move immediately. 'Would you mind if we have a quick look around the house?' His voice was apologetic. 'I know we don't have a search warrant, but just to set our minds at rest, so we don't need to bother you again.' When there was no immediate response, he continued speaking. 'I don't think we'd have any bother *getting* a warrant, sir. This is a high-profile murder case, and a vulnerable lass is missing. Our Police and

Crime Commissioner is desperate to get the whole thing cleared up quickly before the press go into hysterics and start sending out accusations. This way it would be quieter, and we could eliminate the idea from our inquiries.'

Rosie regarded him with increased respect.

Will shot a glance at Stella before answering. 'Sure!' he said. 'Why not? It's not as if we have anything to hide.'

'That's very kind of you,' Joe said. 'We'll start upstairs, shall we? Then we can leave you in peace to go to bed.'

'Why don't we wait here?' Will's voice was dry. 'We wouldn't want to get in the way.'

'Very sensible. We'll not be long.'

And it did take very little time. There were three bedrooms. Will had the biggest at the front of the house. There was a wooden wardrobe that would have been large enough to hide a small girl, but only held clothes. Most were of good quality but old. There was nothing flash or new. Rosie checked under the bed, just to be certain.

Stella's room was a blast of colour, the walls covered in posters. Most were filled with slogans – protesting about the building of new roads, a secure centre for asylum seekers, the destruction of the rainforest – but others promoted gigs and festivals. It wasn't Rosie's choice of music. She hadn't heard of most of the bands. There was a charcoal sketch of Stella leaning against a five-bar gate, her hair blowing loose. That would have been done by Josh, probably when they were still at school together. There was no sign that Chloe had been here, no sleeping bag on the floor, no clothes that would have fitted her.

The last room was tiny and contained nothing but piles of books and luggage: a couple of rucksacks and suitcases. There was certainly nowhere to hide here. The bathroom was basic. An old bath with a shower over it, a sink and a toilet.

Joe stood at the door and looked in. 'Only two toothbrushes. If Chloe was ever in the house, I'd say she's left. Let's have a quick look downstairs and then we'll get off. I'm ready for home. I've already missed the kids' bedtime.'

Will and Stella were still in the living room, chatting a little too loudly about trivial matters concerning the farm, pretending that having a couple of detectives searching the house was nothing out of the ordinary. They'd left the door open, and Rosie could hear them as she continued the search. She looked in the kitchen, peering into a pantry with shelves of tins and dried pulses. She opened a door into a lean-to that housed an old washing machine, a sink and a row of boots. There was a smell of dog, but nothing else. Joe took on the dining room, which, from what Rosie could see from the hall, was dark and gloomy and seemed seldom used.

They landed up together at the door to the living room. Joe called to the father and daughter inside. 'We've finished now. Thanks for your help and sorry to have bothered you. We'll leave you in peace. No need to show us out.'

Before the Marshes could answer, he'd led Rosie outside into the yard, shutting the door firmly behind him. Joe started to make his way straight back to the car, but Rosie touched his arm.

'Hang on a minute.'

They stood under the starry sky, until all the downstairs lights in the house were switched off.

There was enough of a moon to see the silhouettes of the outhouses.

'What are you doing?' Joe was impatient. He obviously thought the whole evening had been a waste of time.

'There's just something I'd like to check.' Rosie started making her way to the smallest shed where the logs and hay had been stored. 'Can you give me a shout if the lights come on down-stairs again, or you see either of them heading this way?'

She was in the outbuilding before Joe could answer. Using the torch on her phone to see into the corner where she'd been looking when Stella had surprised them, she crouched by the pile of hay and raked through it with her fingers until she saw that metallic glint again.

Outside, Joe seemed to be feeling the cold, despite his thick jacket. He'd wrapped his arms around his body. Wuss.

'Well? Found anything?'

Rosie closed the door of the shed quietly. 'I'll show you once we've left the premises. Let's get out of here, shall we, before they come out to check that we've gone?'

They walked the rest of the way to the car in silence. Halfway there, a fox crossed their path, alert but completely unafraid.

Joe drove on until they'd gone through the gate and past the cattle grid, then he pulled to a stop.

'Well?' he said again.

Rosie pulled an evidence bag from her pocket. Inside there was a silver chain with three cheap charms attached. Three letters. Not real silver, but some cheap metal made to look like it. Something you might pick up on a market stall, or in a shop full of tat to attract the kids. C, E and A.

'I thought I saw something in the hay when Stella caught us.' Rosie was feeling triumphant now. This was a trophy to take back to Vera. 'A bit of a glint. It was worth going back to look properly.'

'C, E and A,' Joe said. 'Chloe and Esther? And the lass Alice that the boss was asking about.'

'A bit of a coincidence, if not. I bet the other girls have one too. We can find out.' Rosie paused. 'So it seems that Chloe was there, and she dropped the chain. That means that Stella and Will were lying.'

'Well, that doesn't necessarily follow, does it? There was no sign of the lass inside the house. She could have hidden out there one night without the Marshes knowing.'

'Do you think that's likely?' Rosie couldn't keep the scepticism from her voice.

'I think it's possible.' Joe started the engine. 'We know she felt safe in wild places, and after the common at Longwater, this is as wild as it gets round here.' A pause. 'The other explanation is that they *were* involved in Josh's murder and that they brought her here so she couldn't come to us.'

He drove on down the track. Rosie was glad that they'd come to a real road, other traffic.

'Do you think Chloe is still alive?' Her imagination was working overtime now. She was thinking that there were lots of places to bury a body on a farm. She'd seen stuff on the television. Pigs eating all the evidence of the dead person, even the bones. Were there pigs at the Paradise? She didn't like to mention that to Joe.

He took a while to answer. 'I can't see the Marshes as killers and honestly, what motive would they have? All the evidence shows that Josh Woodburn wasn't any sort of stalker. He was no danger to Stella. And surely the only reason to get rid of Chloe would be if she saw his murderer.' He seemed to be concentrating on the road ahead of him and it was a while before he spoke again. 'They might just have wanted to help the lass when she was confused and in trouble. In that case,

I'm not sure why they decided to lie to us tonight.' A pause. 'Perhaps there *is* a more sinister explanation.'

Joe, it seemed, was as confused as she was. 'I'll give the boss a ring when I get in. Let her know what we've found.'

What I *found!*

He dropped Rosie at Kimmerston police station to pick up her car. Before driving off, he opened the window and shouted out: 'If you're going to stick with this team, Vera thinks you might want to consider moving a bit further north. Get out of the city, be closer to our patch.'

Then he was gone.

Driving back towards Newcastle and the flat that she loved, Rosie wasn't sure what to make of that. Why hadn't Vera passed on the message herself? Was it an order or a bit of advice? Or was Joe Ashworth just stirring? It occurred to her that Vera might want a sign of her commitment, to know that she intended to stay and make a go of it. How could she answer when she didn't know herself?

Chapter Thirty-Three

EARLY NEXT MORNING, VERA CALLED THEM to a briefing in her office. She needed to talk to Joe and Rosie before they set off for the hills.

She was troubled, uncertain. She wasn't hit by a lack of confidence very often, but Rosie's discovery of the silver chain in the shed at the Paradise had thrown her. Her conversation with Jimmy Hepple had thrown her too. Bloody Hector always came back at the most awkward time to unsettle her.

'I feel as if I've lost focus on Brad Russell,' she said now. A confession to her team, but a challenge too, because she thought *they* weren't taking his death sufficiently seriously. 'Just because he was a scally, it's as if his death isn't as important as Josh Woodburn's or as tracking down Chloe Spence. Remember you're going up to Gillstead to get more details on him too. He was his mam's son after all, and she'll be grieving.'

'He made his grandparents' life a nightmare,' Joe said, 'but they're missing him in their own way.'

'Someone took him there to kill him. They must have fed

him some story. He'd be too canny to allow himself to be bundled into a car without any fuss.'

'Brad told his grandparents he'd got a smart new job. He might have been streetwise, but he wasn't very bright. I don't think it'd be hard to con him with tales of a bright new future.'

Vera looked across at her sergeant. 'Even by some stranger?'

'Yeah, by someone who looked neatly groomed and spoke well. He'd be impressed by all that, easily taken in.'

'Aye,' Vera said. 'You're probably right, Joe. We all believe what we want to believe in the end.'

There was a silence, broken by Rosie, impatient. 'So what do you think we should be looking for when we arrive at Gillstead?'

'Well, if I knew that, pet, I'd already have told you!' Vera snapped before she could stop herself, then decided it wasn't the lass's fault that she was getting so introspective. She shook her head. A sort of apology. 'Talk to the kids. You can meet them from the school bus. Find the mysterious Alice. They're more likely to talk to you than to me, even than Joe here, who looks and sounds more like a teacher than one of them. Their parents might all be in bed by ten, but I bet they still have some sort of life, and even if they're in their rooms gaming, they'll still be awake at midnight. So did they see the strange car that Mary Lister described? Maybe catch a glimpse of Brad Russell?' Vera took a breath before continuing. 'And most importantly, have any of them seen Chloe?'

'You don't think she's still at the Paradise then?'

'Nah. It sounds as if the Marshes were far too relaxed when you started searching. Will's not daft. He'd know he didn't have to let you in at all. And it's possible that Stella only let him know that Chloe had been there once she'd left.'

'So you think Chloe might have headed for the hills? Even though Brad's body was found in Gillstead?' Rosie was perched on the radiator. 'Wouldn't she realize the killer might be there?'

'Good point, pet. But she might have headed to the village before news of his death leaked out. Even if she has her phone with her, she won't have been able to charge it if she's been camping out.'

There was a moment of silence while they were all working through the possibilities. 'We know Chloe had some cash with her,' Vera said, 'and she could have made her own way up into the hills. Someone might be sheltering her. She could have woven some tale about being in danger – she was good at telling stories – and for the locals there, Russell's death would have made that more credible.'

Vera was wondering if she should go to Gillstead herself. It wasn't that she didn't trust her team, but she was the fixer, wasn't she? And it was her territory. She'd understand it better than they would. All the same, there was something important she wanted to do on the coast first.

'I'm staying here to see Esther Sullivan.' She looked across the desk at them. She didn't have to explain her movements, but she'd decided, hadn't she, to be more communicative with the team, more collaborative? 'Her mam was going to talk to her last night, but I'm not sure Esther would be entirely truthful.' Vera thought of Gaby, imagined her all weepy and guilty. Not quite saying: *What did we do wrong that you hide things from us?* But certainly passing the guilt trip on to her daughter. 'I thought it would be more straightforward if I saw the lass at school.'

And I want to see those teachers again, now we have other leads to follow. The Salvation Academy would be the sort of place to be hot on extracurricular activities, wouldn't it? Something else to stick in the brochure and impress the inspectors. Things like voluntary service and the Duke of Edinburgh Award Scheme. She could imagine the teachers organizing trips to Paradise Farm. And maybe they'd taken the kids hiking in the hills.

Vera arrived at the school as the mid-morning break was just ending. She waited until the kids had disappeared inside, before going to reception and asking if Miss Wiseman, Chloe's tutor, was available.

'Who wants to see her?'

'Inspector Stanhope, Northumbria Police.' Vera had her warrant card ready to show.

'Oh, I think the head would like to be informed that you're here.'

'I'm sure he would, pet, but I very definitely don't want him sticking his neb in. So unless you'd like to be charged with obstructing the police in their inquiries, perhaps you could tell me where I can find Miss Wiseman. If she's teaching, I'll wait.'

'She's teaching year ten drama. It's a practical session.'

'And where will she be?'

'In the drama studio.'

Vera had seen a sign to the studio on a door on her previous visit and had at least some idea where she was heading. She set off, followed by plaintive calls from the receptionist that she needed to sign in.

In Vera's school days, any performance took place in the hall where the kids would have assembly every morning, belting out hymns and mumbling the prayers. It would also serve as a gym with wall bars, and a stack of vaulting horses and mats in one corner. The stink of adolescent sweat and feet. But this was a real studio theatre, with an area of banked seating and a full lighting system. Inside, the students were working in small groups, sitting on the floor in apparently earnest discussion. Rachel Wiseman was walking around, chatting to them. She looked up when Vera came in and gave a little wave. There was no natural light, and it took Vera a moment to get used to the shadows.

'Impressive facilities,' she said. 'I don't expect you'll get this at Birks.'

'True. But the kids are improvising their own script. They'd be able to do this anywhere.' Rachel shouted to the kids to start blocking out the moves. 'Make some notes on the dialogue. Think about each of the characters, the specific words they'd use.'

She took a seat in the front row and Vera joined her.

Rachel spoke in almost a stage whisper. 'Have you found Chloe?'

'Not yet, but we think she's still alive. She might have been hiding out at a place called Paradise Farm. Does the name mean anything to you?'

Rachel shook her head.

'It's a kind of eco smallholding. They do stuff around sustainability.'

'Sorry, I don't think our kids have been involved.'

Vera thought that made sense. After all, she couldn't see Helen Miles or the school approving of the ageing hippy or his green-warrior daughter. Or the muck and the mess.

'What about the Duke of Edinburgh Award Scheme?'

'Oh, we're a part of that. It looks very good on university applications.'

Of course. Never mind that it'd get town kids out into the fresh air, and that they might actually enjoy it.

Rachel was still talking. 'One of our governors runs the Gillstead Hall hotel. He lets our kids camp in a corner of the grounds, and they walk out from there. It's become a legendary expedition within the school. They do more than twenty miles over the weekend.'

'So Chloe Spence went on the Duke of Edinburgh expedition?'

'She did, though she was a bit young. They don't usually get to take part until they're much older, in the sixth form. But she was desperate to go, and I asked Fred Lee who organizes it if he could make an exception. He took her out on a couple of the practice hikes, and he said she'd definitely cope. I went along too. Of course we had to have a woman with them. It nearly killed me, but Chloe loved every minute. She was a different student out on the hills, chatty, relaxed.'

'When was the expedition in Gillstead?'

'Not long after term started. Mid-September.'

So Chloe would be more familiar with the terrain around Cragside than any of them had realized. She hadn't just been there on that recent day trip with her grandfather. She had a close friend there, and she'd know good places to camp in the hotel grounds. Presumably the kids had been well out of sight of the hotel guests.

'Can you remember exactly where you were camping?'

Rachel shook her head. 'It was nowhere near the main building, and we had to carry all the kit miles from the car park. There was a kind of shed with a composting toilet that we were allowed to use. I guess maybe it had been put there for the gardening staff. No showers. It made me realize that I'm really not into roughing it.'

'Anything else you remember?'

'It was next to a high stone wall. That gave us some shelter from the weather.'

In the body of the studio, the students were getting bored and restive. 'Sorry,' Rachel said. 'I'll have to get back to them.'

'Of course.'

Rachel stood up.

'I don't suppose you can tell me where I can find Esther Sullivan?' Vera asked.

'Sure! She's here, in my drama group.'

'Okay if I have a word with her?'

Rachel hesitated.

'I don't want to go through formal channels! I certainly don't want the school authorities to know. I can just talk to her for a few minutes here.'

Rachel shrugged. Vera could tell what she was thinking: *What have I got to lose? Another couple of months and I'll be out of this place.*

They sat right at the top of the raked level of seating, looking down on the group. Here it was almost dark. They wouldn't be heard, and they'd hardly be seen. The students had started acting out their improvisations and there was a background hum of conversation. Esther was a slight, dark girl, quiet and intense.

'You've been keeping in touch with Chloe. I know you've been a good friend to her.' Vera pulled the evidence bag with the chain and charm out of her pocket. 'I'm guessing you've got one of these too.'

'Yes, we went to Whitley on the bus once and there was a stall on the seafront selling them.' A pause. 'It was a brilliant day. We went swimming, had chips and ice cream.'

'That was while Chloe was still living at home? And before your friend Alice had moved to Gillstead?'

Esther shook her head. 'Alice had already moved, but she came back for the day.' She looked up at Vera. 'It was like she'd never been away. Chloe said we were like the Three Dark Wives and told us a story about the standing stones where Alice lives. One of her mam's friends had come in to keep her company, so Chloe had the whole Saturday free. I told my mother I was out with other friends.'

'So it was after school had warned you to keep a distance?'

'Yes.' Nothing else. The girl's mouth was shut in a straight line. Esther might appear compliant, but Vera thought she was as stubborn as her friend.

'You've seen her since she went missing?'

For a while, Vera thought Esther would stick to the story she'd fed to her mother, but in the end she nodded. 'Only once.'

'When was that?'

'Two days after she stopped coming to school.'

'In Longwater public library?'

Another nod. 'We pretended not to be friends any more in school, but we met there most afternoons after class. I wasn't sure she'd be there, but I went on the off chance.'

Vera thought through the timeline. 'Do you know where she was planning to stay that evening?'

'Chloe said she had an idea where she might go, but she wasn't going to tell me. Not because she didn't trust me, but because she didn't want to put me in any danger. She knew by then that Josh Woodburn had been killed.'

'She didn't see the murder?' This, Vera thought, was important.

Esther shook her head. 'Chloe told me that Josh had saved her. He'd made sure she hid away.'

'But she knew who'd killed Josh?'

'She didn't know for certain, but she'd guessed.' There was a pause. Esther obviously knew the question that would come next. 'She didn't tell me that either. She was really, really scared. She thought I'd go to the police or tell my parents and she couldn't trust anyone. That was what she said. "They could all be in it together."'

'That wasn't one of her conspiracy theories? One of the stories she liked to follow online?'

Esther thought about that for a while. 'Maybe, but she seemed really to believe it. Before, it had always seemed a bit of a joke. Like the Wicca thing and the Three Dark Wives. She didn't take that seriously, but it freaked out the other girls. They really thought she might put spells on them.'

'Do you know where she is now?'

'No! We were supposed to meet in the library again. But she wasn't there. She just left me a note.'

'Yes,' Vera said, 'we found it. Why didn't you take it with you?'

'I panicked,' Esther said. 'I just wanted to get home.'

That made sense to Vera. It seemed that the class was winding up, and she still had a couple of questions. She went on quickly: 'Did you give her any cash?'

Esther nodded. 'I have my own bank card. I went to a cash machine and took out some of my birthday money.'

'How much did you give her?'

'Fifty pounds.' Esther sounded proud. 'I don't care if she never pays it back.'

'You're a good friend to her,' Vera said. But the bell started ringing as she spoke, and she wasn't sure that Esther had heard.

The theatre emptied. Esther got to her feet. Vera put her hand on the girl's arm. 'If you hear from her, you must tell me. Here's my card.'

Esther took it, but still seemed uncertain. 'She's not in bother, pet. She's in danger.'

Esther nodded and ran lightly down the steep stairs to the bottom of the studio and out of the door. Rachel had already left with her students. Vera followed more slowly. She gave a cheery wave to the receptionist and went out through the main doors.

As soon as she got back to Kimmerston, Vera phoned Joe. They were still on their way to Gillstead and Rosie was driving.

'I need you to search the grounds of the Gillstead Hall hotel for signs that Chloe may have been staying there. Follow the wall. The teacher I spoke to said they set up camp right next to it. If you can, do it without letting the hotel staff know what you're up to.'

'Won't that be trespassing?'

'Nah, access to the grounds is free to any of the hotel guests. Go and have a late lunch afterwards. That'll put you in the clear.'

'On expenses?'

Vera could hear Rosie sniggering in the background. 'Aye, but I'll be checking. A sandwich, a coffee and a bag of crisps. Not the full three-course à la carte.'

'Anything else we're looking out for?'

'A shed with a composting toilet. Handy if you get caught short.' She was about to end the call but threw out a last instruction. 'You'd best get a wiggle on if you're going to make the school bus. You might not have time for lunch, after all.

ANN CLEEVES

You might have to make do with a pint and a plate of chips in the Stannie Arms later. We need to track down that Alice.'

There was no response.

Vera could feel the pull of the hills. She wanted to be there with them, sniffing around the woodland of the hotel's estate. Sometimes, there was no pleasure in being the boss, being stuck behind a desk. But in the school with its corporate branding and its logo, she'd started to get an inkling of another explanation for all that had gone on. She thought that Katherine Willmore, the Police and Crime Commissioner, might be the person to help. She socialized with politicians and the great and the good. And she owed Vera Stanhope a favour.

Chapter Thirty-Four

JOE STOPPED AS FAR AWAY FROM the Gillstead Hall entrance as they could. There were three car parks, all surrounded by trees. Always a stickler for rules, Joe suggested they went in for a quick coffee before they started their search. Then they'd be justified in wandering round the grounds. He always felt uneasy in smart places. Confidence seeped away. And this was a very smart place. A huge house, built in the eighteenth century. It was hard to believe that until recently it had been a private home.

Rosie hadn't taken much persuading. 'Sure!'

The coffee was good and the service was swift, so twenty minutes later they were outside again.

'The boss said the school group set up base a long walk from where they left the cars, and it was next to the wall.'

'Well, it's a bloody long wall,' Rosie said. 'Shall we split up? One of us to walk clockwise and the other anticlockwise and when we meet in the middle we'll be about as far from the building as it's possible to get.'

Joe didn't like Rosie calling the shots, but he couldn't think of a better plan. They started off from a walled garden at the back entrance to the hotel. It was close to the house and kitchen staff appeared from time to time to pick herbs, so if Chloe had been hiding out here, she'd soon have been spotted.

Joe's walk led him anticlockwise. At first he was parallel to the road, and glimpsed the tops of tractors, and heard the occasional rumble of a forestry truck. The ground underfoot was slightly boggy, and the wall covered in moss and lichen. The trees were widely spaced here, and the landscape reminded him of parkland, the setting of some grand period drama. He could imagine a carriage arriving down the drive, which he could glimpse in the distance; it would be bearing men in breeches and women in fancy gowns to a ball. There was a background sound of birdsong, which Vera would be able to identify, but which meant nothing to him.

The wall took a right-angle and the woodland became denser, the undergrowth less easy to walk through. Soon he lost all sight of the big house, the drive or the road. Any traffic noise was muffled by the trees. In places, he had to move away from the wall, and fight his way back to it later. There was something intimidating about being alone in a landscape that was so alien to him. Once, he stopped to catch his breath. He heard a scuffling sound. Not Chloe, but some unidentified animal sheltering under a pile of dead branches, blown down in a storm.

The grounds were more extensive than he'd thought. He'd expected a short walk, then lunch and to be well finished in time for the school bus to arrive at four-thirty. It seemed now that lunch might be a hurried affair. He pulled out his phone, thinking to check in with Rosie, but there was no signal. He was beginning to regret the decision to split up. He was uneasy about having agreed to a new young officer wandering here on her own when there might be a killer tracking their moves. He couldn't imagine how Vera would react if anything happened to another of her officers.

At last he came to another corner, another sharp turn. Now he must have reached the area furthest away from the big house. Here the wall was crumbling in places. Perhaps stone had been stolen by long-ago farmers to build barns or repair their own boundaries. There were gaps to see through and beyond there was a bare hillside and grazing sheep. Inside the boundary, the land was still densely wooded. There were indications of forestry work. Dead trees had been felled and stripped of smaller branches. Long straight trunks had been rolled together, apparently awaiting collection.

He heard a sound. Footsteps cracking small twigs, a jacket brushing against overhanging branches. Joe hoped he wouldn't have to explain his presence to one of the estate workers, and the old impostor syndrome kicked in. He stood still for a moment and thought he was being ridiculous. He was a detective with years of experience investigating a double murder. He had every right to be here.

'Hello! Who's there?'

No reply.

'Rosie? Is that you?' Because although he was sure he hadn't reached the centre point of the boundary, Rosie was younger and probably fitter. Her walk might have been less obstructed. She might well have got there before him and carried on, knowing that eventually they'd meet up.

Still there was no response, but the noise of distant footsteps returned, and this time the rhythm was faster, and the sound grew more faint. Someone was running away. He shouted after them. 'Hey! Stop! Who is it?'

Silence. He knew there was no point in trying to follow. They were long gone, and he wouldn't have a clue where to start searching. There was no certainty that the runner was Chloe or anyone who might be looking for her. This place was probably full of fitness freaks running just for the fun of it.

'Hello!' This wasn't the strange runner, but Rosie, her voice very faint. 'Where are you?'

'Here!' As soon as he'd shouted, Joe realized how unhelpful that was.

'I've got something. I'll wait here for you. Follow the wall and you'll come to me.'

So he walked on, scrambling over fallen trees, and at last he caught the flash of colour – her blue down jacket – right next to the wall. She must have moved more slowly than him because she was standing at the furthest corner. Joe had been hoping for something dramatic: a small tent or a sleeping bag, and inside another piece of writing from the missing girl. But all he could see was Rosie, still looking smart in her skinny jeans and her long leather boots and her bright blue jacket.

'What have you got?'

Rosie nodded towards the trees. Nearly hidden was a substantial wooden shed, camouflaged. You could walk within yards of it and still miss it.

'I've checked. It's got the composting toilet inside.'

'So this is where the kids camped.' He couldn't hide his disappointment. There was no indication even that the group from the Salvation Academy had used this as their base. Any ash from a fire had been covered with leaf mould and all rubbish had been taken away. 'No sign that Chloe's been here recently though.'

'Oh, ye of little faith! Take a look.'

He unlatched the door and pushed it open. He'd expected an unpleasant stink, but there was just the smell of damp wood and earth. The toilet was in the furthest corner, half-hidden by a screen made of woven branches. The rest of the space had been used to hold tools. Saws and shears hung from nails on the wall. And here there was a sleeping bag, laid on a plastic sheet, and a small rucksack containing a few clothes.

'I heard someone,' Joe said, 'running away.'

'I know. She must have heard me coming. We were *so* close to finding her.' He could hear the frustration in Rosie's voice now. 'Maybe if I hadn't made such a noise . . .'

'Where did she get the sleeping bag?' Joe thought recriminations were pointless and he'd not been quiet either, had he?

'From Esther Sullivan? Or from the Paradise? Even if the Marshes weren't helping her, she could have nicked it from there.'

'Maybe. Or the boss could be right and one of the local kids has been helping her out.'

'Is it a coincidence,' Rosie asked, 'her being here, so close to where Brad Russell's body was found?'

'I don't know.' But Joe had learned from Vera to be very suspicious of coincidence.

'What do we do now?'

'We go back to the hotel and find some phone reception.' Joe thought this would have to be Vera's call. Besides, the fresh air and exercise had meant that he was starving.

'We shouldn't wait here in case Chloe comes back?'

'We can't even be sure that she's the person who's been staying here, can we?' Joe said. Though he thought that of course this was Chloe's hideout. In one sense, he wished they hadn't found her. At least here she'd been relatively safe. 'And she won't come back immediately, will she? She'll wait until she thinks the coast is clear. As long as we're here when it's dark and she comes back to sleep . . .'

'I don't know . . .'

Joe thought Rosie had a cheek, questioning his decision. 'Let's chat to Vera, shall we? We can decide then.'

'Sure,' Rosie said. 'Sure.' But she still sounded uncertain. He heard her mutter under her breath as they walked away:

'Are we kids? Can't we do anything without checking first with the boss?'

He pretended that he hadn't heard.

They ordered coffee and sandwiches in the hotel bar, looking like any other couple who'd sneaked a day off work to spend some time in the country. While he was waiting for the food to be delivered, Joe went outside to speak to Vera.

The boss was triumphant. 'So I was right. She headed out to Gillstead, her safe place.'

'What do you want us to do next? Should one of us stake out the camp and wait for her to come back?'

The silence at the end of the line went on for so long that Joe thought the connection had been broken.

'Not yet,' Vera said. 'We don't know who else might be around, keeping an eye on you.' There was another long pause. 'I'll head up there later this afternoon. In the meantime, make sure you're in the village when the school bus comes in. Ask all the kids about Brad Russell and the car that the nebby woman saw from her bedroom window. Talk to Alice and find out if she's been in touch. Chloe will be hungry now, won't she? Even if the Marshes gave her food when she was at the

Paradise, it might be worth asking the kitchen staff if they've seen a lass hanging around the bins. These posh places chuck out stuff that can still be eaten.'

'So you're coming to Gillstead yourself?' *Checking up on us. Not trusting us to find the girl ourselves. As Rosie said, treating us like kids.*

'Aye. But not yet. I've got a theory I want to check out. I need a chat with our esteemed PCC first, and she's in a meeting with a bunch of politicians. Definitely not to be disturbed for a couple of hours.'

Vera didn't share her theory with him. Of course not. Joe thought that she might talk about becoming more collaborative since Holly's death, but there was no real sign of her putting the resolution into practice. She was the same control freak, holding her secrets close even when it put herself and others in danger.

Back in the hotel the sandwiches had arrived.

'Well?' Rosie had already taken a bite. It wasn't a good look.

'She's coming up tonight. I'm to book her a room in the pub too.'

'What are we to do about the hideout in the grounds?'

'Nothing. We're not to draw attention to it in case there are people looking out for her. We're to focus on the kids getting off the school bus. And on Brad Russell.'

'Isn't that a bit risky?'

Joe thought that Vera had never been one to shy away from risk. 'She claims to have a theory.'

'Which is?'

He shrugged.

'Does she always work like that? Doesn't it piss you off?'

Joe thought about that. 'I suppose. But she's usually right.

I'd hoped that Holly's death might make her see things differently, but perhaps she's too old to change now.'

Rosie rolled her eyes. She wasn't a woman to hide what she was thinking. Joe wondered how long she'd last on the team.

The bus stop was in the centre of the hamlet right outside the Stanhope Arms. A couple of parents were waiting in their cars. Perhaps they lived on outlying farms and were here to take their kids home. Joe hoped they wouldn't get in the way of the informal questions Vera had demanded.

The bus was fifteen minutes late, but this didn't seem unusual. The passengers rolled off, full of end-of-the-week high spirits, laughing and shouting. There were a couple of adults who'd paid to use the scholars' bus, but the others, eight of them, were students. Joe sent Rosie in to be first point of contact. That, after all, had been what Vera had wanted. He started explaining to the parents who were climbing out of their cars, apologizing for the delay, saying it wouldn't take long. They were curious but understanding.

'Hi, guys!' This was Rosie. 'I'm a detective investigating the death of the lad up at Cragside bothy. Can I ask a few questions?'

They gathered around her, listening. He'd expected more joking, more fooling about. They hadn't known Russell, had they? They were young and would consider themselves immortal. But she'd managed to get their full attention. 'At the moment we're considering it an unexplained death, and we need to know what he was doing there and how he got there.' Rosie looked out at them. 'His name was Brad Russell. He was fifteen years old. About the same age as some of you. He had a mam and a grandma, and they need answers.'

'We were told it was an overdose.' The speaker was a girl, pretty, confident. Long blonde hair.

'We're still waiting for tests to come back. Like I said, at the moment it's unexplained.'

Silence. The older ones at least would draw their own conclusions. True crime podcasts were popular, weren't they? Even among the young.

'Does the name mean anything to you? Brad Russell?'

A collective shaking of heads.

'He grew up on the coast.' Rosie didn't specify Longwater, Joe noticed. Even with its smart new housing estates, Longwater would trigger associations with crime and drugs. The town had a rep. She was playing this well, holding their sympathy.

'We think he was brought here on Tuesday night,' she went on. 'His body was found on Wednesday mid-morning. A witness saw a car that she didn't recognize late on the Tuesday evening. A black saloon, with Northumberland or North Tyneside plates. My colleague Joe over there will be asking your parents if they noticed anything, though I'm assuming they're early to bed. But one of you might have been up late. Studying . . .' They recognized the sarcasm and giggled. ' . . . or gaming or chatting on social media with your mates. Did anyone see a strange car that night?'

There was a moment of silence and then an older lad with the shadow of a moustache and dark hair raised his hand.

'Something pulled in to the house at Cragside that night. You know, the rental home.'

'You live near there?' Rosie knew that there were no houses near the property.

He shook his head. 'I'd been out. I was walking home. I live further out of the village, and I go back that way.'

'What were you doing wandering around at that time of night?'

'I'd been to see a friend. We'd been . . .' A pause. '. . . *studying*.'

Giggles, which is what he'd hoped for.

'And is the friend here?'

A hand went up. It was the bonny blonde lass who'd asked the first question. Joe thought of the excuses *he'd* come up with to his parents when he'd started going out with Sal. They'd been about the same age as this pair.

There were more giggles, which Rosie ignored.

'Did you get a close look at the car?'

'Yeah, I like cars,' the lad said. 'It was high end. A hybrid Volvo. I didn't notice the number plate though.'

'Did you see the driver? There are security lights outside the house. You would have had a good view if anyone got out.'

The teenager shook his head. 'I was in a hurry to get home. I was late back, and I knew my dad would be waiting up. I didn't stop to look. I assumed it was the owner. He lives in town and turns up at odd times and it's the sort of car he'd drive. Every time he's here he seems to have something new.'

'There was just one person? Just the driver?'

The lad thought again, then looked straight at Rosie, his voice eager. 'There were two of them! I'd been almost running, and I had to stop at the top of the bank to get my breath. I glimpsed down the hill and I saw them. Just silhouettes against the security lights. But definitely two of them.'

'Can you tell me anything about them. Build? Height? What they were wearing?'

He shut his eyes for a moment. 'One was smaller than the other, but really that's all. I couldn't make out any detail, and

I only looked at them for a moment before I turned round and ran on.'

'Anyone else see the car that night?'

There was no answer. The group shuffled their feet. Perhaps they thought this was over now and they could be on their way, but Rosie was speaking again. 'I'm sorry, I need to ask you about someone else, and this is probably even more important. A young woman is missing. Her name's Chloe Spence. Some of you will recognize the name because her grandfather owned Cragside Farm while she was growing up and she was a regular visitor. You might have seen from the news that we're all very worried about her. There's some evidence that she's been in Gillstead, at least for the past night or two.'

They stared at Rosie in silence. Joe thought this line of inquiry might be a waste of time. The parents were starting to get restive. Then the bonny blonde lass stuck up her hand.

'We were mates at one time. Years ago, mind. I lived on the coast, and we knocked around together. We've kinda kept in touch.' The words light and easy as if they didn't mean anything at all, but Joe, who had a young daughter, could sense the wariness.

'You're Alice?'

She nodded, surprised.

Rosie directed her next question to the whole group. 'Anyone seen Chloe recently? Seen her around?'

There was a collective shaking of heads. Except by the blonde girl. She just looked down at her feet.

'That's it then,' Rosie said. She handed out cards with her phone number. 'If you see anything or remember anything, give me a call.' She turned to Alice, kind and firm. 'You okay to hang around for a bit, love? I'd like a chat. And we'll ask my colleague Joe Ashworth to join us too. Are your parents here? Will they be anxious if you're a bit late home?'

'Nah, I just live in the village and they'll both be at work.'

There was a bench on the green next to the bus stop and they chatted there. At first Rosie kept it general. No questions about Chloe. Alice told them her parents were both lecturers at Newcastle Uni. They commuted into the city every day. 'They liked the idea of me growing up in the country.'

'And you?' Joe asked. 'Do you like it?'

'I did when I was young. There was a freedom. All this space.'

'And now?' Rosie asked.

'Now, everything happens in town. There's no public transport after the school bus, and my mother and father don't fancy driving me around when they've got in from work.'

'But at least you've got a boyfriend in the village.'

Alice gave a shy little grin. 'I suppose.'

'You said you'd "kind of" lost touch with Chloe. What did you mean? Did you keep in contact at all? Through your socials?'

'Yeah,' Alice said. 'Well, through Snapchat and Insta. She'd been going through a really shit time.' She looked up. 'You know she's been in care? In that dreadful place?'

Rosie nodded. 'Was it so dreadful?'

'It sounded dreadful to me.'

'But you've seen her recently, haven't you?' Joe liked the way Rosie was keeping her voice gentle. There was nothing judgemental about the question.

'No!'

'Come on, Alice. Her grandad bought you a spa treatment at the Hall.'

'Oh, then. Yeah.'

Silence.

'We want to help her. We think she might be in danger.'

'I promised I wouldn't tell anyone.' A pause. 'She was scared and she's so young. The bravest person I know.'

'We want to help her,' Rosie said. 'We need to find her.'

Chapter Thirty-Five

KATHERINE WILLMORE, THE POLICE AND CRIME Commissioner, couldn't meet Vera until the end of the working day. All after-noon, the detective was restless. Since hearing back from Joe and Rosie that they'd found Chloe's hiding place, she hadn't been able to settle to anything. She was itching to be in Gillstead with her colleagues. Willmore arrived just as Vera was about to give up on her. They talked in one of the anonymous meeting rooms. Vera didn't like the idea of the PCC in her office, invading her personal space. She didn't offer coffee.

'I'm glad of a chance to chat,' Willmore said. 'I wanted an update on the Woodburn case.'

'With a bit of luck, we'll get this sorted by the end of the weekend.'

But only if I'm there, keeping them all straight.

'So you've found the girl?' The PCC was obviously relieved.

'Not quite. But they've found where she's been camping, and we know she's still alive.' *At least she was earlier today.*

'So you'll just wait for her to go back to her hideout, and you'll get her, bring her home.'

Vera wondered where home would be for Chloe now, and shook her head. 'We'll check it out of course, but she won't go back there now. She's sharp as a tack that one. She'll know we'll be waiting for her.'

'If she's in Gillstead, she must know Brad Russell is dead. If he killed Woodburn, why doesn't she just come to us? Phone 999 and we'll bring her in.'

'She's young and scared and has got caught up with anxiety about all sorts of conspiracies. She thinks she's being followed and she's probably right. She can't trust anyone.' Vera paused. 'My worry is that the killer will know she's been seen in Gillstead too. Or that they already know.'

'How would they know that?' Willmore's voice was sharp. 'Someone leaking to the press?'

'Not one of my team!' Vera's voice was even sharper. 'But we had to interview some of the village kids about her. And they're all over their socials, aren't they? It won't take long for the news to spread.'

'You couldn't have handled that more discreetly?'

'Not without missing out on important leads.' Vera was tempted to say more, but she needed a different kind of information from the woman. 'There was something you said, when we first found Josh Woodburn's body. It's stuck in my mind.' She leaned forward and spoke softly although nobody could be listening. 'I think this is all about money,' she said when Willmore had finished speaking. 'Power and money. If we can understand that we'll find the killer.'

After talking to Willmore, Vera decided to postpone her trip to Gillstead again. Instead, she headed to Longwater and Rosebank. This had all started in the children's home with the troubled kids and the struggling staff. Her attention had been dragged north and west into the hills, but she was becoming convinced that the answer to the two deaths lay here.

Dave Limbrick, the manager, let her into the building. He looked as tired and grey as he had on her previous visits.

'Any news?' His eyes were slightly feverish. She wondered if he'd slept much since they'd found Brad. Or perhaps his exhaustion was the result of wild nights with Tracey. She hoped that was the case.

Vera didn't answer the question. 'Any chance of a coffee?' She was tired too and she still had to drive to Gillstead.

He nodded and led her through to the kitchen. It was even more depressing than Vera remembered. The bairns were finishing their supper. Tracey was eating with them, and there was a young lass Vera didn't recognize. She was young, hardly into her teens, overweight with small, wary eyes in a round, puffy face. Kath Oliver had been right, it seemed. Places in these homes were at a premium. Rooms wouldn't stay empty for long. Brad Russell had already been replaced.

'The inspector's after a coffee.' Limbrick sat at one of the tables and started chatting to the kids there, asking about their days at school. Vera liked that. Tracey gave a little wave and got up to put on the kettle.

The children dribbled out, after stacking their plates in the dishwasher. Tracey wiped down the table and said that she was on her way home. Limbrick and Vera were left alone. Vera nodded towards the departing care officer.

'Her husband's back from Europe then?'

'Aye, he got in early this morning.'

Vera smiled. 'Eh, man, probably not such a bad thing. You look as if you could do with a rest.'

The coffee was instant but strong. She looked across at him and answered the question he'd posed when she'd first arrived.

'We think we've tracked down Chloe. At least we know she's alive. She's been camping out in the grounds of a fancy hotel in Gillstead.'

'Thank God!' His face relaxed and he seemed younger. He looked up at her. 'That's where her grandparents used to live.'

'Aye. Her happy place.' A pause. 'And that's where we found Brad Russell's body. A strange coincidence.' She let the silence stretch and sensed his discomfort before speaking. 'I was wondering if you could explain that at all.'

He shook his head. Too quickly?

'I need to ask you a few more questions. Just routine. We'll do that in the office, shall we? You'll have the paperwork to hand, and we don't want the youngsters wandering in and earwigging.'

Vera knew there was nothing Limbrick could tell her that she wouldn't find out in other ways, but she wanted to do this properly. However strong the pull of the hills, she owed it to the children here. She repeated their names in her head, because they deserved that at least. Recognition that they were individuals, who'd drawn a short straw in life and been through a crap time. *Mel, George.*

On the walk to the office, she asked Limbrick another question. 'That new lass. What's she called?'

'Amber. Her mam killed herself a week ago. Threw herself off the Tyne Bridge. Her dad's not in the picture. Social services are trying to track down other relatives.'

Vera added Amber to the list.

★   ★   ★

When she met Rosie and Joe in the Stanhope Arms, it was gone eight. Ma was still behind the bar. Vera thought the woman probably worked more hours than she did. The place was rowdy. The Friday-night drinkers were here too. Most of the press had left, though a couple of patient middle-aged hopefuls remained, and they definitely looked brighter when Vera walked in.

'What are you doing here then, Vera?' He was a freelance journo she recognized, though his name escaped her. 'Got something for me?'

'Nah, bonny lad. I'm just here for a pint on my way home.' She gave him a wink because she could tell he didn't believe her, and made her way through to the back, where Joe and Rosie were waiting. It was grandly called a 'private function room' and it was echoey and damp. Locals had held wedding parties and dances here, before the Hall had been turned into a hotel. Now it was decorated with witches and cats made from black card. And wide, staring eyes. And the Three Dark Wives cut out of polystyrene blocks and spray-painted black. They were stuck on the walls and over the windows. Fake cobwebs hung in drifts from the ceiling. There was a lot of fake blood. Maybe with the proper lighting it would be a bit spooky, but now, in the glare of the neon strips, it was sad. It looked like the stage set for a kids' performance.

'What's all this?' Joe was looking around the room as if he'd seen the decorations for the first time. 'They're a bit late for Hallowe'en, aren't they?' The pair had set up on a small table in the corner of the room.

'Not Hallowe'en,' Vera said. 'Tomorrow's the Witch Hunt. A local tradition. The first Saturday past Bonfire Night.'

Ma had noticed Vera come into the bar and wandered through with a pint for her, and a food menu.

'You'll need to be quick. We're closing the kitchen in fifteen minutes.'

The inspector turned to her. 'You're going ahead with the hunt, then? Even with one teenager killed and another missing . . . That's not enough horror for you?'

'We talked about cancelling, but the village wouldn't hear of it. Not the real locals. They reckon it'd be bad luck. Besides, folk come from all over the county to take part.' Ma gave a wide smile. 'We couldn't disappoint them. We always start off with an early supper in here, and party games for the kiddies, before the witch goes onto the fell.'

'And I bet it's a good night for business,' Vera said. 'Though it seems a tad tasteless to me.'

Ma smiled again. 'Oh aye. The takings are higher on Witch Hunt night than on Christmas and New Year's Eve put together.' A pause. 'You'll all have to move out tomorrow. The rooms have been booked for months.'

Vera didn't reply to that. She hoped it would all be over by the following evening. If it was, she thought she could invite Joe and Rosie to her house. They'd have a celebratory bite to eat. She'd even send them home in a taxi, so they could all have a few drinks. Then she thought she was getting ahead of herself. Nothing was guaranteed. The meeting with Limbrick hadn't helped and the PCC had been more than sceptical about Vera's theory. Willmore had just shaken her head. Sad and disappointed because she'd hoped Vera would have a better answer. 'I'm sorry, Vera. I just don't see it.'

They ordered food and waited for Ma to disappear into the main body of the pub. 'So you spoke to this lass Alice. What did she say?'

Rosie answered: 'That she and Chloe had been mates since

they were very young. They kept in touch through socials and caught up occasionally when Alice had a day out at the beach. They met up when Gordon brought Chloe here for her special treat from the kids' home.'

'Did Alice know she was camping out here?'

'Yeah.' Joe jumped in, wanting to take at least a bit of the credit. 'We spoke to her on her own after letting all the others go. She admitted giving Chloe the sleeping bag and has been supplying her with food. Chloe had insisted she keep the whole thing secret. Alice hadn't told *anyone* – not even her parents or the lad she's smitten with.'

'Has she heard from Chloe today?'

Joe shook his head. 'She claims not. And that's unusual. Usually, they message regularly. Alice charged the lass's phone for her, and Chloe knows a spot near the hotel where there's Wi-Fi. Alice is worried she'll think Alice grassed her up. How else would we know to be searching the hotel grounds for her?'

'Do we believe her? This Alice . . .'

Joe shrugged. 'Yeah, I think so. But teenagers . . .'

'So as far as we know the lass is on the run again?'

'Seems like it.'

'Bugger.' In the silence that followed Ma brought their food, and for a while they concentrated on eating.

'Do you want us to go back to the camp tonight, in case she's gone there?' Joe set his knife and fork on the empty plate.

'Aye. Like you say. Just in case.' Vera thought that would be a wild goose chase, but it wouldn't do the pair any harm to be wandering round the woods last thing at night. It would be a kind of team-building exercise. Watkins, her boss, was a great one for those. Though she'd never known him participate himself. He seldom left his office.

'Should we check that Alice isn't hiding her mate away at home?' Rosie didn't seem so keen on the midnight ramble.

Vera thought briefly about that and then she shook her head. 'Nah, if Chloe is there, she's safe. We don't want her running away again, disappearing into the night as soon as one of us rings on the doorbell.'

'What's the plan?' This was Rosie once more. Her voice was demanding. Vera liked a bit of spark, but if the lass carried on challenging her superiors like this, she'd need to be put in her place.

'We make the most of the situation as we find it.' Vera emptied her glass and wondered if she could be arsed to go back to the bar for another drink. 'The press know that we're here. The kids will be all over social media telling the world that we're asking about Chloe. The killer will be scared witless, losing their reason. They'll want to get to our Chloe before we do.'

'You think the killer will come here looking for her?' Rosie sounded horrified. 'You've set this up as a kind of trap?'

'Not on purpose, pet. I didn't know that you'd find Chloe camping out here, did I? We were just following leads. Routine policing.' Vera paused for a moment, staring at a limp cut-out witch hanging just above Rosie's head. 'And if you find Chloe in the hut in the hotel grounds, you can bring her in. We'll see that she's safe, and she might have useful information for us. Though I don't think she knows the full story around Josh Woodburn's death. I think that's something that we'll have to work out for ourselves.'

'You know what happened, don't you?' Joe said. 'We're supposed to be a team. Share what you've got with us.'

Vera shook her head. 'I *know* nowt, Joe lad. I've got a few theories floating around in my head, but they're still stories.

And we need more than make-believe to end this. We're not like Chloe Spence with her fantasies and tall tales.' Vera's meeting with Katherine Willmore had dented her confidence, and sitting here in this gloomy barn of a room, she didn't want to make a fool of herself again.

But she could sense their disappointment as they looked at her from the other side of the table over the sad remains of another unhealthy meal. 'I tell you what,' she said suddenly. 'I'll come with you out into the woods to look for the bairn. I could do with a bit of an adventure. We're a team, aren't we? Let's see if we can find her and bring her into the warm. Just give me a couple of minutes to fetch my boots from the Land Rover.'

It was cold and clear. Very still. Here in the hills, winter came early, and they might wake to a frost. Vera was enjoying herself. Being outside, and breathing in this sharp, clean air with its scent of pine needles and ice, was a hundred times better than sitting in the pub and waiting for Joe and Rosie to come back. Then the guilt set in, because what right did she have to be enjoying herself when two young men had been killed and a lass was in danger?

They walked along to the hotel, and even when there were no further street lamps, they could make their way easily by the light of the full moon. Only one vehicle passed them: a battered mini driven too fast by a young lad. No black Volvo.

In the woods there was less light, and they had to use torches. It came to Vera suddenly, that if Holly had been with them she'd have had a head torch. She'd been a runner and had pounded the streets before dawn and after dusk in the dark days of the year. Vera found that there were tears in her eyes and was glad that the other two couldn't see.

Because she'd been the person to find it, Rosie led them to Chloe's campsite. Vera was aware of the wall on one side of her and the trees in the shadow beyond. And that she couldn't breathe as easily as she once had. Perhaps she should listen to her doctor and take up a bit of exercise again. Rosie stopped suddenly. They stood for a moment in silence. Vera could hear a faint noise ahead of them, then saw a badger, its eyes reflecting the torchlight. It was years since she'd seen a badger and it was smaller than she'd remembered, solid and low to the ground. It stamped away into the undergrowth, and they walked on.

When they were approaching the shed, Rosie stopped and pointed. Vera whispered: 'Let's lose the light.'

They stood for a moment, while their eyes got used to the darkness. Moonlight slanted through the trees, and above them there was a sky full of stars.

Vera motioned for Joe and Rosie to stay where they were and walked towards the building. Her steps made no sound on the leaf mould that was deep underfoot. As she pushed the door open, she had a moment of doubt. They should have come earlier. The killer would have been there ahead of them. She imagined a body. Blood. A pale face drained of all colour because a lass was dead, not because she'd chosen the goth white make-up. In the seconds before looking inside, Vera thought that if Chloe was dead, she would of course resign. How could she have been so cavalier with a young person's life? So arrogant as to think that she knew best?

Her hand holding the torch was shaking. The beam shivered a little as she shone it inside. The sleeping bag was still there, lying on the bare floor, as Rosie and Joe had described it from the morning's visit. But there was no sign of Chloe. No body.

Vera thought that unless somebody was sheltering the lass, she would be very cold.

She moved outside. 'It's as we thought. She knew we'd come looking for her and she's scarpered.' She stamped her feet. She'd thought to bring boots but not thick socks, and the cold was seeping into her bones. These days she spent too long in the office. She'd forgotten what she needed to be prepared.

They were about to turn and walk back to the hotel and the road, and Vera was hoping there might be a lock-in at the pub so she could get a dram or two. Suddenly, there was a disturbance ahead of them. A noise that was louder than the scuffling of a badger or a fox. In the silence it sounded thunderous.

'That's a person!' Joe was setting off after them, crashing through the undergrowth, wild and unfocused.

'It's not Chloe.' Rosie hadn't moved. She was trying to listen to the direction of the footsteps.

Wise young woman, Vera thought. *You know better than to charge off into the night. No way will Joe catch them.*

Rosie was still talking. 'When we surprised Chloe earlier today, her footsteps were lighter. This is an adult.' She didn't bother to whisper now. What would be the point?

Vera agreed. So who was crashing through the woods at this time of night? A poacher, maybe, but that would be too much of a coincidence. And someone hoping to get a photo of the badger sett wouldn't run away like that if they were disturbed. So, most likely, this was the killer. What were they doing there? Had they followed Vera and the team? Or had they worked out already where Chloe might be hiding? If so, where had they got that information?

Vera's mind was jumping, making connections. Very unlikely

connections. She and Rosie followed the wall back to the hotel and the road. Joe was waiting for them, bent double, breathless.

'Sorry, I lost him. He was miles ahead of me.'

'Was it a "him"? Could you see?'

Joe shook his head. 'I didn't get close. I couldn't see a thing. They were way ahead of me.'

And fitter. Perhaps you should be upping your exercise regime too.

Vera wondered where the intruder was now. Sitting in the hotel lounge with a beer or a coffee? In one of the fancy bedrooms, cleaning themselves up? Her team would check the hotel register of course. And the vehicles in the car park. Rosie and Joe could do that now. She didn't need to stay here to do that. No point in having climbed the greasy pole if you couldn't find minions to do your dirty work, and the bar at the Stanhope Arms with its big fire was calling. But Vera thought it more likely that their killer was driving away from Gillstead now, either back to the coast or to some anonymous B&B. They were probably on their way home, she decided. After all, it was the Witch Hunt the next day. And as Ma had said, all available accommodation would already be taken.

Back at the pub, the bar had officially shut, but Ma was still serving, and she'd just thrown another couple of logs on the fire when Vera came in, so she wasn't looking to close up shop anytime soon.

Vera sat on a stool by the bar. Unladylike, but then she'd never been considered a lady.

'I'll have whisky please, pet. A double. It's chilly out there now. And whatever you're having. I don't need anything fancy, mind.' She'd never been a whisky snob.

Ma nodded and poured herself the same.

'Can I have a look at your register? I'd like to see who you've got staying tomorrow night.'

'Is that legal, like? With data protection?'

Vera thought about that. 'Well, I can't encourage you to break the law, can I? Just leave the book on the bar and clear a few glasses. I assume it is all in the book and you don't do fancy computer booking?'

'We do both,' Ma said. 'Belt and braces.' She reached under the bar and brought out a heavy diary. Then she wandered away to the furthest corner of the room to chat to a couple of locals, leaving Vera to look at whatever she wanted.

Vera was in bed when the text came through from Joe. It said that they'd looked at every car in the place. There were no dark-coloured Volvos. And nobody involved in the case had booked into the Gillstead Hall hotel.

Vera turned over and gave a little sigh of satisfaction. It was just as she'd thought. But there was nothing to say that the person Joe had chased through the woods wouldn't come back the next day. In fact, Vera thought, she'd bet on it.

Chapter Thirty-Six

JOE HADN'T SLEPT WELL. HE'D GOT cold wandering around the hotel grounds, and the duvet provided by the Stanhope Arms was skimpy, the double glazing let in the draughts and the heating had been switched off long before he'd got to his bed. There'd been a text from Sal with a photo of his oldest daughter, Jess, in costume, just before her Youth Theatre performance. Jess had a starring role and he'd promised he'd be there.

She was brilliant! Such a shame you couldn't make it.

The tone was sad and disappointed, but the implication was clear: he was a crap dad. It came to him that it would never be possible to please the two strong women in his life, but that *he* wasn't strong enough to let either of them go. Maybe it was time to break free of Vera at last.

At breakfast, he thought that Rosie had also had a bad night. She looked red-eyed and bleary.

'It's the silence,' she said, 'and the dark. I'm a city girl. There's always a bit of noise in town, something to remind you that you're not alone.'

'You *are* alone, though, aren't you?' In contrast Vera was chirpy, full of energy. 'You've not got a partner of any description?' And when Rosie didn't answer immediately: 'Sorry for being nosy. It goes with the job, doesn't it?'

Then Rosie laughed. 'I suppose it does. And no, no partner of any description. I was engaged to a lovely lad, but he wanted someone to have his kids, not share his life, and I ditched him at the last moment. My work was too important for him and for me.' She looked up at them both. 'My mam had already bought the hat and shoes for the big day. I'm not sure she'll ever forgive me.' A pause. 'I'm a bit more wary these days.'

Joe was expecting some wisecrack comment from the boss maybe about *his* marriage – but she only gave a sympathetic nod of her head.

'Are we calling in the troops to do a search?' he asked. 'Is Charlie coming across to join us?'

'Not yet,' Vera said. 'I've got him chained to a desk. He's doing some work for me.'

The mood she was in, Joe knew better than to ask what sort of work, and Vera continued:

'I'm thinking we need a more discreet approach. It'll be a madhouse here today. The chaos starts in the early afternoon with the bairns' fancy dress parade. There'll be lots of strangers about. Let's just keep our eyes peeled, shall we, for someone who's not quite a stranger. Not to us at least. The last thing we need is a load of plods in uniform spoiling the enjoyment.' Long pause. 'And scaring off our killer.'

'So what do you want us to do? Precisely.' Joe was thinking he could be at home, placating Sal and spending some time with his children.

'A bit of surveillance,' Vera said. 'Otherwise known as sitting on your backsides and keeping your eyes peeled. I want to find out where Chloe is. We think she's in the village some-where, and if she wasn't sleeping rough, there are a couple of possibilities – she might have found a corner in that fancy hotel, and she might be at her friend Alice's. She persuaded Alice to keep her secrets for this long, and there's still a chance that she's hiding her without letting us know.' Vera paused. 'Our Chloe's had good mates throughout all this. Esther and Alice. It gives you hope for the future.'

Joe thought Vera was going to say something more, but she didn't.

'So,' he repeated. 'Precisely?'

'Eh, if you want me to do your job for you, this is how I suggest you organize your day. So, Joe, I'd like you to take on the hotel. Have a chat with the manager and get them to set you up with a uniform of some kind. Then you can wander round the corridors without being stopped. See if Chloe has found a little hidey-hole where's she's spent the night. I'm thinking a laundry or utility room. Or a pantry. She'll be starving. She might not be there now. Once the staff started their shifts this morning, she might have done a runner again, but there could be a sign of her somewhere. She might still be keeping that diary of hers. Seems to me the only way she can make sense of her life is to write about it.'

Joe thought this didn't sound much like sitting on his arse all day, but at least he'd be indoors. It was better than being out on a hill getting frozen.

The boss was in full flow now, hardly stopping for breath. 'Rosie, you do a recce of Alice's place. We haven't been there, have we? You picked her up at the bus stop and interviewed her on the green. See if there are any places where Chloe might be hiding. Garage, outbuildings. Her folks are academics, aren't they? I presume they've got a pretty big gaff. But be discreet. I don't want the parents calling you in as a potential thief or murderer. And I don't want Chloe knowing you're there and legging it.' She looked directly at the DC. 'And to be fair, you stick out like a sore thumb. Let's see if Marie has an old jacket and a pair of boots you could borrow, so at least you can pass yourself off as a walker who's lost her way.'

Rosie looked horrified at the prospect of wearing Ma's cast-offs and Joe restrained a snigger.

'Shame we can't borrow a dog,' Vera said. 'Nobody takes any notice at all of a dog-walker.'

'I'll be careful, boss. I can't do dogs. I'm allergic.'

'Ah.' Vera was finishing off her full English. 'Pity.'

Joe was scared for a moment that Vera would suggest he and Rosie swapped roles. He was already trying to come up with an excuse of his own, but she just wiped a bit of egg yolk with her bread, and stuck it in her mouth.

'And you?' Rosie turned to Vera. 'What will you be doing? In case we need to get hold of you quickly and there's no reception.'

Joe expected an angry response, but Vera just tapped the side of her nose. 'I'll be looking out for the lass too, but you don't need to know the details. I'll know where to find you, and that's all that matters.'

Joe thought that was odd. Vera could always be secretive, but not like this. Not deliberately holding back details. It was almost as if she didn't trust them. Joe knew that she had faith in *him*. The boss could be sarky and annoying, but she'd never once accused him of disloyalty. He wondered if she had reason to question Rosie's ability to keep details of the investigation to herself. He couldn't see the young DC as a leaker of secrets, but perhaps Vera had evidence that had led her to doubt her. The thought unsettled him, and he felt edgy all day.

At the hotel, he introduced himself to the duty manager, who kitted him out with uniform black trousers, white shirt and gold waistcoat. The man was obviously enjoying the drama and the disruption to his routine, but he was busy.

'If you fancy carrying a few bags and showing guests to their rooms, we wouldn't mind at all. It'd add to the disguise, and we're rushed off our feet! It's always the same at Witch Hunt weekend.' He was only half-joking.

But Joe knew he wouldn't be spending time in the public areas of the hotel. He'd be backstage, going through the doors that said STAFF ONLY and walking down bare concrete floors looking for signs of Chloe.

He spent the first hour trying to understand the layout of the place. When the Hall had been built there would have been an army of servants, hidden from the family and their guests, appearing like magic from the narrow staircases and chilly spaces that were their domain. Sal liked the period dramas on telly, and he watched them with her. Service would have been mostly invisible: fires lit and meals appearing on tables as if by magic. Those below-stairs places were still used by house-keepers, by kitchen porters and cleaners. The attic rooms where servants had once slept still housed the live-in staff, and they took their breaks, chatted and laughed in a dark, windowless room not far from the kitchen.

He couldn't find anywhere that Chloe could have been hiding. She'd not have fitted in any more here than in the front-of-house glamour of the hotel. Even the cleaners wore a uniform with a company logo, and they knew each other. Joe might pass for a staff member in the public rooms, but here he'd been challenged.

'Are you new then?' A curious skinny man in checked trousers and white clogs.

'I haven't seen you before.' A large bossy woman wearing the same gold waistcoat, who'd caught him peering into a cold store.

In the end, he gave up his wandering and sat in the subterranean staffroom. Beyond a closed door, and across a corridor, he could hear the clatter and rattle of the kitchen, and the shouts of the chefs. He took off the ridiculous waistcoat and explained to the people who came in for coffee from the machine in the corner, or to rest for a few minutes, who he was and what he was doing there.

'You haven't seen a lass? Young. She's only fourteen but could pass for older. We think she was camping out in the gardener's shed in the grounds, but she's not there any longer.'

He was greeted by shakes of the head and blank faces, and by early afternoon he'd decided this was a wild goose chase. He considered phoning Vera first but thought that she might tell him to stay there anyway. So he changed back into his own clothes, handed the uniform to the harassed receptionist, and set off for the Stanhope Arms to face Vera's wrath.

As he approached the centre of the village, he heard music. He rounded a bend in the road and saw that a procession was taking place down the main street. A brass band led a straggling line of boys and girls dressed up in elaborate costumes. There were cats, witches and warlocks. The smaller ones were holding on to parents' hands, but there were older teenagers there too. He wouldn't have been seen dead taking part in this sort of thing if he'd been that age, but perhaps there was a kind of ironic cool in their participation. He recognized Alice, her face painted green, in a tall witch's hat and a long flowing cloak holding hands with her boyfriend who had become one of the characters from Harry Potter. Jess had moved on from Potter now, but Joe had had to sit through all the films. More than once. The couple were leading the procession and waving to the crowd on each side of the road. Any traffic had been forced to stop.

At the pub, the couple paused for a moment, before, like adolescent pied pipers, leading the band and the children down an alley to the back of the building and the big barn-like function room where Vera's team had eaten the night before.

Joe, and the watching crowd, followed. He stood aside and waited while they all filed in to the room. For the first time, he saw how close the pub was to the open hillside. At the end of the yard, there was a drystone wall with a gate in the middle. Beyond that, a wide meadow and another gate on to the fell. From there, the hill rose steeply, and then flattened again, to the plateau where the standing stones stood guard over the valley.

Inside the event space, it seemed that a rowdy competition was taking place. The costumes were being judged. A big man with a microphone was shouting instructions. He seemed to know all the kids and there were jokes with the parents. Joe watched for a moment from the open door, then made his way into the bar proper. If Vera was still around, surely that was where she'd be.

The pub was full, and Ma was busy. Joe waved across to her. 'Have you seen the boss?'

The landlady continued pulling the pint, and barely looked up. 'Sorry, I've not seen her since breakfast. I was expecting her in for her lunch. You know what she's like about her scran.'

Then a tide of punters washed up between him and the bar and she was lost to view.

Joe went outside and stood in the courtyard, looking out on the hills. He walked as far away from the sound of the fancy dress competition as he could get, and phoned Vera. No reply, but he only had one bar of reception and perhaps she had none.

He was wondering what he should do next when Rosie landed beside him. She was still wearing one of Ma's water-proofs. It was enormous and reached to below her knees. It took him a moment to recognize her.

'I don't know about you,' she said. 'But I could use a drink.'

Chapter Thirty-Seven

ROSIE HAD FELT LIKE A RIGHT fool leaving the Stanhope Arms in a waterproof that smelled of dog and would probably set off her wheezing, and wellington boots a size too big that flapped around her legs. But she was excited too. She'd picked up Vera's energy, her sense that the killer could be here in the village. Since she'd ditched Daniel almost at the altar, Rosie had been floundering and distracted. Before deciding that marriage, to *him* at least, wasn't for her, life had seemed settled, her future sorted. Then there'd been that moment when they'd been sitting in his parents' cluttered front room working on the last-minute details of the wedding, and she'd been hit by a sense of dread. She couldn't be the wife he wanted. It would be, she'd known suddenly, a dreadful mistake. Too much compromise. Too little fun.

Since then, perhaps there had been too much fun. Too many nights with her mates in the bars on the Quayside. Too many cocktails. Too many hangovers. This investigation was giving her the same buzz. Even wearing a stinky jacket and boots that would certainly give her blisters on her toes and ankles, she felt very alive.

Alice's family lived almost in the centre of the village. It was a grand house behind a wrought-iron gate, with a garden at the back which seemed to lead down to the river. Rosie knew nothing about architecture but guessed it was Georgian – stately with a flat face and symmetrical windows. It was hard to see if there were any hiding places in the back garden. The house was tall and narrow, three storeys high. No garage. There might be attic rooms, unused – they knew that Alice was an only child, so the family would hardly use all that space – but it would surely be risky to hide Chloe away there. It was much more likely that there was a shed or outbuilding where the lass might be.

The gates weren't locked, but Rosie had known she wouldn't get in that way without someone noticing. There were two cars parked on the gravel drive. Alice's parents would be at home. Aware that she'd already been here too long and that she didn't want to be caught staring, Rosie walked on to the edge of the village to look for another way in. The pavement quickly petered out after she passed the house. The road came to a narrow bridge crossing the river. Traffic seemed to be pouring into Gillstead now. Rosie kept her eyes peeled for a black Volvo, but she saw none of the vehicles from their suspects' list.

Just before the bridge, a footpath led down a grassy bank towards the river, and Rosie took that. The path followed the river and was parallel to the road towards the village. From here, she could see the backs of all the houses in the main street. Some had built high fences or planted a hedge of leylandii to protect their privacy, but it seemed that Alice's parents were more interested in keeping the view than hiding from prying eyes. There was a low stone wall, with a wrought-iron gate providing access to the path, and Rosie could see all the details of the house on the other side.

The garden was well tended. A few autumn flowers were still in bloom in the borders. On a terrace, halfway between the house and the path, stood a wooden summer house, with windows looking out to the water and the hills on the other side of the river. Beside it, a pizza oven and a wood-fired hot tub. Everything the family would need to entertain guests on summer evenings. Rosie felt a twinge of envy. It was a bit different from her parents' home and her flat in Heaton. But if Alice had provided a place of safety for Chloe who was, it seemed, almost a younger sister to her, perhaps the summer house was where the girl had been staying.

Rosie stood for a moment, just outside the line of sight from the house, listening. Nothing but the sound of the river behind her.

Vera had said this would be boring, and Rosie wasn't sure she had the patience to wait for some indication of Chloe's presence. From here, she couldn't see inside the summer house. It was frustrating to think that Chloe might be inside, and that she could be standing just metres away.

The back door of the house opened, and a middle-aged couple came outside. Rosie walked on a few paces so there was no chance of them seeing her, but she could still hear the conversation.

'It's no good,' the woman said. Her voice was Southern educated, anxious, fraught. 'I might have to go to Waitrose in Hexham. I promised hot dogs for the kids' party this afternoon. I was sure I had sausages in the freezer but when I looked there were only half a dozen there. I'll just check in the chest freezer in here.'

'Here' was an outhouse attached to the main building. Rosie stood behind a tall elder, covered in purple berries, and watched.

This was another possible hiding place for Chloe. Perhaps Alice's mother would do the police's work for them and find the lass. But through the outhouse's open door all Rosie could see was a large bum, as the woman bent to look inside the freezer. She was pondering what a family of only three people would need with two freezers, when the woman straightened and turned.

'No, nothing. I'll just have to go into town and face the traffic on the way back to the village.'

'Why don't I come with you?' The man's voice was calm, easy. He seemed to find the lack of sausages less of a catastrophe than his wife. 'We can go for a coffee, maybe have brunch in Gianni's. There'll still be time to do everything you need for the party. And I'm sure that Alice will be glad of the house to herself while she prepares.'

'We'll need to go now!' The woman sounded panicky. She was, Rosie thought, a real drama queen.

'No problem. We can do that. I'm ready. We can text Alice and tell her what we're doing.' He reached into his pocket and pulled out a set of car keys. 'You see, all prepared!'

'You do realize,' the woman said, 'that as soon as we leave, her *friend* will turn up.'

'That's not a problem, is it?' Rosie thought the man must spend his life calming and reassuring the woman. What sort of relationship was that?

'I do worry, you know, that they're probably breaking the law.'

If the man answered, Rosie didn't hear the response. The couple disappeared into the house. Soon after that there was the sound of a car engine. Then silence.

★ ★ ★

Rosie sat on a fallen log and looked out at the river, as if she were here to study nature or indulge in some open-air meditation. There were walkers now dragging dogs along the footpath, stopping to scoop up their shit into plastic bags, and she didn't want to be seen staring into a private garden. This seemed the best place to wait. If Chloe *were* the friend Alice's parents had been discussing, it was surely unlikely that she'd approach the house from the main street, especially as it seemed they disapproved of their daughter helping the girl. Wouldn't she come in this way? Rosie thought the friend they'd referred to must be Chloe. Why else had they mentioned the law in that context? And why the sneering tone when the mother had spoken of the 'friend' if they'd only been speaking about someone Alice knew from school?

The log was cold, and patience wasn't one of Rosie's virtues. It wasn't uncomfortable here now that the sun was burning off the frost on the grass and the mist over the river, but she was bored. She stood up and stretched and looked up and down the path. The early-morning dog-walkers must be back at home having a late, lazy breakfast. There was nobody to be seen. If Alice's parents were driving to Hexham, even if they decided against coffee and brunch, they'd be away for a while. And if Alice was like any other teen Rosie knew, she'd still be in bed at this time on a Saturday morning, even if she was expecting Chloe to turn up later. She walked to the gate in the low wall and lifted the latch. The runaway might not be in the outhouse that held the family's second freezer, but she might be in the summer house.

She walked along the wall to the boundary hedge, hoping for a little cover from the house and the neighbours, then up the bank until she was level with the stone terrace that held the pizza oven and hot tub. She bent double so the oven and tub sheltered her from the windows while she made her way to the summer house. She tried to pull open the door, but it didn't move. Rosie wondered if it had been locked from the inside by Chloe, or simply if the family was security conscious.

The windows had been covered in ice overnight, but the sun had melted it and now they were streaming with moisture. It was still impossible to see what was inside. Rosie used the sleeve of Ma's jacket to wipe it away, but the coat must have been grubby, because she was left with smears that did nothing to improve visibility.

'Hey, what do you think you're doing?' It was a hefty man on the path. He wore a Toon Army strip and jeans that were too big for him and sagged to allow a view of his underpants. No dog. 'We've thefts in the village all summer and I know fine well you don't live there. I'm calling the police.' His voice was very loud.

'Don't do that sir.'

In her haste Rosie slid down the bank, her boots leaving a muddy gouge in the lawn.

'Why not? Someone nicked my bike from my shed two weeks ago. I've still not got it back. Folks say there's no point phoning the police, but if they don't know what's going on . . .'

'I did try the front door, but nobody's at home.'

Still he stood, blocking the way, extending his frame by keeping his legs wide apart, his elbows out. 'No reason to be snooping around someone else's property.'

'I *am* the police!'

He stared at her, at the disgusting jacket and the over-sized wellingtons. 'Nah! Behave!'

She'd transferred her warrant card to the back pocket of her trousers, and now she pulled it out and showed him.

'That's you?' The voice disbelieving and still very loud.

'I'd welcome a little discretion, sir.' Rosie looked at the house, expecting the door to open and Alice to appear.

'What were you doing there then?'

'I'm looking for a teenager. A lass. She's only fourteen. She's been missing for more than a week.'

'You think she's in Gillstead?' At least he'd lowered his voice.

'We think that she might be.'

'We could get the word out among the young farmers. Set up a search party.' Now he was excited and eager to help.

Rosie could imagine what Vera would make of that! A posse of equally loud young men and women scaring off the killer. She shook her head. 'I can't go into details but this is a sensitive operation. Clandestine. I'm sure you understand.'

He nodded wisely. He'd probably watched too many cop dramas on television. But still he didn't move. 'You think they've got her hidden in there somewhere?'

'You know I can't answer that, sir.' Playing along.

'It wouldn't surprise me,' he said darkly. 'A snooty pair. Moved from the city. You know the sort.'

Rosie gave a little smile, feeding his fantasy.

'I'd best let you get on with it then.'

She nodded, before adding: 'Not a word to anyone, sir. As I said, this is a secret operation, and I'll know who to blame if word gets out in the village.'

'You can trust me!' And off he went, with a bit of a swagger.

She doubted his promise of secrecy would last once he'd had a few pints, but Rosie thought there was nothing else she could have done.

★ ★ ★

She waited, not wanting to risk being caught again, but time was passing. Alice's parents could be back from Hexham at any time. The garden was long, and she wasn't sure that she'd hear a car pulling in to the drive. She didn't want to be seen snooping. This time, when she opened the gate, she strode straight to the summer house as if she had every right to be there. Let the neighbours think that she was a friend of the family.

She found a large white handkerchief in the jacket pocket and cleaned the summer house window with that. A complete anticlimax. Inside there was a garden table and chairs, and a lounger, folded against one wall. A shelf containing glasses and bottles of wine. No sign of Chloe and nowhere she could be hiding. Rosie swore under her breath. Bloody Vera, with her weird ways of working and her refusal to bring in a full search team!

She went back to her position on the riverbank. Every time she heard footsteps, she tensed. Now she really needed a piss, and was wondering if she could get away with climbing further down towards the river and going there, when there was the click of the latch on the gate. She turned slowly and saw the back of the person walking up the steep garden towards the house.

She knew immediately that it wasn't Chloe. This figure was male, and he had dark hair. Even from behind, Rosie recognized him. This was Alice's boyfriend, the lad who'd glimpsed the Volvo outside Cragside Farm on the night before Brad Russell's body had been found.

Suddenly Alice's mother's words slotted into place. This was the 'friend' the woman had spoken about with a sneer. Perhaps she despised his accent, and the probability that he'd leave school early to work on his father's farm. And any anxiety about a brush with the law was about the possibility of the two young people having sex. Alice wasn't sixteen and so was below the legal age of consent.

This had been a wild goose chase. Rosie suspected that she and Joe had been sent on their respective tasks of surveillance to keep them out of the way, while Vera followed an inquiry of her own. The boss was treating them as children who couldn't be trusted. She felt a rising anger. How had Joe put up with this behaviour for so long? Rosie began to plan her own escape route back to a job in the city. But still she stayed where she was and watched, reluctant to leave her post while Alice was still inside. It came to her suddenly that Vera had a habit of being right.

The lad had reached the house. He looked up at an upstairs window and whistled. The window opened and Alice looked out. She was wearing a cream silk dressing gown, and her hair was long and loose. The scene had the look of a contemporary staging of *Romeo and Juliet*, which was just, Rosie thought, what they intended. Not for an audience but as their own personal performance. She could almost smell the chemistry between them. They were young and caught up with their own romance. She felt a stab of envy. Had she ever felt like that about a man?

'I'll come down,' Alice's voice was light and warm, 'and let you in. It's time we got ready for the procession. I've got your costume. Hurry up! We'll be late!'

The boy disappeared into the building. Rosie knew this was a waste of time. The couple wouldn't want Chloe there to disturb them. Besides, the parents would soon be home. But still she waited for them to show themselves, intrigued by the idea of the costumes, of teenagers dressing up.

It occurred to her then that the couple would leave through the front door if they were going to the village centre, and that she might already have missed them. Rosie hurried along the riverside path and back to the bridge. There, her way was blocked by hundreds of people. The road was closed, and people were pushing to get to the front. There was an air of anticipation. Something was about to happen, but Rosie was so far back in the crowd that she couldn't tell what it was.

She heard music. A tune she might have heard when she was a child. Then the crowd started singing. The noise had all the grace and sophistication of a football chant and she struggled to make out the words. The chorus, shouted rather than sung, was clearer.

'Hunt the witch! Hunt the witch! Eyes open. Eyes open. Keep Gillstead clear of evil!'

It was, she supposed, just a bit of community fun, but somehow it struck too close to home. The message was inappropriate. Scary. The music faded and the crowd started to clear. She saw people turn in to the alley beside the pub and followed them. In the big room where they'd eaten the night before, she saw Joe Ashworth. Suddenly, she realized, she was ridiculously pleased to see him.

Chapter Thirty-Eight

VERA HAD WAITED UNTIL JOE AND Rosie left the pub before phoning Charlie. She'd taken her mobile outside so she wouldn't be overheard and stood looking out over the hill. Holly had spoken sometimes about 'headspace' and Vera had mentally rolled her eyes and scoffed. Here though, in this place, with the huge sky and the moor stretching out to the horizon, and the background music of sheep and curlew, Vera thought that her mind was as clear and sharp as it would ever be.

'You were right.' Charlie seldom showed any emotion, but even though the reception was poor, Vera thought she could hear something in his voice. Triumph? Admiration?

'So,' she said, 'it was as we thought.'

'As *you* thought.'

She allowed herself a moment of pride before continuing: 'There's a link then?'

'More than one.' A pause, and then he explained his discoveries.

'Well,' she said when he'd done. 'Who'd have thought?' But *she'd* thought. She'd had an inkling. An idea.

'Do you want me to head over?'

'Aye.' In the pub behind her, there was a loud bang, then swearing and then laughter. 'It's chaos here. Another couple of hours and the village will be *full* of strangers. It'll be possible then for them to hide in plain sight. We'll need you and your sharp eyes.' Now it was her turn to pause. 'We have to find the lass before they do.'

'You still don't know where she's hiding out?'

'I've got Joe and Rosie on it.' Which, they both realized, wasn't any kind of answer, but Charlie knew better than to push it.

'When do you want me to come along?'

Vera thought about that. 'Why don't you do a bit of a detour? See what's happening with our main player. I'll leave the rest up to you.'

Charlie didn't reply. He didn't need to.

When Vera left the pub, there was already a sense of excitement in the village. People were decorating their houses, not with the bright orange pumpkins of Hallowe'en, which Vera found rather jolly, but with strings of witches' hats, fake cobwebs. Everything black and grey. On all the windowpanes in the main street, more images of single eyes had been stuck. Some hooded and half-closed, all sinister. All of them signalling the same thing. *We're watching, we're looking for you.* Eyes had been the symbol of the Witch Hunt for generations.

She crossed the road and headed up the track to Cragside Farm. The owner had said he'd closed the house down for the season, but Vera thought he might have had a change of heart. The Witch Hunt had only been a local event in her youth, but surely the businessman wouldn't resist renting the house out now that people from all over the county wanted to take part.

Perhaps he'd turned up himself with a bunch of friends to party and to mock the plebs. Vera had asked Charlie to dig more deeply into the man's background, still on the lookout for connections. Her own form of witch hunt.

But when she approached the farm, she saw that the yard was empty. No sign of the big SUVs she might have expected. She headed up the path towards the bothy where she'd found the body of the young addict. *Brad. He was more than an addict.* She thought again that everyone deserved to be remembered by name. The bothy was still covered in police tape and they'd put a padlock on the door to keep out the curious after the team had finished their investigation, but she made no attempt to go inside. Instead, she sat with her back to the wall looking down at the valley, and the village. She fished a pair of binoculars from the pocket of her jacket. They'd belonged to her father. Hector had been a tight-fisted man, thrifty to the point of meanness, except when it came to his optical equipment. She remembered Jimmy Hepple, who could afford his own good binoculars now.

This pair had cost Hector more than a thousand pounds. They were light but very powerful. Occasionally she focused them on the fell beyond. Any stray walker would think she was looking out for peregrine or goshawk on the hill. Or that she was focused on the Three Dark Wives, which looked enormous now in the low autumn light. Brooding. Dominating the landscape. Peregrine had bred halfway up one of the stones when she was a girl. Hector and a climbing friend had made it to the eyrie to steal the young. Or she could be counting the thrushes – the redwing and fieldfare – arriving for the winter from the north. More often though, the binoculars were trained on the village and the farmhouse below.

Joe thought her impatient, lacking in caution, and if she'd been watching a city street, she'd have given up long ago. Here though, halfway between the sky and the hill, she was at home and calm and prepared to wait. She watched the crowds gather in the street and heard the first strains of the band. She tried to phone Charlie to check if he was on his way, but she must have hit a patch with no reception. A kind of lethargy had overtaken her, and she stayed where she was.

She was about to give up, to admit to herself that she'd been wrong and that she should move on to check in with the rest of the team, when she saw movement through one of the downstairs windows in the fancy farmhouse below. Only a glimpse, a ghostly shadow through the binoculars, but she'd been right after all; there was somebody inside.

Not rushing, the binoculars still strung around her neck, Vera started strolling down the hill. The slope was steep, and she could feel the stretch in her calves. She tried to keep out of the line of sight of the window, while making sure that she'd see if anybody left the house.

She knew she should wait. It was ridiculous to handle this herself. There was a back door and as soon as she knocked at the front, whoever was inside would leg it onto the hill. Because this wasn't the owner or a holidaymaker. Not without a vehicle. She tried to call Joe, but still, with the racket going on in the street below, he wasn't hearing his phone.

Now she was right at the house. Standing close to the wall, she moved around it, looking through windows into tastefully furnished rooms, the incomers' version of farmhouse chic. Vera's neighbours were farmers and their home was cluttered and mucky, smelling of dog and woodsmoke and Joanna's cooking. This was all pale grey paint and stripped pine, and in contrast, there was a modern kitchen straight out of *Homes and Gardens*, (which Vera had only read once, at the dentist). The shadowy silhouette Vera had seen from the hill had been in the kitchen. She stood for a moment, looking in at an angle so she wouldn't be seen from inside. There was a mug on the workbench and a plate with crumbs. A pot of instant noodles, empty. Someone had stayed here the night before.

She came to a window with curtains drawn, and put her ear to the pane, listening for movement. There might have been something, but there was double glazing, and she couldn't be sure. Besides, by now her imagination was working overtime. She decided this was ludicrous. She was a senior detective, not a lass playing at cops and robbers or hide-and-seek.

She marched up to the front door and knocked loudly, then pushed open the door, which wasn't locked.

Oh, pet, what were you thinking? Anyone could have come in. Because Vera was sure that this was Chloe and she'd been here the night before once her camp had been discovered. Though it was a mystery how she could have let herself in.

'Chloe? Are you there? I'm a police officer and we've been looking for you. We just want to check that you're safe. You're not in any bother.' She paused, listening. 'Your mam and your grandad are worried about you.'

She walked further into the house. No sound. Vera felt breathless and a little light-headed, her thoughts racing. She'd imagined that Chloe might have found her way here – this was where she'd spent much of her childhood – but now, in the silence, she wasn't sure. Perhaps it wasn't the girl she'd glimpsed through the window, but the killer.

She pushed open a door with her elbow. This was the room with the drawn curtains, but there was enough light to see a small space, with bookshelves from floor to ceiling, a couple of comfortable chairs and a low table. In the advertising copy for the holiday rental, it might be described as the library. Vera had been expecting signs that Chloe had been sleeping here, but there was nothing to suggest it. On the table there was a notebook and pen, and Vera was excited by that. Had Chloe been writing about her experiences again, exploring her thoughts and her fears in words? Vera pulled on a pair of gloves and was about to check its contents when she heard a faint sound from upstairs.

The stairs were carpeted and, despite her weight, there were no creaks. Halfway up, she stopped to catch her breath and to listen again. Perhaps her imagination had run away with her. All she could hear was the bleating of the sheep on the hill and the background noise of the music and the crowd. Vera continued to the top of the stairs. There, she waited.

She was on a square landing flooded with light from a long window looking out to the road and the village, with a comfortable chair. She could imagine sitting here and staring out at the world. There was a short corridor, with four doors leading off it. They were all closed. She stood, quite still, at the top of the stairs, her attention caught by a car that seemed to be approaching the house. Then, in a moment, before she had a chance to turn, there was a noise behind her. One of the doors had been pushed open and somebody flew past her, knocking her off balance. She reached out for the banister but missed it and toppled down the stairs, head over heels, her speed increasing until she reached the bottom. There was a surreal moment when she wondered if she'd be moving more slowly if she was less heavy. Did gravity work like that? Then she hit her head on the stripped wood floor of the hall, and everything went dark.

Chapter Thirty-Nine

JOE STOOD AND WAITED WITH ROSIE, watching the children's party in the big event space. He saw he'd had a missed call from the boss. No message. Of course not. He resented her disappearances, her insistence that she could look after herself. The last case they'd worked on should have made her more cautious. She'd promised that she'd do things differently, but now, when he phoned, there was no reply.

Rosie had been talking to some of the young parents, and had worked out what would happen next, what the Witch Hunt was actually about.

When the tea was served they moved outside, so she could explain. Conversation inside was impossible because of the noise. The place was chaos now, with over-excited children, fuelled by sugar and the joy of being the centre of attention, yelling and giggling and running around. Soon, Joe thought, there'd be a food fight. The parents with the Southern accents tried to exert some control, but the locals let the kids get on with it. This was Witch Hunt night, when confusion and disorder ruled. They'd been the same when they'd been that age.

'So what exactly happens?'

'The fun begins,' Rosie said, 'when it gets dark.'

Joe thought this was fun enough, but Rosie was still speaking.

'That's when the witch hides on the fell.'

'What witch?'

'This year it's Ma who runs the pub. Apparently the usual witch is in rehab drying out.'

Joe knew better than to ask for details; they'd only get distracted. 'What happens then?'

'The kids go and look for her.'

'What? On their own? Bairns running round on the hill in the dark?' Joe knew what Sal would say if he suggested his brood took part in the hunt.

'According to the parents I was speaking to, they haven't lost a child yet.' A pause. 'I think the younger kids have parents with them and the older ones are allowed head torches now. In the past, apparently, it was like a glorified game of blind man's bluff. The idea is for them to find the witch before she finds them. If she touches one on the shoulder, they're out of the game. If they see her before she touches them, they shout: "Witch, witch, I see you." The first one to shout out is the winner. They reckon there'll be a moon tonight so it'll be a doddle. It'll be over in a few minutes. If the weather's bad it can last for hours.'

Joe couldn't imagine anything more reckless. Many of the parents had been in the bar drinking since lunchtime and they'd be in more danger than the children, staggering around the hill. 'You wouldn't think it'd be allowed.'

'I think the council tried to shut it down a couple of years ago, but the village took no notice, so they turned a blind eye.' Rosie grinned. 'Hey, see what I said there. Blind eye. Have you seen there are eyes everywhere?'

'The evil eye,' he said. 'Apparently that's what it's about.'
The idea made him uncomfortable. He'd thought the Witch
Hunt would be a glorified village fete, manufactured for
tourists, but this felt more edgy and horribly chaotic. His
idea of a nightmare. He'd been brought up a Methodist,
singing rousing hymns in a plain chapel, with no element of
ritual. His faith had slid away from him over the years, but
this seemed blasphemous, a celebration of evil and the supernatural.

'What do we do now?'

Joe didn't know what to say. Without Vera he was lost, inde-
cisive. Sal thought he hadn't applied for promotion because
Vera had put blocks in his way, but it was fear that stopped
him too. Fear that he'd not be able to handle the responsibility
of being in charge, and anxiety that he'd shy away from the
difficult decisions.

The sun was setting behind the hills to the west. There'd
been a fierce red glow on the horizon, but now the light was
fading. The hill was a dark silhouette and soon that would
merge into the black sky. The few street lights in the village
were suddenly turned off – this too was a prearranged part of
the evening's event – and above them Joe could already see a
scattering of stars and a half-moon.

A cheer rose from the party space, and Ma walked out
through the wide-open doors towards them. She was dressed
in black with a grey straggly wig under her black witch's hat.
Her face had been painted white. In the half-light, that was all
he could see with any clarity. The startling white face. And
her staring eyes.

The witch turned back to the room and the crowd fell
silent. She raised her hands in the air. A young child started

to cry, obviously terrified, but Ma took no notice. She shouted at her audience:

'You know the rules. Half an hour by the clock on the wall, and then the hunt begins.'

Joe turned to look for the clock, which he hadn't noticed before. It was on an outside wall of what once had been stables, caught in a spotlight, the only light in the place now apart from the party room and that in the bar. When he turned back, Ma had disappeared.

Chapter Forty

WHEN VERA CAME TO SHE WAS confused, unsure of her surroundings. She knew at once that she wasn't at home in bed. Her house still smelled of Hector, of the chemicals he'd used in his taxidermy, with a back note of damp. And she couldn't feel the weight of blankets and old-fashioned quilt. Sometimes, though, she fell asleep at work in her chair in her tiny office, because she couldn't be arsed to drive home or because she'd had a drink, or because she was exhausted. Now she felt the same stiffness in the limbs, and the same headache.

She pushed herself up to a sitting position and realized at once that this was a different sort of pain. She'd ricked her shoulder and she hadn't had a headache like this through drink for years. Slowly she remembered where she was. In the farmhouse at Cragside, at the bottom of the stairs, on the hard wooden floor of the hall. The door opposite was open. There was still a little light, but it was fading. She must have been unconscious for a while.

Suddenly there was even less light. A figure stood in the doorway, and she squinted towards it, still too dazed and uncomfortable to be scared at this point. Everything was blurred, and there was a halo effect behind the newcomer's head. It could be an angel. Or a devil. She shook her head a little, hoping to see more clearly, but that only made the pain worse. She shut her eyes for a moment in the hope that when she opened them, the figure would have disappeared.

'Vera, man, what have you done to yourself now?'

Charlie. Not an angel, but her saviour all the same. If she'd been on her feet, she'd have kissed him. She could tell he was concerned. He'd never have used her first name in a work situation, even though they'd been together for years.

'A bit of a trip.' Her voice sounded croaky and distant. 'Nothing to get into a state about.'

'A trip?' His voice suspicious.

'Well,' she conceded. 'Maybe a push.'

'What are you doing here on your own? You could have been killed.'

'Not me!' Her head was already starting to clear. It was the relief, and her heart rate returning to normal. 'You know me, Charlie, as tough as old boots.'

'Where are the others? What were they thinking, letting you out on your own?'

'I'm not a bairn. I don't need my parents' permission.' Now she felt able to move without throwing up on the waxed wooden floor. 'Give me a hand up. How did you find me?'

'I thought you might come here looking for Chloe.'

'Then you're a better detective than Joe Ashworth or Rosie Bell.' He gave her a hand and helped her gently to her feet. 'Though don't you dare tell them I said so.'

They stood for a moment.

'Can I get you anything? A glass of water?'

'Water would be champion.' Suddenly, she realized she was very thirsty.

As he disappeared into the kitchen, she held on to the banister to steady herself. She still felt a bit wobbly on her feet, but she released the hold when he returned.

She tried to focus on the matter in hand. 'Is our killer here?'

'Well, your suspect is. Not enough evidence yet to convict.' Charlie was always a realist, but this time she knew he was right.

'Where are they?'

'Mingling with the crowd.' Charlie paused, apologetic, guilty. 'I lost track when I tried to find somewhere to park. It's a madhouse out there, and I wanted to find you.'

Vera's thoughts were sharp now and her mind was racing. 'Even if we find Chloe before they do,' she said, 'that won't help us much.'

'So what are we thinking?'

'We need our own witch hunt. To catch the killer as they're approaching Chloe.'

'Eh, you can't do that! It'd put the lass in danger.'

'She's in danger already.' A pause. 'We find her and stick to her. Like glue.' She turned to the man. 'Has the Hunt started?'

'It hadn't when I came to find you. They were just about to start the thirty-minute countdown.'

'We'd best get a wiggle on then. Let's find the others. Between us we should be able to find her.' She tried a smile, attempted a lightness that she couldn't quite feel. 'After all, we don't want to miss the drama.'

They got to the Stanhope Arms with ten minutes to spare before the start of the Hunt. It was dark apart from a glow from the moon, and Vera thought this was ridiculous. How would they find one child in this crowd? But what else could they do? They'd lost the killer too. Charlie spotted Joe and Rosie first and pointed them out. They were standing in the pub's yard with the rest of the crowd. The kids were tugging at the adults' arms, like leashed hounds, desperate to start.

'Where have you been?' That was classic Ashworth. There was the same sort of fury as when a missing child suddenly appears. Relief masquerading as anger.

'I had a bit of a trip and Charlie here came to my rescue.'

'So what's the plan?' Rosie was less bothered about Vera's health than about getting a result. Vera could appreciate that. She'd be the same.

'I think Chloe will be out on the hill. Hiding in plain sight. She'll see it as the best form of escape. I surprised her in the Cragside farmhouse, and she did a runner. I tried to explain who I was, but she's scared of the world now. Of her own shadow. She grew up here. She knows about the Witch Hunt. She'll have taken part herself as a kiddie. The trouble is that our suspect knows she's in Gillstead and they'll be on the hill too. We need to find her before they do.'

'And bring her in?' Joe was looking at the clock. Vera could tell that he'd been hanging around here for too long and he wanted to be away.

Vera shook her head. 'We stick with her. We need proof. At the moment we've got no evidence to charge our suspect.'

'You're using a fourteen-year-old lass as a decoy?' Joe was horrified. She thought he was about to explode into a tirade of criticism and jumped in before he could continue.

'We stick with her. We protect her.'

'In the dark? With all this madness going on around us?'

'We know the killer's out there,' Vera said. 'Charlie followed them to the village, but he lost them. Our perpetrator will be looking for Chloe anyway. At the moment she's safer on the hill with all the others than she would be in an empty village. The killer would look for her here first.'

'Tell us.' Joe was still furious. 'Who exactly are we talking about? Who is this mysterious killer? You haven't exactly told Rosie and me what's going on here. Are we supposed to guess?'

'We still don't know. Not for sure.' Vera was feeling very tired. 'But this is who *I* think we're looking for.' She gave them a name. They deserved that at least, though when she shared her suspicion, she wasn't sure that they believed her. 'Charlie, explain what we think has happened.'

Charlie explained. His voice was diffident, quiet. It was as easy to forget as his appearance. Impossible to describe. Vera had to strain to hear him, and there were moments when she lost concentration altogether. Instead, she focused on Joe and Rosie, on their faces. They were certainly listening. At first they seemed sceptical, but he was beginning to convince them, and in the end they were nodding.

'So,' Vera demanded, 'you do see that we've only just made the link.'

In the silence that followed the crowd began to count down the seconds to the beginning of the Hunt, roaring out the numbers, the sound increasing with each one. Vera could sense their excitement.

'Ten, nine, eight, seven, six, five, four, three, two, one!' Then after a brief pause: 'Witch, witch, we're coming for you! We're looking for you, looking for you!'

And the stampede began. Vera felt suddenly faint. The rushing crowd blurred in front of her eyes. She knew then that she wasn't up for a tramp on the fell in the dark. She'd be no good to the team if she passed out again. She'd only distract them. 'I'll stay here,' she said. Her words seemed to come from a long way off. She couldn't believe that she was losing strength at this particular moment. 'Just in case they come back.'

Charlie became solicitous again. 'Maybe I should call an ambulance.'

'Get on with you!' She made a shooing gesture with her hands. 'Make sure you come back. With them both.'

Chapter Forty-One

THEY FOLLOWED THE FAMILIES THROUGH THE five-bar gate that led from the meadow at the back of the pub, and on to the open hillside. Rosie thought this was madness. Flashes of light from the head torches scattered around her like sparks or fireflies. She could see shadows in the moonlight, but how could she tell if one of these was Chloe Spence? Or the killer? There were small children with their parents, but the older teens were alone or in small giggling groups. She guessed it was a rite of passage to be allowed on to the fell without an adult, and perhaps the inhabitants of Gillstead knew this place as well as she knew the streets of Heaton, but still the whole thing seemed ridiculously risky. A health and safety officer would have a fit.

It occurred to her then that there were no lone adults here. If they came across one, they would have found their killer. And, she thought, *they* would arouse suspicion too: three adults without a child between them. Perhaps they should tag on to a group of youngsters. If they could find one. The groups had scattered. The rules said that they should stick to this piece of fell, surrounded by a drystone wall. It had been cleared of sheep and there were no obvious hazards, but there was space enough to make the search almost impossible.

Her eyes got used to the dark and she could see the outline of the prehistoric standing stones, hard and black, the moonlight throwing faint shadows. Vera had pointed them out as the Three Dark Wives.

The witch never strays far from there.

In this light, it was hard to believe that the stones had been dragged here, pulled into place by teams of men. They looked organic, grown from the earth. Or supernatural. Vera had been right: this was a place where the witch could hide, while the children whirled on the open moorland all round her. Rosie was aware of the kids chasing across the grass. She couldn't see them, but she could hear them; excitement and fear made their voices high-pitched, piercing.

Joe and Charlie seemed as stunned as she was about everything that was going on. They'd all grown up in towns. They were streetwise, could read dodgy characters, knew the places and the people to avoid; but here with the dizzying stars, endless space and no street lights, they were out of their depth.

'Shall we just wait here?' Joe was speaking. They were in the shelter of one of the huge rocks, not too far from the gate and the pub, their silhouettes masked by the stone. 'Better than wandering around aimlessly, and they'll have to come past this way eventually.'

Rosie thought he found the space as disconcerting as she did and was as sceptical as she was about Vera's insistence that they should be here on the hill. 'Sure,' she said, relieved that at least there was some sort of plan. 'Why not?'

There was a scream behind them. So loud and terrified that it was impossible to tell whether it was a child or an adult. Rosie swung round to see. There was a white face, up-lit by torchlight. Ma in her witch's costume. Not kitsch now. Not something to laugh at. But sinister. She'd crept behind a child and his father and touched a shoulder. The scream subsided and the pair walked off. They were out of the game.

'Bloody hell,' Joe said. 'Those kids will be scarred for life.'

Rosie thought they couldn't have been the only people to see the encounter, but nobody shouted out the magic words. *Witch, witch, we've been looking for you and now you're found.* Perhaps, like riders on a scary fairground ride, they wanted the experience to continue.

There were fewer lights now. Ma must have found most of the younger kids. Perhaps their parents had wanted them found so they could be taken home and put to bed. Perhaps their chatter had given them away. It was the lone teenagers who were left. They slunk around the hillside, crouching so they were harder to see. Many had turned off their head torches so they wouldn't be noticed. They flitted about, ghostly in the moonlight. Rosie had the feeling that only now was the real game beginning. The previous chase had been a show for the little ones. She felt the same stress as she did on surveillance, the same anxiety. And really, she supposed, that was what this was. But how could she tell a killer from an almost grown teenager when she could see no detail? And how would she know the supposed victim, when all she'd seen was a photo?

Charlie, standing beside her, was still alert though. She sensed a sudden tension in his body, and she was focused, her eyes wide to take in as much light as she could, before he nudged her and nodded in the direction of a figure standing a little apart. There was something about the shape, the bulk and heft, that made her think that this was an adult. There was no movement. A stillness that suggested someone watching and waiting, as concentrated as they were. As determined.

Rosie understood at last why the killer had chosen this pantomime to search for their prey, and why Vera had insisted on their presence. A troubled lass, who'd been missing for a week, might have an accident on the hill while taking part in the Hunt. She might trip in the dark and hit her head on the rocky ground. People would blame the organizers, the village for persisting with such an outdated ritual. The press would take up the story. What sort of community was this that allowed such a dangerous event to take place? Besides, if it were tucked in a fold in the fell or hidden in a ditch, the body might not be found for days. There were animals and raptors which fed on carrion. There might be so little of her left that it would be hard to distinguish accident from murder.

The watcher moved, very suddenly, with a speed and agility that surprised them. From his different viewpoint had he seen the girl? The ground underfoot was uneven, boggy in places, so the pace seemed reckless. Rosie could tell that their killer was desperate. A little further down the hill, there was another flurry of activity. Rosie thought this must be Chloe, aware that she'd been seen, trying now to escape back to the safety of the village and the people waiting for the winner of the Hunt to be announced.

Charlie was already running, surprisingly light on his feet. Rosie followed and was aware of Joe a little ahead of her. Then a big brown cloud covered the moon, and there was no light at all. Her foot caught a hard clump of reed and cotton grass and she fell.

Chapter Forty-Two

When the moon was covered, Joe lost all sense of where he was, and the direction in which he was running. He'd never been anywhere quite so dark. He'd been on holiday to wild places with Sal and the kids, but there'd always been a glow on the horizon, a hint of the nearest town. The Gillstead street lights had been switched off and the doors of the Stanhope Arms firmly shut. In the cottages, curtains had been drawn so no light would escape.

It seemed that most of the remaining Witch Hunt participants had stood still when the moon was covered. They'd be as disorientated as he was, and suddenly careful of their own safety. He and Charlie and the two people ahead of them were the only ones running. He couldn't tell where Rosie was, but he could hear footsteps, and he followed the sound. In the back of his mind was fear of Vera's reaction if any harm came to Chloe or they let the killer go. Her disappointment that they'd let her down, that they could never be trusted if they were on their own.

Slowly, the cloud slid away from the moon, and he lost the

confusion and the lack of spatial awareness. He couldn't see the two figures running ahead of them, but he could make out Charlie's shadow, slight, as easily hidden here on the hill, it seemed, as he was in everyday life.

Behind him a bell was being rung. Loud and incongruous, it reminded him of his schooldays: a big brass bell had called them into school from the playground. This was the sign that the Hunt was over. The witch had been found. The equivalent of the white smoke once a pope had been chosen.

There was a distant cheer from the village below and Gillstead was light again. Not brightly lit, because it was still surrounded by darkness, but the street lamps had been switched back on and the doors of the barn at the rear of the pub had been thrown open. If anything, those lights made the hillside seem even darker, and now all the remaining hunters were making their way down the hill to the gate. He was overtaken by chasing teenagers who were fitter and less risk averse than him. He had a moment of panic when he was certain that this had all been a waste of time, and the killer would escape.

How hard would it be, in all this confusion, to put an arm round a young lass, pretend to be a parent, and drag her away back on to the hill? When everyone else was yelling, who would take any notice of her screams for help?

There was a bottleneck at the gate, with people jostling to get through, the crowd impatient, curious and wondering at the hold-up. And there was Vera, implacable, legs apart, hands on hips, chatting to a young girl with a round face that was white in the moonlight. And Charlie, who'd wrestled a man to the ground, was pulling his hands behind his back and speaking the words of arrest. As he got closer, Joe saw Charlie, surprisingly strong, lift the man to his feet. Chris Woodburn stood blinking, as if he didn't know how he'd come to be there, his face mud-stained and streaked with tears.

Chapter Forty-Three

EVERYTHING WAS CONFUSION. VERA'S TEAM WAS blocking the path back to the village and hordes of people – participants and watchers – were swirling around them. Ma was the centre of attention, playing up to her audience. The crowd parted and clapped her back to the yard at the rear of the Stanhope Arms, and she bowed towards each side with a flourish as she walked. The winner of the Witch Hunt was Alice's boyfriend, and he was being carried, shoulder high, by a group of his friends across the meadow towards the pub. Vera was crouched next to Chloe, trying to reassure her that now all would be well. That the danger was over.

Suddenly, there was a shout from the crowd. High-pitched and aggressive. Directed, Vera realized, at Charlie, who was holding on to Chris Woodburn.

'Hey! What the fuck are you doing? Let that man go. And shift so we can get past.' It was impossible to tell if the shriek had come from the mouth of a man or a woman.

The mood of the group changed immediately. As if a switch had been thrown, good-natured impatience turned to alcohol-fuelled anger. It rippled through the crowd, charged like electricity, sparking and fuelling the locals who wanted more drink and home, and the visitors aware of the packed streets, the chaos they'd face driving out of the village.

Charlie was still restraining Woodburn, but the DC was jostled, elbowed until he lost his balance and almost his footing. He was trying to steady himself, when an arm shot out and suddenly Chris Woodburn was tugged out of his grasp. When Vera looked next, the man had disappeared into the throng, pulled by a person she'd only glimpsed. In the darkness she couldn't make any sort of ID. The action had happened so quickly that she could scarcely believe it.

Charlie started to heave his way through the people, trying to follow the man, but the crowd became even more hostile. Perhaps they believed that Charlie was jumping some sort of invisible queue and they moved together to block his path, but Vera, watching, still with a protective arm round Chloe, thought this was more orchestrated than a few lairy locals fighting for their patch. Woodburn's rescuer had come mob-handed or paid some local thugs to make a scene. She should have been expecting the intervention and could have kicked herself. She shouted to Joe:

'Take Chloe here back to the Stanhope and have a word with Ma. See if she can find somewhere quiet for her to rest. Stay with her, eh? Don't let her out of your sight. Just in case.' Then, crouching so she was on the same level as the girl: 'You go with my sergeant here. He'll look after you. He has a lass about your age.'

She turned to Rosie: 'I've got people watching the roads out of Gillstead, but let's see if we can find them before then, eh? The two of us can show them how it's done. I want to end this thing tonight.'

They moved off, Rosie fierce and strong in her bright blue coat despite her twisted ankle. Vera felt a sudden surge of energy and anger and was close behind her.

Chapter Forty-Four

AWAY FROM THE GATE, THE CROWD thinned a little. Most of the villagers had headed back to the pub, aware that there'd been some sort of scuffle, but thinking that was par for the course on Witch Hunt night. Rosie could sense Vera by her side, matching her step for step, despite her age and the knock that she'd taken in the Cragside farmhouse. Rosie had started off in the direction that Woodburn had taken, but now the boss touched her arm.

'Slow down a bit, pet. Let's think about this. If they're in the village Charlie will track them down. He's like a terrier that one. No point us running around like headless chickens.'

They were in the corner of the meadow, where the grass was longer and starting to be sugared with frost. In the distance, the last shadowy silhouettes were clearing the hill. Reluctantly, Rosie slowed to a stop, and Vera continued talking.

'You know Chris Woodburn well, better than anyone else on the team. Let's be clever about this and put ourselves in his shoes. Where do you think they might be hiding?'

Rosie thought about that. Woodburn's rescuer might not be at home in the hills, but Chris had walked them regularly with his son. Surely, he would run away from the village and the people milling around the streets, and into the uplands where there was space to disappear.

'Woodburn knows this place,' she said. 'I think he'd stay away from the village. He'd be more in his comfort zone up on the fell.'

She was aware of a slight movement: Vera nodding in agreement. Rosie remembered one of the photos in the Woodburns' kitchen, pictured it clearly. The Three Dark Wives with Chris and Josh standing beside them.

'They'll have circled back and be heading to the standing stones. That part of the hill will be empty now. Nobody will expect them to return to the site of the Witch Hunt! It'll make sense for them to wait out there, with a view of the village, until the streets are clear and they can drive away.'

'Good thinking!' There was admiration in Vera's voice, but Rosie thought the boss had been ahead of her, had probably had exactly the same idea. Rosie wasn't sure what she made of that. Was the woman being patronizing? Or encouraging? She shook her head to clear the thought from her head. This wasn't a time for navel-gazing.

There was nobody now at the gate where they'd caught Chloe. At least the girl was safe, Rosie thought, overwhelmed suddenly by a sense of relief. She pushed her way through and waited while Vera fastened it behind them.

'It might not be much of a barrier,' the DI said, 'but it'll slow them down a bit if it comes to a chase.'

Rosie was all set to march up the hill then, but Vera stood quite still, listening. If Charlie was a terrier, Rosie thought, the boss was some other kind of hunting dog. Patient now, sniffing out the scent of its prey.

'No rush.' Vera's voice was a whisper, no louder than the wind in the reeds where the ground was boggy. 'If they're there, you're right and they'll wait until the roads have cleared.'

There was still a moon, and they kept low to the hill, so they wouldn't present a silhouette to anyone watching. Vera controlled their movements, pointing for Rosie to climb up one side of the hill while she took the other. Rosie could tell that her idea was to walk around the back of the slope, so they'd meet behind the standing stones. The couple on the hill wouldn't be expecting that, if they were expecting anyone at all. Surely they'd be watching for people to come directly towards them from the village.

Rosie was glad of Vera's instruction to move slowly. Her ankle was still sore, and she didn't want to twist it again, or trip, or make any kind of noise. From the valley there was a faint rumble of traffic, and headlights shifting slowly, like a line of worry beads being moved along an invisible thread. She stopped and listened, thought she heard a faint murmur of conversation, felt the exhilarating sense that her judgement had been right. She had no fear at this point. She still couldn't picture Chris Woodburn as a man who might be dangerous. She turned to see Vera moving to join her.

Now they were on the plateau behind the standing stones. The moon threw their shadows onto the hill towards her. Vera had told her their story and she saw them as monumental: three strong women, protective and solid. The sound of voices was louder now, and she could hear something of what was being said. Chris Woodburn:

'It wasn't supposed to happen like this.'

Rosie remembered a phone call she'd heard when she'd been invited to the Woodburns' Cullercoats house for dinner and had sat at the table, swamped by their grief. Chris had said something similar then. Perhaps he'd been speaking to the same person.

Another, different voice: 'I can get you away. You can start a new life. Anywhere you like.'

'No!' A pause. 'I was pleased, actually, when they caught me. It's gone too far. I can't stand it. I'll go back. Hand myself in.'

A silence. 'Really, I don't think that's a good idea.' The pitch had dropped again and was so quiet that Rosie struggled to hear it, but it was icy, threatening. 'Not a good idea at all. I have too much to lose.'

Rosie inched forward, hoping to see beyond the stones to the speaking couple. She'd lost all sense of where Vera might be and was completely focused on Woodburn and his companion. As she edged towards them, her ankle twisted again on an uneven clump of dead heather and gave way beneath her. She fell. She managed to stifle a scream as the pain hit, but the sound of her body thudding against the ground was so loud in the silence that they must have heard it.

The stranger's voice shouted into the darkness: 'Who is it? Who's there?'

Rosie said nothing. She stayed where she was, close to the ground. Perhaps they'd think they'd heard an animal, something wild and feral living off the fell. At first she thought she'd got away with it. Then there was a sharp, white light, and the beam of a powerful torch scoured the hill and came to land on her. She struggled to her feet, blinking and blinded, wincing as she tried to put some weight on her foot.

'Chris!' she shouted. The bowl of the valley created an echo and the word seemed to roll around her. 'It's Rosie Bell. You know me. I'm on my own and I just want to talk to you.'

'He's a killer!' That sharp, piercing voice again, with an edge of panic. 'Don't believe what he tells you.'

The torch beam moved, this time providing a spotlight on Woodburn. He'd moved from behind the largest of the Wives. His shadow was thrown forward, so he could have been a smaller version of them. A stone son. He was implacable too. With Josh dead, perhaps he thought he had nothing to lose.

'I'll come with you,' he said, 'and tell you everything.' He walked towards Rosie. The torchlight was behind him, and the shadow grew longer. 'I'll plead guilty to murder.'

Then the beam shifted back and was focused once more on Rosie. It got closer and closer, but she knew she couldn't run. Her ankle wouldn't hold her or allow her to do more than hobble. Soon her opponent was only feet from where she was standing. The light hurt Rosie's eyes and she turned away. Then the torchlight was no longer directed immediately at her. It swung skyward, like the beam of a tipsy lighthouse. Rosie glanced back to check what was happening and saw a woman, arm raised, the heavy torch a weapon now and about to hit her. There was a second when she was frozen, imagining Josh Woodburn as she'd seen him on the mortuary table. Skull split, splintered bones and dried blood.

Then there came a noise like the roar of an enormous animal. It shocked them both; the woman lost concentration and looked towards the sound. Rosie, fascinated, saw Vera, large and strong as a bull charging towards them. Before the woman could move, Vera's shoulder had made contact with her body and shoved her to the ground. The torch slipped away, and for a moment everything was dark.

'Who is it?' Rosie had stooped to pick up the torch and was shining it into the woman's face. 'Is it who you were expecting?'

'Oh aye.' Vera was out of breath but still triumphant. 'This is her. This is Helen Miles.'

They made a strange procession down the hill. Vera had tied Miles's hands behind her back, but held on to her, an arm linked through the woman's. In the shadow they could have been lovers. Rosie found enough reception to phone for a van to be waiting for them in the yard of the pub. She limped her way slowly, with Woodburn beside her. He was compliant now – relieved, it seemed, that the chase was over. He wouldn't try to run again.

At the bottom of the hill, they stopped to open the gate, and pushed the suspects through. With her free arm, Vera nudged Rosie.

'There, pet, didn't I tell you we'd show the men how it was done.'

Chapter Forty-Five

MA HAD OFFERED HER HOUSE FOR Joe and Chloe to wait for news, and that's where Ma took Vera and Rosie when they arrived at the Stanhope. Charlie turned up soon afterwards. It was next door to the pub, rather grand, which would have surprised Vera's team but didn't shock Vera herself. The landlady had inherited the Stannie Arms from a pair of elderly aunts, spinster sisters – even more formidable, according to local legend, than Ma herself. There was no mortgage, no rent, no slavery to a big brewery. No husband to fritter away the profits. She'd be a wealthy woman. And uppity. Another Dark Wife.

'No point sitting in a traffic jam for hours and that lass could do with a rest,' Ma said. She'd changed and cleaned most of the make-up from her face, but there were still streaks of white on her cheekbones, giving that strange ghostly look which somehow suited her. She was imperious as ever and disappeared back to the Stanhope Arms as soon as she'd let them in. Vera suspected there'd be a lock-in until the early hours.

As soon as she'd had signal, Vera had been on the phone to

Chloe's grandparents, and the hospital where her mother was still a patient.

'The lass is quite safe.'

Her father and grandfather were on their way. Chloe had been terrified when Vera had stopped her after she'd raced down the hill, with Woodburn at her heels. She'd kicked and lashed out, until Vera had wrapped her arms around her, holding her tight, murmuring reassurance.

Joe had walked the girl to the pub and then Ma had almost carried her to the house, and straight into the bedroom. The curtains were so thick that no light or sound came through. She'd stooped to take off the lass's shoes, before lying her on the bed and carefully covering her with a fleecy blanket.

Vera went in to see her as soon as she and Rosie arrived. She was light-headed for a moment. There'd been times when she'd thought they'd never find the girl alive.

'We'll chat in the morning, pet. But you're safe. And that's all that matters. We're on your side.'

It didn't matter that Chloe was fast asleep.

Woodburn and Miles had been taken to Hexham nick, where they'd be kept for the night before being driven to Kimmerston in the morning. Vera had decided that they could wait for interview until then.

Now Charlie was making tea, and Ma had given them a tin of home bakes left over from the kids' witchy party. They were sugary and covered in butter cream, and just what was needed. The team sat in Ma's comfortable living room, quiet, waiting for the adrenaline to seep from their systems.

'Poor lass,' Vera said.

She sent Rosie into the bedroom to check on the girl again. When Rosie limped back into the room, nodding to show that

Chloe was still sleeping, Vera continued talking, her focus at first on the lass:

'The past few days she's not been thinking straight. She didn't know who to trust, so she didn't trust anyone. Except her two mates – Alice and Esther. No wonder, when everyone in authority seemed to have let her down and she'd become obsessed with conspiracies. You can understand why though. This was all a conspiracy of a sort. When I went into Cragside she rushed past me and joined in with the other kids in the parade and on the hill. Woodburn was already hiding out there. He saw her before you lot did, and she did a runner.'

'How did she get into the farmhouse?'

'The new owner had upgraded a lot since her grandfather sold it, but he hadn't changed the front door. There was always a spare key hidden in one of the outhouses.' Vera paused. 'I shouldn't have charged into the place. I should have realized it would freak her out. Like I said, by then she wasn't thinking straight. She'd been on the run for a week, not sleeping or eating properly. No wonder she bolted. She must have thought she'd be safe on the hill, with all the other kids.' Another pause. 'She's brave, that one.'

The room was full of furniture that Ma had inherited from her aunts: a large dark wood sideboard, a leather chesterfield, a couple of armchairs that looked less comfortable than they were. It was lit by a standard lamp, the shade decorated with a hunting scene. Vera supposed Ma would spend little time in here. The pub was her real home. It was a bit like *her* and her cottage in the hills. That still felt as if it belonged more to Hector than to her. Perhaps one day she would have to move. When she retired and she didn't have her office at the station as a base.

Her team were staring at her, waiting for an explanation. In the end, Joe lost patience: 'You're not saying that Woodburn killed Josh. His son!'

She shook her head. 'Of course that was never meant to happen. Brad was just supposed to frighten him off. Nothing more than that. But Brad was never the most reliable person. Volatile. Addicted. To drugs and to violence, despite his attempt to charm. Kath Oliver told us that.'

'But Chris Woodburn didn't even know that Josh was working at Rosebank.'

'Of course he did! The family was close. Josh went back to see them, and he often talked to his father about what he was doing at university. His mother might not have known. She was busy, working as a GP over in Gateshead. But Chris and his father went walking together. They'd have talked about it, even if Josh wanted to keep it as a surprise for his tutor.'

'I don't see where the university comes into it.'

'Josh was doing a course in film and media. He was interested in broadcast journalism. For his final degree piece, he'd decided to make a documentary about children's homes. He was idealistic, and he genuinely enjoyed working at Rosebank, and of course he wanted to impress Stella Marsh, but he only got a job there to do research into the system.'

'That's why he spent so much time with Chloe?'

Vera nodded. 'She'd have been an ideal interviewee, wouldn't she? Bright. Articulate. Sparky. She'd even started on her own script. All those diary pieces he encouraged her to write.' She paused for a moment, scrolling back through the conversations she'd had at the start of the investigation. 'You told me his tutor said Josh was excited by his new project. He thought he'd be producing a piece that was important.'

'I still don't understand how that gave Chris Woodburn a motive for murder.'

Vera looked across the room. In the past, she might have taken credit for making the connections, and of course the initial idea had been hers. They couldn't take that away from her. She was still as sharp as she'd ever been, whatever the team thought. But Charlie had done the graft. They'd never have reached the right conclusions without his patience. 'Why don't you explain, Charlie?'

'Woodburn's an accountant. Not the sort that does the books for small businesses, but high-powered. One of his most lucrative contracts is with a firm that has fingers in a lot of pies throughout the North of England. Including privately run children's homes. They're known as Seaview Holdings. A man called Stamoran runs the kids' home side of the business, and I've been digging around into his background. He's changed his identity a couple of times and is also known as Cornell Charles. He grew up here in the North-East.'

'He couldn't have been involved in Josh's murder though,' Rosie said. 'You told us he was on a cruise on the other side of the world.'

'No,' Vera said, 'and I don't think he dreamed up the whole plan, but he was certainly involved. He was a small-time crook when he was living in the North-East, a fraudster, charming old ladies out of their pensions, stealing from his employers. A horrible man, but without a record of violence. The real power behind the throne was Helen Miles. She was behind Seaview, just as she was behind other companies with a shady reputation.' A pause. 'Imagine if Josh's film came out. She'd built her reputation on being a born-again Christian giving back to the community, founding a school to give local kids a chance of a better life, and all the time she owned a business that ripped off troubled teens.'

'Would it really look that bad?' Rosie sounded sceptical. 'Enough to trigger two murders?'

Charlie took up the explanation: 'On the surface, Seaview seems very respectable. The caring face of capitalism. But if you dig a bit deeper, it's all rather . . .' He hesitated, looking for the right word. '. . . unsavoury. We suspect it's more engaged in criminal activity than social justice, so yeah, it really would have looked that bad.' Charlie stared out at them, his face bleak. 'It seems that a private equity firm based overseas is close to investing in Seaview. Now wouldn't be a good time for unfavourable publicity.'

'Would Woodburn have known who he was working for?' Joe sounded as if he could hardly believe what he was hearing. This was like the most dramatic form of television drama. But Charlie was reliable. Understated. He wouldn't have passed on information that hadn't been thoroughly checked.

'He might not have known everything that was going on, but he must have guessed that at least some of their dealings were extremely dodgy.' Charlie paused. 'My contact in serious crime described Seaview as being like some sort of weed, with roots going underground and coming up in the least expected places.'

In the street outside there was a burst of laughter. Some of Ma's customers were on their way home.

'It must have been a shock,' Rosie said, 'when Woodburn found out that his son intended to expose the system, what was going on at Rosebank at least. Josh would have been able to find out how much the local authority was paying for their troubled kids, and he'd see how little was actually feeding into their care.'

Vera nodded her approval. Rosie Bell might be nothing like Holly, the team member who'd died, who still haunted them all, but she had the same good brain. She'd do very well.

'I think Chris tried to persuade his son to consider another project,' Vera said, 'but he couldn't be too forceful without explaining his own involvement with the company. Instead, he fed his concerns to his employers. A big mistake. The information went right to the top. To Miles.'

Charlie came back in then. This was his story after all, and he didn't often have a chance to shine. 'In the end, they took matters into their own hands. Miles hired Brad Russell to frighten off Josh – she'd grown up in Longwater and still had her contacts there. She thought the student would easily be scared into dropping the project altogether. But as we know, Brad was unreliable. Volatile. He got a kick out of violence.'

'The person in the car outside the home.' Rosie was ahead of them again. 'That was Miles, watching what was happening.'

'I think so. And the person who scared Chloe in the library. We know from her involvement in the school that Miles likes to be hands on. She's never been one to delegate. No wonder Chloe was freaked out when at last she got a glimpse of the woman in the car. The woman she'd been taught to consider as almost a saint. That would make anyone believe in weird conspiracies.'

Charlie took over the story again. 'Seaview Holdings lease a small fleet of cars, some based in the North-East. That gave us our first lead. They're all black Volvos. Chris Woodburn brought Brad here in one of them. He wouldn't have wanted to use his own vehicle.'

There was a moment of silence before Charlie continued: 'I think that the company would have tried flattery and an incentive to stop making the film. Maybe offering another project, money to make something? But he refused to be bought off. They could have sacked him, but he still had all the dirt.'

Vera thought that he'd been brave too. A son you'd be proud of.

'Why did Woodburn bring Brad to Gillstead to kill him?' Rosie asked. 'I suppose by then he did know Brad had murdered his son.'

'Brad knew that Chloe had roots here,' Vera said. 'Woodburn could have convinced him that they were looking for the lass, that they needed to get to her before she spoke to the police. Brad told his grandparents he'd been offered new and important work. Woodburn persuaded him that they needed to track down Chloe. Chris was under a lot of pressure by now and he was desperate.'

'Pressure from Seaview?'

Vera nodded. 'Right from the top. From Miles.'

'So,' Joe asked, 'the night Josh died. What happened?'

'Brad was hyper. Everyone says so. He'd been hired to scare off Josh and he was restless and he couldn't keep still. I think he was wandering in and out of the common room all evening and nobody really noticed. Not with the film running and the lights off, and anyway he was always like that. He'd have been listening out for Josh's car, but Chloe had heard it too and was outside waiting for him. The hammer would have been in Brad's room. He'd needed something to nail that dartboard to his door! Josh would have seen the sort of mood Brad was in and he sent Chloe away. 'Go to your safe place and wait for me.' He would have said something like that. We'll find out the details when we get a statement from her. She never thought of Rosebank as a safe place and she'd told Josh about the boys' den on the common, so that's where she went to wait.'

Vera imagined the lass running away from the home, into the dark and the murk, and on to the common, feeling her way through the undergrowth until she was safe. Had she emerged the next morning, to see the police cars and the activity? She'd contacted Esther for help, before moving on to Paradise Farm. Then she'd thought of Alice and the hut at Gillstead Hall, believing that there, at least, she'd be safe.

'What about the lack of blood on Brad's clothes?' Rosie broke into her thoughts.

'He always wore a big parka, didn't he, according to Chloe's diary? Even indoors. But we never saw him wear it after the murder. Chloe saw it though, late that night on the common. It was in her first piece of writing. She thought it was a dead child, covered in blood. Brad went and burned it the following morning. He was in a rush to get out, if you remember. It would just have been one of the fires that were always being set on the common. We'll check with the lass in the morning what he was wearing when she saw him, but I bet it was the parka.'

On cue, the doorbell rang. Vera went to let in Gordon and John. Chloe was still asleep when they carried her into the car. Her place was with her family now.

Chapter Forty-Six

ROSIE STOOD OUTSIDE THE HOUSE WITH its view over Cullercoats Bay. It was only eight o'clock and she'd not had much sleep. When she'd got home to Heaton the night before, she should have gone straight to bed, but there was the wine in the fridge, and she'd been tempted. That, and all the sugar she'd eaten in Ma's house, had kept her awake until the early hours.

It had been her idea to talk to Chris Woodburn's wife. She'd discussed it with the boss the night before. 'I'm the nearest she had to a Family Liaison Officer, and it must be awful. She's lost a son and it seems that her husband was responsible, even if only indirectly. He'll be in prison for years so she's lost him too. Besides, she might have some idea what was going on with that company he was working for.'

Vera had nodded. 'But just think on! You're a cop, not her therapist.'

Standing on the doorstep, waiting for an answer to her knock, Rosie remembered the inspector the night before, tenderly laying Chloe Spence to sleep in the landlady's house,

352

and she couldn't help smiling. There were times when Vera acted like a social worker herself.

She hardly recognized the woman who answered the door. Anna Woodburn was wearing sweatpants and a sweatshirt and looked as if she'd been in them all night. It was clear that she hadn't slept.

'Oh, it's you. You'd better come in.' Hostile, but still somehow needing the company. A chance to talk. Or the hope of some honesty after all her husband's lies.

They sat in the kitchen again, and the woman made coffee. 'I'm not going in to work tomorrow.'

'Of course not!' Rosie was shocked that she'd even considered it.

'Naturally, my colleagues will find out in the end that my husband's a killer. And that he has to take some responsibility for the death of our son. But I can't face them. Not yet.'

'They'll understand that you had nothing to do with it.'

'Will they? Or will they be enjoying the drama and the gossip? They were always jealous of us. GPs are well enough paid, but Chris's income took us to a different level. First-class flights and a holiday home in Tuscany. The mortgage paid off. I never flaunted it. I found the wealth rather embarrassing, and we supported our charities, but all the same I loved the spontaneity that money can bring. Fancy a weekend in Venice? Let's go! You become accustomed to a certain level of comfort and support. Never checking the prices when you go shopping. The lack of anxiety. The roof's leaking. No worries, we can get a new one. We married when we were still students and madly in love. Everything was a struggle. Perhaps I thought we deserved the good life now. I became entitled.'

'So you never asked questions about where the money was coming from? Why Chris was so well paid?'

She shook her head. 'I don't think I wanted to know. I convinced myself that he was just very good at his job. He tried to tell me a couple of times. When he'd had one glass too many. He said he might apply for something less stressful. I shut the conversation down, told him he was brilliant and that he should have more confidence in himself. But really? I thought I had the best life ever and I didn't want anything to change.' She looked up at Rosie. 'Which makes me complicit, doesn't it?'

Rosie shook her head.

There was a moment of silence. 'Is he okay?' Anna Woodburn paused. 'I still care about him. I can't help it.' She looked around the room, at the reminders of her old life. Family snaps and appointment cards on a cork board. The photo of Chris and Josh against the Three Dark Wives. A couple of theatre tickets for the following week.

'He spent last night in the police station in Hexham. We'll be interviewing him later this morning. He was upset but holding it together. If he pleads guilty, there won't be a trial. There'll still be publicity, but it'll soon be over.' A pause. 'It wasn't his idea, you know, hiring someone to scare off Josh.'

'The solicitor was on the phone last night. He explained the background. He told me that Chris intends to admit everything and to tell you all he knows.' She looked up. 'He's frightened that he'll be under pressure to keep quiet, that they might threaten me to get at him. But I said I didn't care. I've got nothing to lose now. And that's how all this started, isn't it? Keeping quiet about something that needs to be exposed. Josh was the person who was going to let the light in.'

'You must be very proud.'

'I am.' She sobbed and put her hand over her mouth. 'But I'd give anything, anything, to have my son back. To know that he was about to walk in through the door.'

'You know that your husband's charge will probably be for murder? The murder of Brad Russell, the young man who killed Josh?'

She nodded.

'He was a troubled young man, an addict.'

'Don't ask me to feel any sympathy for him!'

'He was under the same sort of pressure as your husband,' Rosie said. 'I think it's the people in charge we should target, don't you?'

Anna Woodburn nodded again.

'So we'd like access to all the computers here in the house. In your husband's office and to all individual laptops. We'll be able to get a warrant, but if you give us permission, we can move more quickly.'

'Sure! Anything you need!'

'Is there anyone I can get to be with you?'

'No, the last thing I need is to have to explain.'

Rosie started getting to her feet, but Anna Woodburn continued: 'I know you're busy, but would you stay for a coffee? Just for a short while. Until I'm more myself. You can phone your colleagues and tell them I'll be here all day if they want to check the computers.'

'Of course,' Rosie said. 'Coffee would be champion.' She took out her phone to call Vera, to tell her she'd be delayed for a while, but that the search team could come in.

* ★ ★

355

Back in Kimmerston, she found Vera and Joe in the boss's office. There'd been a delay getting Woodburn and Miles back from Hexham, but they were buzzing. The serious crime team had been digging into Seaview Holdings.

'It's a huge operation. They run children's homes that we weren't aware of, one in Oldham and one in Morecambe.' Joe was fizzing. Too much coffee and like her, too little sleep. Rosie thought he'd been up late boasting to his wife about the success of the investigation, making himself the hero of the story. That was what men did.

'What about Stamoran?'

'He's in custody in Cumbria. They picked him up early this morning. I think he'll talk, and the digital team is already working on his devices.'

Rosie's next question was for Vera. 'How did you first think that it was all a scam? That some shady operation was running the kids' home. And that Helen Miles was involved.'

'It was something Willmore said, soon after the first murder. She hated the fact that someone was making a profit out of troubled young people. Then Kath Oliver explained how hard it was to find a place for adolescents in care.' Vera looked up. 'That's competition, isn't it? Supply and demand. And when you have competition, someone's going to be making a profit. As to Miles, Charlie followed the money trail. It's often the boring work that pays off.'

Rosie nodded, but that sounded too much like politics and politics had always turned her off. 'Were the Rosebank staff aware of what was going on?' She pictured Dave Limbrick with his ponytail and his shabby clothes, the affair with Tracey that would clearly lead nowhere. It was hard to think of him as a master criminal.

'No!' Vera obviously agreed with her. 'He's a good man doing his best under the most difficult circumstances.'

'What will happen to the home?'

Vera shrugged. 'That's not our business.' But she frowned and Rosie could tell she was worrying about it too. 'Maybe social services will take it over. In the short term at least. Those kids don't need any more disruption in their lives. I've talked to Kath Oliver, but it's all down to politics, isn't it? Politics and money.' Exactly echoing Rosie's thoughts.

Chris Woodburn was pale. Hexham must have found him a place to shower or to wash at least, because he was no longer spattered with mud. Perhaps his lawyer had provided clean clothes. He looked just as he must have seemed throughout his life: respectable, professional. Vera and Joe conducted the interview while Rosie looked on with Charlie in the viewing room. She didn't resent being left out. Not too much.

'Tell me about Brad Russell.' Vera's words were sympathetic, almost motherly. 'Why did he have to die?'

There was a moment's silence. Rosie wondered if the man was having second thoughts. Perhaps he'd been got at, after all.

But he sat straight and looked at Vera.

'Because I was told to do it. But because he'd killed my son, if I'm honest there was, I suppose, an element of revenge. I'd never thought I could be so angry.' A pause. 'Of course most of my anger was directed at myself. I should have left the organization as soon as I suspected just how deep the care home fraud was, and who Seaview was linked with. But they always came up with plausible explanations and I wanted to believe them.' He paused again. 'We'd become seduced by the lifestyle. We all had. I'm rather old-fashioned and saw myself as the provider. I didn't want to disappoint my wife. Now, that seems ridiculous.'

'You hadn't realized that Brad had been asked to scare Josh off?'

'No! Of course not! I'd have done something to stop it.' A pause, then a shred of honesty. 'I'd have warned Josh at least.'

Rosie remembered her first encounter with the Woodburns. Chris had been convincing then. He'd persuaded her that he had no knowledge of Josh's involvement in the care home. She'd believed him.

Perhaps Joe remembered that first conversation too, because the next question came from him. 'When we arrived to inform you of Josh's death, you claimed not to know that he'd been working in Rosebank. That was a clever response on the spur of the moment.'

Woodburn turned towards him. 'Over the years,' he said slowly, 'I've had to become a good liar.'

'You hadn't already been informed of your son's death?'

Woodburn shook his head. 'I was devastated. There was nothing false about that.'

'How did you persuade Russell to come to Gillstead with you?' Vera asked. 'And why there? A place where Chloe Spence might be hiding out. Were you looking for her too?'

Woodburn answered the last question first. 'I needed to find the girl. I wasn't sure how much Josh had told her.'

'How did you know about her association with Gillstead, and that she might be there?'

There was a silence. 'I was told that she might be. I was obeying orders. But that's always an excuse, isn't it, when people do bad things?'

'Who gave you the orders?' Vera wasn't motherly anymore. She was steely.

There was a moment of silence before Woodburn spoke again. 'Helen Miles.'

'Do you have any record of that conversation?'

'It was a message through WhatsApp. I'll give you the password to my phone.'

Vera nodded again. 'Talk me through the evening you took Brad up to Gillstead.'

Woodburn shut his eyes briefly before telling his story. 'Russell thought he was coming to help me find the girl. He didn't realize I was Josh's father. He was obeying orders too, but he was excited. All the way on the journey, he couldn't stop talking, bouncing around in his seat, like a hyperactive toddler. I just wanted peace.'

'You walked together up to the bothy?'

Woodburn nodded. 'By then Russell was calmer. I supposed it helped, being out of the car, having some exercise and fresh air. We went up quietly, in case Chloe was there, but there was no sign of her. I had a rucksack with some food, bottles of water. There was already wood in the grate and we lit a fire, boiled a kettle. Brad was like a different kid then. Joking. Normal, almost, but it didn't last. Soon he was tense and aggressive again.'

'He was an addict,' Vera said.

Woodburn nodded.

'And you had something to make him feel better.'

'Yes.'

'Who gave it to you?'

'I didn't see. The packet was left for me in a bin in Longwater.'

By someone else, Rosie thought, who'd been following Miles's orders, someone she'd known before her conversion and wealth.

'You knew the gear had been doctored?'

'I guessed. I was told Russell would be taken care of.'

'You do realize –' Vera was at her most impressive – 'that makes you guilty of murder? An accessory at least.'

'Of course.'

Now, Rosie thought, Woodburn was impressive too. Taking responsibility at last.

Chapter Forty-Seven

VERA WAS IN THE INTERVIEW ROOM with Rosie beside her. Miles was daunting, and Vera had decided that this was a job for the women. Joe and Charlie were hidden but watching. On the other side of the table sat Helen Miles and her brief, both channelling impatience and righteous indignation.

'This is ludicrous, of course,' the lawyer said. Another woman, power-dressed, skinny, heels. Vera thought she'd had work done. There was something of the puppet about the face. 'Helen Miles is famous in the region for her philanthropic work. A committed Christian, she founded and funded the Salvation Academy to provide opportunities for local young people that were never available to her. She's never hidden her convictions as a juvenile, but she turned her life round as a young woman.'

Miles had managed to get hold of some make-up. She sat there silent, granite-faced. Her body was toned and hard too. It was easy to see how she'd pulled Woodburn from Charlie's grasp.

Vera's voice was mild. 'Your client helped a murderer to escape last night.'

They'd obviously prepared for this. 'Nonsense. Miss Miles had no knowledge that Mr Woodburn was being arrested. She thought he was a victim of a robbery. It happens in crowds everywhere. Gangs come from the city to steal wallets and phones.'

'Did she recognize him as a colleague? An employee?' There was a moment of silence before Vera continued talking. 'We have a Mr Stamoran in custody in Carlisle. He confirmed that Seaview Holdings is wholly owned by one of Miss Miles's companies. We are, of course, talking to Christopher Woodburn, who helped to arrange the purchase. We have WhatsApp messages and a trail of evidence. We have witnesses who put Miss Miles outside Rosebank Care Home in the run-up to Josh Woodburn's murder.'

Helen Miles reverted to her juvenile self then and all other questions were answered with: 'No comment.'

It was Sunday and Vera had sent most of the team home. They deserved a break and besides, there was no need to keep paying overtime. Woodburn and Miles had been charged. They'd be kept in the cells overnight to appear in court the following morning, before being remanded in custody.

Vera had a lunch date, though that was work of a kind too, she supposed. First she drove out to Longwater and parked outside Rosebank. The grey November weather had returned and the common at the end of the track was hidden by a damp mist. Kath Oliver had said she'd go to the home to let the residents and staff know what was happening, and Vera thought she should show her face too. It'd be good to put in a joint presence.

Kath was already there, in the office, talking to Dave Limbrick. Vera stood outside the door for a moment, listening to her explanation. She'd arrived close to the end of the social worker's little speech:

'So the local authority will take over for a bit, until the situation becomes clearer. You and the other staff will still be paid. We can work together to make the kids feel safe. It's been a terrible time for you all.'

'You'll be in charge then?' Limbrick sounded relieved, almost animated. 'You'll be my boss?'

'Well, I'll be your first point of contact if you need any help or support.' Vera could hear the amusement in the woman's voice.

'Eh,' he said. 'I could almost kiss you! Just knowing you understand and that there's somebody to share the load.'

'Is there anything you need now? How are the kids?'

'A bit quiet. We've talked it through – Brad dying. It's a lot to take in after Josh . . . When they've already put up with so much.'

'You think they need some specialist mental health support?'

'Well, of course they do! They did before. Poor George was still wetting the bed when he came to us. But I might as well be asking for the moon on a plate. A three-year waiting list for CAMHS, the last time I checked. Most of our residents would be adults before they got an initial appointment, and they'd end up back at the bottom again, this time of the grown-ups' list.'

'You'd be surprised what can be achieved,' Kath's voice was steely, 'when there's a high-profile case and the press are involved.'

This seemed like a good time for Vera to make an entrance. She tapped on the office door and went in. Limbrick was looking more relaxed than she'd ever seen him. He was sitting behind his desk, actually looking as if he belonged there.

'I just wanted to update you,' Vera said. 'It'll be all over the media later today. I'm sure Kath's told you that Chloe's home, safe and well.'

Limbrick nodded. 'I told Mel and George. They're delighted.'

'We've got someone in custody for Brad's death. It's Josh's father.' A pause. 'It was Brad who killed his son.'

'So it was revenge?'

Vera shook her head. 'It was a bit more complicated than that. He was working for the company that owns Rosebank, and as Kath will have explained, they're under suspicion for fraud and other criminal activities. We have another individual in custody. We think they planned the whole scheme.'

'We had nothing to do with that!'

'I know. You're victims too. But you might be able to help us get a conviction. Not just of Mr Woodburn, but the people who were pulling his strings. So I'll need a statement from you. And I wanted to warn you that a team will be in here first thing tomorrow, checking on your records and all your devices. But it's not you or your staff who are under suspicion. That's why I'm here. To let you know and to make that clear.'

Vera and Kath stood outside for a moment before driving away. The mist was rising a little. There was a view of the estuary, the rusting pier, where once the coal boats had moored.

'So,' Kath said, 'we're still here and we're still fighting.'

Vera chuckled. 'Oh aye, I'm off for my next battle now.' She clapped her hand on the social worker's shoulder and got into her car.

★ ★ ★

Vera knew she'd be late for the next appointment, and she sent a text before driving away. Apologetic but not grovelling. She'd never grovelled. It was the weekend after all, and she was in on her own time.

Katherine Willmore was waiting in a window table in the Marine Centre where they'd met the time before. This too, it seemed, was an unofficial meeting. Vera waved as she got in but queued up to order food before joining the PCC. She was starving. She mouthed across at the woman to ask if she wanted anything. Katherine shook her head.

'So,' she said when Vera joined her, 'you have a suspect in custody. Congratulations!'

'We do. And a confession. And we have the brains behind the organization. Woodburn might have fed the doctored heroin to Brad Russell, but he wouldn't have had the nerve or the contacts to make it happen.'

'So who has he implicated? Anyone we know?' Willmore was interested, relieved that a double murder had been wrapped up so easily. Vera could tell she was already planning a triumphant press conference. She might be a lawyer by training and trade, but hers was a political appointment.

'A guy called Stamoran heads up the children's home arm of the business, but he's based in Cumbria. We have the organizing force in custody.'

'And who's that?'

Vera's pie and chips was arriving, carried by a young lass with arms as thin as twigs and shaky hands. They waited until the plate had safely landed on the table before continuing.

'Helen Miles.'

Katherine Willmore raised an eyebrow. 'And you have proof?'

'Oh yes.'

'It could be sensitive. She's very popular locally.' Willmore didn't sound *too* upset though, because she *was* a politician, and she was already working out the optics, seeing how the story might play with the electorate.

'I know.'

Willmore caught Vera's eye and smiled. She looked at her watch. 'Well done.' It seemed as if she was about to go, to leave Vera to finish her meal alone.

'There is one thing more, ma'am. In your role as Police and Crime Commissioner. Something you might like to highlight. Not entirely your sphere of influence, but relevant when it comes to crime prevention.'

'Yes?' Willmore was suspicious, anxious even. She regarded Vera as if she was a dog, usually friendly enough, but given to unexpected attempts to bite the hand that fed her.

'Privately owned care homes for troubled kids. This case has shown that they're a breeding ground of crime and anti-social behaviour. If we're putting an emphasis on prevention, I wonder if we should be making a case for bringing them back into local authority control.'

'I'm not sure.' Willmore looked at her warily. 'The way council finances are at the moment . . .'

'Scotland has done it and Wales intends to bring them all back as soon as they can. Some English local authorities have seen the benefit.'

'All the same . . .'

'Do you know how much these companies are making out of our troubled teens?' Vera kept her voice even, reasonable. No point frightening the woman off with emotion. That wasn't the way her brain worked. 'Look at the profits they're making, and this case has highlighted a connection with criminal activity!

Besides, we all know how much it costs to keeps an offender in prison. In the long term it would be saving you a fortune, if we could turn these kids' lives around.' A pause. 'I'd say it'd be a vote-winner.'

'Well . . .' Willmore seemed more interested now. 'I'll certainly think about it.'

'Social services have already taken over Rosebank. They had no option in the circumstances. You could view it as a pilot project. See how they get on, how the kids improve with proper support.'

'Yes.'

Vera could sense the battle shifting her way.

Willmore was still speaking: 'That makes a lot of sense.'

In her head, Vera was composing a triumphant text to Kath Oliver.

Chapter Forty-Eight

THEY SAT IN VERA'S HOUSE IN the hills. It was evening and the sun had gone and Rosie had never seen so many stars. Gillstead had felt remote enough, but this was the top of the world. Apart from the farm at the end of the track, all she could see were pinpricks of light in the valley. She couldn't believe that the boss actually lived here, miles from civilization, and yet she'd had the nerve to tell Rosie to move out of the city and closer to their patch.

She and Joe had been driven up by Kath Oliver, the social worker who'd looked after Chloe and Brad. Vera had offered them all a lift in the Land Rover and to stand them a taxi home, but Kath had said she'd need to get back before it got too late. Rosie had had quite a bit to drink by now and couldn't quite remember the excuse. Something about dogs to feed, or an elderly mother to look after. Rosie had expected Charlie to be there too, but when she'd asked about his absence, Vera had said she hadn't been able to persuade him.

'He's not very comfortable in company, our Charlie. And he's still going through all the Seaview stuff with the forensic accountant. He's like a terrier. Nothing he likes better than digging for the truth.'

Vera had lit a fire, and the place smelled of woodsmoke and the soup she'd heated up in the kitchen to feed them all. They sat in the living room at a battered pine table and ate the soup with chunks of fresh bread. Rosie thought it was like being a character in a fairy tale, though she couldn't work out if Vera was the wicked witch or the good fairy. Or one of the Three Dark Wives.

Usually, white wine was Rosie's drink of choice. Or gin and tonic. Here there was nothing but beer and whisky. She'd started on the beer, which was cloudy and smelly, and was, according to Vera, her neighbour's home brew.

'Nothing like Jack's beer if you're having a celebration.'

And this was, it seemed, a celebration. Charlie had dug up all they needed to connect Miles to the two murders, and Stamoran had recovered his memory. Better to implicate his boss than be charged with planning the murders himself. They already knew that Woodburn would be an excellent witness.

Vera carried the soup bowls and plates into the tiny kitchen, and they moved to the comfortable chairs staring into the fire. Except for Rosie who sat on the hearthrug. It seemed that there weren't enough chairs to go round. Vera couldn't have company very often. Joe and Kath were drinking mugs of coffee. Rosie was still on the beer.

Despite having drunk as much as Rosie, Vera's explanation was clear. 'Stamoran and Miles knew each other long before they set up in business together, but the care home racket was definitely Miles's idea. She grew up in care. I don't think she just bought into Seaview. I think she set it up. Charlie's probably working on it now, digging up the details.'

But tonight the details didn't seem to matter. Chloe Spence was safe, the CPS was happy with what they'd achieved and Charlie would provide them with the details they needed. And Rosie had found a team to belong to.

'What will happen to the school?' Rosie asked.

'I chatted to Susannah Hepple earlier,' Vera said. 'She was shocked of course. She'd worked with Helen Miles for years and was a true believer, but she's a bright woman and came to the evidence with an open mind. She reckons it can carry on. Some of the middle-class parents, who fought to get their kids in there, might be scared away by all the bad publicity, but that means there'll be more places for the bairns it was intended for.' There was a pause. 'Perhaps some of the teachers who didn't like the regime might be persuaded to stay on.'

Kath Oliver started making moves to leave.

'We'll meet up next week, shall we?' she said to Vera. 'With Miss Willmore, your PCC. Have a look at developing a pilot project to bring Rosebank back into local authority control.'

'It's in the diary.'

'It's worth fighting for, eh, Vera?' the social worker said as she rose out of her chair. 'No point thinking about retiring while there's still work to be done.' Then to Rosie and Joe:

'I'll drop you two back in Kimmerston and you can get taxis from there.'

Rosie stumbled as she got to her feet, and Joe helped her outside. The cold hit her and sobered her. She turned back to look at Vera as Kath drove slowly down the pitted track. The boss was standing in the doorway, watching them go. The light behind her made her silhouette look black and as solid as one of the standing stones above Gillstead. She had a huge grin on her face – pleased, it seemed, to be alone again.

Chapter Forty-Nine

A WEEK LATER, VERA ARRIVED BACK at the cottage after a day in Kimmerston tying up loose ends. Another weekend's overtime that she wouldn't bother claiming. It was already dark. It was only the middle of November, but winter came early here in the hills. There was a light in her neighbours' house, and she thought she might wander down in a bit, take a bottle to share with Jack and Joanna, talk about sheep prices and Joanna's writing instead of the case.

She hung her jacket on the hook by the door and felt in the pocket for an envelope that had arrived for her at the police station the day before. Delivered by hand. She'd recognized the writing. It had been in her pocket all day and was crumpled. She opened the envelope and straightened out the piece of paper inside.

Dear Inspector Stanhope
I just wanted to tell you how thankful I am that you're heading up the investigation into Josh's death. I think you're the best detective in England!

371

Living with my mam is going really well. She seems happy and I'm so glad to be away from Rosebank. Without you, I don't know where I'd be. Still scared and hiding probably. Maybe I'd be dead – definitely not safe and back at home.

In a weird way, everything that's happened has brought my family together (or at least more together!). I'd forgotten how nice it is to be someone's sole focus. Nana and Grandpa are being lovely. At Rosebank there was always someone screaming louder, so it was impossible to be heard. Josh was the only one who ever heard me. I'm so sorry that he's dead.

I've been thinking I could be a copper when I'm older. Like you. I want to help people when they're at their lowest. I want to help victims get justice. There are too many bad people out there. I want to rescue someone like you rescued me.

I'm going back to school tomorrow. I'm scared, but not quite so scared, because I know you're in my corner.

So, many thanks.

Chloe

The letter ended with a smiley face. Vera smiled too and pulled on her jacket to go and visit her friends.

About the Author

David Hirst

Ann Cleeves is the multimillion-copy bestselling author behind three hit television series—*Shetland,* starring Douglas Henshall; *Vera,* starring Academy Award nominee Brenda Blethyn; and *The Long Call,* starring Ben Aldridge—all of which are watched and loved in the United States. All three are available on BritBox.

The first Shetland novel, *Raven Black,* won the Crime Writers' Association Gold Dagger for best crime novel, and Ann was awarded the CWA Diamond Dagger in 2017. She was awarded the OBE in 2022 for services to reading and libraries. Ann lives in the United Kingdom.